# Tradition and Innovation
# in Folk Literature

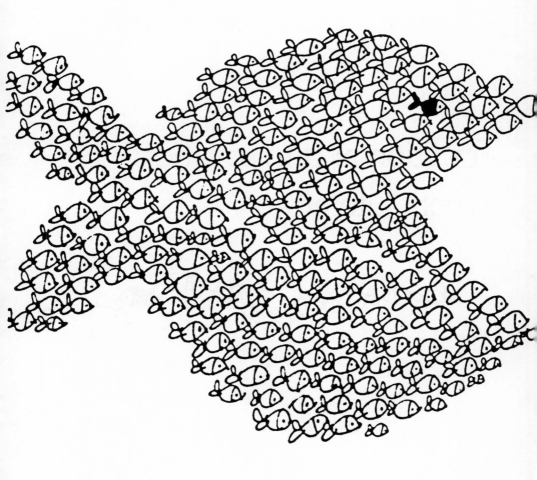

Published for University of Vermont
by University Press of New England
Hanover and London, 1987

# Wolfgang Mieder

# Tradition and Innovation in Folk Literature

Printed in the United States of America

LIBRARY OF CONGRESS CATALOGING IN PUBLICATION DATA
Mieder, Wolfgang.
   Tradition and innovation in folk literature.
Bibliography: p.
   Includes index.
   1. Folk literature—History and criticism.
2. Folklore in literature.   I. Title.
GR72.M53   1987      398.2      86–21206
ISBN 0–87451–387–1

## Text Permissions

John Ashbery, "The Pied Piper," from *Some Trees* (New York: Ecco Press, 1956) copyright ©
   1956 by John Ashbery. Reprinted by permission of Georges Borchardt, Inc. and the author.
W. H. Auden, "Leap Before You Look," copyright 1945 by W. H. Auden. Reprinted from W.
   H. Auden: *Collected Poems*, edited by Edward Mendelson, by permission of Random House,
   Inc. and by permission of Faber and Faber Ltd.
Vincent Godfrey Burns, "Man Does Not Live By Bread Alone," from *Redwood and Other Poems*
   (Washington, D.C.: New World Books, 1952).

(*Permissions continued on p. 292*)

For my wife Barbara

# Contents

# Introduction

"Dauer im Wechsel" (Constancy in change)
(Goethe, 1803)

There have been many poets, philosophers, and scholars who have reflected and commented on cultural changes. Johann Wolfgang von Goethe's poem "Dauer im Wechsel"[1] is only one poetic expression of how prevalent the concept of change is in all aspects of our existence. However, although he stresses the important element of change, he also demonstrates how art can transcend the ephemeral nature of most of our endeavors. Art can overcome the transitory quality of life and secure for us a certain "constancy in change" as the title of Goethe's poem claims. But in a world of constant changes it is, of course, not only art in the rigid sense of that word that provides a certain continuity through the ages. Language, social norms, beliefs, customs, and innumerable traditions of all kinds help in establishing a structure for our lives, and although they provide a certain permanence, they are at the same time in a process of continual change. Traditional modes of expression such as fairy tales, legends, nursery rhymes, and proverbs, to name but a few, have for a long time been part of a verbal folk art giving durability to our understanding of the world. As part of the larger field of folklore they have played a major role in maintaining a basic framework for generations of people who have used them as common philosophical guides from childhood to old age.

It is not surprising, therefore, that folklorists and cultural historians have for a long time looked upon such traditional expressions as "survivals."[2] They were seen as ancient and unchanging reflections upon life that had to be collected and preserved in print before they disappeared in a rapidly changing world of industrialization. Dozens of superb collections of fairy tales, legends, folk songs, riddles, proverbs, and so on were published, particularly in the nineteenth century, and this "preservation" activity continues to the present day. Many of the introductions, especially in the earlier collections, repeatedly stress the need to amass these old survivals of times long past before such gems of folk wisdom were forever lost. In such publications the static, constant, and traditional aspects of the various folklore genres were usually stressed, and very little attention if any was paid to the innovation processes that have always been part of any tradition no matter how small the changes might be.[3] Because the survivalists wanted to preserve, they stressed the conventionality of folklore as such, and they blatantly ignored the modern variations of traditional expressions that were taking place while they argued for the static nature of anything falling in the realm of folklore.

More modern folklorists, however, have begun to stress exactly the opposite point. In a seminal paper, Hans Moser talks of the "constant changes"[4] all traditions undergo over time, and he argues strongly that it is this innovative phenomenon that scholars should address today. Kurt Ranke, while stressing the importance of a combined study of folklore and cultural history, has argued successfully that scholars should heed the "processes of stylistic change"[5] that occur in any traditional form of expression over the generations. Other scholars have pointed to such dichotomies as "variability and stability,"[6] "new creations of traditional forms,"[7] "traditions and change,"[8] "cultural continuity and discontinuity,"[9] "simultaneity of tradition and innovation,"[10] and so on. The renowned American folklorist Richard Dorson summarized this stress on the dynamic and innovative processes that are part of tradition by talking of "the contemporaneity and modernity of folklore."[11] From the modern point of view it is difficult to understand why it took folklorists such a long time to look at the fascinating survival forms of traditional motifs in modern societies, but it obviously was not easy to redirect scholars' interests from supposedly static traditions to dynamic changes in these very traditions. Due to the increased relationship between present-day folklore and popular culture, the interplay of tradition and innovation now belongs to the serious concerns of folklorists and cultural and literary historians, as well as other scholars who occupy themselves with universal cultural expressions.

In the meantime an international congress on "Tradition and Originality"[12] has taken place, and we also have an entire volume of essays by internationally renowned folklorists dedicated to the question of "continuity."[13] The editors of this book placed an appropriate question mark after the word "continuity" that functions as its main title. The subtitle (in English translation Historicity and Constancy as a Folkloric Problem) alludes to the dichotomies mentioned above. In the lead article, Hermann Bausinger stresses the fact that continuity is a relative concept,[14] that is, we have no precise measurement of time that defines continuity. While many folklore motifs might easily be traced back to classical antiquity, others are definitely of a much more recent origin. Traditions obviously can also die out while new ones are created. Traditionality in and of itself is in fact irrelevant if we don't consider at the same time the context, use, and function of fairy tales, proverbs, and so on over certain time periods. The fact that a certain proverb might reappear again and again in printed collections is by no means a sign of continuity. The solidified and rigid text in a collection might in fact be nothing but a relic or survival that is "dead" as far as its currency among the folk is concerned. If we want to study the cultural significance of traditional stories, motifs, and expressions, it is of the greatest importance that their existence with and without their textual changes be studied diachronically and synchronically. To this fundamental aspect of folklore must also be added comparative cultural and linguistic considerations on a national and, where possible, an international basis.

What we have to realize is that even the world of folklore is based on historical development and constant change. Oral traditions especially have clearly been prone to changes in form and wording. Fairy tales after all were not blindly learned by heart in former times. They "lived" because they were told by individuals who added or deleted words or sentences as they saw fit. Oral folklore therefore is to a certain degree unstable and only the literary fixation of fairy tales, legends, and even proverbs in collections has given them their stable character. Such traditional texts, certainly in oral contexts, exist by repetition and therefore in numerous variants. This variability is the fascinating part of studying them since the variants indicate that the texts are indeed alive and not mere relics. We might be able to reconstruct the arche-type for some fairy tales, nursery rhymes, and so on by painstaking research, but at the same time it becomes extremely clear that the "original" version never remained constant and that variation is intrin-sically related to tradition.[15]

These innovative textual changes are not restricted to orally trans-mitted folklore. They are very much present in the written use of verbal folklore genres. Poets, journalists, advertisers, politicians, preachers, artists, cartoonists—in fact all people who communicate through language—rely on traditional expressions and make them fit new social environments. In a society where people have the tendency to question traditional values, it should not be surprising that the use and function of oral folklore has changed considerably. No longer does it necessarily serve as an edifying moralistic or didactic comment. Rather it is employed in playful and witty variations fitting our cynical times. By altering traditional texts to make ironic, if not satirical, commentaries on societal ills, the old standbys of folk wisdom take on a new meaning and importance as reflections of modern life. Parodies in the form of wordplay, jokes, or humorous retellings of longer narratives are very popular and show the remarkable adaptability of seemingly "antiquated" texts. The study of such new uses and func-tions of verbal folklore is, in fact, the study of innovation, a far cry from the study of folklore relics that occupied scholars for so many genera-tions. Studying innovation and its processes leads to the investigation of human communication, which ought to be at the heart of folklore scholarship.[16] But we must be careful not to let the scholarly pendulum swing to a new extreme by concentrating only on innovative uses of folklore in our modern age. The mere study of folklore as rigid surviv-als was one extreme. Folklore studies should now not swing to the other extreme and merely deal with the innovative survival of texts in the world of popular culture and mass media. The historical aspect of traditional materials must play a role in serious folklore scholarship. Folklore at its best addresses both tradition and innovation and shows how constancy and change are interlinked in the dynamic process of civilization.

The six chapters of this book all address the theme of tradition and innovation while dealing with such different verbal folklore genres as fairy tales, legends, nursery rhymes, and proverbs. They all are histor-ical and comparative studies, and, with the exception of the two more general chapters on fairy tales and proverbs in the modern age, they trace one particular legend, nursery rhyme, or proverb from its earliest reference to present-day uses. Such investigations cover a time span of many centuries; they treat European, American, and Asiatic cultures; and they are truly interdisciplinary in nature, drawing on such fields of study as anthropology, art, classics, folklore, history, linguistics, literature, mass communication, philology, philosophy, political science, psychology, religion, and sociology. The many examples of the use of folklore in texts from literary sources in the form of poems, prose, songs, aphorisms, epigrams, and dramas, in the numerous references of advertising slogans, newspaper headlines, greeting cards, and graffiti, as well as in the dozens of illustrative references from medieval woodcuts and artists such as Hieronymus Bosch, Pieter Brueghel, and Francisco Goya all the way to emblems, engravings, cartoons, caricatures, and comic strips attest to the all-encompassing presence of traditional folklore genres in our cultural development. While textual references could be cited in relatively large numbers we obviously had to restrict ourselves in the use of actual illustrations in this book. But the included pictures certainly provide an idea of the iconographic use of folklore motifs from the late Middle Ages to modern times.

It should also be mentioned that the majority of references stem from Anglo-American and German sources because of my own background in these two cultures. However, some texts and illustrations from Belgium, China, France, Holland, Israel, Italy, Japan, Spain, and the Soviet Union have also been included to add to the international aspect of the phenomenon of tradition and innovation. Where a national tradition of a folklore text such as the proverb "Big fish eat little fish" exists in a specific country, it is hoped that another colleague might subsequently study its history, dissemination, and innovative survival in this country. In order to give a complete world history of this particular international proverb the help of many experts would obviously be necessary. We hope, however, that our multicultural and interdisciplinary studies in this book are steps toward such global investigations of tradition and innovation in particular folklore texts.

While the titles of the six chapters speak for themselves, nevertheless a very short general overview of their content follows here in order to introduce the reader to the specific problems raised in each. The first chapter on "Grim Variations: From Fairy Tales to Modern Anti-Fairy Tales" is the most general and least historical of all the chapters. The question raised here is what value and meaning fairy tales have for adults. It is argued that they are symbolic comments on basic aspects of social life and modes of human behavior. While the fairy tales end with positive resolutions of all conflicts, the modern adult often identifies with the more negative individual scenes or motifs in the tales since they appear to reflect real-life problems. In three sections of the chapter, such negataive and often cynical or satirical reactions to the traditional fairy tales "The Frog Prince," "Snow White," and "Hansel and Gretel" are presented by analyzing modern "anti-fairy tales" in the form of lyrical poetry, aphorisms, prose texts, caricatures, cartoons, comic strips, and so on. Poems by Randall Jarrell, Anne Sexton, Galway Kinnell, Robert Gillespie, Sara Henderson Hay, Louise Glück, John Ower, and Dorothy Lee Richardson show serious reflections on the appropriateness of fairy tales in the modern age. Some of these texts are in fact "grim" reactions to the old Grimm fairy tales, and it is amazing to see how the perfect world of the fairy tales can be brought into contrast with political and social issues, marriage problems, economic uncertainties, and even the dangers of nuclear power. But if we interpret fairy tales as emancipatory tales for people of all ages, then even the anti-fairy tales, as modern reactions, take on deeper significance in a complex world that is anything but a fairy tale. Tradition and innovation clearly complement each other in these modern adaptations, and together they express a hope for a better world in which injustice, cruelty, and other unfair practices may cease. Fairy tales as well as anti-fairy tales are seen as universal expressions of the human condition, and they are powerful comments on the continuous struggle toward a better world.

The second chapter traces the complicated origin and history of the well-known legend of "The Pied Piper of Hamelin." Some of the earliest references from the late Middle Ages are presented and discussed, and a number of theories regarding the historical truth of this legend are analyzed. Literary reinterpretations by such authors as Johann Wolfgang von Goethe, Robert Browning, Bertolt Brecht, and many others are interpreted. Many detailed comments center on the iconographical history of the famous Pied Piper. Included is a discussion of the proverbial expression "To pay the piper," and much emphasis is given to the way this German legend became one of the most popular Anglo-American children's stories. The second half of this chapter treats the Pied Piper as a universal symbolic figure, an ambivalent leader who encompasses both positive and negative values. We see various politically dangerous and evil Pied Pipers such as "communism," Hitler, and Richard Nixon, but there are also Pied Pipers of religious sects, television, disco dancing, hula-hoop, advertising, and many more. Everywhere we look Pied Pipers seem to be ready to lead us astray. From the many texts, cartoons, and caricatures it becomes evident that the Pied Piper is a most convincing universal symbol for the ambiguous character of "leaders" of all types. The city of Hamelin in Germany has, of course, made a whole industry out of its Pied Piper association, and the result is the mercantile packaging of the legend for ready consumption by eager tourists who purchase books, postcards, bumper stickers, carved rats, and beautiful figurines of the Pied Piper in this small Pied Piper town. Hamelin itself has become the symbol for the tourist industry acting as a Pied Piper. The end of this chapter attempts to analyze the way folklore is being used today for commercial purposes,[17] another aspect of the innovative adaptability of traditional folk narratives.

Following the two chapters on fairy tales and legends respectively is a study of the "Modern Variants of the Daisy Oracle," which traces the popular divination rhyme "He (she) loves me, he (she) loves me not" and its variants from the Middle Ages to its varied survival in advertising, caricatures, and modern greeting cards. Once again texts from children's books and literary references from such authors as Walther von der Vogelweide, Goethe, A. A. Milne, John Ruskin, James Lowell, and John Le Carré are cited. English, French, and German variants in particular are analyzed, and illustrations by such well known artists as Gérard Grandville, Ludwig Richter, and Norman Rockwell are also mentioned. It is also shown how this universal flower oracle has found its way into numerous political caricatures, into Valentine cards, modern lyrical poetry, economic commentaries, and the world of advertising. In some of the modern variants, the old daisy that used to be plucked in this divination game has been replaced by other devices such as a gold-plated mechanical daisy divination charm. Taken together the many variations of the daisy oracle over several centuries and across national boundaries show that, while the simple daisy nursery rhyme has become adapted to the complexities of our modern life, the traditional game of plucking a daisy to find out one's fortune in love is still very much present among children and lovers everywhere.

The fourth chapter deals with "The Proverb in the Modern Age" and shows how old proverbial wisdom survives in new clothing in today's world. It is argued that while proverbs continue to be used in their original wording with the intention of teaching, moralizing, prescribing a course of action, or simply commenting on a common experience of everyday life, they are also often varied to fit the changing times and situations that require forms of expression the traditional proverb no longer can supply. The chapter has been divided into four parts. First there is a discussion of proverb illustrations, which centers around Pieter Brueghel's famous picture commonly called "The Netherlandic Proverbs" (1559) and its later variations, but there are also many examples of woodcuts, emblems, oil pictures, caricatures, and cartoons by other artists. The second section analyzes the relationship of the at times antiquated and questionable traditional proverbial wisdom to the concerns of modern sexual politics. The obvious antifeminism prevalent in so many proverbs is discussed, and many examples are given to show how innovative changes attempt to overcome the chauvinistic attitudes of the old stereotypical proverbs. The third part consists of numerous poems by such authors as John Heywood, John Gay, Samuel Taylor Coleridge, W. H. Auden, and Arthur Guiterman, which are all based on well-known proverbs or their critical variations. Many of these lyrical poems show dissatisfaction with the one-sidedness and apparent narrow-mindedness of certain proverbs. The fourth and final part summarizes some of the points raised in the other sections by discussing the origin, history, and modern use of one specific proverb, "Who does not love wine, women, and song, will remain a fool his whole life long." Martin Luther's possible coinage of this proverb is commented upon, and variants by Robert Burton, Lord Byron, William Makepeace Thackeray, Johann Strauss, and others are also presented. This epicurean proverb has been reduced to the proverbial triad "wine, women and song" by now, and it lives a popular existence in modern cartoons and on T-shirts. The entire chapter clearly demonstrates that both the traditional proverb and altered anti-proverbs are part of modern communication and that people switch back and forth between them just as they oscillate between the traditional values and new mores.

East and West are linked in the fifth chapter concerning "The Proverbial Three Wise Monkeys" and the proverb "Hear no evil, speak no evil, see no evil." The seemingly independent origin of this proverb in both Europe and the Far East is traced, first by discussing its early

European appearance in medieval Latin proverb collections, in the *Gesta Romanorum*, and in a French ballad by Eustache Deschamps. Then the possible Eastern origin of the proverb is discussed by analyzing so-called Japanese Koshin stones that display three monkeys carved on the pedestal of the stone covering their ears, eyes, and mouth. The two origins of the proverb in far-removed cultures are taken to be proof of the possibility of polygenesis in the creation of proverbs, but then it is shown how the proverb and the three monkeys became molded together once East and West came into closer contact towards the latter part of the nineteenth century. The proverb has become extremely popular due primarily to the image of the three monkeys that so vividly illustrates its basic wisdom. Small ivory, clay, stone, brass, or wooden figurines of the three monkeys can be bought in curio and gift shops almost anywhere in the world, attesting to the international dissemination of the proverb and its attached monkey symbol. But the three monkeys are also used in political caricatures, on serious and silly posters, on greeting cards, and on bookmarks, as well as on T-shirts. There are also American and German poems by such authors as Florence Boyce Davis and Günter Kunert that praise the traditional wisdom of the proverb or find issue with the philosophy of passivity and non-involvement expressed in it. We even have figurines and cartoons showing a fourth monkey doing exactly what the traditional three monkeys are not to do. Once again we have a traditional folklore text to which modern people react ambivalently. While it might appear prudent at times to adhere to the advice of not hearing, seeing, or saying anything, it is also argued in modern parodies of the three monkey group that such an attitude leads to serious social problems by accepting the status quo without questioning any of its values. The wisdom of the proverb is as ambiguous as life itself, a fact which has led to fascinating traditional and innovative uses of this truly international expression.

The sixth and final chapter presents the "History and Interpretation of a Proverb about Human Nature," the widely known proverb "Big fish eat little fish." Again the chapter points out that for this internationally disseminated proverb polygenesis cannot be ruled out. Its Indo-European origin and history are painstakingly investigated from the earliest reference in Hesiod (eighth century B.C.) to modern times. While the appearance of the proverb in other European languages is referred to in passing, it is the Anglo-American history of this proverb that is traced by discussing variants of it in the writings of John Lydgate, Alexander Barclay, George Herbert, William Shakespeare, Jacob Thomas Middleton, Mateo Alemán, Roger Williams, William Penn, Jonathan Swift, John Adams, Bertolt Brecht, and many others. The proverb is also often illustrated, in a number of paintings by Hieronymus Bosch and Pieter Brueghel, in emblems, and in modern caricatures that use the big fish eating little fish as symbols for the stronger oppressing the weaker, the rich usurping the poor, and so on. Right from the beginning the proverb was interpreted as a reflection of the rapacious and aggressive nature of mankind, and this has not changed in the modern texts and iconographic representations.

The rich illustrative materials in this chapter are divided into five basic groups: (1) one large fish randomly pursuing several smaller ones, (2) a big fish planning to devour one specific fish, (3) a sequence of three or more fish trying to swallow each other up, (4) a vicious circle of fish of the same size trying to incorporate each other, and finally (5) the attempt of many small fish to gang up on the larger one. The references come from American, English, German, and Russian publications, and this linguistic and cultural spread proves that such reinterpretations of a classical proverb are an international phenomenon. What is interesting about this proverb is that its basic wisdom appears to hold up in the modern age as well. Greed and aggression are present everywhere and big fish are in fact still eating little fish. Even the symbolic inversion of this proverbial law in some aphoristic writings, graffiti, advertisements, and caricatures, where the solidarity of many little fish overcomes the power of the big fish, seems only momentarily to be able to free mankind from rapacity and other societal ills. We continually find new shapes for the perpetrators—loan sharks, business giants, monopolies, powerful countries, and so on—but with few exceptions this is as far as the innovations go. The actual wisdom of this ancient proverb is so strong that it continues to express the constant struggle between good and evil, strong and weak, rich and poor, as convincingly now as thousands of years ago.

It is clear from these short comments about the six chapters that they are tied together by the common theme of tradition and innovation. The purpose of each chapter has been to show how traditional folklore genres such as fairy tales, legends, nursery rhymes, and proverbs survive, either in their commonly known wording or in innovative variations in a modern technological society. The dozens of references to art, literature, and the mass media make it clear that folklore studies cannot possibly be static or antiquarian in nature. While folklore does, to a certain degree, stand for tradition, stability, and continuity, it also includes innovation, dynamics, and change. In order for innovations to take place, the traditional text must be alive. But through the juxtaposition of the common text and the altered expression we gain new insights into the complex aspect of human existence. It is to be expected that verbal folklore will be questioned in the modern age, but we are all programmed to the basic truths expressed in many of the texts so that we quote them even when actually wanting to negate them. We can reinterpret, change, and question traditional texts, but we will not be able to escape their wisdom completely. Fairy tales, legends, nursery rhymes, proverbs, and other genres not discussed in this book contain certain universal truths, and it is for this reason that people of all walks of life return to them in order to communicate their innermost feelings, anxieties, thoughts, and hopes. Over the centuries some of the texts were changed, and today more than ever before we consciously alter traditional expressions to fit our new needs, but often we are in fact only adhering to the ever present and fundamental process of tradition and innovation.

At the end of this introduction I have the pleasant task of thanking the following relatives, friends, and colleagues for helping me to locate some of the many references in this book. They are, in alphabetical order, Dan Ben-Amos, Melissa Brown, George B. Bryan, Walter and Lee Busker, Walter and Lucille Busker, William and Barbara Busker, Peter Christiansen, Jennifer Davis, Alan Dundes, Rickie Emerson, Howard Fitzpatrick, Karen Hurwitz, Malcolm Jones, Marilyn Jorgensen, Henny Lewin, Kevin McKenna, Dennis Mahoney, Barbara Mieder, Horst and Elfriede Mieder, Kenneth Nalibow, Kate Olshki, Richard and Francine Page, Ann and Dick Park, Carolyn Poley, Christine Reimers, Veronica Richel, Lutz Röhrich, Barbara Schermerhorn, David Scrase, Trixie and Eric Stinebring, Helmut Walther, Helen Walvoord, Jared and Beatrice Wood, and Jack Zipes. Special thanks are also due to the inter-library loan librarians Sandy Gavett and Betty Hoose for their untiring efforts in obtaining research materials for me. Our secretary Janet Sobieski was of fantastic help in typing parts of the manuscript, and I also would like to express my appreciation to Hank Steffens, John Jewett, and Robert Lawson for their constant support of my research efforts. No scholarly work can go on in isolation, and I am most appreciative for the help that I have received from the people mentioned above and for the support of many others.

But above all I would like to express my deep thanks to my wife Barbara for the steady help, support, and interest that she provided as usual on this book. Without her presence, her understanding, and her willingness to forego such pleasures as weekend excursions, vacations, and leisure time spent together, this book would not have been completed. There is much of her in this book, especially since she also edited each chapter for me. I owe her much thanks, and would like to dedicate this book with much love and appreciation to her.

*Burlington, Vermont*                                                    W. M.
*Spring 1986*

# Tradition and Innovation
in Folk Literature

# 1 Grim Variations

## From Fairy Tales
## to Modern Anti-Fairy Tales

The appearance of the two volumes of *Kinder- und Hausmärchen* (Children's and Houshold Tales) by the Brothers Grimm in 1812 and 1815 marked not only the publication of one of the true bestsellers of the world, approaching the international and multilingual dissemination of the Bible, but also the beginning of a large global scholarly field commonly referred to as folk narrative research. While scholars of the nineteenth century assembled significant national and regional fairy tale collections that paralleled those of the Grimms, serious investigations into the origin, dissemination, nature and function of these texts also began to appear in a steady flow that has not ebbed.[1] In fact, interest in fairy tales has increased considerably in the past three decades, and obviously the bicentennial celebration of the births of Jacob and Wilhelm Grimm marked a high tide not only in scholarship on their fairy tale collection and their philological, folkloric, mythological, legal, and literary endeavors[2] but also in research concerning the fascinating question of what their work and in particular "their" fairy tales mean to people in modern technological societies.

At the present time, beautifully illustrated editions of Grimms' tales can be found in bookstores everywhere, attesting to the ongoing fascination of fairy tales even for children of the computer age. The modern child can still learn from these tales that certain problems, dangers, and ordeals can be overcome, that transformations and changes must occur, and that everything will work out in the end. They will learn to solve their problems imaginatively, and if we can give credence to psychological interpretations of the tales, the children will become independent and socially responsible citizens whose naive search for personal pleasure is replaced by an analytical understanding of social reality. Above all, children will learn from fairy tales to have an optimistic and future-oriented world view, and they will realize and understand universal human problems, which in turn will be a key to coping with their own individuality and the world at large. Child psychologists, in particular Bruno Bettelheim,[3] have made a strong case for the didactic value of fairy tales for children as they go through various rites of passage in their maturation process to adulthood, and there appears to be no need to argue with the contention that these tales of times gone by seem to be appropriate literature for young and innocent children.

But what about the adult? What value and meaning do these children's stories, as they are commonly referred to, have for people who have long passed their childhood? Do fairy tales have some universal appeal to mankind of all age groups and social classes, or are they today only for children and scholars who study them for various reasons? Why is it that cultural and literary historians, folklorists, sociologists, psychologists, and others have studied and continue to investigate the deeper meaning of fairy tales? Surely not simply because they love children's literature and in a wave of nostalgia long to return to those cozy moments when a beloved family member read or perhaps even told them one of those old stand-by Grimm tales many years ago. The reason is that scholars have long realized that these tales were originally not children's stories but rather traditional narratives for adults, couching basic human problems and aspirations in symbolic and poetic language. Even though they present an unreal world with miraculous, magical, and numinous aspects, fairy tales nevertheless contain realistic problems and concerns that are universal to humanity. They are symbolic comments on basic aspects of social life and modes of human behavior. Presented are not only such rites of passage as birth, adolescence, courtship, marriage, old age, and death, but also typical experiences and feelings in people's lives. Emotions such as love, hate, joy, sorrow, happiness, and sadness are found again and again, and often the same tale deals with such phenomena in contrasting pairs, that is success versus failure, wealth versus poverty, luck versus misfortune, kindness versus meanness, compassion versus indifference, or, simply put, good versus evil.

Fairy tales present the world in black and white, but in the end this conflict is resolved, and happiness, joy, and contentment become the optimistic expression of hope for a world as it should be. This trust in ultimate justice and the belief in the good of humanity must be of significance to adults today if hope is to exist for mankind at all in an age that is anything but a fairy tale. It is not surprising, therefore, that the Marxist philosopher Ernst Bloch talks so much about the utopian function of fairy tales in his monumental work *Das Prinzip der Hoffnung* (The Principle of Hope), which appeared from 1954 to 1959. For him, at least some fairy tales contain emancipatory potential for mankind, liberating people from oppression and leading to more just societies.[4] Read and interpreted in this way, fairy tales clearly contain elements of social history from a time far removed from the present. They often camouflage the trials of oppressed people facing malevolent rulers, the ever-present conflict between the haves and the have-nots, the desire for a fairer political system and social order, and so on.[5] The stories supposedly for children conceal in part the frustrations of adults who to this day long for a better and fairer world, where people can in fact finally live happily ever after.

This element of hope for social justice, fairness, and humanity is what enables these traditional fairy tales to survive today among children and adults. Their universality in dealing with human questions as well as their universal appeal as aesthetic expressions of the resolutions of these queries have occupied more psychologists and philosophers than Bruno Bettelheim and Ernst Bloch. The scholarship on the Grimm fairy tales alone is so vast by now that an individual researcher can hardly claim to know it all. There now exist superb critical editions with voluminous notes by such renowned scholars as Johannes Bolte, Georg Polívka,[6] and Heinz Rölleke,[7] several detailed studies concerning the aesthetics of fairy tales by Max Lüthi,[8] fascinating structural investigations by Vladimir Propp,[9] significant historical studies by Lutz Röhrich,[10] socio-political interpretations by Jack Zipes,[11] and many more.[12] Mention should also be made at least in passing of the inclusive tale-type studies that have been carried out using the Finnish geographic-historical method of analyzing the origin and dissemination of individual fairy tales. There are among others

Ernst Böklen's two volumes of *Schneewittchenstudien*, Anna Birgitta Rooth's *The Cinderella Cycle*, Marianne Rumpf's *Rotkäppchen: Eine vergleichende Untersuchung* and more recently Michael Belgrader's *Das Märchen von dem Machandelboom*.[13] But the basic problem with these otherwise excellent studies is that they document variants of these major tales only through the nineteenth century. While they present attempts at finding the archetype of each tale and discuss its historical dissemination more or less world-wide (or at least throughout the area of Indo-European tradition), they concern themselves not at all with what is happening to such well-known fairy tales in the present century. There is no immediate need for additional tale-type studies of such detail (although they obviously have their intrinsic and respected value). What is really needed is to bring the existing studies up-to-date, taking them from the Brothers Grimm to the present day.[14] Dozens of variants in the form of rewritten children's stories, literary reworkings, parodies, and satires exist, and there are also many uses of fairy tales in movies, caricatures, cartoons, comic strips, advertisements, and graffiti, which all need to be documented and interpreted in regard to their function and significance.

For the incredibly popular fairy tale of "Little Red Riding Hood" there have appeared a number of studies which in fact go far beyond Marianne Rumpf's earlier tale-type study. Hans Ritz (pseud. Ulrich Erckenbrecht) published his German *Die Geschichte vom Rotkäppchen. Ursprünge, Analysen, Parodien eines Märchens* in 1981 and one year later Jack Zipes followed in the United States with his *The Trials and Tribulations of Little Red Riding Hood: Versions of the Tale in Socio-Cultural Context*. Both books deal with numerous new literary versions of the fairy tale. Zipes includes various illustrations of the fairy tale and adds insightful interpretataive comments regarding its socio-political and moralistic significance. In my independently formulated study "Survival Forms of 'Little Red Riding Hood' in Modern Society" I include not only many additional texts but also modern reinterpretations of certain motifs of the tale in cartoons, caricatures, comic strips, and advertisements. In 1982 Zipes's book appeared in German translation. There have even been three major popular magazine and newspaper reports on this modern scholarly preoccupation with "Little Red Riding Hood."[15] It will surprise no one, therefore, if in this study no further mention is made of this particular tale except to say that such detailed studies of newer variants and allusions are needed for other very popular Grimms' fairy tales.

Before presenting and commenting on modern variations and reminiscences of "The Frog Prince," "Snow White" and "Hansel and Gretel," a few general observations concerning the modern survival of fairy tales are necessary. Doubtlessly traditional fairy tales are still told, read, heard on the radio, or watched on the television or movie screen, and it appears that children for many generations to come will continue to be enchanted by them. But these children are bound to grow up and mature, carrying with them consciously or subconsciously some of the archetypical motifs and structures contained in the fairy tales. In a most enlightening essay concerning the possibility of fairy tales in the modern age Hermann Bausinger argues successfully that humanity is predestined toward a type of "Märchendenken" (fairy tale thinking), that is, that we long for and strive toward the happy end so vividly expressed in fairy tales. Even though there might be moments of regression or deviation from this path, people will always try to escape the status quo of social reality in their longing for happiness. He, too, refers to Ernst Bloch's view of the fairy tale as a future-oriented departure toward utopia and to the fact that the biographical plots of many fairy tales thus become reflections of people on their path to a better life.[16]

On this subject, Max Lüthi speaks of the fairy tale as presenting people with "opportunities" for "purposeful motion" toward a world as it ought to be.[17] Jack Zipes refers to this aspect as the "emancipatory potential" of fairy tales "chart[ing] ways for us to become makers of history and our own destinies."[18] Lutz Röhrich even talks of the "Modell-Charakter" (model character) of many fairy tales for human emancipation from certain role expectations.[19] In this regard, the traditional fairy tales are in fact therapeutic, didactic, and optimistic expressions couched in symbolic language. How fitting, therefore, for Max Lüthi to state rather poetically that "fairy tales present an encompassing image of humankind and the world."[20]

But it is also Max Lüthi who has repeatedly pointed out the "Freiheit" (freedom) with which each individual can react to any given tale.[21] It must, therefore, come as no surprise that adults often respond quite differently from the way these scholars predict when rereading or remembering the fairy tales with which they became so well acquainted as children. While they might appreciate a fairy tale from time to time for the reasons discussed above, adults tend to understand fairy tales critically rather than symbolically. Having relinquished their naive dreams of a perfect world of happiness, love, and optimism, they often question the positive value system of the fairy tales. Many adults are unwilling to or incapable of accepting the positive value system of the old fairy tale as even a possibility to be hoped for, since they are too occupied with real-life problems. If suffering and oppressed people of earlier ages created these fairy tales to provide an escape from an unhappy and ugly reality, modern people, adhering to a pessimistic if not cynical world view, at the expense of the optimistic nature of the fairy tales, identify instead with the societal problems of former times, which appear to resemble their own. It has often been remarked that the fairy tale contains its antipode in its very essence. That is, while certain characters ultimately achieve happiness, others very drastically go to their doom. To many people of the present day the actual fairy tale is simply too far-fetched to accept, and it is the anti-fairy tale that appears to give a clearer symbolic view of what the human condition is really like.[22]

The moment one ceases to look at a fairy tale as a symbolic expression of the idea and belief that everything will work out in the end, the cathartic nature of the tale vanishes. Rather than enjoying the final happy state of the fairy tale heroes and heroines at the very end of the fairy tale, modern adults tend to concentrate on the specific problems of the fairy tales, since they reflect today's social reality in a striking fashion. Who, after all, would ever admit to being so naive and trusting as to believe in the optimism and hope of fairy tales? A good dose of negativism is present in this intellectual view of the world and also in its pragmatic reaction to the ills of modern society. Although at times we may wish and hope for a better or even fairy-tale existence, we are in fact preoccupied and burdened with real problems that prevent us even from longing for, let alone finding, that marvelous happy end. The positive and emancipatory vision of the fairy tales appears more often than not to be buried in a world where one tragedy or crime chases the next. Pessimism, skepticism, and cynicism are rampant and perhaps too much even for the traditional fairy tales to overcome.

Nevertheless, one thing is certain; fairy tales belong to our cultural heritage and common knowledge. They are familiar to almost everybody in our society as only the Bible and a few other written works are. According to a recent survey of two thousand representative West Germans by the Sample Institute (Mölln), 94 percent knew "Hansel and Gretel" very well, 93 percent "Snow White," 91 percent "Little Red Riding Hood," 90 percent "Sleeping Beauty," 89 percent "Cinderella," and 86 percent "The Frog Prince."[23] The picture is most likely similar in the United States, where "Snow White," "Cinderella," and "Sleeping Beauty" might rank higher due to the effect that the Walt Disney movies have had on large segments of the population.[24] Nonetheless, Linda Dégh is correct in assuming that in general we can talk of "superficial familiarity with not more than about a dozen [Grimm] tales"[25] in America. Obviously "Rapunzel" and "Rumpelstiltskin" would belong to this list in addition to the ones mentioned above.

Small as the number may be, these fairy tales represent part of our common heritage, making it possible to communicate with them and through them. We constantly reinterpret this handful of tales, not necessarily by recalling them in their entirety, but rather by looking critically at particular problems in the individual tales. When the final positive resolution of all problems at the end of the tales is neglected, certain of their episodes come to be seen as reflections of a troubled society, as a critical view of the belief in perfect love, or as a concern with social matters. Such modern reinterpretations of fairy tales gain in poignancy when contrasted with the traditional tale, that is when reality is juxtaposed with the world of wishful thinking. The resulting interplay of tradition and innovation takes place not only in the reinterpretation, sometimes poetically, of these fairy tales or segments of them by individuals, but also in the many modern allusions to fairy tale elements in movies, advertisements, comic strips, caricatures, cartoons, greeting cards, and graffiti. The popularity in the mass media and elsewhere in written and oral communication of playing with the motifs of no more than a dozen Grimm fairy tales is ever more obvious, as a questioning reaction to the positive and optimistic world view expressed in the fairy tales increases. The tendency to confront the fairy-tale world through humor, irony, or satire with a more realistic analysis had already begun by the turn of the century. Questions of guilt, deception, fairness, and so on began to be asked, and by today most of the realistic reinterpretations of entire fairy tales or certain motifs have become the general rule except when the fairy tales are intended for the pleasure of children.

Such modern reinterpretations often deal with sexual matters, which should be of no surprise considering the many psychological interpretations of fairy tales. But many of them also deal with such serious problems as greed, insensitivity, deception, cruelty, vanity, selfishness, hate, power, irresponsibility, and inhumanity. The adult world is filled with frustrations and disappointments, and often it appears absolutely void of the hope for happy endings. But by couching these disappointments in reinterpretations or allusions to positive fairy tales, are we not actually concealing behind these negative statements the glimmer of hope for a better world in which anti-fairy tales will once again become fairy tales? As Randall Jarrell states in "The Märchen: Grimms' Tales," written in 1945:

> Had you not learned—have we not learned, from tales
> Neither of beasts nor kingdoms nor their Lord,
> But of our own hearts, the realm of death—
> Neither to rule nor die? to change, to change![26]

Changes are necessary, and by concentrating on the anti-fairy tale side of the coin mankind might awaken to the fairy tale's emancipatory potential. Fairy tales show us the progress of their heroes toward a happier life by overcoming obstacles of all kinds. Perhaps the modern transformations of these fairy tales will teach humanity meaningful solutions to its difficult and complex problems. An adult who deals with any aspect of fairy tales today, be it in a joke, a cartoon, a literary text, an advertisement, or whatever, must obviously also recall the actual fairy tale and its happy end. By showing the ills of society using fairy tale motifs and by not giving up hope of creating the state of bliss expressed in them, we are in fact acknowledging the steady influence that these old tales have on us.

But let us now turn to a short analysis of three well-known fairy tales to show how these traditional stories survive today in the form of questioning anti-fairy tales. A *New Yorker* cartoon can serve as a starting point for some of the grim variations which are to follow. In it a car is approaching a large road sign with the inscription "You are now entering Enchantment—'Gateway to Disenchantment.'"[27] One can well image a somewhat archaic town-crier walking through the streets of the town lying ahead calling out the following news stories of the day: "'Snow White kidnapped. Prince released from spell. Tailor kills seven. These are the headlines. I'll be back in a moment with the details.'"[28] Fairy tale violence appears to be making the big news, and even the children seem to react negatively to the more gruesome aspects of some fairy-tale episodes, as is made clear by another cartoon, in which a small boy comments to his mother who is reading him Grimms' tales for the umpteenth time: "'Witches poisoning prin-

*"Witches poisoning princesses, giants falling off bean-stalks, wolves terrorizing pigs . . . and you complain about violence on TV!?"*

cesses, giants falling off beanstalks, wolves terrorizing pigs . . . and you complain about violence on TV!?' "[29]

Other such smart-aleck responses to the old stories by children deny the special magic of the tale by putting into question the formulaic beginning of many of them. A little boy simply interrupts his father's fairy tale reading by stating " 'Once upon a time. . .' You read that one before, Daddy!"[30] Another bright kid exclaims: "You read me that one before, so now it's 'TWICE upon a time,' right?"[31] And a third lad working with a construction kit even goes so far as to say to his well-intentioned dad with a fairy tale book in hand; "Les' [sic] deine dummen Märchen der Großmutter vor, ich habe hier einen Konstruktionsfehler auszumerzen!"[32] (Read your stupid fairy tales to grandmother. I have to get rid of a construction error here). But there is also the brainy girl who reacts to her father by impatiently asking: "Once upon a time, once upon a time! When was it, anyway?"[33] And so it is also not surprising when a school child whispers to a friend, "If it starts with 'once upon a time' I'm leaving,"[34] as the teacher prepares to read a story to the class. One wonders how psychologists as Bruno Bettelheim would react to such questions and statements by modern children, questions that destroy the gateway into the enchanted world of fairy tales.

The picture is no different as far as the concluding formula "and they lived happily ever after" is concerned. There is not only the realistic question of a youngster, "If they lived happily ever after, does that mean they're still alive?"[35] which might cause a mother problems. Another child wants to know the answer to the following justified question: "Doesn't anybody ever live happily ever after WITHOUT gettin' married?"[36] Keeping this question in mind, we have the following three cartoons in which the experienced parents themselves change the traditional formula that was already questioned by their observant youngsters. There is the father who ends his fairy tale with "And they lived happily for quite some time."[37] Alluding to the situation of separated parents a mother closes another story with "And they both lived happily ever after—she in New York, he in L.A."[38] And a third cartoon carries the following explanatory caption: "The beautiful princess married the handsome prince and they lived happily ever after until the children were grown and she decided to pursue a career and his masculinity was threatened."[39] It must not come as a surprise that parents today wonder if they should read fairy tales to their sophisticated children at all, when their happy endings appear to be so far removed from the reality of the adult life lying ahead of them. This conflict is convincingly expressed by Lisel Mueller in her poem "Reading the Brothers Grimm to Jenny" (ca. 1976):

> Jenny, your mind commands
> kingdoms of black and white:
> you shoulder the crow on your left,
> the snowbird on your right;
> for you the cinders part
> and let the lentils through,

*"And they both lived happily ever after—she in New York, he in L.A."*

and noise falls into place
as screech or sweet roo-coo,
while in my own, real world
gray foxes and gray wolves
bargain eye to eye,
and the amazing dove
takes shelter under the wing
of the raven to keep dry.

Knowing that you must climb,
one day, the ancient tower
where disenchantment binds

the curls of innocence,
that you must live with power
and honor circumstance,
that choice is what comes true—
O, Jenny, pure in heart,
why do I lie to you?

Why do I read you tales
in which birds speak the truth
and pity cures the blind,
and beauty reaches deep
to prove a royal mind?
Death is a small mistake
there, where the kiss revives;
Jenny, we make just dreams
out of our unjust lives.

Still, when your truthful eyes,
your keen, attentive stare,
endow the vacuous slut
with royalty, when you match
her soul to her shimmering hair,
what can she do but rise
to your imagined throne?
And what can I, but see
beyond the world that is
when, faithful, you insist
I have the golden key—
and learn from you once more
the terror and the bliss,
the world as it might be?[40]

If children question the utopian world established at the end of fairy tales, adults are bothered even more by the wide chasm between what the world is and what it ought to be, as is expressed in this poem. Adult reactions to the traditional "and they lived happily ever after" are therefore predictably highly negative. While in 1935 Fisher Body could still use an advertisement in which a bride and groom drive off in a beautiful car to a "happily ever after"[41] life after the prince had rescued his Cinderella from the ashes, modern scenes from a marriage present anything but a happy state. Chas Addams drew a cartoon of a royal couple at a marriage counsellor's admitting, "Wir leben aber seit Jahren nicht glücklich und zufrieden"[42] (We haven't lived happily and contentedly ever after for years). Another young king is more explicit about his marriage problems, asking the counsellor, "How can we live happily ever after if she refuses to have oral sex?"[43] In the palace such marital confrontation might also be put more generally in the simple accusation, "You're not even *trying* to live happily ever after!"[44]

But obviously this formulaic phrase, and even entire fairy tales, are not reinterpreted only from a marital point of view by adults today. They also serve as symbols for universal human problems and affairs, which are usually not particularly enchanting. A German cartoon expresses this splendidly by taking the formula "and they lived happily ever after" literally and juxtaposing it with present day reality. The caption of this cartoon showing a couple sitting in front of a television set explains: "'. . . so leben sie noch heute.' Verlaß dich drauf, in den Grimmschen Märchen steckt mindestens ein halbes Dutzend todsicherer Grusicals und Kriminalthriller drin!"[45] (". . . they lived happily ever after." You can bet that there are at least half-a-dozen sure horror and detective thrillers in Grimms' fairy tales).

Fortunately not all modern variations and allusions to Grimm fairy tales are gruesome and grim; some, in fact, are extremely humorous or positively ironic. All of them, however, question the traditional beliefs expressed in the utopian fairy tales, thus liberating us from some of the stereotypical roles and expectations presented in the tales. After all, it is not just the perfect ending of the fairy tale on which we must concentrate, but also the various steps that might lead us there. And often it is exactly these steps or episodes in the fairy tales that are placed into striking juxtaposition with today's realities by the modern adult reactions to the Grimm fairy tales. Usually the deeper symbolism of the fairy tales is lost in such modern reinterpretations, but the contrasts between the symbolic original and the realistic variation brings about a most effective communication of the present imperfections, be it on the level of the individual, the family, or the society at large.

The first fairy tale in the Brothers Grimm collection, "The Frog Prince," certainly has been reinterpreted along these lines numerous times, probably due to the fact that it deals with obligation, transformation, maturation, sex, and marriage.[46] Such universal themes are particularly relevant to the adult world, even though Dennis the Menace might naively ask his mother upon having this fairy tale read to him, "How long was Dad a frog before you kissed him?"[47] Let us at least hope that Dennis's mother and father are happily married and that his mother does not reproach her husband with, "You kissed better when you were a frog,"[48] or that the father does not conclude, "If you must know, yes! I was happier when I was a frog!"[49] Next we have the unhappy father sitting in a frog-like position at a pond and the mother explaining to the child, "Don't worry about it, dear. Your father's just reliving his youth."[50] And if fairy tale transformations were possible, he might even change back into a real frog and leap back into the water, with the woman left to comment, "He's opted out of society again."[51] While these cartoons might be joking reversals of the fairy tale, they put into question the truth of the tale by secularizing and demythologizing its symbolic content.[52]

On a more serious literary level, Susan Mitchell has expressed this longing to get out of a marriage in a caring and understanding fashion in her poem "From the Journals of the Frog Prince" (1978). What seemed to be a fairy tale transformation at first has proven to be a curse in a world where perfect marriages are not possible:

> In March I dreamed of mud,
> sheets of mud over the ballroom chairs and table,
> rainbow slicks of mud under the throne.
> In April I saw mud of clouds and mud of sun.
> Now in May I find excuses to linger in the kitchen
> for wafts of silt and ale,
> cinnamon and river bottom,
> tender scallion and sour underlog.
>
> At night I cannot sleep.
> I am listening for the dribble of mud
> climbing the stairs to our bedroom
> as if a child in a wet bathing suit ran
> up them in the dark.
>
> Last night I said, "Face it, you're bored
> How many times can you live over
> with the same excitement
> that moment when the princess leans
> into the well, her face a petal
> falling to the surface of the water
> as you rise like a bubble to her lips,
> the golden ball bursting from your mouth?"
> Remember how she hurled you against the wall,
> your body cracking open,
> skin shrivelling to the bone,
> the green pod of your heart splitting in two,
> and her face imprinted with every moment of your transformation?
>
> I no longer tremble.

Night after night I lie beside her.
"Why is your forehead so cool and damp?" she asks.
Her breasts are soft and dry as flour.
The hand that brushes my head is feverish.
At her touch I long for wet leaves,
the slap of water against rocks.

"What were you thinking of?" she asks.
How can I tell her
I am thinking of the green skin
shoved like wet pants behind the Directoire desk?
Or tell her I am mortgaged to the hilt
of my sword, to the leek-green tip of my soul?
Someday I will drag her by her hair
to the river—and what? Drown her?
Show her the green flame of my self rising at her feet?
But there's no more violence in her
than in a fence or a gate.

"What are you thinking of?" she whispers.
I am staring into the garden.
I am watching the moon
wind its trail of golden slime around the oak,
over the stone basin of the fountain.
How can I tell her
I am thinking that transformations are not forever?[53]

What this person (or rather, frog) is in fact saying is that marriage should not force a person to lose his identity. Another cartoon shows this splendidly, when a frog faced with a princess about to kiss him argues, "But I don't want to be turned into a prince. I want you to accept me for what I am."[54] Life at court or in the materialistic world of today is not necessarily desirable, especially not if it means giving up a more contented life. Thus a frog can even be ridiculed by his peers for having such transformation thoughts: "I'm a frog, you're a frog. Hell, we're all frogs. Except, of course, for Prince Charming over there."[55] And then there is the simple frog who will not let himself be seduced by a princess into being unfaithful to his family: "Please don't kiss me! I have a wife and children, and they're all frogs!"[56] We have a poetic reworking of this idea in a poem by Hyacinthe Hill appropriately called "Rebels from Fairy Tales."

We are the frogs who will not turn to princes.
We will not change our green and slippery skin
for one so lily-pale and plain, so smooth
it seems to have no grain. We will not leave

our leap, our spring, accordion. We have
seen ourselves in puddles, and we like
our grin. Men are so up and down, so thin
they look like walking trees. Their knees seem stiff,
and we have seen men shooting hares and deer.
They're queer. . . they even war with one another!
They've stretched too far from earth and natural things
for us to admire. We prefer to lie
close to the water looking at the sky
reflected; contemplating how the sun,
Great Rana, can thrust his yellow, webbed foot
through all the elements in a giant jump;
can poke the bottom of the brook; warm
the stumps for us to sit upon; and heat
our backs. Men have forgotten to relax.
They bring their noisy boxes, and the blare
insults the air. We cannot hear the cheer
of crickets, nor our own dear booming chugs.
Frogs wouldn't even eat men's legs.
We scorn their warm, dry princesses. We're proud
of our own bug-eyed brides with bouncing strides.
Keep your magic. We are not such fools.
Here is the ball without a claim on it.
We may begin from the same tadpoles, but
we've thought a bit, and will not turn to men.[57]

Consider finally the wonderful German cartoon, shown from the perspective of the frogs, where a kid-frog begs his mommy, "Lies noch
mal den Teil vor, in dem der hässliche Prinz ein hübscher Frosch
wird!"[58] (Read that part again where the ugly prince becomes a beautiful frog!). What a wonderfully humorous and yet telling inversion of
the fairy tale motif!

In the modern world of disbelief and non-magic not even spells by
witches work correctly. In one cartoon a witch pursues a half-
transformed frog screaming "Come back—I haven't finished with you
yet!"[59] A second humorous illustration shows two frogs commenting
on yet another hybrid frog/man: "They don't cast spells like they used
to."[60] Anyway, who would believe today that the magic of a kiss could
possibly transform the frog or any human being into a more desirable
person? Opposing this belief is first of all the fear of the unknown, be it
merely a sexual encounter or a more lasting relationship. Chas
Addams, for example, drew a somewhat timid young woman next to a
large overwhelming frog with the caption, "Aber woher soll ich denn

wissen, daß du ein verzauberter Prinz bist?"[61] (But how am I supposed to know that you are an enchanted prince?). A more sophisticated modern princess doubtingly confronts the would-be seducer with the question, "You really expect me to believe that you're a prince?"[62] Another young woman is concerned about sexual promiscuity and first asks the frog, "How do I know you don't have herpes?"[63] Finally there is the basic question, "But how do I know you'll turn into a prince?"[64] in a clean cartoon from *Playboy* that shows beauty and the beast confronting the only-too-human concern about beginning a meaningful relationship.

This fear of sexuality also plays a major role in the fairy tale of "The Frog Prince." It is not surprising to see it reinterpreted today, with the big difference that the sexual context of the episode is much more blatantly expressed. This is particularly true in parts of Anne Sexton's lengthy poem "The Frog Prince" (1971) in which the fear of sexual maturation is put into the following words:

> Frog has no nerves.
> Frog is as old as a cockroach.
> Frog is my father's genitals.
> Frog is a malformed doorknob.
> Frog is a soft bag of green.
>
> The moon will not have him.
> The sun wants to shut off
> like a light bulb.
> At the sight of him
> the stone washes itself in a tub.
> The crow thinks he's an apple
> and drops a worm in.
> At the feel of frog
> the touch-me-nots explode
> like electric slugs.
>
> Slime will have him.
> Slime has made him a house.[65]

It is, of course, the possibility of a sexual interpretation of this fairy tale that has made it so popular in the adult world. Such magazines as *Playboy*, *Penthouse*, and worse, as well as films of erotica abound in allusions,[66] of which only a few of the less indecent ones will be included here to indicate the possible perversion of Grimms' fairy tales. In a harmless cartoon the deceptive frog has obviously gotten the young woman to kiss him without miraculously changing into a

*"I lied!"*

prince. His sly comment is simply, "Funny! I usually turn into a handsome prince."[67] But in a *Penthouse* cartoon we find the frog in an animalistic sex act with the princess who can only comment, "Hey, I thought you were supposed to change into a prince first."[68] A second cartoon from this magazine shows the frog putting on his frog-suit after the sexual act and slyly saying, "I lied!"[69] A poem by Phyllis Thompson entitled "A Fairy Tale" (1969) may bring the sexual preoccupation with this tale to a close. She too describes the bedroom scene

of the fairy tale, but with a vocabulary and directness that destroy the
magic of human love involving sex:

> Prince, when I found you downwind of the toadstools
> In the spring wood clearing, gaping with heartache,
> And you gulped, swollen under your sad jewels,
> I took you in a cold passion, for pity's sake,

> For the ludicrous white belly and bulging head.
> You jumped, suddenly, long green legs outsplayed,
> To my cupped hand. So was I brought to bed
> By a pledge, my white flesh by your green skin laid.

> How shall I tell the shapely change that fell
> On us as we embraced, reluctant? When
> You kiss my glistening skin I feel a spell
> Dissolve, and I come green to your hands again.

> I do not know the seeming from the true
> As we slip into our unambiguous climax!
> I, last and loveliest born, most happy—you,
> Prince, still humped like a frog in the slime of sex![70]

Luckily we also have more humorous interpretations of the kiss
scene, although they are still negative comments on our society. In a
cartoon from the solid *Audubon* society magazine we find another lying
frog who at least offers the cheated princess some consolation: "So I
lied to you. I'm not a prince. But marry me and you'll never be
bothered by flies."[71] But there are also other disappointments, for just
as spells of witches don't work perfectly anymore, so kisses do not
result in Prince Charmings either. Much black humor is contained in a
cartoon from an issue of the *Field and Stream* magazine in which a
young woman has just unsuccessfully kissed a frog who answers her:
"Thanks for the kiss, but I'm not the prince. A poacher got him."[72] We
are reminded of another disenchanting kiss-scene in the poem "Kissing the Toad" (1980) by Galway Kinnell:

> Somewhere this dusk
> a girl puckers her mouth
> and considers kissing
> the toad a boy has plucked
> from the cornfield and hands
> her with both hands;
> rough and lichenous
> but for the immense ivory belly,
> like those old entrepreneurs
> sprawling on Mediterranean beaches,

with popped eyes,
it watches the girl who might kiss it,
pisses, quakes, tries
to make its smile wider:
*to love on, oh yes, to love on.*[73]

Another princess transforms a frog into a prince all right, but he is old and decrepit; the appropriate caption reads, "And about time, too!"[74] When a kiss only changes a frog partially into a prince, his upset question is, "You call that a kiss?"[75] and in a similar comic strip from *The Wizard of Id* series such a poor creature exclaims, "How 'bout once more with feeling?"[76] Little wonder that a more sexually intended cartoon concerning the unsuccessful kiss scene has the seducer demand, "Perhaps you could break the spell if you'd kiss me somewhere other than the mouth."[77] Yet even complete transformations seem to be problematic, for now and then the prince lapses into aspects of his former froghood. When an elderly royal couple goes for a walk, for example, the king suddenly flashes out a grotesquely long tongue to catch a fly, in a cartoon with the caption, "You can take the Prince out of the frog, but you can't take the frog out of the Prince!"[78] A German counterpart by the well-known artist Horst Haitzinger shows the prince leaping from a banquet table to catch a fly in the air with the caption, ". . . er war einfach zu lange Frosch!"[79] (. . . he simply was a frog for too long!). But even these hilarious illustrations only show once again that no magic kiss will change a person's identity and idiosyncrasies.

Talking about human oddities, we have also the absolutely ungrateful person who, after being rescued as it were, has the audacity to confront the princess with, "Marriage! Good heavens woman! Royalty marrying a bird who goes round kissing frogs?"[80] The poor rejected princess will obviously wind up on the couch of the psychiatrist, the modern intepreter of fairy tales, confessing to him that, "I started out looking for a prince, but now I just like to kiss frogs."[81] Alas, in *New Woman* magazine appeared the absolute reversal of ridiculing the woman searching for her lovely prince. This time she is the frog and says to the male, "Kiss me and I'll turn into a beautiful princess!"[82] It remains to be seen whether a whole new series of cartoons and literary variants will follow this new perspective. Judging by the fact that this variation appeared in 1982 and that I have located no others this far, we might have to conclude that this inverted motif has not caught on as yet.

The final examples of grim reinterpretations of this popular tale are drawn from the larger social sphere of politics and economics. The frog motif is used to satirize the problematic state of the modern economy, which is not free of worries as it would be in a fairy tale. There is, for example, the king just changed into a frog by the witch who, rather than being upset, declares, "Frankly, now that I've found out the size of my kingdom's national debt, I'd rather remain a frog."[83] Or we have the bankrupt king sitting at the Internal Revenue Service office lamenting, "Between 1962 and 1974 I was a frog. Then in 1975 I was crowned king, and 1975 was a very bad year for kings."[84] Perhaps he might be helped by the new tax bill, which was caricatured as two frogs with signs reading "Kiss me—I'm really a handsome GOP Tax Bill."[85] Maybe even the prime rate might go down if someone dares to kiss yet another obese frog, claiming that, "He's an enchanted prime rate."[86] While these cartoons use the positive symbol of the kiss scene of the fairy tale, they are in fact negating its utopian significance. There is no hope expressed in these modern variations but instead one senses an overpowering clash of the magic and the real. Even if the kiss were to take place, the economic problems would remain only in the form of a slightly deflated frog.

Turning to a few last political allusions to the fairy tale of "The Frog Prince" we have one frog commenting to another, "I can only hope when I become a prince again it [my kingdom] hasn't changed into a democracy."[87] Hope springs eternal for the prince, but obviously he doesn't want any change in the political status quo. There was also the interesting cartoon in 1983 showing the entire women's vote represented by a princess confronting the democratic contenders with the comment, "Just wait a minute now! Let me get this straight. . . . A kiss will turn one of you Democrats into a President?!"[88] But the magic didn't work, since political reality refuses to be patterned after fairy tales. Even more bitter in its satire is an anti-Reagan caricature that shows Reagan trying to convince the Statue of Liberty turned princess to look at the apartheid government of South Africa as a prince: "C'mon, Lady, loosen up and give my buddy here a little kiss. . . . I'm telling you he's a prince."[89] And finally there appeared a political caricature showing the strained relations between the Reagan administration and the Soviet Union. Since Reagan is a male, the artist has changed the Soviet Union into an ugly toad called Olga whom Prince Reagan is about to kiss. The stage directions for this absurd encounter read ". . . Then, when I kiss you, Olga, you turn from an ugly old toad into a not-so-bad looking broad, and we live more-or-less happily ever after."[90]

All that we can hope is that our political leaders will at least succeed in maintaining a world balance in which we can, in fact, live "more-or-less happily ever after." They have already succeeded in alienating us from the belief in magic fairy tales, but the fact that we continually draw on old fairy-tale motifs to comment on our human comedy here on earth is ample proof that we still hope for a transformation of humanity onto a higher level of social consciousness. In every humorous or satirical allusion to a fairy tale is hidden a statement of how things ought to be. In this emancipatory thrust as well as in fond memories of childhood days long passed lies the significance of fairy tales such as "The Frog Prince" for adults.

Modern reinterpretations of certain parts of the fairy tale "Snow White" also reflect human follies and vices. This tale of narcissism, beauty, jealousy, competition, temptation, and eventually maturation once again addresses basic conflicts that are parts of any socialization process. As a symbolic account of the pitfalls of wanting to be the very best, this fairy tale can serve as a parody of a society in which outside appearance is valued more highly than ethical convictions. The obsession with an artificial ideal of external beauty is present in the movies, on television, in magazines, and elsewhere, and the old fairy tale is used by the mass media both to encourage this preoccupation and to ridicule it. We want to concentrate more on the satirical view here, but folklorists, psychologists, sociologists, and others should pay much more attention to what effect both types of fairy-tale allusions in advertisements, cartoons, caricatures, and so on have on the mentality of the public.[91] They are clearly not used to keep certain fairy-tale episodes in our consciousness but rather to shock us into critical thinking by confronting the fairy-tale images ingrained in us with novel interpretations of them. The parodied fairy tales become significant forms of communication for the adult world, forms which, in a few words and often with an appropriate illustration, can be more effective than long commentaries on a particular subject matter.

Obviously certain formulas or rhymes are particularly suited for such innovative interpretations, and in the case of "Snow White" it is the universally known verse, "Mirror, mirror on the wall, who is the fairest of them all?" that has served innumerable times as an attention-getting device to shock people into a critical analysis of their own selves or of problems surrounding them. After all, this question, even in its original wording, does not necessarily only ask about beauty, and by varying it only slightly all kinds of enlightening queries intended to lead to new insights can be posed.

At its root this famous two-liner is, of course, the question that stems from naracissism and vanity. Almost everybody has asked this question during the maturation process or later in life, and the numerous greeting cards that play with this verse are humorous reactions to this fact. They also show the trivialization and demythologization of the actual fairy tale and of its important message about the need to overcome excessive self-love. One such greeting card, for example, has a ridiculous figure ask, "Mirror, mirror on the wall, who's the fairest of them all?" The response on the inside of the card is, "It's still Snow White, but keep trying, kid!"[92] The verse was slightly changed for the following birthday card: "Mirror, mirror on the wall, who's the youngest of them all" is printed outside of the card over a mirror, and the inside shows the broken mirror with the caption, "Oh, well, Happy Birthday, anyway!"[93] We see that fairy tales aren't possible anymore, not even on lighthearted greeting cards except, of course, a wonderful Valentine's Day card that hopes to make a dream come true. "Mirror, mirror on the wall who's the nicest, most wonderful, lovable person of them all?" is the almost-expected question, and the perfect fairy-tale answer is "That one! The one who's reading this card! Happy Valentine's Day."[94] Even the mirror has a heart shape, and the fairy tale has been reduced to commercial kitsch. Here we have folklore motifs used as a panacea, creating a sweet and mushy perfect world, at least for one day of romanticism a year. Such silly greeting cards have become extremely popular in recent years, and perhaps we should not simply brush this phenomenon aside. People are obviously buying them, thereby indicating that fairy tale motifs, even when used humorously, can help them express their feelings about another person. Behind these cards are hidden the traditional fairy tales with their positive message, and their jokes, puns, and ridicules are nothing less than hidden hopes for a fairy tale utopia.

Turning to the actual question of beauty, let us quote the end of a lengthy poem on "Snow White and the Seven Dwarfs" (ca. 1970) by Anne Sexton, which illustrates splendidly this only too human obsession:

> And thus Snow White became the prince's bride.
> The wicked queen was invited to the wedding feast
> and when she arrived there were
> red-hot iron shoes,
> in the manner of red-hot roller skates,
> clamped upon her feet.
> First your toes will smoke
> and then your heels will turn black
> and you will fry upward like a frog,
> she was told.
> And so she danced until she was dead,
> a subterranean figure,
> her tongue flicking in and out
> like a gas jet.
> Meanwhile Snow White held court,
> rolling her china-blue doll eyes open and shut
> and sometimes referring to her mirror
> as women do.[95]

Sexton seems to imply that Snow White really hasn't learned much from her stepmother and that the cycle of narcissistic rivalry will start over again. The famous mirror question is a universal one, and it has been the subject of many cartoons and caricatures showing both women and men asking the oracle about their beauty or other such important matters. In an imperfect world these artistic interpretations are usually negative in their humor or social commentary, once again indicating that modern life is not a fairy tale and that we must cope with what we are.[96] Certainly visual beauty is not going to be the answer to all our frustrations, even though it might help.

Imagine the disappointed look on the face of a woman who, after having asked the standard question, "Mirror, mirror on the wall, who is the fairest one of all?" receives the answer "Elizabeth Taylor"[97] in a 1957 New Yorker cartoon. Other women, realizing that they are no match for such competition, rephrase the question to a safer, "Who's the greatest Mom of them all?"[98] or "Who is the fairest one of all, and state your sources!"[99] And if the mirror, as it is likely to do, gives an unsatisfactory answer, the reaction is quick and to the point: "Well, then, who's the most intelligent?"[100] or "Oh, yeah? Well, I've seen better-looking mirrors, too!"[101] Of course there are also the defeatists who don't give the mirror a chance since they know that some "Snow White" will obviously beat them out: "Mirror, mirror—I know, why belabor the point . . ."[102] or "Mirror, mirror, on the wall, go to hell."[103]

*"It says I'm the fairest one of all! So there!"*

But there is always hope, and in the modern technological world an aggressive woman would definitely turn from a mirror to a much more objective and reliable computer. After complicated calculations she is able to read the print-out to her female competitors with much spite and self-assurance: "It says I'm the fairest one of all! So there!"[104] Even though she might have won this grotesque beauty contest, the cartoonist clearly wants to satirize this preoccupation with appearance. The ends that some people are willing to go to in order to beautify themselves are fittingly ridiculed in a cartoon where a woman sits in front of a mirror surrounded by dozens of cosmetic items. She too asks the traditional question, "Mirror, mirror, on the wall, who's the fairest of them all?" but the answer by the mirror is, "Just keep spending, sweetheart, it could be you!"[105] We wouldn't be surprised if along with her cosmetics this woman were to buy a new type of handy mirror that was advertised with four pictures and the appropriate slogan: "Mirror Mirror. On the wall. On the desk. On the shelf. On the door."[106]

In comparison, how much more relevant and significant was an article on various concepts of female beauty at different ages, from Nefertiti to Rubens' female figures and others. Befittingly the journalist chose the headline "Mirror, Mirror on the Wall . . ."[107] for this intriguing essay. And finally, the British satirical magazine *Punch* included a short text entitled "Snow White and the Sincere Mirror," which, with much irony, makes the same point that tastes vary and that beauty after all is in the eye of the beholder:

> "Mirror, mirror on the wall, who is the fairest one of all?" the Queen asked her new mirror. The old one had smashed itself rather than give an opinion.
>
> "I'll be honest with you," replied the mirror. "The fact is that there are no absolute standards. Among the Eskimos, for instance, your kind of beauty would cut very little ice. Ha ha! On the other hand, send you somewhere East of Suez where the best is like the worst, and they might go for you in a big way. Yes sir, a very big way. You look like Joan Crawford, actually. Except younger," the mirror added quickly.
>
> "I asked a simple question," said the Queen. "Who is the fairest of them all? Yes or no."
>
> "That's what I'm saying," explained the mirror. "Tastes vary. The kind of mirror I am, with my socio-economic conditioning, personally, I like somebody along the lines of Snow White—kind of a younger Natalie Wood."
>
> "And of all the mirrors I could have had," the Queen complained, "I had to get a culturally deprived one with integrity."[108]

The problems of narcissism, beauty, and greatness are not restricted to the female population. Men too are riddled by such insecurities and the cartoons that I have located of men speaking to the mirror appear to be even more absurd in their use of questions for which the mirror has no answers. Picture a poor fellow in the morning in front of a mirror shaving and putting the following question to this bathroom oracle: "Mirror, mirror on the wall, who's the most successful regional manager of computer-systems analysis in East Orange, New Jersey?"[109] And a king, who doesn't have such mundane worries, stands in front of the mirror wondering while exposing himself, "Mirror, mirror on the wall, whose is the largest . . ."[110] Just as ridiculous is a third man with his query, "Mirror, mirror, on the wall, who is the most unself-consciously hipper-than-thou-almost-over-thirty-type-person of them all?"[111] In these cartoons the mirror symbolizes people's concern with their identity and shows some of the anxieties and fantasies that prevent us from finding self recognition and maturity.

In addition to answering questions of this type the mirror has also become a political looking glass in which the future of politicians is put under scrutiny. From 1960 dates a fascinating cartoon in which Richard Nixon is shown as the witch-like stepmother getting the poisoned apple ready for Snow White and asking evilly, "Mirror, mirror on the wall, who's the fairest one of all?"[112] This is a splendid satire of dirty and tricky politics which is matched by a German political cartoon showing Indira Gandhi standing in front of the mirror wearing a banner with the inscription "Bürgerrechte" (Civil Rights) and holding a club in her hand. The mirror, probably in this case the people, will not dare to answer her question, "Wer ist die Schönste im ganzen Land?"[113] (Who is the fairest one of all?), negatively. Her son, Rajiv Gandhi, was recently shown in quite a different predicament on the cover page of *The Economist*. As he strikes a meditative pose looking ahead, his head is flanked by pictures of Reagan and Gorbachev. Alluding to Gandhi's attempt to steer India between the two super-powers the caption to this photo montage reads, "Picture, picture on the wall I would like to love you all."[114] The cartoons show us how infantile our behavior can be, and they are grim variations on the same question raised in "Snow White" in a poetic fashion. Once taken literally and placed in the adult world, the symbolic fairy tale of narcissism becomes a telling mirror of our societal and psychological reality. If fairy tales, as such, represent archetypical problems of humanity, then the transposition of certain of their motifs into the realistic world can help us to understand mankind better. The innovative use of traditional folklore materials thus takes on the significance that the actual fairy tales had once upon a time when they were told for adult entertainment. The fairy tales have been reduced to cartoons in our world of images where the reading of cartoon captions has taken the place of enjoying the longer traditional fairy tales.

In "Snow White" there are, of course, also the seven dwarfs who have captured the fantasy of the adult world and that of modern children. Two telling cartoons might be mentioned here where a child gets the traditional fairy tale mixed up with the more realistic problem of divorce. Dennis, the Menace asks his dad to entertain him with the "Snow White" tale by requesting, "Read me about Snow White and the Seven Divorces."[115] And his German female counterpart asks her mother about the marital state of the dwarfs' mother to which the mother responds matter of factly, "Tut mir leid, die Geschichte sagt nichts darüber, ob die Mutter der sieben Zwerge Witwe oder geschieden war"[116] (I'm sorry, the story doesn't mention whether the seven dwarfs' mother was a widow or divorced). Such fairy tale cartoons become telling commentaries on societal problems like divorce, and they also show that children or adults are prone to place certain fairy-tale motifs in contrast with realistic situations facing them. Seen like this, the cute little dwarfs, which were saccharinized even more by Walt Disney's movie version, become much more significant figures. Often they are seen by adults as representing multiple concerns in sexual or international politics.

Returning for a moment to the Walt Disney version of *Snow White* that gave the dwarfs their famous silly names, we would like to show at least some examples of how this movie has resulted in a trivialization of the dwarfs who in the traditional fairy tale represent the solid work ethic. In one cartoon the funny little dwarfs come home to a room where all their little beds are arranged with their Disney names on them. But there is one with a new name and the surprised question is, "Chubby! Who the hell is Chubby?"[117] There is also a Frank & Ernie comic strip that pictures a patient in a physician's office with the humorous statement, "I don't know what's the matter with me, Doc. I feel sneezy, bashful, sleepy, dopey, and grumpy, but I'm still happy."[118] Little wonder that Anne Sexton in her already mentioned poem, "Snow White and the Seven Dwarfs," writes equally disrespectfully:

> The dwarfs, those little hot dogs,
> walked three times around Snow White,
> the sleeping virgin. They were wise
> and wattled like small czars.
> Yes, It's a good omen,
> they said, and will bring us luck.
> They stood on tiptoe to watch
> Snow White wake up. She told them
> about the mirror and the killer-queen
> and they asked her to stay and keep house.[119]

The sarcastic tone of these lines was matched by the headline of an advertisement that appeared in the *Good Housekeeping* magazine in which a modern emancipated woman declares "I'm not Snow White but I'm not Dopey, either."[120] While this person might not be the fairest of them all, she is also not "stupid" as the dwarf's name "Dopey" would imply. We obviously have a woman here who is liberated enough to negate the beauty ideal and the servant role that play such a major part in this particular fairy tale.

The personalized dwarfs, and also the old anonymous ones, have been interpreted sexually by adults for quite some time, in ways ranging from light-hearted humor to crude obscenity. Robert Gillespie wrote his poetic reinterpretation "Snow White" (1971) along these lines, clearly wondering about the sexual activities of the Disney dwarfs and moving the underlying fairy tale once again into the original realm of adult entertainment.

> She found herself 7 no less
> dwarfs!
> Such disney images—where did they come from, the yellow pages?—
> grumpy sleepy sneezy happy dopey doc
> Doc?
> So why didn't she ever have any little dwarfs?
> She was afraid of her father's handlebar moustache?
> Who does she think she is, no hostility like the rest of us
> toward stepmother? Her mother for dying?
> What is really going on out there in that house in the woods?
> Do they really know?
> Does it ever get dirty and dull
> fishy-stale in her innocent linens?
> What are their little penises like, Snow White?
> Does one finger
> one lap another hump?
> Does one sneeze? Unnatural
> this absence of the natural. This division.
> 7 safe little men to father Mommy.
> Why are they stay at homes?
> Does she do the wash and cook casseroles or just be beautiful?
> What was she *doing* out there in the wilderness in the first place,
> looking for dwarfs?
> Who made Snow White her big bed and cookies
> letting her sit there and eat?
> Home from their gold mine the swarthy dwarfs she inspires bring
> bacon and mayonnaise. With love. They make spring
> look like a dwarf.

Oh that lovely garden of a girl,
they stay because she takes their seed, because a garden stays.
They grow. Get roots down. Better men for it.

(And the apple woman and her uxorious
sidekick, what the fuck what a drag why not be the most beautiful
move on freak out kick *free*,
kicked out)
nibble nibble pick pick at the core of civilization
arch-fear proto-hate ur-guilt
their balls fall off like ripe peaches
pussy snow
beautiful sweet and kind and good.
Everybody agrees.
You soak me up, I'll cut you down;
*because* they soak her up. Because
they *like* it. Like looking up the blood-red and ebony snow
white they wish they came from.
Save us from our littleness
our ugliness without any beautiful touches
oh lift us up.
Now she is home, a king's son's wife, she is fairy tail
she eats roast beef with crackers
listening to the birds chirp
watching the snow melt
wondering where the brave woodcutter
where the men on white horse[121]

   As in this poem, the dwarfs in sexual cartoons also seem to be unable
to forget the wonderful girl with whom they enjoyed common sexual
activities. That such activities went on is well documented as far as the
adult interpretation of the fairy tale is concerned, for instance by a
cartoon in *Playboy* magazine in which the dwarfs are listlessly showing
up for their morning work. The explanation given is, "Snow White
withheld her favors this morning, so we all got up Grumpy."[122] There
are also American and German cartoons showing the dwarfs at the
window of the palace where Snow White now lives her life with her
prince husband. The American caption quite pointedly has Snow
White send her former "lovers" away with the statement: "Can't you
get it through your heads? That part of my life is over!"[123] while the
German drawing by Horst Haitzinger has the prince ask his bride,
"Hast du eigentlich noch Kontakt zu deinen Freunden von früher,
Schneewittchen?"[124] (Are you still in contact with your former friends,
Snow White?). There is also a cartoon in which the prince finds the

seven dwarfs in bed with Snow White. This scene results in his reso-
lute declaration, "Jetzt will ich aber mit diesen sieben Zwergen ein
Wörtchen reden, Schneewittchen!"[125] (Now I really want to have a
word with these seven dwarfs, Snow White!). The sexual interpretations even entered a cartoon depicting the fairy-tale relationship between Prince Charles and Lady Diana, who had been working as a
nursery school teacher (i.e. caring for small children or "dwarfs"). In
the cartoon Queen Elizabeth leans over to her son Charles while Lady
Diana is surrounded by the dwarfs and asks, "Tell me, Charles . . .
exactly what do you know about this girl?"[126]

Yet there are obviously more serious reinterpretations of the seven
dwarfs as well. While it might be funny to draw a comic strip in *Mad*
magazine in which the tall Snow White smashes her head against the
door frame, which results in her head being bandaged up by the
ever-caring dwarfs,[127] a cartoon showing Snow White leaving the
house and singing a 1977 hit, "Short people got no reason to live,"[128] is
a sad satirical commentary on some of the lyrics of popular music. It's
only proper that one of the dwarfs is trying to stop this insensitive
Snow White by hitting her with a chair, and I report with some
satisfaction that this ridiculous record was taken off the market.

Even more serious are four political cartoons making U.S. presidents
into grotesque Snow Whites. Ridiculing our involvement in Southeast
Asia, a *Punch* cartoon from 1970 shows former President Nixon as a
democratic peace-bringer followed by seven dwarfs turned generals,
each with a briefcase naming his respective country: "South Vietnam,
South Korea, Cambodia, Thailand, Taiwan, Indonesia, and Laos." The
caption puts this entire democratization plan into question by stating:
"Snow White and the Seven Experiments."[129] During the Watergate
scandal Nixon also was drawn as Snow White, surrounded by his
dwarf-like cronies. This time the caption is merely "Snow White,"[130]
which suffices to place the conniving Nixon into a shocking juxtaposition with the pure Snow White of the fairy tale. The presidential
advisors involved in the cover-up also absolutely negate the innocent
dwarfs of the traditional tale. This is also the case in a cartoon in which
President Reagan accuses his White House staff members of being
responsible for having obtained some Carter documents during the
presidential debates: "Some of you dwarfs are going to take the rap for
the Carter papers or my name isn't Snow White!"[131] Here Reagan, who
is as big, relatively, as Snow White, is clearly shown to be untouchable

in this small scandal, and his underlings or dwarfs will have to cover for him. In a final political caricature we have one more time Reagan as Snow White with his little helpers surrounding him. No caption is necessary, but seven of the politicians with whom Reagan has surrounded himself have names on their shirts that pervert those sweet Walt Disney labels in a most telling manner: "Sleazy, Shifty, Cozy, Slick, Easy, Porky, and Grabby."[132]

On a more serious note yet is a German poem, "Der Spiegel" (The Mirror, ca. 1940) by Max Herrmann-Neiße, about a mirror that miraculously survived a major war. The poem closes with the question that all people ask their politicians: "Spieglein, Spieglein, an der Wand, wann kommt der Friede diesem Land?"[133] (Mirror, mirror on the wall, when will peace come to this land?). No doubt the mirror oracle will be questioned for many centuries to come, since questions of identity, beauty, and the like will always plague mankind. The fairy tale of "Snow White" will continue to exist at least in its printed or film versions, but judging by the decreased knowledge of fables and other traditional lore in our society, one wonders if some day the allusions in these cartoons and other texts will no longer be recognized. It would certainly be a great loss to communication and understanding if that were to occur, for our modern children's stories don't even come close to the universal applicability to life's complexities that the traditional fairy tales have.

In his interpretation of the "Hansel und Gretel" fairy tale Bruno Bettelheim states that "the gingerbread house is an image nobody forgets,"[134] and judging by the many allusions to it in modern texts and illustrations it has definitely been implanted in our consciousness. Who wouldn't want to give in to his oral greed and nibble on all those wonderful goodies? The temptation is always there for children and adults to give in to the drive of the taste buds. Even if Hansel and Gretel stand in front of a marvelous gingerbread house displaying a sign that draws attention to the fact that it "Contain[s] glucose, dry skimmed milk, oil of peppermint, dextrose, etc.,"[135] they probably will not be able to control their desire. And in one cartoon there is even a sophisticated witch who lures her victims to the sweets with a sign that states "Contains no saccharin."[136]

Little wonder that another cartoon pictures an equally tempting gingerbread house whose sign in the front yard labels it as the "American Dental Association National Headquarters."[137] If in the fairy tale the children are supposed to learn that they should not succumb to uncontrolled desires, we have here a cartoon based on the gingerbread motif that draws attention to what will happen to those who eat too many sweets. Of course the first consequence will not be the need for that evil dentist, the modern witch. There is always Alka-Seltzer® for immediate relief after gorging oneself, as can be seen from a splendid three-frame comic strip: the first frame shows Hansel and Gretel munching away, the second pictures them suffering indigestion and burping, and the third drawing has them hurry toward a house made up of Alka-Seltzer® tablets.[138] This satire is clearly directed at the quick and ready cures our modern pharmaceutical products seem to offer us. The same point is made in a more serious cartoon in which the ginger-bread or Alka-Seltzer® has been transformed to that universal drug "Valium."[139] A truly perverted gingerbread house offers even more potent stuff as Hansel finds out by sniffing the chimney on the top of the roof, his eager message to Gretel being "Let's go inside. Someone's smoking pot."[140] Two really up-to-date Swiss kids are, however, too bright to let such a modern witch lead them astray. Their short remark to the eternal temptress while turning away from that unhealthy stuff is simply, "Nein danke, wir essen nur Bio-Kost"[141] (No thanks, we only eat health food).

Such mutations of the traditional gingerbread house show how the dangers for children have changed in the modern world. The fact that people will always be confronted by new ills makes this motif a most convincing symbol of human problems. This is also the case in two very innovative cartoons that show the witch traveling in a trailer gingerbread house. In one she stops on the road and attempts to pick the children up by asking, "Hi, kids! Want a lift?"[142] and in a very similar illustration two years later in the same magazine we see only the evil witch in her mobile home looking for possible victims.[143] Such cartoons obviously amuse adults at first, but once we are reminded of the evil witch in the fairy tale, the many stories of child abductions come to mind and turn these seemingly funny picture-jokes into grim black humor.

This is also the case with the numerous cartoons that choose the gingerbread motif as a way to comment on today's construction indus-try and all the problems associated with it. There is first of all the wisecrack of two know-it-all children who confront the witch with the perfectly realistic question: "Gingerbread? Really? How did you get a mortgage?"[144] Much more serious, however, is another cartoon in which a bank official gives the witch the following sad news: "I'm from the marshal's office. Nabisco has foreclosed on your mortgage."[145] Once the "witch" is seen as an elderly single person this cartoon becomes a telling satire on how people lose their homes because of financial problems.

Of course people also lose their homes because of larger and higher buildings or because of the epidemic of town houses and condominiums. In front of a quaint and charming gingerbread house we find the sign of a large construction firm explaining that "This structure will be torn down and replaced by a new 44-story cookie."[146] And if it weren't a tall office building that would replace this family homestead, some contractor would certainly put up a whole array of little homes, trying to sell them as a little fairy-tale village for rich suburbanites with the claim "Gingerbread Village—105 Tasty Units—Immediate Occupancy."[147] And what if the old witch were to fight city hall and actually win the case and retain her beloved home? Someone would soon put up a highrise right next to her, and a young concerned couple called Hansel and Gretel would only say to each other, "Beats me how they got planning permission."[148] Or the city would simply build the needed highway over the house that it could not destroy since "She fought the court order to the hilt."[149] Progress will win out, and the fairy-tale world will be squeezed underneath the superhighway of our busy society.

Such disenchantments also exist for the buyers of the few lovely gingerbread homes that might still be available. Some dreamers regress into childhood if only confronted by a house bearing any resemblance to their image of the witch's house in the fairy tale. Thus a grown-up Hansel and Gretel marvel at a shingled country home and romantically exclaim "And look—she's got an outside gingerbread toilet."[150] The next step is to nibble at the house, at which point the man, being a bit more realistic in his analysis of the dream home, remarks, "For Heaven's sake, Hilda–this is *mock* gingerbread."[151] The fairy-tale element is also lost in a closer scrutiny of the caption, "Had any nibbles?"[152] of yet another cartoon, in which the witch is actually trying to sell her house. Here the old verse, "Nibble, nibble, little mouse, who is nibbling at my house?" is reduced to a mercantile matter by the dwarf-like neighbor asking the question. And finally consider a cartoon in which a realtor leads the prospective buyers Hansel and Gretel to the house explaining, "We just listed it . . . some young punks vandalized the place and cooked the owner."[153]

The last cartoon leads us to an interesting anti-fairy tale poem by Sara Henderson Hay with the curious title, "Juvenile Court" (1963):

> Deep in the oven, where the two had shoved her,
> They found the Witch, burned to a crisp, of course.
> And when the police had decently removed her,
> They questioned the children, who showed no remorse.
> "She threatened us," said Hansel, "with a kettle
> Of boiling water, just because I threw
> The cat into the well." Cried little Gretel,
> "She fussed because I broke her broom in two,
>
> And said she'd lock up Hansel in a cage
> For drawing funny pictures on her fence . . ."
> Wherefore the court, considering their age,
> And ruling that there seemed some evidence
> The pair had acted under provocation,
> Released them to their parents, on probation.[154]

Just as in the cartoon, Hansel and Gretel are interpreted here as juvenile delinquents who really won't get much of a punishment. This opens up a whole new question about the character of Hansel and Gretel, who, like so many primitive fairy-tale heroes, have committed a most serious crime. The German poet Josef Wittmann treats this question in his short poem, "Hänsel und Gretel" (1976):

> Nichts als die Not gehabt,
> erwischt beim Stehlen,
> eingesperrt,
> ausgebrochen
> und ihren Wärter dabei umgebracht.
> Und aus denen,
> meinst du,
> soll noch mal was werden?![155]
>
> (Nothing but rough times,
> caught stealing,
> locked up,
> escaped
> and the warden murdered.
> And of them,
> you think,
> something will come some day?!)

When the story is looked at realistically and episode by episode, the children do in fact commit a criminal act. This is also very evident from another most telling poem by Louise Glück, where we find "Gretel in Darkness" (1971), that is, tortured by nightly attacks of a terribly guilty conscience about having pushed the witch into the oven.

> This is the world we wanted.
> All who would have seen us dead
> are dead. I hear the witch's cry
> break in the moonlight through a sheet
> of sugar: God rewards.
> Her tongue shrivels into gas. . . .
>
> Now, far from women's arms
> and memory of women, in our father's hut
> we sleep, are never hungry.
> Why do I not forget?
> My father bars the door, bars harm
> from this house, and it is years.
>
> No one remembers. Even you, my brother,
> summer afternoons you look at me as though
> you meant to leave,
> as though it never happened.
> But I killed for you. I see armed firs,
> the spires of that gleaming kiln—
>
> Nights I turn to you to hold me
> but you are not there.
> Am I alone? Spies
> hiss in the stillness, Hansel,
> we are there still and it is real, real,
> that black forest and the fire in earnest.[156]

Interpreted in a realistic and isolated fashion, the burning of the witch is in fact a gruesome act by the young Gretel, who however kills the witch only to protect the life of her brother. In the fairy tale the killing is but one symbolic step in dealing with an evil force and a way toward liberation and independence. At the end of the tale the children are shown as benevolent people who have learned to cope with their own needs and those of others. Momentary regressions even into criminal acts function as a contrast to the fairy-tale path toward eventual bliss and fulfillment. Black and white are in continuous struggle until the inherent good of the fairy-tale hero triumphs. As modern interpreters of the tale, unwilling to accept the symbolic nature of these tales, we often emphasize the gruesome isolated scenes, since they reflect life all around us. But the fact that fairy tales, too, appear to have scenes of inhumanity should certainly not be an excuse for realistic actions. Fairy tales must be seen in their entirety, otherwise they will be as disenchanting as the news of the day. Once again, given the pessimistic world view that, understandably, surrounds us, it is only natural that such negative reinterpretations have become popular. But in all of that despair there is also always the glimmer of hope that something will some day come of us, just as it did of Hansel and Gretel.

Our final examples will turn grimmer yet, commenting on various additional social problems. As early as 1920 the American journalistic writer Bert Leston Taylor published a telling variation of the "Hansel and Gretel" fairy tale titled "The Babes in the Wood," with the ironic subtitle "Revised and Regilded for Comprehension of the Children of the Very Rich." In this account Taylor satirizes the materialistic and superficial behavior of the wealthy, even having the children use pearls instead of bread crumbs to find their way back to this lifestyle.

*I*

Once upon a time there dwelt in a small but very expensive cottage on the outskirts of a pine forest a gentleman with his wife and two children. It was a beautiful estate and the neighborhood was the very best. Nobody for miles around was worth less than five million dollars.

One night the gentleman tapped at his wife's boudoir, and receiving permission to enter, he said: "Pauline, I have been thinking about our children. I overheard the governess say to-day that they are really bright and interesting, and as yet unspoiled. Perhaps if they had a fair chance they might amount to something."

"Reginald," replied his wife, "you are growing morbid about those children. You will be asking to see them next." She shrugged her gleaming shoulders, and rang for the maid to let down her hair.

"Remember our own youth and shudder, Pauline," said the gentleman. "It's a shame to allow Percival and Melisande to grow up in this atmosphere."

"Well," said the lady petulantly, "what do you suggest?"

"I think it would be wise and humane to abandon them. The butler or the chauffeur can take them into the wood and lose them and some peasant may find and adopt them, and they may grow up to be worthy citizens. At least it is worth trying."

"Do as you please," said the lady. "The children are a collaboration; they are as much yours as mine."

This conversation was overheard by little Melisande, who had stolen down from her little boudoir in her gold-flowered night-dress for a peep at her mamma, whom she had not seen for a long, long time. The poor child was dreadfully frightened, and crept upstairs weeping to her brother.

"Pooh!" said Percival, who was a brave little chap. "We shall find our way out of the wood, never fear. Give me your pearl necklace, Melisande."

The wondering child dried her eyes and fetched the necklace, and Percival stripped off the pearls and put them in the pocket of his velvet jacket. "They can't lose us, sis," said he.

## II

In the morning the butler took the children a long, long way into the woods, pretending that he had discovered a diamond mine; and, bidding them stand in a certain place till he called, he went away and did not return. Melisande began to weep, as usual, but Percival only laughed, for he had dropped a pearl every little way as they entered the wood, and the children found their way home without the least difficulty. Their father was vexed by their cleverness, but their mamma smiled.

"It's fate, Reginald," she remarked. "They were born for the smart set, and they may as well fulfill their destinies."

"Let us try once more," said the gentleman. "Give them another chance."

When the servant called the children the next morning Percival ran to get another pearl necklace, but the jewel cellar was locked, and the best he could do was to conceal a four-pound bunch of hot house grapes under his jacket. This time they were taken twice as far into the wood in search of the diamond mine; and alas! when the butler deserted them Percival found that the birds had eaten every grape he had dropped along the way. They were now really lost, and wandered all day without coming out any-where, and at night they slept on a pile of leaves, which Percival said was much more like camping out than their summer in the Adirondacks. All next day they wandered, without seeing sign of a road or a chateau and Melisande wept bitterly.

"I am so hungry," exclaimed the poor child. "If we could only get a few *marrons glacés* for breakfast!"

"I could eat a few macaroons myself," said Percival.

## III

On the afternoon of the third day Percival and Melisande came to a strange little cottage fashioned of gingerbread, but as the children had never tasted anything so common as gingerbread they did not recognize it. However, the cottage felt soft and looked pretty good to eat, so Percival bit off a piece of the roof and de-

clared it was fine. Melisande helped herself to the doorknob, and
the children might have eaten half the cottage had not a witch
who lived in it come out and frightened them away. The children
ran as fast as their legs could work, for the witch looked exactly
like their governess, who tried to make them learn to spell and do
other disagreeable tasks.

Presently they came out on a road and saw a big red automobile
belonging to nobody in particular. It was the most beautiful car
imaginable. The hubs were set with pigeon blood rubies and the
spokes with brilliants; the tires were set with garnets to prevent
skidding, and the hood was inlaid with diamonds and emeralds.
Even Percival and Melisande were impressed. One door stood in-
vitingly open and the children sprang into the machine. They
were accustomed to helping themselves to anything that took their
fancy; they had inherited the instinct.

Percival turned on the gas. "Hang on to your hair, sis!" he
cried, and he burnt up the road all the way home, capsizing the
outfit in front of the mansion and wrecking the automobile.

Their mamma came slowly down the veranda steps with a
strange gentleman by her side. "These are the children, Edward,"
she said picking them up, uninjured by the spill. "Children, this
is your new papa."

The gentleman shook hands with them very pleasantly and
said he hoped that he should be their papa long enough to get really
acquainted with them. At which remark the lady smiled and tapped
him with her fan.

And they lived happily, after their fashion, ever afterward.[157]

The author doesn't tell us whether this woman bothered to get a
divorce first before picking up the new papa for the children. But there
exists an interesting allusion to the gingerbread house of the fairy tale
in John Ower's short but revealing poem, "The Gingerbread House"
(1979), in which the separation of parents has caused much emotional
stress for their little girl. The toy gingerbread house that the parents
had made for their Gretel was interpreted not as a doll's house but
rather as a witch's house by the child, an allusion to her unhappy
homelife, which resembled that of Hansel and Gretel. The old fairy-
tale spell of the witch, perhaps here standing for marital problems of
various kinds, brought hate to the parents. The poem ends with them
"gobbling up" their child, which is clearly meant to show that their
broken home has consumed the life of the child:

> We made our little girl
> A gingerbread house.

Despite sweet cement
It leaned as if it yielded
To a hurricane wind.
Our baby took one look at it,
Said it was a witch's house,
And burst into tears.
She was a prophet in her way.
During our estrangement
The witch flew out the window
Riding on the storm.
She cast a wicked spell
That made us hate each other.
And now between the two of us
In the finest fashion
Of the old fairy-tales
We gobble up our child.[158]

Looking at the uses of motifs from this fairy tale that comment on national and even international problems, we find a magazine cover of *The Economist* with a rather traditional drawing of Hansel and Gretel approaching the witch's house but with the interesting headline, "West Germany's Greens meet the wicked world."[159] Implied is, of course, the idea that the young people of this new German political party with their idealism concerning the environment, disarmament, and social justice will have to realize that "Realpolitik" is as mean and unpleasant as the witch in the fairy tale.

Talking of the environment, consider also the appropriate comment of a little boy to his father who is reading him the part of the fairy tale where the children drop the bread crumbs: "They shouldn't have been dropping that bread. That's littering."[160] Better yet is a more serious interpretation of a touching passage in the traditional fairy tale. In 1973 the German news magazine *Der Spiegel* included a cartoon with the altered quotation " . . . da nahm Hänsel Gretel an die Hand und ging den Plastiktüten und Cola-Flaschen nach, die zeigten ihnen den Weg zu ihres Vaters Haus"[161] (Then Hansel took Gretel's hand and followed the plastic bags and cola bottles that showed them the way to their father's house). Almost ten years later Horst Haitzinger published a full-page colored caricature depicting this scene with an almost identical caption: "Da nahm Hänsel Gretel an die Hand und ging den Plastiktüten und Blechdosen nach, die zeigten ihnen den Weg zu ihres Vaters Haus"[162] (Then Hansel took Gretel's hand and followed the plastic bags and tin cans that showed them the way to their father's house). It is interesting to note how certain fairy tale motifs in their modern reinterpretations seem to take on a tradition of their own. Since people are experiencing environmental damage everywhere, the changed motif of the universal fairy tale becomes a most convincing and appropriate statement on today's realistic concerns.

The same process can be shown, as a final point in this section on "Hansel and Gretel," in four cartoons, caricatures, and poems that bring the sweet gingerbread house into striking juxtaposition with the anxiety over nuclear power. With the atom bomb that fell on Hiroshima still fresh in mind, Dorothy Lee Richardson in 1949 wrote her poem, "Modern Grimm," which starts and ends with the traditional verse, "'Nibble, nibble, little mouse, who is nibbling at my house?' 'Only the wind. Only the wind.'" But this quiet wind in the poem becomes the terrible whirlwind of self-destruction that mankind has made for itself. In a land that might have had its magic once upon a time, a terrible bomb has killed all magic, leaving us without the reassurance of the safe home as we know it from the end of the *Hansel and Gretel* fairy tale.

> "Nibble, nibble, little mouse,
> Who is nibbling at my house?"
> "Only the wind.
> Only the wind."

"What have you sown, O darling children?
 What have you grown in the land of magic?"
"Only the wind. Only the wind."

"What chroma of wind, O clever children?
What brilliant shade have you made with your magic?
What color of wind?"

"A rich red wind over Hiroshima,
Darkly blowing, brightly glowing.
A red-black wind

"We have sown the wind. Its seed we found
And dropped it lightly to the ground.
We have sown the wind.

"The small thing split. It branched to bear
A thousand red-black fruits in air.
We have sown the wind.

"We have sown the wind. It rises high
Till it beats the ear and blinds the eye
And sweeps a hole in the crouching sky
Where the whirlwind rushes in!"

*"Nibble, nibble, little mouse,*
*Who is nibbling at my house?"*
*"Only the wind.*
*Only the wind."*[163]

Nothing has changed since this poem was written and the threat of a nuclear accident, if not war, hovers over us. To illustrate this danger, a 1981 caricature transformed the chimney of the gingerbread house into a cooling tower with the caption, "Nuclear Power."[164] The witch has become the personification of this dangerous force and the innocent children walking toward it symbolize mankind's path toward possible annihilation. And following the actual nuclear accident at Three Mile Island, I located two bitter satirical reactions in recent publications. The cartoonist Mike Peters has placed the gingerbread house in front of two nuclear cooling towers and has the witch step out to lure the children inside. But to her amazement she finds them not alive anymore. Her short remark is the apocalyptic, "That's odd . . . They're cooked already . . ."[165] This reinterpretation of the gingerbread scene was repeated with the identical caption in a very recent "Mother Goose and Grimm"[166] comic strip.

But what kind of comics are these? They are certainly not funny but are, rather, grim statements of the dangers mankind has invented for itself. The fact that these comments are expressed through altered motifs of fairy tales is yet another proof of mankind's desire to find utopian solutions to these problems. By effectively alienating the adults from their fairy-tale dreams through perverted fairy-tale motifs in literary texts or cartoons, these comments always express the hope that this shock therapy might recall the emancipatory goals of fairy tales. "Hansel and Gretel" and its many reinterpretations are certainly ample proof that such disenchanting reactions are at least small moralistic attempts to bring about such a change. For the adult world these modern survival forms of traditional fairy tales are, without doubt, of much importance, since they will always remind us of how the world really is and how it ought to be.

Materials similar to the ones we have presented for "The Frog Prince," "Snow White," and "Hansel and Gretel" are available for other well-known Grimm fairy tales. Everywhere we look the surprising adaptability of these tales, or at least their motifs, becomes obvious. In the introduction to an important essay collection, *Fairy Tales as Ways of Knowing*, the editor, Michael M. Metzger, speaks of "the

*That's odd . . . They're cooked already . . .*

flourishing renewal of scholarly interest in fairy tales.''[167] We want to add that there also exists a fascinating upsurge in innovative survival forms of the fairy tales, which deserves much more attention from the scholarly world. Movies, television, all types of literature, caricatures, cartoons, and comic strips frequently play with the archetypical contents of traditional fairy tales. Viewers or readers can identify with such reinterpretations or they can oppose them, according to their own experiences. But communication of some sort is assured, since modern film makers, authors, and illustrators can count on the almost universal knowledge of the basic Grimm tales in our society.

The simple telling of the fairy tales or their satirical, parodistic, or alienating changes all signify the "Erneuerungsmöglichkeit"[168] (re-juvenation possibility) of fairy tales. This is possible only because fairy tales are "welthaltig"[169] (world-encompassing) as Max Lüthi declared almost forty years ago. They contain universal human experiences of love, hate, fear, anxiety, and so on, and that is why they can be applied to the modern age as well, even though their symbolic language might need to be changed to express today's reality. No matter which tech-nological or epistemological advances mankind may undergo, the fairy tales will always "represent the diverse possibilities of actual existence. Although they themselves are scarcely real, they represent real things. The glass beads of the fairy tale mirror the world."[170] As has been discussed, fairy tales contain a drive toward the positive solution of all conflicts, where good wins out over evil in the end, and the modern anti-fairy tales represent, in spite of their grim variations on traditional Grimm fairy tales, a continuous move toward improving the human condition. Fairy tales were always meant to be emancipatory tales for people of all ages, and we need them as well as their survival forms, to cope in an ever more complex world.

# 2 The Pied Piper of Hamelin

## Origin, History, and Survival of the Legend

Of all the German legends, "The Pied Piper of Hamelin" has without doubt attained the greatest popularity, not only in the country of its origin but also in other European nations, as well as in the United States. Shortly after its seven-hundredth anniversary, scholars can look back upon a truly amazing amount of research attempting to solve the riddle of why 130 children left the town of Hamelin on 26 June 1284, and where they might possibly have gone. As early as the eighteenth century, Christoph Friedrich Fein attempted to find a solution to this sudden exodus of young people, in a short essay,[1] and since then there have appeared at least a dozen scholarly dissertations, monographs, and books, as well as numerous journal articles, all of which have investigated the origin, meaning, and history of this legend.[2] Above all, the studies of Willy Krogmann (1934), Wolfgang Wann (1949), Heinrich Spanuth (1951), and Hans Dobbertin (1970), have assembled a detailed account of the history of the legend.[3] With much philological skill they have explained the departure of the children of Hamelin and reinforced the conclusion that they were most probably led voluntarily or abducted forcefully to a new settlement in Moravia.

In his superb study on the historical sources of the Pied Piper legend, Hans Dobbertin has assembled 140 texts and references dating from approximately 1300 to 1816, when the legend appeared in its commonly cited and known form in the first volume of the *Deutsche Sagen* (German Legends) of the Brothers Grimm. Clearly, this is not the place to discuss every one of these references, but at least a few must be mentioned here in order to give a fragmentary picture of the origin and history of the legend. The earliest source is a stained-glass inscription from around 1300 on the Market Church in Hamelin, which was restored in 1572 but is now lost. The fragmented inscription referred to the day of John and Paul (26 June) and attempts at reconstruction from the few words remaining show that the inscription might have read, "Am dage Ioannis / et Pauli / cxxx sind binnen / Hamelen ge/varen tho Kal/varie vnde / dorch geledt / allerlei gevar / gen Koppen ver/bracht vnd verloren" (On the day of John and Paul 130 [children] in Hamelin went to Calvary and were brought through all kinds of danger to the Koppen mountain and lost). The picture itself showed a man in colored clothes surrounded by children, and it is for this reason that the word "children" and of course the reference to the "Pied Piper" could be left out of the inscription, which was limited in space.[4]

Of the greatest importance is the fourteenth century Latin chronicle *Catena Aurea* (The Golden Chain), written by the monk Heinrich of Herford, since one of the manuscripts found in the city of Lüneburg contains a Latin report concerning the children of Hamelin, which was probably added to the back of the last page between 1430 and 1450. This "Lüneburg manuscript," which was found only in 1936 by Heinrich Spanuth, gives a precise account of the exodus of the children, mentioning the exact date, the number of children, and a young man with a silver pipe:

> Here follows a marvelous wonder, which transpired in the city of Hamelin in the diocese of Minden, in the Year of Our Lord 1284, on the Feast of Sts. John and Paul. A certain young man thirty years of age, handsome and well-dressed, so that all who saw him admired him because of his appearance, crossed the bridges and entered the city by the Weser Gate. He then began to play all through the city a silver pipe of the most magnificent sort. All the children who heard his pipe, in number around 130, followed him to the East Gate and out of the city to the so-called execution place or Calvary. There they proceeded to vanish, so that no trace of them could be found. The mothers of the children ran from city to city, but they found nothing. It is written: A voice was heard from on high, and a mother was bewailing her son. And as one counts

the years according to the Year of Our Lord or according to the first, second or third year of an anniversary, so do the people in Hamelin reckon the years after the departure and disappearance of their children. This report I found in an old book. And the mother of deacon Johann von Lüde saw the children depart.[5]

In a Bamberg chronicle from the year 1553 by Hans Zeitlos, we find the first written German report of the legend with a number of important new additions. Zeitlos calls the pipe player a "spilman" (musician) and gives him a magical if not devilish nature, saying that he might return three hundred years later to fetch more children. For the first time there are also two children who return—one blind and the other mute so that they could not explain the actual happenings. This realistic addition clearly is meant to increase the plausibility of the events described, but it also immediately adds to the mysterious nature of the tale since these two "witnesses" cannot communicate their impressions.

There is also a mountain which lies approximately a rifle shot away from this city, called Calvary, and the citizens say that in 1283 a man was seen, possibly a musician, wearing clothing of many colors and possessing a pipe, which he played in the city. Whereupon the children in the city ran out as far as the mountain, and there they all disappeared into it. Only two children returned home, and they were naked; one was blind and the other mute. But when the women began to look for their children, the man said to them that he would come again in 300 years and take more children. 130 children had been lost and the people of this place were afraid that the same man would come again in 1583.[6]

While the Lüneburg manuscript and the Bamberg chronicle give us early Latin and German variants of the legend, it is the Pomeranian theologian Jobus Fincelius who provided the first printed German version about three years after the latter in his *Wunderzeichen*. Here the piper is described as a devil, and the fact that the children were led away is seen as an example of God's anger against human sin. The evil character of the townspeople in the legend is already foreshadowed here, and the "Pied Piper" is seen as a figure who brings severe judgment by taking away the children. It is also important to note here that Fincelius refers to a different date, the Feast of Mary Magdalene (22 July) of the year 1376, a date that was later picked up by Robert Browning who found it in an English manuscript from the year 1605 that was based on this German text from 1556.

I wish to report here a true story concerning the devil's power and evil nature. About 180 years ago it happened in Hamelin on the Weser in Saxony, that the devil, on the Feast of Mary Magdalene, appeared on the streets in men's clothing. As he went he piped, enticing many children, boys and girls; and he led them out of the city to a mountain. When he arrived there he disappeared with the children, who numbered very many, so that no one knew where the children went. A young girl, who had followed them afar, told her parents this, and shortly thereafter the painstaking search began, on land and on sea, to discover whether the children had perhaps been stolen and led away. But no one found any trace of where they had gone. This greatly saddened the parents, and it serves as a frightful example of God's anger over sin. This report is recorded in the Municipal Report in Hamelin, and many people have read and listened to it.[7]

In addition to these three early written or printed texts, three significant short references to the children's exodus still exist in Hamelin. The Hamelin museum exhibits a large stone, part of a town gate from the year 1556, that has the following inscription:

ANNO 1556 / CENTU(M) TER DENOS
CUM MAG(US) AB URBE PUELLOS /
DUXERAT A(N)TE A(N)NOS 272.
(CON)DITA PORTA FUIT.[8]

(In the year 1556, 272 years after the magician led 130 children out of the city, this portal was erected.)

The other two extant inscriptions are on the fronts of houses in Hamelin. The first is inscribed under the gable of the so-called *Rattenfängerhaus* (Pied Piper House), which was constructed in the year 1602/03.

ANNO 1284 AM DAGE IOHANNES ET PAVLI WAR DER 26 IVNII
DORCH EINEN PIPER MIT ALLERLEI FARVE BEKLEIDET GE-
WESEN CXXX KINDER VERLEIDET BINNEN HAMELEN GEBON
TO CALVARIE BI DEN KOPPEN VERLOREN[9]

(In the year 1284 on the Feast of Saints John and Paul, the 26th of June, 130 children were led astray by a pied piper and led out to Calvary by the Koppen where they all disappeared)

The other inscription is to be found on the *Hochzeitshaus* (Wedding House) dating back to 1610, another magnificent example of the northern Renaissance in architecture. The verse is quite similar to the previous one, and both of them recall the earliest inscription on the stained-glass window discussed above.

NACHT CHRISTI GEBVRT 1284 IAHR
GINGEN BI DEN KOPPEN VNTER VERWAHR
HVNDERVNDDREISSIG KINDER IN HAMELN GEBORN
VAN EINEM PFEIFFER VERFVRT VND VERLOHREN[10]

(In the year of Our Lord, 1284, 130 children from Hamelin, in the custody of a piper, were led out of the city to the Koppen, and there they disappeared)

Thus far all references and texts have been relatively short and they have simply stated the fact that on 26 June 1284 a man led away 130 children from the town of Hamelin. Only the first printed prose text from 1556 tried to explain that the children might have been led away as punishment for the sins of the people of Hamelin. Plausible as this explanation may be, we must stop here to see what other possible reasons there might have been for such an exodus. It seems clear that the actual departure of 130 children took place, but the question is why? Many theories exist which will be mentioned here only in short summary:

1. As early as the seventeenth century, the German philosopher Gottfried Leibniz theorized that the children might have been lured away by someone who wanted them to take part in the Children's Crusade of 1212.[11]

2. A number of scholars attempted to trace the legend to the Battle of Sedemünder which took place on 28 July 1259. This battle was a result of the decision of the Bishop of Fulda to place Hamelin under the jurisdiction of the Minden Diocese. Several hundred young men from Hamelin fought in this fierce battle and hardly anybody returned to the city of Hamelin.[12]

3. It has been argued that the legend might have had its origin in the dance epidemic in the Middle Ages known as St. Vitus' or St. John's dance. People went through a literal *Tanzwut* (dance mania), which is considered to have been an attempt to counteract the plague. Large groups of people could be seen dancing and calling upon St. Vitus to cure them from the plague or other epidemics.[13]

4. There have been proponents of the theory that the departure of the children was a direct result of the Black Death, which is especially

plausible when one considers that rats are associated with the plague. It must be added here, however, that rats are never mentioned in any version of the legend until 1565. This theory goes as far as to connect the Pied Piper motif with that of the *Totentanz* (Dance of Death).[14]

5. There are theories that claim to trace the legend back to mythological sources. The piper has been compared to Orpheus, Wainamoinen (Finnish), and Gunadhya (Sanskrit), and his pipe is likened to the horn of Oberon or the lyre of Apollo. These explanatory attempts ignore the historical documentation that has been amassed for this local Hamelin legend.[15]

6. The most plausible theory, which is also based on most convincing historical facts, claims that the children (or rather, young adults) took part in the colonization of the East. It has been shown by Wolfgang Wann and Heinrich Spanuth that Bishop Bruno of Olmütz in Moravia had a castle on the Weser river only about ten miles away from Hamelin. In the second half of the thirteenth century Bishop Bruno, formerly Count von Schaumberg, established over two hundred villages and cities in Moravia and for this purpose he sent recruiters or "locatores" to lure people into resettling in the East. One such recruiter must have come to Hamelin between 1250 and 1285 and taken 130 people with him. Wann has found family names in the archives of Troppau in Moravia that seem to mirror those of Hamelin. It is also claimed that there was good reason for the young people of Hamelin to look for a new place to settle since the town had experienced a considerable increase in population. Many walled-in cities of the time had similar problems, creating social friction among the population and making the climate right for the emigration to a better land in the East.[16]

It is doubtful that this last theory will ever be discredited since it is based on too many solid historical and philological facts such as parallel names. But there is, of course, another considerable problem to be reckoned with—the entire part of the legend dealing with the rats and the rat-catcher, as well as the metamorphosis of the recruiter into the figure of a piping rat-catcher who leads the children away only as a punishment after their parents refuse to pay him for ridding the town of a plague of rats. The earliest recorded version of the legend that contains a rat-catcher who leads first the rats and then the children out of Hamelin comes from 1565 and was included in the so-called *Zimmer Chronicle* by Count Froben Christof von Zimmer of Swabia and his secretary Johannes Müller.

Several hundred years ago the inhabitants of the city of Hamelin in Westphalia were plagued with such a large quantity of rats, that it became unbearable. It so happened that a foreigner, an unknown or traveller, much as the travelling students of long ago, came into the city. Hearing the troubles and complaints of the burghers, he proposed whether they would consider a reward for him if he were to remove the rats from the city. They were overjoyed with such news and for his offer they promised to pay him a sum of several hundred guilders. With that he went through the city with a little pipe, which he then placed to his mouth and commenced to play. Immediately all the rats in the city came running out of the houses and in unbelievable numbers began to follow at his feet as he walked out of the city. He banished them to the nearest mountain and no more rats were seen in the city. This accomplished, he demanded his promised reward. But they had hidden it away, confessing that although they had been in agreement with the sum, that since the matter had caused him no difficulty, but rather he had dispensed with his task so easily, not by hard work, but by an unusual art; therefore, they felt that he should not ask for so much, but lower his sights and take less. The stranger, however, insisted on keeping the original agreement and he persisted in seeking the sum promised him, and if they didn't give it to him they would rue it. The citizenry, however, stayed with the opinion that this was far too much money, and they no longer wished to give it to him. When he realized that he was not going to receive anything, the stranger began to walk through the streets with his pipe as before. There crowded the majority of the children in the city under eight or nine years of age, and they followed at his feet and out of the city to the nearest mountain. This mountain miraculously opened up and the stranger and the children went inside. Immediately afterwards it closed up again and neither stranger nor children were ever seen again. Now there was a great wailing throughout the city and the people could do nothing but commit themselves to God and admit their guilt. The city reported this wondrous story in all its correspondence as an eternal reminder and added the right number on the date according to the birth of Christ; on the end, however, they added the departure of the children in such and such a year. One cannot be too amazed, for we know that it is customary in Trier, that when the new year begins, one doesn't write it according to the year of Christ's birth, which is the custom everywhere, but one writes after the year in which Christ became man, and that year began on the day of the Annunciation.[17]

In this chronicle the rat-catcher is a stranger from a foreign land, with somewhat the same low social status as the musician in Hans

Zeitlos' earlier version of 1553. But where did Zimmer and Müller get the rat-catcher motif from and what possessed them to link it with the exodus from Hamelin? We know today that there were a number of similar rat- and mouse-catcher legends attached to certain localities current in Germany and other parts of Europe. Hans Dobbertin prints fourteen of them[18] and Leander Petzoldt also included several variants, which all show how a person playing on an instrument (pipe, horn, etc.) frees a town from various types of animal plagues.[19] Since the actual profession of the rat-catcher existed in the Middle Ages, it is not surprising that legends were in circulation about an especially good rat-catcher who cleared a whole town of the vermin. There are also woodcuts attesting to this important profession from 1430[20] and from the sixteenth century,[21] which show an almost magical power of the rat-catcher over the rats even though no musical instrument is illustrated.

What we will probably never know is whether Zimmer and Müller were the first to link a variant of the rat-catcher tale with the account of the children's exodus. What we do know is that this chronicle, which was also a much more literary work, did not have much of an influence, since it existed only in two manuscripts that were edited for the first time in 1881. Perhaps the two tales were already linked in oral tradition by 1565, even though variants of the account with only the children continue through the seventeenth century. In any case, in another chronicle written by Augustin von Mörsperg in 1592 the two tales are also linked, but the entire legend is different enough to show that it was not copied from the unpublished Zimmer chronicle. This chronicle adds support to the idea that combined versions of the legend did exist orally by at least the middle of the sixteenth century. The Mörsperg chronicle also contains the first illustration in color of the Pied Piper leading the children away from Hamelin.[22]

We can only speculate why the *Wandersage* (migratory legend) of the rats was attached to the "historical" account of the exodus of the children of Hamelin. Most likely it was the people from Hamelin themselves who accomplished this tour de force. The oldest accounts state very matter of factly the truth that 130 children left Hamelin and were lost forever. As time passed, the person who led them away was called a "spilman" (musician) or even a devil, perhaps a conscious attempt to put the blame for the departure of the children on a person of low social esteem, while the fault actually lay with the ruling towns-

people. It might simply have become unthinkable to later generations of Hamelin that 130 innocent children were permitted to be abducted. So we might have an actual ''cover-up'' here, to use a modern descriptive phrase. Why not blame the exodus of the children on some evil musician or rat-catcher, who, because the ruling class broke a promise, had the audacity to punish the children? A little guilt the burghers could accept, as long as they had their scapegoat in the rat-catcher for the actual loss of the children. The rat-catcher legend, therefore, helps to explain the exodus of the children, that is, it becomes an etiological first half of the actual legend of the Pied Piper of Hamelin as we know it today. It is the motif of revenge on the part of a more positively seen musician and rat-catcher in later years that links both parts of the legend together and makes it a moral tale of crime and punishment, showing that above all promises must be kept.[23] The didactic marketability of the legend was recognized as early as 1622 when someone printed a broadsheet about the departure of the children from Hamelin in rhymed couplets and with a detailed illustration. The verses end with the statement, "Darumb ihr lieben Christen fein! / Last solchs Vns auch ein Beyspiel seyn!"[24] (Therefore you dear, fine Christians! / Let this be an example for you!). Clearly it is this didactic idea that has attracted the authors of so many children's books to this particular legend.

By the time the Brothers Grimm finally printed their variant of the legend in 1816, it had long become a unified whole in oral tradition. They themselves were able to cite nine sources, the earliest being from the year 1573. Their own text is a conglomerate of these various sources, but it is this published German version that became the primary text, in the same fashion that the rewritten fairy tales by the Grimms became the standard German versions picked up by later compilers in Germany and for translations into other tongues. Since so many translations exist of the Grimm tales, it is surprising that Donald Ward could still note in a commentary of his superb translation of 1981 that "their version has never before been translated into English."[25] Here is Ward's English text:

### The Children of Hameln

A wondrous man appeared in the town of Hameln in the year 1284. He wore a coat of many bright colors from which he is said to have acquired the name Pied Piper. He proclaimed himself a ratcatcher, and he promised to rid the city of all mice and rats in exchange for a certain sum. The citizens accepted his offer and promised him the requested amount of money as his reward.

The ratcatcher then drew out a small fife and began playing. The rats and mice immediately came creeping out of all the houses and gathered around him. When he was certain that none remained behind, he began marching out of town with the entire horde following after him. He led them down to the Weser River where he rolled up his clothes and marched right into the water, followed by all the creatures, who then drowned.

After the citizens had been delivered from this plague, they regretted having promised so much money. Using all kinds of excuses, they denied the man his reward, and he departed in bitterness and anger. Then, on the morning of June twenty-sixth, St. John's and St. Paul's Day—some say at seven o'clock, others say at noon—he reappeared as a hunter with a terrifying countenance, wearing a strange red hat.

Once again the sounds of his fife were heard in the streets and alleys. This time, however, instead of rats and mice came children. Boys and girls from four years of age on ran after him in great numbers, among them the grown daughter of the town mayor. The troupe of children followed him as he played, and he led them outside the town where they disappeared with him into a mountain.

A nurserymaid with a child in her arms, who had been approaching the town from afar and witnessed all this, brought the report to the city. The parents ran en masse to the gates, seeking their children with grieving hearts. All the mothers were weeping and wailing. Messengers were sent out in all directions by land, sea, and riverways to discover if anyone had seen or heard of the children—but all in vain.

Altogether, one hundred and thirty children were lost. Some people say that two of them returned some time later, but one was blind and the other dumb. The blind one could not point out the place but was able to tell how they had followed the Piper, and the dumb one could point out the place though he had heard nothing. One child joining the others was in his nightshirt and turned around to get his coat. He thus escaped the tragedy, for when he returned, the others had already disappeared into a cave in the hillside, which people still point out today.

The street on which the children marched out through the gate was still called—in the middle of the eighteenth century and probably still today—the Silent Street because no dance could be held and no musical instrument could be played there. Indeed, even when a bride was led to church in a procession, the musicians had to cross that street in complete silence.

The mountain near Hameln where the children disappeared is called Mt. Poppen. Two stone crosses have been erected to the right and to the left of the mountain. Some say the children were led into a cave and emerged again in Transylvania.

The citizens of Hameln recorded the event in their city register, and ever since have been in the habit of dating all their announcements from the day that their children were lost.

According to Seyfried, the date recorded in the city register was the twenty-second, not the twenty-sixth, of June. The following lines are inscribed on the City Hall:

> In the year of our Lord 1284
> from Hameln were led away,
> 130 children who here were born,
> lost by a piper inside the mountain.

And on the new gate are the lines:

> *Centum ter denos cum magnus* [sic] *ab urbe puellos*
> *Duxerat ante annos CCLXXII condita porta fuit.*

In 1572 the town mayor had the entire story illustrated in
stained glass windows for the church with an accompanying text
inscription. This, however, has become largely illegible. A coin
commemorating the event was also printed.[26]

But the English public did not need to wait to become acquainted
with the Pied Piper legend until this very recent translation. As early as
1605 the first English version of the legend appeared, written by
Richard Verstegan, who most likely knew Jobus Fincelius' German
version of 1556, and who is even listed as one of the sources of the
Brothers Grimm. For the English-speaking world it is significant that
Verstegan talks of a "pyed pyper." Even more important is that Verstegan's is absolutely the first reference to the possibility that the children
from Hamelin might have migrated to "Transiluania." The Brothers
Grimm also, it will be remembered, referred to the possibility that "the
children were led into a cave and emerged again in Transylvania," and
they most likely got this idea from Verstegan. What seemed mere
conjecture in 1605 and 1816 is now thought to be the closest we will
ever get to the actual reason for the exodus of the children. Verstegan's
English version was also a major source for Robert Browning's celebrated poem "The Pied Piper of Hamelin," and is thus of considerable
importance for both the German and English tradition of the
nineteenth and twentieth centuries. Verstegan's text reads as follows:

And now hath one digression drawn on another, for beeing by
reason of speaking of these Saxons of Transiluania, put in mynd
of a most true and maruelous strange accedent that happned in
Saxonie not many ages past, I cannot omit for the strangenes
thereof briefly heer by the way to set it down. There came into the
town of Hamel in the countery of Brunswyc an od kynd of com-
pagnion, who the fantastical cote which hee wore beeing wrought
with sundry colours, was called the pyed pyper; for a pyper hee
was, besydes his other qualities. This fellow forsooth offred the
townsmen for a certain somme of mony to rid the town of all the
rattes that were in it (for at that tyme the burgers were with that
vermin greatly annoyed.) The accord in fyne beeing made; the
pyed pyper with a shril pype went pyping through the streets,
and foorth with the rattes came all running out of the howses in
great numbers after him; all wich hee led vnto the riuer of Weaser
and therein drowned them. This donne, and no one rat more per-
ceaued to bee left in the town; he afterward came to demaund his
reward according to his bargain, but beeing told that the bargain
was not made with him in good earnest, to wit, with an opinion
that euer hee could bee able to do such a feat: they cared not what

they accorded vnto, when they imagyned it could neuer bee de-
serued, and so neuer to bee demaunded: but neuerthelesse seeing
hee had donne such an vnlykely thing in deed, they were content
to giue him a good reward; and so offred him far lesse then hee
lookt for: but hee therewith discontented, said hee would haue his
ful recompence according to his bargain, but they vtterly denying
to giue it him, hee threatened them with reuenge; they bad him
do his wurst, wherevpon he betakes him again to his pype, and
going through the streets as before, was followed of a number of
boyes out one of the gates of the citie, and coming to a litle hil,
there opened in the syde thereof a wyde hole, into the which himself and all the children beeing in number one hundred and thirty,
did enter; and beeing entred, the hil closed vp again, and became
as before. A boy that beeing lame and came somwhat lagging be-
hynd the rest, seeing this that hapned, returned presently back
and told what hee had seen; foorthwith began great lamentation
among the parents for their children and men were sent out with
all dilligence, both by land and by water to enquyrie they could
possibly vse, nothing more then is aforesaid could of them bee
vnderstood. In memorie whereof it was then ordayned, that from
thencefoorth no drum, pype or other instrument, should bee
sounded in the street leading to the gate through which they
passed; nor no osterie to bee there holden. And it was also established, that from that tyme forward in all publyke wrytings that
should bee made in that town, after the date therein set down the
years of our Lord, the date of the years of the going foorth of their
children should bee added, the which they haue accordingly euer
since continued. And this great wonder hapned on the 22. day of
July, in the years of our Lord one towsand three hundreth seuen-
tie, and six.

The occasion now why this matter came vnto my remembrance
in speaking of Transiluania, was, for that some do reporte that
there are diuers found among the Saxons of Transiluania to haue
lyke surnames vnto diuers of the burgers of Hamel, and wil seem
thereby to inferr, that this iugler or pyed pyper, might by negro-
mancie haue transported them thether, but this carieth litle appar-
ence of truthe; because it would haue bin almost as great a wonder vnto the Saxons of Transiluania to haue had somany strange
children brought among them, they knew not how, as it was to
those of Hamel to lose them: and they could not but haue kept
memorie of so strange a thing, yf in deed any such thing had
there hapned.[27]

But Verstegan's text, important as it is for the historical scholarship
(he is the first to mention the lame boy left behind), did not have much
influence in helping to spread this migration and abduction legend in

the English-speaking world. Much more influential, but of course also much later, was Andrew Lang's translation of a nineteenth century French adaptation of the legend by Charles Marelles in his popular *Red Fairy Book* (1890), since Lang's books were read widely in the Anglo-American world.[28] Lang's "The Ratcatcher" is considerably longer than all versions mentioned thus far, and he also included direct discourse to add a dramatic immediacy to the folk tale. The Grimms' text was, of course, not translated in the nineteenth century and so it could not have had any direct influence on the general population. But it was not a prose version of the legend that immortalized it for the English world in any case. Rather it was a highly poetic literary text, the classic poem "The Pied Piper of Hamelin" (1842) by Robert Browning, that made this tale a true legend for English speakers. The German legend had to go through the craftsmanship of a great author in order to be made accessible and eventually to become a folk legend in the English language as well.

We know that Robert Browning must have been acquainted with Richard Verstegan's English prose account of 1605. In a splendid paper on "Browning's Source for 'The Pied Piper of Hamelin,'" Arthur Dickson proved convincingly that this version must have been in Browning's hands, since the following parallels exist in only these two texts:

1. The date of the occurrence—22 July 1376.
2. The invitation to the piper, at the climax of the controversy, to "do his worst."
3. The statement that there was a little boy who was lame and couldn't keep up with the rest.
4. The statement that no tavern was allowed on the street.
5. Concluding remarks about the possibility of the children's having been carried off into Transylvania.[29]

Dickson lists fifteen other possible sources that Browning might have known, including the German version of the Brothers Grimm. It must be remembered that Browning did spend some time in Germany in 1834 and that he might have come into contact with the German legend then. In any case, the legend was well known in the Browning house, since Robert Browning the elder himself had started his own Pied Piper poem in 1842. He did not complete it at the time, after learning that his son was writing a similar poem. The father's manuscript, in which the Pied Piper takes on evil character traits, was only published in 1912.[30]

The younger Robert Browning wrote and published his poem in November 1842 independently from his father. That he intended his poem for children is clear from the dedication to a little boy by the name of William Macready, for whose entertainment the poem was written. Browning's text is composed of fifteen uneven stanzas containing 303 lines, and it basically retells the Pied Piper legend as a lyrical and descriptive children's story. Doubtless its particular charm to children lies in the marvelous description of the rats, such as this exerpt from the seventh stanza:

> Into the street the Piper stept,
>   Smiling first a little smile,
> As if he knew what magic slept
>   In his quiet pipe the while;
> Then, like a musical adept,
> To blow the pipe his lips he wrinkled,
> And green and blue his sharp eyes twinkled,
> Like a candle-flame where salt is sprinkled;
> And ere three shrill notes the pipe uttered,
> You heard as if an army muttered;
> And the muttering grew to a grumbling;
> And the grumbling grew to a mighty rumbling;
> And out of the houses the rats came tumbling.
> Great rats, small rats, lean rats, brawny rats,
> Brown rats, black rats, grey rats, tawny rats,
> Grave old plodders, gay young friskers,
>   Fathers, mothers, uncles, cousins,
> Cocking tails and pricking whiskers,
>   Families by tens and dozens,
> Brothers, sisters, husbands, wives—
> Followed the Piper for their lives.
> From street to street he piped advancing,
> And step for step they followed dancing,
> Until they came to the river Weser,
>   Wherein all plunged and perished![31]

Since Browning intended his poem for children, it is not surprising to see a moralistic message at the end of his account:

> And, whether they pipe us free from rats or from mice,
> If we've promised them aught, let us keep our promise![32]

Such an entertaining didactic story in rhyme caught on quickly in the nineteenth century. In the period from 1882 to 1983 alone there were almost fifty different editions of the poem as illustrated children's books, some quoting the poem exactly, others being prose renderings for very young children.[33] The most beautiful was surely the 1888 edition with thirty-five illustrations by the English artist Kate Greenaway, which in 1983 was reprinted as a small gift book, attesting to its appeal even today.[34] Browning's poem has been translated into numerous languages, and its German translation by Walter Ruhm[35] has given a certain popularity to this version in the land of the legend's origin, thus completing the cycle of this migratory (in all senses of the word) legend.

With the Grimm text in Germany and the Browning poem in the English-speaking world, the legend of the Pied Piper had become one of the best known folk tales in both languages by the middle of the nineteenth century. In fact, it gained so much popularity that literary adaptations abound in both cultures during the remainder of the century. It must, however, be stated that these new renditions are by and large only longer poetic reworkings, without substantial changes in the basic plot of the legend. We have poems by Johann Wolfgang von Goethe (1804), Joseph von Eichendorff (1840), Gustav Freytag (1844), Karl Simrock (1864), and Joseph C. Cotter (1898), a short novel by Wilhelm Raabe (1863), an epic poem by Julius Wolff (1875)—which was used as the libretto for Victor Nessler's opera (1878)—and a play *The Piper* (1909) by Josephine Preston Peabody.[36] German folk songs also exist that basically retell the legend, the most important of which is the song "Der Rattenfänger von Hameln," which was included in Achim von Arnim and Clemens Brentano's famous collection, *Des Knaben Wunderhorn*, published in 1806, ten years before the Brothers Grimm printed their version. It is interesting to note that this song interprets the Pied Piper quite negatively, as can be seen from the first stanza:

> Who is that colorful man in the picture?
> He is probably up to something bad,
> He pipes so wildly and so deliberately;
> I would not have taken my child to him.[37]

Goethe also saw the Pied Piper as an evil, demonic, or even devilish figure, who doesn't just catch rats and children but also deceives young and beautiful maidens, as is indicated in the following three stanzas of "The Rat-Catcher," the freest poetic rendition of the legend in nineteenth-century Germany. Since Goethe wrote his poem in 1804, a good dozen years before the Brothers Grimm wrote down their version, we can see that the tale must have been very well known orally in the eighteenth century as well.

> I am the bard known far and wide,
> The travelled rat-catcher beside;
> A man most needful to this town,
> So glorious through its old renown.
> However many rats I see,
> How many weasels there may be,
> I cleanse the place from every one,
> All needs but helter-skelter run.
>
> Sometimes the bard so full of cheer
> As a child-catcher will appear,
> Who e'en the wildest captive brings,
> Whene'er his golden tales he sings.
> However proud each boy in heart,
> However much the maidens start,
> I bid the chords sweet music make,
> And all must follow in my wake.
>
> Sometimes the skilful bard ye view
> In form of maiden-catcher, too;
> For he no city enters e'er,
> Without effecting wonders there.
> However coy may be each maid,
> Howe'er the women seem afraid,
> Yet all will love-sick be ere long
> To sound of magic lute and song.[38]

In his *Faust* (1808), Goethe goes so far as to call Mephistopheles a "vermaledeiter Rattenfänger"[39] (accursed [or damned] Pied Piper), and it is this negative aspect of the Pied Piper figure that appears to be stressed in the more modern adaptations of the legend as well. We must realize that the legend itself actually portrays the Pied Piper as an ambiguous figure, both good and evil. As a rat-catcher he is an altogether benevolent and welcome magician, but as an abductor of innocent children he becomes as malevolent and evil as the devil himself. Whatever the reason for the popularity this legend had for children, it is exactly this ambiguity in the character of the Pied Piper that appeals to the adult today, as can be seen in modern poetic texts, in caricatures, and in advertisements.

This fact is clearly noticeable in both German and English in the positive and negative connotations of the mere word "Rattenfänger" or "Pied Piper." The well-known legend has been reduced to a mere proverbial expression that only alludes to the legend. For the English language there is an additional curiosity that must be looked at here, since many people connect the proverbial expression "To pay the piper" with the Pied Piper of Hamelin legend. Checking standard proverb collections reveals that this is actually a shortened version of such proverbs as: "Who pays the piper, calls the tune" (1611), "Those that dance must pay the music" (1638), "He who pays the piper may order the tune" (1874), and "He who pays the piper can call the tune" (1910). While 1611 is the earliest reference given, these proverbs are probably much older.[40] The proverbial expression "To pay the piper" is recorded for the first time in 1638,[41] so that it could in fact refer to Verstegan's Pied Piper version in English from the year 1605. However, that account had no popular currency and could hardly have been the source for the expression, which must be looked at as a shortened version of the proverbs mentioned. Many proverbial expressions are shortened versions of proverbs, which can also be seen from two parallel texts that have the same meaning as the ones discussed here, namely "He that dances should always pay the fiddler" and "To pay the fiddler."[42]

But there have been and continue to be scholars who claim that the phrase "To pay the piper" in its figurative sense originated with the Pied Piper legend. Cobham Brewer argued this first in 1870 in his famous *Dictionary of Phrase and Fable*, but he was rebuffed in a short note by A. C. Mounsey in 1884:

> In his *Dictionary of Phrase and Fable*, Dr. Brewer tells us that the phrase "To pay the piper" comes from the tradition about the Piper of Hamelin, who was not paid. But England, I fancy, had from early times pipers who lived by their piping, the expense of which was, doubtless, on frequent occasions defrayed by one out of the many that had enjoyed the pleasure of the dance. The passage from the literal to the figurative meaning is very easy, and it would seem unnecessary to fetch the phrase from so far. The French have managed, without the help of foreign tradition, to give a proverbial form to the same idea. "Payer les violons" has long been used in the sense of paying the expense of something of which others have all the profit or pleasure. But Dr. Brewer has, no doubt, good reasons for what he affirms.[43]

It might be added here that parallels from other European languages can easily be found, and as a matter of fact, the editor of the centenary edition of Brewer's *Dictionary* has dropped the claim that the phrase originated from the legend altogether.[44] But the die-hards remain nonetheless. In 1922, Albert M. Hyamson stated that "To pay the Piper" is "an allusion to the legend of the Pied Piper of Hamelin concerning the payment for whose services a dispute arose."[45] Charles N. Lurie also claims that "we owe to this story also the ancient saying about 'paying the piper,'"[46] and as recently as 1980 there appeared the claim that "this expression probably alludes to the 13th-century legend of the Pied Piper of Hamelin in which the piper, upon being refused the payment promised for ridding the town of rats, played his pipe again; this time, however, it was the children who were led out of town to their death. Thus, the residents suffered the consequences of their decision, having 'paid the piper' with their children's life." The author continues, "the derivation may be more literal, that is, it was customary to pay a piper or other street musicians for the entertainment he supplied."[47]

There is, as I see it, an easy way out of this seeming controversy. There is enough evidence, due to the general European currency of the actual proverb, to insist that it itself gave rise to the shortened expression "To pay the piper." However, due primarily to Browning's poem, people have associated the legend and the proverbial expression and continue to think of one when using the other. Browning's poem and the legend can, therefore, be regarded as a secondary and somewhat later additional source of the expression, but they were not the primary origin. The legend is, however, the definite source for the simple expression "To be a Pied Piper" or the even shorter mere name "Pied Piper" in its figurative sense. In 1928 we find it referenced for the first time: "Pied Piper—anything or anyone that lures or leads may be referred to as a 'Pied Piper.'"[48] The figurative meaning is also listed in a number of the large dictionaries of the English language, of which three must suffice as examples:

Pied Piper—a person who induces others to imitate his example, esp. by means of false or extravagant promises.[49]

pied piper—one that offers strong but delusive enticement; a leader who makes irresponsible promises.[50]

pied piper—a person who entices or misleads others.[51]

Judging by these figurative meanings, the negative characteristics of the legendary Pied Piper are definitely being stressed. Yet the following examples will clearly show that modern mankind sees in the Pied Piper an ambiguous person who can fit almost any leadership situation.

Consider, for example, the poem "The Pied Piper of Brooklyn" (1910) by Ambrose Bierce, in which the Pied Piper not only finds himself transplanted to New York, but also transfigured into the Congregational preacher Henry Ward Beecher. This pastor had led the fight against slavery, and in his eulogy Bierce compares him to the Pied Piper because his voice had aroused many followers in this noble cause.

> So, Beecher's dead. He was a great soul, too—
>    Great as a giant organ is, whose reeds
>    Hold in them all the souls of all the creeds
> That man has ever taught and never knew.
>
> When on this mighty instrument was laid
>    His hand Who fashioned it, our common moan
>    Was suppliant in its thundering. The tone
> Grew more vivacious when the Devil played.
>
> No more those luring harmonies we hear,
>    And lo! already men forget the sound.
>    They turn, retracing all the dubious ground
> O'er which he'd led them stoutly by the ear.[52]

This great soul piped like a giant organ the tune of freedom, and his beliefs enticed people to follow him on this positive path. But with Beecher's death, Ambrose Bierce fears that people will soon forget his mighty piping, retracing their old questionable steps and actions.

There were, of course, many negative Pied Piper figures as well, especially in the tumultuous political arena of Europe. A 1906 German political caricature, for example, shows a Russian bear that leads along European rats (each country is illustrated as a rat). The title reads "Der Rattenfänger von St. Petersburg"[53] (The Pied Piper of St. Petersburg) and the illustration satirizes the extent of Russian borrowing from other countries which, it is implied, will lead them to their financial ruin. Much more drastic is a caricature from the German satirical magazine *Kladderadatsch* from 1929, with the caption "Der Rattenfänger von Moskau,"[54] in which a skeleton leads a demonstration of Communists to what will obviously be death by drumming with two

Der Rattenfänger von Moskau

Kommunistischer Demonstrationszug

large bones on a drum. Once the Nazis came to power such fascist anticommunism took hold of the entire German press, and in 1933 there appeared a cartoon that once again shows a skeleton leading communists to their doom.[55] Four years later, we find yet another reddish and devilish Pied Piper with the caption "Die Komintern pfeift" (The Comintern pipes), and all the communist "rats" of the world following him to their destruction.[56] Even in 1944 the Nazi propaganda machine had the audacity to print a caricature showing Joseph Stalin talking to the Pied Piper of the Comintern and asking him for a national anthem since international communism was a lost cause.[57] Hidden or covered up, of course, is the fact that it was Germany that was in a losing position at that time. Of interest is that this blatant denunciation of communism was continued almost immediately after the war by the United States, as can be seen from a political cartoon that appeared in the *Saturday Review* in 1947 showing the familiar Pied Piper as a communist trying to lead the miserable people astray once again.[58] Any undesirable leader or movement can obviously be projected into a Pied Piper figure who leads people by evil magic or deception to their doom.

The most notorious of such questionable Pied Pipers was Adolf Hitler who, at least in Germany, was often and still is referred to as the most evil Pied Piper of them all. This can be seen from Erich Weinert's poem "Hitlers Nachtlied" (Hitler's Nightsong), which he wrote in 1941 while in exile in Moscow, and which by its titular allusion to Goethe's peaceful poem "Wanderers Nachtlied" (Wanderer's Nightsong) warns the reader that the new poem will be a biting satire:

> What should this old Pied Piper do?
> The "Blitzkrieg" lasts longer and longer
> I don't find any more rats
> Where can I get new rats from
> And my old accustomed pipe
> Is shrill and off-key
> They're not listening to my pipe
> And they're already leaving my ship.
>
> It crashes and crumbles at all fronts
> What am I to do with my affairs
> Now I am an established man
> But what am I to do with it?
> Where am I to move to
> If my rats are no longer dancing?

I am seriously in danger
They devour me with skin and bones.

How good it was in the old days
When one after all bankruptcies
Was only sent to St. Helena
But today one isn't human any more
Also today's rats probably
Will not give me thanks
And if I am lucky, I will
Die one day in a Hottentot kraal.[59]

Weinert lets Hitler refer to himself as a Pied Piper, even comparing himself to yet another infamous Pied Piper of the past—Napoleon. The poem illustrates how Hitler's army of rats (the Wehrmacht) is being bogged down by an ever-expanding war and how Hitler's pipe (his appeal, the Nazi propaganda machine) is becoming weaker, so that the grotesque Pied Piper cannot lure any more rats (Nazis) into his devilish service.

Bertolt Brecht wrote a somewhat longer poem around the same time called "Die wahre Geschichte vom Rattenfänger von Hameln" (The True Story About the Pied Piper of Hamelin), in which the piper (Hitler) at first appears as a savior who excites the naive population because of his wonderful piping (rhetoric, promises, etc.). While he tries to deceive people, he is driven to madness by his own music (power) and leads everybody back to Hamelin, where this devil's circle closes with his death and the end of the senseless pact with evil.

The Pied Piper of Hamelin
Through the town he went
And caught with his piping
Thousands of little children
  He piped nicely. He piped long.
  It was a marvelous song.

The Pied Piper of Hamelin
From the town he wanted to save them
So that the little children would have
A better place to grow up.
  He piped nicely. He piped long.
  It was a marvelous song.

The Pied Piper of Hamelin
Where did he lead them astray?
For the little children were all
Deeply stirred up in the heart.

He piped nicely. He piped long.
It was a marvelous song.

The Pied Piper of Hamelin
When from the town he went
His piping, it is said, captivated
His own mind as well.
  I pipe nicely. I pipe long.
  It is a marvelous song.

The Pied Piper of Hamelin
Around the mountain he turned
And led the little children
Back into the town again.
  Piped too nicely, piped too long
  It was too marvelous a song.

The Pied Piper of Hamelin
They hung him in the marketplace
But about his piping, piping
People talked for a long long time.
  He piped nicely. He piped long.
  It was a marvelous song.[60]

Such poems had to be written in exile, for nobody could have dared to publish such visions in the dark ages of Nazi Germany. There were obviously also no cartoons against Hitler to be found in Germany, but the *New York Times* published a fascinating caricature in 1934 that depicts a National Socialist piping the tune of "Deutschland über alles" and "Heil Hitler," while he leads little children screaming "Heil" out of a medieval town. Even a black stork with a baby in its beak follows the leader, indicating with obvious symbolism at this early date the demise of the "Crazy Piper" and his followers.[61] While this caricature is indeed an appropriate reaction to Nazi Germany by the American press, one does wonder about a wartime advertisement by Bell Aircraft that appeared in 1943 in *Time* magazine. In a colorful illustration a proud American fighter pilot looks up to a sky filled with Airacobra fighter planes. The headline praises him as the "Pied Piper of the Pacific" and, as the copy explains, "with the devastating fire power of his cannon-bearing P-39 Airacobra, this modern Pied Piper of the air destroys the rats which threatened to overrun civilization. When the rats are gone, he'll come back to a world in which technical advances that war has brought to Aviation will be put to even greater use."[62] In other words, once the Japanese "rats" are killed, which is now the

rtoon supplied by permission of the Daily Express, London.

*The crazy piper. Der Rattenfänger.*

major purpose of these planes, they will be used for civil aviation. It is amazing to see what sickening levels war propaganda can reach when it begins to demonize the enemy into subhuman creatures.

More recently we have had other political Pied Pipers who have attempted to lure people into their questionable schemes. One of the most fascinating caricatures concerning a modern German Pied Piper appeared 1969 in the news magazine *Der Spiegel*. It depicts the drumming neo-Nazi Adolf von Thadden as he and his fascist followers pass between representatives of the two major German political parties. The caption warns "Hameln ist überall" (Hameln is everywhere), meaning that people could fall under the spell of a dangerous leader, not only in Germany, but anywhere in the world, at any time.[63] A clear example of this is Iran's Khomeni, who has been shown in two recent cartoons as a medieval Pied Piper leading his people back to the dark

ages[64] and as a skeleton who plays his grotesque song of the Iranian revolution on a machine gun.[65] Violence and the threat of war are also the subject of a Soviet cartoon depicting Uncle Sam in the role of the Pied Piper blaring out the notes "Soviet Threat" while leading a procession of Pershing-2 missiles from New York to Western Europe.[66] It is not surprising that the Polish Solidarity Union has also been the subject matter of a Pied Piper cartoon. Here the Pied Piper is Solidarity, which is being followed by the Polish people in the shape of an innocent sheep, while Brezhnev is trying to catch the sheep with a lasso.[67] Since this illustration appeared in a Bombay/New Delhi newspaper, we can assume that the Pied Piper is interpreted positively. A rather satirical if not humorous Egyptian cartoon depicts Henry Kissinger as a Pied Piper on his Middle East missions, while some of the sheiks do not wish to follow him and his ideas: "We listen to him, but we choose our own paths."[68] Finally, there was the humorous and almost tragicomical caricature of former President Jerry Ford attempting to lead the Puerto Ricans along to "Statehood for Puerto Rico."[69] But his dreams of a fifty-first state were shattered when, as the illustration shows so effectively, the people, in an absolute reversal of the Pied Piper motif, ran in the other direction instead of following him. In other words, not every modern Pied Piper succeeds, nor are they necessarily so evil any more.

But we are surrounded by more than political Pied Pipers in our modern complex society. There are plenty of opportunities for us to be tricked into following the most varied Pied Pipers in the most differentiated disguises. There was the terrible event in 1978 in Jamestown where the religious leader Jim Jones led his blind and obedient followers to mass murder. A German cartoon illustrates such a religious Pied Piper who is blindfolded and whose adherents follow him covered with his veil. The satirical-ironical caption reads "Der Erleuchtung entgegen"[70] (toward enlightenment), and the reader cannot help but wonder how such gurus can have so much power over other people's minds. But how about such other harmless crazes and fads as the hula-hoop fashion, which, as one cartoon shows, led hundreds of people to follow the hula-hoop Pied Piper?[71] The disco craze also has had a Pied Piper effect, as can be seen from a Swiss cartoon where a disco-playing Pied Piper has created a big traffic jam.[72] And of course there has been the fad for carrying large transistor radios around, which can have a Pied Piper effect since people just have to follow those tunes, as a cartoon shows with happily dancing people following a surprised radio owner.[73] This person obviously has no evil intentions with his transistor music, and people are following him freely. The danger of television's luring people into watching it too much was the subject of two cartoons. One shows a Pied Piper carrying a portable television and having children follow him, just as in the legend.[74] The second cartoon is more universal, since here adults and children reading TV Guide follow the Pied Piper who carries a giant television set.[75] The message is clear; we should be careful not to come too much under the magic spell of this modern Pied Piper.

From these examples it can be seen that the Pied Piper legend or at least the figurative meaning of the phrase "To be a Pied Piper" appears with considerable frequency. To complete this picture, let me add here at least a small selection of such allusions as they appear in book titles and as magazine and newspaper headlines:

Raddall, Thomas H., *The Pied Piper of Dipper Creek and Other Tales*. Toronto: McClelland & Stewart, 1943.

Shayon, Robert Lewis. "The Pied Piper of Video." *The Saturday Review of Literature* (25 November 1950), pp. 9–11 and 49–51.

Sayles, Arlen A. *The Pied Piper of Heaven*. Philadelphia: Dorrance, 1971.

McCarthy, Edward U. *The Pied Piper of Helfenstein*. Garden City, New York: Doubleday, 1975.

Anon. "The Pied Piper of Peace." *Time* (6 September 1976), p. 27.

Beck, Marilyn. "Pied Piper of NBC Plans Book." *Burlington [Vt.] Free Press* (12 April 1977), p. 5C.

Groenfeldt, Tom. "Pied Piper Lures Kids with Ice Cream." *The Record* (25 July 1977), pp. B1–2.

Adams, Dan. "The Pied Piper of '78." *Vermont Cynic* (2 February 1978), p. 39.

Loeb, Marshall. "Pied Piper for Industry." *Time* (18 December 1978), p. 70.

Green, Kate. "A Modern Pied Piper Leads Young and Old." *The South County News* (10 March 1980), p. 3.

Sheraton, Mimi. "Kansas City's Pied Piper of Chickendom." *The New York Times Magazine* (18 May 1980), p. 106.

Candido, Judy. "Sue Morse: The Pied Piper of Forestry." *The South County News* (9 June 1980), p. 14.

Gelb, Barbara. "Jacques D'Amboise. The Pied Piper of Dance." *The New York Times Magazine* (12 April 1981), pp. 50–53, 56, 58, 60, 62, 64, 66.

Swan, Annalyn. "Pied Piper [Oboist Heinz Holliger]." *Newsweek* (14 September 1981), p. 83.

Harwood, Madeleine. "Voters Should Check Pied Piper of Nuclear Weapon Resolution." *Burlington Free Press* (25 February 1982), p. 8A.

Rich, Alan. "Pied Piper of the Clarinet [Richard Stoltzman]." *Newsweek* (19 March 1984), p. 105.

These are just a few recent examples that show the generally positive connotations of the figuratively used "Pied Piper" in modern journalism. The positive interpretation is even more prevalent in the world of advertising. A cartoon even exists that reduces all advertising to a positive Pied Piper effect. Two shopkeepers have obviously hired a traditional Pied Piper who has gone through town to lure prospective customers to the store. When he arrives with his eager followers, the merchants exclaim with delight "It works!"[76] A music store in Vermont used this idea as an actual advertisement, adding the headline "Follow the Piper"[77] and an illustration of a pleasant Pied Piper to the layout. When advertising agents look for new people or slogans to market a product, they are in fact on the watch for a Pied Piper of sorts. Such a person was, for example, David Naughton whose Dr. Pepper commercials earned him the title "The Pied Pepper of soft-drink commercials."[78] Quite appropriate was a bright red merchandise bag that had printed on it the store's name, "The Pied Piper," and a traditional silhouette picture of a Pied Piper followed by children; in this case they are following him right to a toy store in St. Armonds Key, Florida.[79] And just as fitting was the illustration of a Pied Piper on a poster for a theatre production of a Pied Piper play that the University of Vermont Players wrote and presented in 1979.[80]

We should now return to the survival of actual motifs of the legend in modern society. The rats and the influence that the Pied Piper had on them continue to fascinate us, and there are a number of cartoons reflecting the rat problems that some of our big cities experience just as the medieval city of Hamelin did. The British satirical magazine *Punch* published two cartoons depicting the rat problems of London. One shows the rats not responding properly to the tunes of the Pied Piper, and the caption declares, "This looks bad—they're showing distinct signs of immunity."[81] The other cartoon, printed ten years later, is very similar, but here the rats are ridiculing the Pied Piper, and the towns-people proclaim nervously, "My God, they've become piper re-sistant."[82] But then there is also the cartoon that shows the Pied Piper having great success attracting the rats out of a rat-infested New York city school building,[83] and another one in which a specially contracted rat-catcher succeeds in getting the rats out of a large city garbage pile. The caption of the last mentioned cartoon reads "I see they got a private contractor in."[84] Perhaps he came from Baltimore, for in the "Yellow Pages" of that city we find an advertisement for an extermina-tor of termites, roaches, and pests who is appropriately called "Pied Piper."[85]

It is time to ask whether rats would in fact react to certain musical tunes or whether the entire legend motif of a musician attracting rats or mice is absurd. In an article in *Science* magazine, two Harvard profes-sors published a serious article on the ability of rats to hear at high frequencies and found that their hearing surpasses that of humans, cats, and dogs. They also report "that rats sometimes display epilepti-form seizures when they are exposed to frequencies of 21 kilocycles."[86] All that the medieval Pied Piper might have had is a pipe that produced particularly high frequencies that attracted the rats. If this sounds too far fetched—and of course the two Harvard professors do not mention the legend once in their erudite article—then consider a report that went through the media in 1977–78 with the fascinating title "California Man Goes From Rats to Riches," illustrated with a picture of a young man playing an electrical guitar that repels rats.

> HIPASS, Calif. (AP)—A sound so shrill it drives rodents wild, kills cockroaches and sends fleas flying is whistling up a fortune for Bob Brown, a polio-crippled guitar player who retired in 1965 on a $235 monthly Social Security check.
>
> In his garage one day six years ago, Brown was putting together an electric guitar when he tangled some wires. He recalled Tuesday that he saw rats scattering. He crossed the wires and the rodents ran again.
>
> Brown, 51, built what he called a rat repellant box and since then, 18,000 have been produced in Los Angeles and Tijuana, Mexico.
>
> A chicken farmer north of San Diego, about 50 miles west of Hipass, bought the first one when "about 10,000 mice were bothering the chickens every night. It cleared his place in four or five days," Brown said.
>
> The government of Venezuela recently ordered 300 to kill cockroaches in food stores in Caracas, and 1,000 were sent to Spanish granaries in Barcelona. Brown plans to fly to Brooklyn, N.Y., next Tuesday to talk to U.S. Housing and Urban Development Department officials about placing 9,000 units in low-rental apartments.
>
> "We flew to Hawaii and discovered the antennae on roaches just fold up when they hear it—they're on their backs, out of touch, without any balance," said Brown.
>
> Brown, a native of Fairmont, Minn., said the frequency is "over a million cycles a second." The human ear can hear up to about 20,000 cycles. Said Brown, who played with bands in Las Vegas: "Musicians know of the overtones, the harmonics which is what excite rock musicians—the frequencies that go through your head and you don't even know what's doing it to you.
>
> Brown said the net profits of his Amigo Ecology Corp. were about $800,000 last year and the gross "about a million and a half."
>
> "A millionaire? I guess I am," said Brown.[87]

It is most surprising that this account does not make a reference to the Pied Piper legend either. Did the journalist not recall the famous legend, or just not mention it for fear of taking away from the authenticity of the newspaper report?

About forty years ago there was a similar report concerning a conscious revival of the legend in order to rid the California town of Albany from its rats.

The United Press carried a story under date of October 15, 1943, to the effect that the waterfront town of Albany, California, had been requested by its harried citizens to appropriate one thousand dollars for freeing the town of rats. In a revival of the "Pied Piper of Hamelin" legend, Red Nichols, noted band-leader, paraded through the streets of the town playing the most weird notes that he could produce on his famous trumpet. Unlike their famous legendary forbears, the rats resisted the dulcet strains. The incident, intended, of course, as a parody, is of interest primarily for the fact that the town of Albany, engrossed in the war effort as are few towns anywhere, should take time out to express a common anxiety in terms of a legend eight centuries and a whole continent removed. Even if the spirit that obtained as the dashing band-leader "did his stuff" was nothing like that which pervaded quaint Hamelin town as the sinister piper Bundting trod its cobblestone streets, or nothing like modern commemorative festivals in the same town—which paid for its perfidy, so the legend runs, with the lives of one hundred thirty of its children—it is nevertheless heartening to know that an average American city like Albany can lose itself, if only for a day, in reliving a legend.[88]

This type of dramatization of a folk legend is ample proof of its continual popularity. In fact it might be seen as one of the conscious attempts to perpetuate folk narratives. Speaking of this publicity stunt in Albany, Wayland Hand noted that "this was an outright spoof, of course, but it does show how an ancient legend can be dramatized by the modern miracle of mass media and communication in a place far removed from the area of the legend's origin."[89]

The problem in Albany was, of course, that the famous American jazz trumpeter Red Nichols did not play high enough frequencies on his trumpet, for otherwise the rats would have followed him the way we saw in some of the cartoons of a Pied Piper ridding large cities of their rats. Judging from a few additional humorous interpretations of the piper motif, we can see that people still believe in rats following a piper. By the looks of a German cartoon, it is clearly dangerous to go to a carnival party as a Pied Piper since the rats will immediately follow you.[90] Even more humorous was a cartoon in the *New Yorker* that transfigured the Pied Piper into a marathon runner who is chased by a large pack of rats, each with its registration number.[91] Or picture a little boy confronting the Pied Piper and his army of rats with the frustrating statement, "You have my hamster in there, somewhere."[92] More serious is yet another cartoon, which depicts a poor street musician at a

*"You have my hamster in there, somewhere."*

street corner who can attract only a lonely rat by his music, but nobody who would spare him a dime.[93]

There is no reason why in the world of fantasy an animal should not take on the role of the piper for once. An intelligent cat might well take up flute playing and attempt to lure a mouse out of its hole,[94] and even Snoopy might feel like a Pied Piper when Sally is joyously following him.[95] And, in a wonderful reversal of the entire legend, how about a cartoon showing a rat that takes on the role of the Pied Piper and is followed by adult people saying "I like that tune"?[96] One wonders where this grotesque crusade might end.

With this cartoon we might turn to a strange reinterpretation of the second part of the legend by the American poet Ronald Koertge. In "The Pied Piper" (1971), it is once again the Pied Piper who leads, but, as in the cartoon, it is adults, the parents of the children, who are being abducted, leaving their offspring behind to care for themselves.

> None of their children trusted him, but
> even that didn't make any difference.
>
> Beside themselves with his melodies
> they left, congesting streets and
>
> avenues, parkways and lanes, raising
> great clouds of dust. For themselves
>
> they went in what they had on, but for
> their offspring—on clotheslines that

> stretched for miles—they left clean
> clothes: mantles and gowns, jumpers
>
> and frocks, tunics and slips. And when
> they were gone and the fierce wind had
>
> blown the air clean, there was absolute
> silence except for the tentative giggles of
>
> the children and the uproar of their new attire.[97]

It is not absolutely clear who the Pied Piper is, but he might well represent the materialistic goals of our society, which the parents aspire to attain. While letting the children fend for themselves, they are hustling and bustling about to live their own lives, hoping to pacify the children with newly-bought clothes. But with a "fierce wind" and an "absolute silence" after their departure, the children can only voice "tentative giggles," which soon are replaced by an "uproar" of despair and unhappiness. This poetic reversal of the legend shows the freedom of interpretation that is possible with traditional narratives once they are put into the service of social satire.

And how about the "tentative giggles" of the children who, just like the children in Hamelin seven hundred years ago, are unhappy, frustrated, and worried about their future in modern society? Will they ever laugh happily again, and will they be able to cope better than their parents with the ills of society? How do they know that they are following the right Pied Piper instead of one who, as it turns out, might not care at all about them? This idea is expressed in a short poem "The Pied Piper" (1950) by Mac Hammond, which summarizes the second part of the legend in a mere four-line stanza:

> The tune I played was only music;
> Only the tone of my flute was magic,
> Was what the children of that tropic,
> That winter, heard and found so tragic.[98]

Who is this piper? Does he know what he is doing? What direction is he pursuing? Is he, as a sexual cartoon suggests, a homosexual whose evil plans are quickly recognized by some children exclaiming, "I say he's a fag and I say let's split"?[99] How well does the piper know his own strengths and weaknesses, his ability to lead young people in new directions? Another humorous cartoon shows how quickly he might deviate from his path when he is attracted to a woman who immediately takes over the Pied Piper role, now being followed by both the original Pied Piper and the children.[100]

But one shouldn't be too pessimistic, as another recent cartoon illustrates by means of some science-fiction creatures who follow their futuristic Pied Piper, with much confidence, to a better place to live, saying: "Patience, darling, our leader will find us a suitable planet."[101] Perhaps there will be laughter and happiness on this new planet. This hope for a new and better life is also expressed in Gwendolyn MacEwen's poem "The Pied Piper" (1963), where an equally "absurd" piper, perhaps a "momentary messiah" brings laughter and hope to the young generation, telling the older generation to let the children go.

> was he only
> I ask you
> a magnet, radical
> and yellow in their towns
> or a gay science, I ask
> you, was he only
> momentary messiah, was
> he only these?
>
> children still wait
> for the absurd
> red and yellow music; they
> have not forgotten
> him tho you wish
> they would
> forget, always forget
> the piper, the pied
> piper, the red and yellow
> piper. O gentlemen,
> in your cities of rats
> someone hears a gentle music,
> someone laughs.[102]

This sentiment is also expressed in another lyrical reinterpretation of the legend by David Curry, which is simply called "Piper" (ca. 1965–69). Referring to the end of the actual legend, where it is stated that a law forbade any singing in the street through which the children left Hamelin, Curry asserts that a new piper, perhaps symbolically standing here for life and hope, will come, that he will play new tunes and that happiness and laughter will once again be felt and heard.

> After they pass a law against singing,
> someone will stumble into a clear place
> and, without thinking, make such notes
>     and words

that all the children will come
   tumbling after.
Eyes will open again,
and all things will be neighbors. The birds
will never have stopped their sounds,
   but suddenly
they will be heard again.[103]

After these positive interpretations of the second part of the legend, one might well ask what has happened to the supposedly tragic end in the old legend where, after all, 130 innocent children are led to their doom? The modern poems and cartoons have in fact shown the Pied Piper to be an ambiguous figure, a metaphor that can be interpreted negatively or positively. It is probably fair to assume that most poets, journalists, and cartoonists, as well as the general public do not know the massive scholarship that exists about this legend, but were they to be aware of it, they would probably agree that the Pied Piper should be interpreted as a much more positive image. As discussed at the beginning of this chapter, the Pied Piper was most likely a recruiter for young people (children in the legend) to settle Eastern colonies. In Hamelin's case there was probably a need for young people to leave an overcrowded medieval town and to look for a better future in a far distant land. There were population, social, and economic problems in Hamelin, and above all there must have been a serious generation conflict between old and young in this city. This conflict has been shown with the type of insight that only a great poet can have by John Ashberry in his poem "The Pied Piper" (1956), where the old people stay behind in misery, while the children leave with a much more "civil" recruiter, "laughing not to return," that is, happy to leave this rats' nest.

Under the day's crust a half-eaten child
And further sores which eyesight shall reveal
And they live. But what of dark elders
Whose touch at nightfall must now be
To keep their promise? Misery
Starches the host's one bed, his hand
Falls like an axe on her curls:
"Come in, come in! Better that the winter
Blaze unseen, than we two sleep apart!"

Who in old age will often part
From single sleep at the murmur
Of acerb revels under the hill;

Whose children couple as the earth crumbles
In vanity forever going down
A sunlit road, for his love was strongest
Who never loved them at all, and his notes
Most civil, laughing not to return.[104]

Two longer reworkings of the legend, published in Germany in 1975, are also based on this idea of a serious generation conflict and the desire and willingness of the young people to leave Hamelin. The two writers involved did a considerable amount of research into the origin of the legend and they portray the entire exodus from Hamelin in a positive light. In Ingeborg Engelhardt's novel, *Der Ruf des Spielmanns* (The Call of the Piper),[105] the young adults marry each other before leaving the corrupt city of Hamelin for a better and freer life in Moravia, where such conflicts as rich and poor, burgher and peasant will, they hope, not exist. Engelhardt is so interested in the socio-economic problems of the late Middle Ages that she leaves out the entire first part of the legend. The Pied Piper's appearance has enough motivation in providing an opportunity for the young people to get out of this miserable place.

Carl Zuckmayer in his play *Der Rattenfänger*[106] kept both parts of the legend, but he too sees the basic conflict as the social tensions in the town. As in Engelhardt's novel, the Pied Piper is a positive figure who enters a love relationship with a young woman from Hamelin. Eventually he leads Hamelin's youth to the East and they follow him with their own free decision and free will. There is nothing magic here anymore; there is no need to make an evil musician out of the recruiter, for he is looked at as the only salvation for the young people.

But there is also Gloria Skurzynski's American novel, *What Happened in Hamelin* (1979),[107] which can best be described as a plausible recreation of the legend in its negative interpretation. The Pied Piper is not a magician here either, but he plans his evil abduction of the children very intelligently and carefully. First he rids the town of the rats by feeding them salted meat and then having the children club them to death as they come to the river to quench their thirst. The children become his prey by his use of ergot poisoning. Everything starts positively and there is even a flickering of love between the Pied Piper and a young girl. But this man is the old evil monster that the creators of the early legend wanted us to believe in. He is a "locator" who is paid to abduct children for the settlements in Moravia, and he succeeds in his devilish scheme by using dope, love, force, intimidation, and any other possible trick. Skurzynski retains the medieval character of the legend and she even adds details reminiscent of the children's crusade and the bubonic plague, but despite all her research it becomes clear that her book is intended to steer juvenile readers away from evil Pied Pipers, particularly those who would sell them dope and thereby lead them to their death. The novel ends tragically for the children who, as in the legend, "vanish into Calvary Mountain" (p. 161), and we will never know whether they arrived in Moravia or not. In any case, the warning is clear, and who would ever have thought that this legend could be reworked into a novel warning against dope-pushers? What one does see is that the Pied Piper legend is still open to many reinterpretations, since the Pied Piper can represent any imaginable type of leader, fad, or cause.

Finally we must turn our attention to the spectacular way in which the city of Hamelin itself perpetuates the life of the legend that has made it so famous around the world. Wherever one turns in this charming town one senses the spirit of the Pied Piper. The city lives from the commercialization of the legend. Tourism is a major source of income, and every year hundreds of people from Germany and the rest of the world come to witness the reenactment of a small Pied Piper play put on every Sunday at noon from June through September.[108] The children of Hamelin take great delight in playing either the rats or the children who followed the piper. And while they run and dance through the picturesque narrow streets of Hamelin, they pass the famous *Rattenfängerhaus* (Pied Piper House) with its glorious *Gaststätte* (restaurant), a modern Pied Piper sculpture, a rotating musical sculpture depicting the exodus of the rats, and other sights recalling the legend. The entire old part of the town is Pied Piper land, and the visitor marvels at the ingenuity of the tourism industry in packaging Hamelin's attraction for ready consumption by eager tourists. Bumper stickers and postcards are sold everywhere, and in 1977 the German post office even issued a stamp, showing the exodus of the children.[109] It is high time that someone studies the importance of this *Folklorismus* (modern perpetuation of folklore through tourism) for the socio-economic structure of Hamelin and also for the legend itself. The commercialization of the legend does not stop in Hamelin itself. Children's literature and toys reach as far as the United States, where one can buy puzzles,[110] children's books, educational tape recordings with slides,[111] and greeting cards that declare lovingly, "I'd follow you anywhere!"[112] under a drawing of young people following a joyful and trustworthy Pied Piper.

Such commercial, educational, and entertainment use of the old legend obviously presents the Pied Piper in a more positive fashion in order to appeal to the consumer or tourist. But all of our texts and examples from the thirteenth century to the present have shown that the Pied Piper must be seen as an ambiguous figure, as abductor *and* savior. It is time that we begin wondering why a Pied Piper appears at all at any given time. After all, a Pied Piper or rat-catcher can perform his tasks only if there are "rats" who wish or need to be led. Whether he is a human or inhuman Pied Piper, he is dependent on his followers. Consider in this regard the short aphorism by Nikolaus Cybinski: "Hörst du die Ratten? Sie pfeifen dem Fänger"[113] (Do you hear the rats? They are whistling for the catcher). Does this not mean that people get the type of Pied Piper they select for themselves? Should we not be careful that we don't continue to make the Pied Piper into a scapegoat as the legend of the "Pied Piper of Hamelin" did so well seven hundred years ago? We really don't want to be completely under the spell of a Pied Piper in the way shown by a recent caricature, where the old Pied Piper takes the entire wintry city of Hamelin under his ambivalent wings.[114] Only a critical analysis of our own problems can protect us from the demonic powers of the Pied Piper. An understanding of one last Pied Piper reference in the form of an aphorism by Sigbert Latzel might help us to reach this insight: "Man spricht in der Geschichte oft von den Rattenfängern, seltener von den Ratten"[115] (One speaks in history often of the Pied Pipers, but seldom of the rats). When we look at the Pied Piper legend from this point of view, it becomes clear that it is meant not only for children, but even more for adults, who all need to be careful that they don't become mere "rats" and that they choose carefully which Pied Piper they might follow. The fact that leaders will always emerge and that there will always be people to follow makes the legend of the "Pied Piper of Hamelin" a universal statement of the human condition, and it is for this parabolic reason that the legend as an expression of basic human needs and fears has survived to this day. Hamelin is indeed everywhere, and the next Pied Piper is right around the corner—so watch out and be on your guard!

# 3 Modern Variants of the Daisy Oracle

## He Loves Me, He Loves Me Not

There exists a long history of love oracles or divinations, and in all European languages one can find the custom of counting out cherry stones, apple pips, buttons, beads, or petals of a daisy to find out such things as whether one is loved, whom one is going to marry, or what profession the person will have. Since these games are usually played by children, or perhaps young adults in love, it is not surprising that the traditional statements or chants that go along with them have been collected in books of nursery, jump-rope, and street rhymes as well as in books of children's games. While many different divination formulas have been assembled over the years, one can talk of three standard fortune-telling rhymes.[1] There is first of all the familiar

> Tinker, tailor, soldier, sailor,
> Rich man, poor man, beggar man, thief,
> Doctor, lawyer, Indian chief

which helps in predicting the profession or social status of a future husband. Next one might cite the following verse, which playfully analyzes various stages of courtship:

> One I love, two I love,
> Three I love, I say,
> Four I love with all my heart,
> Five I cast away;
> Six he loves, seven she loves, eight both love.
> Nine he comes, ten he tarries,
> Eleven he courts, twelve he marries.

And thirdly one must mention the internationally known short formula

> He [or she] loves me,
> He [or she] loves me not,
> He [or she] loves me. . .

and the many variants that have been registered of this simple expression. The following remarks will concern themselves above all with the "loves me, loves me not" formula, which is traditionally spoken while plucking one by one the petals of a daisy. Particular emphasis will be placed on some of its common variants and its modern survival forms in literature, art, postcards, comic strips, and advertisements.

One of the earliest written sources of a divination formula concerning love that uses a plant can be found in a Middle High German love poem by Walther von der Vogelweide from about 1203. In the second stanza the poet describes using a blade of grass to determine whether his lady truly loves him.

> Mich hât ein halm gemachet frô:
> er giht, ich sül genâde vinden.
> ich maz daz selbe kleine strô,
> als ich hie vor gesach von kinden.
> nu hoeret unde merket ob siz denne tuo.
> "si tuot, si entuot, si tuot, si entuot, si tuot."
> swie dicke ichz alsô maz, so was daz ende ie guot.
> daz troestet mich: dâ hieret ouch geloube zuo.[2]

> (A spire of grass hath made me gay:
> It saith, I shall find mercy mild.
> I measured in the selfsame way
> I have seen practised by a child.
> Come look and listen if she really does:
> She does, does not, she does, does not, she does.

Each time I try, the end so augureth.
That comforts me—'tis right that we have faith.[3])

The young poet explicitly points out that he is employing a children's game, which consists of measuring off a blade of grass with the thumb and index fingers while alternating the right and the left hand and saying "she does [love me], she does not, she does, she does not . . ." Ignaz Zingerle quotes another medieval German poem, in which Heinrich von Meißen also uses a blade of grass to find out whether his love will be returned or not. Alas, the oracle does not give a reassuring answer.

Weiz aber ein man, ob ich noch rehte milte müge erwecken?
"ich tuon, ichn tuon, ich tuon, ichn tuon: troestet baz ir werden recken!
ich tuon, ichn tuon—ich mizze ein halm ze lange."[4]

(Does any man [knight] know whether I shall find real love?
"I will, I will not, I will, I will not: console better you noble knights!
I will, I will not—I measure a blade of grass too long.")

Besides quoting this example from medieval literature, Zingerle points out that he was unable to find any references in Middle High German literature to using a daisy as a love oracle.[5] The same seems to be true for medieval English literature, for Geoffrey Chaucer, who often refers to daisies in his works, neglects to mention their use for divinations. What is more surprising, not even William Shakespeare quotes or alludes to the practice of plucking the petals of daisies in his dramas, which are so rich in traditional elements, including flower lore.[6] And yet the divination game with the daisy must have already been popular in Europe, if not in the Middle Ages then certainly very soon thereafter, for in a manuscript by the nun Clara Hätzlerin (fifteenth century) from Augsburg one finds the following short comment:

*Rupff plůmen.*
Wer rupffs plůmen tregt, maint, er sey in zweifel, ob In sein lieb
gerecht main! Wer sy aber tregt gerupfft vîz, on die zwey pletter,
vnd die geleich stånd, Bedeüttet, das er gantzer gerechtikaitt
gewert ist von seinem liebsten! Wellichern aber ain plettlin allain
ist beliben stån, Das maint, Im sey vngeleich geschehen![7]

*(Plucking flowers.*
Whoever carries flowers to be plucked indicates that he is in doubt
whether his loved one truly loves him! Who however carries them
already plucked except for two petals which remain standing that

means that he will receive justice from his loved one! But for whom only one little petal has remained standing that means injustice has happened to him!)

This *Rupfblume* (plucking flower) is most likely one of the numerous names for the daisy that can be found in various dialects of the German language, and such similar names as *Zupfblume* (plucking flower) and *Reißblöaml*[8] (pulling flower) leave little doubt that this fifteenth-century statement refers to the daisy and its use as a love oracle.

As Walther von der Vogelweide used blades of grass in the Middle Ages to determine the fate of his love, children (especially girls) of Erdington in the county of Warwick in England pluck a holly leaf to find out whether or not their mothers love them and want them, saying:

> I pluck this holly leaf to see
> If my mother does want me.[9]

They then count the prickly points of the leaf by repeating "yes, no, yes, no . . ." and accept as the answer the word that tallies with the last point.

A similar game can be played by simply counting the buttons on one's coat, jeans, blouse, or anything while chanting:

> Tinker, tailor, soldier, sailor,
> Rich man, poor man, beggarman, thief

to see whom one is going to marry.[10] Whichever name one stops at will indicate the status of the future husband. The game is splendidly illustrated in *A Rocket in My Pocket* by a drawing of a little girl counting the buttons of her coat and saying:

> Whom shall I marry?
> Rich man, poor man,
> Beggar man, thief,
> Doctor, lawyer,
> Merchant, chief?

> What shall I be married in?
> Silk,
> Satin,
> Calico,
> Cotton?

> Who will be best man at my wedding?
> Tinker,
> Tailor,

Cowboy,
Sailor?

Where shall I live?
Brick house,
Log house,
Frame house,
Cabin?

How many children shall I have?
One, two, three . . . [11]

A more modern allusion to this children's game was the descriptive headline in a German woman's magazine concerning a skirt with thirty-three buttons, which read "Ein Rock mit Abzählorakel" (a skirt with a counting oracle).[12]

This divination game can also be played with prune stones. After having found out whom one will marry one can continue to discover what sort of dress (silk, satin, muslin, rags) the bride will wear and where she will live (big house, small house, pigsty, barn).[13] Actually any fruit stone will serve for this type of fortune-telling count and the questioning of the oracle might be repeated ad infinitum. The game usually starts with the question, "Does he love me?" answered by a simple "yes, no, yes, no . . ." sequence. Subsequent questions and counts are:

What is the first letter of my husband's name? A, B, C, etc.
What is he? Tinker, tailor, soldier, sailor, rich man, poor man, beggar man, thief.
On what day shall I be married? Monday, Tuesday, Wednesday, etc.
What shall I wear? Silk, satin, cotton, rags.
How shall I get it? Stolen, borrowed, bought, or given.
How shall I go to church? Coach, carriage, wheelbarrow, dung-cart.
Where shall I live? Big house, little house, pigsty, barn.
How many children shall I have? One, two, three, etc.[14]

This same game has also been recorded for apple seeds and cherry stones.[15] An interesting poetic version with ten small drawings by Ernest Shephard was published by the British poet A. A. Milne with the title "Cherry Stones" (1927):

*Tinker, Tailor,*
*Soldier, Sailor,*
*Rich Man, Poor Man,*

*Ploughboy,*
*Thief—*

And what about a Cowboy,
Policeman, Jailer,
Engine-driver,
Or Pirate Chief?
What about a Postman—or a Keeper at the Zoo?
What about a Circus Man who lets the people through?
And the man who takes the pennies for the roundabouts and swings,
Or the man who plays the organ, and the other man who sings?
What about a Conjuror with rabbits in his pockets?
What about a Rocket Man who's always making rockets?

Oh, there's such a lot of things to do and such a lot to be
That there's always lots of cherries on my little cherry-tree![16]

Milne includes some of the newer professions in his children's poem
such as engine-driver, postman, and rocket man. The common preoccupation of a child with his possible future profession led Alan Patrick
Herbert to give his book, subtitled *A Child's Guide to the Professions* the
title "*Tinker, Tailor*" (1923) in obvious allusion to the divination rhyme.
He even included a short introductory poem, "The Problem," that
uses elements of the folk rhyme.

Child, your life is just beginning;
    You must look ahead.
Life, alas! consists of winning
    Little bits of bread;
Pause and ask yourself a minute:
    "How do *I* propose to win it?
    How shall *I* be fed?"

Tinker? Tailor? Soldier? Sailor?
    Which is it to be?
"Sailor's" life is seldom merry
(Not unless he runs a ferry)—
    "Gentleman" for me!
Let me give you one more cherry—
Goodness! that's "Apothecary"!—
    Let me give you three.

Burglar? Baker? Undertaker?
    Artist? Auctioneer?
What about the Engine-Driver?
    What about the Peer?
Author earns at least a fiver
    Every other year;

I should like to be a Diver,
  But the clothes are dear.

Roué? Rector? Tax-collector?
  Docker? Diplomat?
People say the Ironmonger
Never feels the pinch of hunger;
  Butcher runs to fat.
If you don't know *what* your groove is,
Courage, there are still the Movies!
  But I tell you flat—
Author is the least inviting,
You will win no bread at writing—
  Don't go in for *that*.

Cowboy? Cutler? Broker? Butler?
  Clergyman or Cook?
Yes, it is an awful question;
I have only one suggestion:
  If I'm not mistook,
You'll discover which you'd rather
If your admirable father
  Buys this little book.[17]

The popularity of the divination rhyme "Tinker, tailor, soldier, sailor, / Rich man, poor man, beggar man, thief" is well attested in the many variations recorded in books on nursery, jump-rope, and skipping rhymes.[18] That such variations can contain serious subject matters is well illustrated by the following skipping rhyme collected in 1949 in Ireland:

A tinker an'
A tailor an'
An I. R. A.
An Auxie man,
A Black-and-Tan
A thief . . . [19]

This street chant drastically embodies the ingredients of the Anglo-Irish War (1921–1922) and is a clear indication how the ugly adult world usurps the playground of children. But the reversal is also true; that is adults borrow from children lore, as the American novelist Irwin Shaw does in the title of his novel *Rich Man, Poor Man* (1969), which depicts the life of three children of an embittered German immigrant in the United States after the Second World War. For the sequel to this novel, which tells about the life of the next generation of this family in the sixties and seventies, Shaw very appropriately chose the title *Begger-man, Thief* (1977). One wonders if he might not come out with a third volume that could easily be entitled *Doctor, Lawyer*, thereby continuing the rhyme. The beginning of the original rhyme, with one small but necessary change, was used by John Le Carré for the title of his extremely successful spy novel *Tinker, Tailor, Soldier, Spy* (1974). Le Carré acknowledges his debt to the fortune-telling rhyme by citing it from the *Oxford Dictionary of Nursery Rhymes* as a motto on the first page of the book. In the novel the author explains his title in the following way: "Tinker, Tailor, Soldier, Sailor. Alleline was Tinker, Haydon was Tailor, Bland was Soldier, and Toby Esterhase was Poorman. We dropped Sailor because it rhymed with Tailor."[20] The individual words of the nursery rhyme thus become code names for four staff members of the British Secret Service in the novel, and the change from "Sailor" to "Spy" in the title helps to identify the genre of the novel. The altered nursery rhyme title "Tinker, Tailor, Solider, Spy" became instantly celebrated when PBS broadcast a thirteen-episode television series dramatizing John Le Carré's best-selling spy novel during the fall of 1980,[21] a fine example of how a traditional rhyme might gain revitalized currency among adults through mass media.

It has been shown that the divination rhyme "Tinker, tailor, soldier, sailor . . ." is spoken or chanted while counting fruit stones or jumping rope or skipping. It is, however, also often used while plucking one by one the petals of a daisy.[22] As has been explained, children can inquire about the social status or profession of the person they will marry, or, of course, they can ask the flower oracle about their own professional future as well. Most Anglo-American versions follow more or less the wording already discussed, but in continental Europe the daisy oracle is able to give answers to different problems as well. Due to the different social structure of Europe, even the rhymes that deal with professions are quite different, as in the long German example that follows:

> Kaiser, König, Edelmann,
> Bürger, Bauer, Bettelmann,
> Schuster, Schneider, Leineweber,
> Doktor, Kaufmann, Todtengräber.[23]

> (Emperor, king, gentleman,
> Burgher, farmer, beggar,
> Cobbler, tailor, linen weaver,
> Doctor, merchant, grave-digger.)

In Switzerland one can also find out one's future place in heaven by plucking a daisy and reciting:

> Himmel, Höll, Fegfü'r, Paradies?[24]
>
> (Heaven, hell, purgatory, paradise?)

The Swiss girls can also inquire, whether they will marry at all:

> Ledig sî, Hochzig ha,
> is Chlösterli ga?[25]
>
> (Be single, have a wedding,
> or go into the cloister?)

And if they are to get married, the daisy will tell them what their social status will be:

> Edelfrau, Bettelfrau, Bûrefrau.[26]
>
> (Noble lady, beggar wife, peasant wife.)

Yet the most common use of the daisy flower as an oracle is, of course, simply to answer the question of whether one is loved or not, and in the shortest possible answer there is no difference in the European and American versions. A laconic "yes, no" or "He loves me, he loves me not" pattern suffices to answer this universal concern.

Before we concentrate on this short divination formula and its modern variants, one other very popular but longer fortune-telling rhyme must be considered, which deals explicitly with the question of love. Once again the rhyme can be recited when counting fruit stones, jumping rope, skipping, or, of course, when plucking daisy petals. The standard Anglo-American version (the rhyme is not known in continental Europe) can be cited as:

> One I love, two I love,
> Three I love, I say,
> Four I love with all my heart,
> Five I cast away;
> Six he loves, seven she loves, eight both love.
> Nine he comes, ten he tarries,
> Eleven he courts, twelve he marries.[27]

A more modern version from a child whose parents' marriage has broken up adds the following sequel:

> Thirteen they quarrel,
> Fourteen they part,
> Fifteen he dies of a broken heart.[28]

In the more traditional state of Vermont one can hear children recite the following more positive addendum:

> Thirteen honor, fourteen riches,
> And all the rest are children, letters, and kisses.[29]

Of particular interest is the following variant, since it already contains to a certain degree the formula of "he loves me, he loves me not":

> One I love, two I loathe,
>   Three I cast away;
> Four I love with all my heart
>   Five I love, I *say* (emphasis on 'say').
> Six he loves me, seven he don't,
> Eight he'll marry me, nine he won't,
> Ten he would if he could, but he can't,
> Eleven he comes, twelve he tarries,
> Thirteen he's waiting, fourteen he marries.[30]

The three center lines of this rhyme are basically what make up this next much shorter variant, which brings us almost to the simplest love divination formula:

> He loves me,
> He don't
> He'll have me,
> He won't
> He would if he could,
> But he can't
> So he don't.[31]

In a two-page note from the year 1888 Felix Liebrecht assures us that the shortest or most universal counting-out rhyme, the "Volksvers" (folk verse) "He loves me, he loves me not," is well known all over Europe, and he quotes Icelandic, Portuguese, Italian, Spanish, and German variants that are recited while plucking the petals of a daisy.[32] While Anglo-American tradition adheres rather strictly to the simple statement of "loves me, loves me not," or an occasional triadic structure: "yes, no, maybe so,"[33] French youths seem to be a bit more imaginative in testing the sincerity of their affections:

> La blanche et simple pâquerette,
> Que ton coeur consulte surtout,
> Dit: ton amant, tendre fillette,
> T'aime, un peu, beaucoup, point du tout.[34]

> (The white and simple daisy,
> Which your heart consults so often,

Says: your lover, tender little girl,
Loves you, a little, much, not at all.)

Some more elaborate yet simple French rhymes expressing various degrees of love are:[35]

Il m'aime—un peu—beaucoup—mais guère—patiemment—constamment—de tout son coeur—en marriage—pas du tout.

(He loves me—a little—a lot—scarcely—passionately—constantly—with all his heart—in marriage—not at all.)

Il m'aime—un peu—beaucoup—tendrement—constamment—à la folie—point du tout.

(He loves me—a little—a lot—tenderly—constantly—madly—not at all.)

Il m'aime—un peu—beaucoup—par amour—par fantaisie—par jalousie—pas du tout.

(He loves me—a little—a lot—with love—with imagination—with jealousy—not at all.)

Similar rhymes can also be found in the German language, and it is interesting to note that the colloquial names for the daisy in German reflect its use as a love oracle:[36]

Orakelblume (oracle flower)
Liebesblume (love flower)
Schatzblume (treasure [love] flower)
Wahrsageblume (prophecy flower)
Massliebchen (little measure of love)

Three more or less common German divination rhymes that show the reason for these names are:[37]

Sie liebt mich von Herzen,
Mit Schmerzen,
Ein wenig
Oder gar nicht.

(She loves me from the heart,
Painfully,
A little
Or not at all.)

Sie liebt mich von Herzen,
Mit Schmerzen,
Über alle Massen,

Kann von mir nicht lassen,
Ein wenig
Oder gar nicht.

(She loves me from the heart,
Painfully,
Above all measure,
Can't let go of me,
A little
Or not at all.)

Sie liebt mich von Herzen,
Mit Schmerzen,
Insgeheim,
Ganz allein,
Ein wenig
Oder gar nicht.

(She loves me from the heart,
Painfully,
Secretly,
Completely alone [i.e. only me],
A little
Or not at all.)

All the cited examples are ample proof that children and young lovers seem to be drawn towards the daisy oracle to find out whether they are loved and if so in what measure. And as luck would have it, this natural oracle is a more positive and reliable one than its ancient counterpart in Delphi. For John Ruskin, the nineteenth-century British author and scholar, has this unromantic comment to make concerning the fortune-telling qualities of the daisy:

> I must be so ungracious to my fair young readers, however, as to warn them that this trial of their lovers is a very favourable one, for, in nine blossoms out of ten, the leaves of the Marguerite [daisy] are odd, so that, if they are only gracious enough to begin with the supposition that he loves them, they must needs end in the conviction of it.[38]

This unpoetic and scientific analysis of the flower oracle has not and will not prevent the traditional game from being continued. One of the most touching literary allusions to the daisy divination is found in the "Garden" scene of the first part of Johann Wolfgang von Goethe's drama *Faust* (1808), which was splendidly illustrated by the artist Friedrich August Moritz Retzsch in 1840.[39] In this scene Gretchen

plucks the petals of a daisy playfully to see whether perhaps Faust
loves her, and the dialogue between Faust and her is as follows:

> [*Sie pflückt eine Sternblume und rupft die Blätter ab, eins nach
> dem andern.*]
>
> *Faust:* Was soll das? Einen Strauß?
> *Margarete:* Nein, es soll nur ein Spiel.
> *Faust:* Wie?
> *Margarete:* Geht! Ihr lacht mich aus.
>
> > [*Sie rupft und murmelt.*]
>
> *Faust:* Was murmelst du?
> *Margarete:* [halb laut] Er liebt mich—liebt mich nicht.
> *Faust:* Du holdes Himmelsangesicht!
> *Margarete:* [fährt fort] Liebt mich—Nicht—liebt mich—Nicht—
>
> > [*Das letzte Blatt ausrupfend, mit holder Freude.*]
> >        Er liebt mich!
> *Faust:* Ja, mein Kind! Laß dieses Blumenwort Dir Götterausspruch
> sein. Er liebt dich! Verstehst du, was das heißt? Er liebt dich![40]

> ([*She picks a star flower and plucks the petals off it one by one.*]
>
> *Faust:* : What is it? A bouquet?
> *Margaret:* No, just a game.
> *Faust:* What?
> *Margaret:* You'd laugh at me if I should say.
>
> > [*She murmurs something as she goes on plucking.*]
>
> *Faust:* What are you murmuring?
> *Margaret:* [not quite aloud] He loves me—loves me not.
> *Faust:* You lovely creature of the skies!
> *Margaret:* [continuing] Loves me—not—loves me—not—
>
> > [*with delight as she reaches the last petal*]
> >        He loves me!
> *Faust:* Yes, my child! And let this language of the flowers be your
> oracle. He loves you! Do you know what that means? He loves you![41])

Gretchen uses the shortest and simplest divination formula to learn
the truth about Faust's feeling towards her, and as is usually the case,
the last petal answers with "He loves me." A later poetic interpretation
of this garden scene between Gretchen and Faust by the British poetess
Letitia Elizabeth Landon expresses the same joy over the positive
outcome of her count, but it is interesting to note that Landon for once
starts the rhyme negatively with "He loves me not":

> And with scarlet poppies around like a bower,
> The maiden found her mystic flower.

"Now, gentle flower, I pray thee tell
If my love loves, and loves me well;
So may the fall of the morning dew
Keep the sun from fading thy tender blue;
Now I number the leaves for my lot—
He loves me not—he loves me—he loves me not—
He loves me! Yes, the last leaf—yes!
I'll pluck thee not for that last sweet guess;
He loves me!" "Yes," a dear voice sighed;
And her lover stands by Margaret's side.[42]

Of great interest also is a poem by James Lowell entitled "With a Pressed Flower" (1840). Not only does the poet mention the fact that the custom of plucking daisies is known in both Germany and New England, but he also seems to be acquainted with the fact that daisies usually have an odd number of petals. For this reason he can express the maiden's expected last count, "He loves me," poetically by saying, "glad tears have filled her eyes / To find the number [of petals] was uneven":

This little blossom from afar
Hath come from other lands to thine;
For, once, its white and drooping star
Could see its shadow in the Rhine.

Perchance some fair-haired German maid
Hath plucked one from the selfsame stalk,
and numbered over, half afraid,
Its petals in her evening walk.

"He loves me, loves me not," she cries;
"He loves me more than earth or heaven!"
And then glad tears have filled her eyes
To find the number was uneven.

And thou must count its petals well,
Because it is a gift from me;
And the last one of all shall tell
Something I've often told to thee.

But here at home, where we were born,
Thou wilt find blossoms just as true,
Down-bending every summer morn,
With freshness of New England dew.

For Nature, ever kind to love,
Hath granted them the same sweet tongue,
Whether with German skies above,
Or here our granite rocks among.[43]

The daisy oracle is described as an international phenomenon and the universal feeling of love is expressed by the pressed German daisy that is sent to an American woman. Somehow one also is reminded of Elizabeth Browning's famous sonnet beginning "How do I love thee? Let me count the ways" (1847). Browning never makes a direct allusion to any of the divination formulas discussed above, but who is to say that she did not have the plucking of the petals of the daisy in mind when she counts the different ways she loves? Ludvig Sandöe Ipsen, the illustrator of a beautiful 1886 edition of Browning's *Sonnets from the Portuguese* chose the Passion Flower to frame in the sonnet,[44] but a lesser and more down-to-earth artist might perhaps have chosen the daisy to represent the various forms of love expressed in the poem.

This romantic and touching use of flower symbolism in literary sources from the nineteenth century is paralleled by artistic illustrations of the daisy motif from that time. The finest and most sensitive illustration is to be found in a collection of fifty colored metal etchings called *Les fleurs animées* (1847) by the French artist Jean-Ignace-Isidore Gérard Grandville. The picture called "Marguerite"[45] shows a young woman in the form of a daisy, plucking the petals of another daisy and surrounded by several smaller animated figures that are half flower and half person. Certainly Grandville's illustration depicts the daisy divination, and it is interesting to note that he made this etching in 1847, the same year that Browning wrote her poem about counting various measures of love.

Equally sincere and traditional is a woodcut entitled "Von Herzen" from the year 1846 by the German illustrator Ludwig Richter.[46] A young woman uses a daisy to find out how much her young friend loves her while he looks on over her shoulder. The title, which means from the heart, is an appropriate shortening of the German divination rhyme, "Er liebt mich von Herzen, mit Schmerzen, ein wenig, oder gar nicht" (He loves me from the heart, painfully, a little, or not at all). Thirteen years later Ludwig Richter returned to this motif in a second woodcut simply called "Er liebt mich" (He loves me), which basically repeats the previous illustration, but perhaps in an even more bourgeois, nineteenth-century setting.[47] The bliss and happiness of this middle class couple is even enhanced by an attentive and loving dog.

This kind of oversentimentalization of the old love divination game reached its peak at the turn of the century on postcards and valentine cards. Often they include little poems like this one:

Lovely daisy
    meekly hiding
Flower of spring time
    white as snow.
With your silver
    petals tell me,
Does he love me,
    yes or no?
All my hopes would
    fly and leave me
Should you say
    he was not true
So fair floweret
    don't deceive me
His love will last
    all ages through.[48]

A similar sentiment is expressed by a valentine card showing a young woman and a young man with a sort of cupid beginning to pluck the petals of a daisy.[49] The card is addressed "For my valentine" and the first petal being plucked has "He loves me" inscribed on it. Another card from 1907 simply states "To my valentine" and pictures a pretty young girl who has just pulled off the first petal of the daisy.[50] Implied is, of course, that she says "He loves me" while performing the divination game. There is also a fancier valentine card sold in 1913, which contains a picture of a young woman plucking a daisy accompanied by the following poem:

The Daisy may not
    tell me true—
It cannot know as
    well as you,
And that is why I
    send this line
To ask *you* for my
    Valentine.[51]

One detects a certain element of doubt about divination abilities of the daisy in this playful poem, and this questioning of the traditional oracle is also indicated on the smirking face of the woman who needs a good reason to send her lover a valentine card to express her love for him.

It might be interesting to note here that the traditional examples cited thus far always depict the woman as asking the oracle, not the man. One could perhaps argue that this is only one more indication of how folklore and its adaptations in earlier literary or artistic works reflect a stereotypical view of women—that they are the more sentimental and unsure members of society who must question a flower to find out whether they are truly loved or not, while men are obviously sure about their amorous feelings and conquests. A recent romantic novelette entitled *He Loves Me, He Loves Me Not* (1979) certainly supports this notion, for the main characters are portrayed in exactly this fashion.[52]

Norman Rockwell's colorful drawing, which appeared in a 1947 calendar with the title "Man and Boy," is quite different in this regard.[53] As the title suggests, it is a young boy who is plucking a daisy here while he sits next to a man who is lying in the grass. The young lad is obviously not asking about whether some young girl loves him or not but rather what he will become one day, probably reciting the verse "Tinker, tailor, soldier, sailor, beggarman, chief . . . " a good pastime for a little boy who will grow up in the still unliberated world of the forties. An interesting little children's book by Robert Keeshan, *She Loves Me . . . She Loves Me Not* (1963), does, however, overcome this role-playing.[54] Twenty-five cute illustrations show how a girl and a boy play the daisy divination game and the laconic captions contrast the "She loves me, she loves me not" formula with the "He loves me, he loves me not" variant until the happy ending.

But this is a picture of the perfect world as seen by innocent and naive children. The modern adult, who sees things quite differently, is certainly aware that love is not always returned in an imperfect world inhabited by troubled people. Little wonder that most modern illustrations of the daisy divination appear in the form of ironical or satirical caricatures, which usually put into question the possibility of finding true love. A German cartoon from 1919 illustrates this notion by depicting a young woman who is insulted by a rogue while plucking a daisy: "'An Ihrer Stell' tät' ich keine Gänseblümchen mehr zupfen, Fräulein!'—'Warum denn nicht?'—'Weil Sie immer die falschen erwischen!'"[55] ("In your place I wouldn't pluck any more daisies, Miss!"—"But why not?"—"Because you always pick the wrong guy!"). A similarly doubtful sentiment is expressed in another recent cartoon, in which a bride in her wedding dress is still asking the daisy oracle whether her husband to be does in fact love her or not: "Er liebt mich—er liebt mich nicht—er liebt mich . . . "[56] (He loves me—he

«Er liebt mich—er liebt mich nicht—er liebt mich. . .»

loves me not—he loves me . . . ). Yet not only the modern woman faces such uncertainties; males are confronted with the same problems and anxieties. Another modern cartoon shows a young and virile man flirting with the wife or girlfriend of a smallish and rather meek man while the latter desperately plucks a daisy saying "She loves him, she loves him not, she loves him, she loves him not . . . "[57] The real irony is that the man doesn't even ask the flower any more whether he is loved by her, which the traditional formula "She loves me" would have demanded. Instead he changes the rhyme into "She loves him" and seems to surrender to the intruder without much of a fight. Even more depressing is the cover illustration from a 1979 *Punch* magazine, where a young lad who has just been rebuffed by his female friend sitting on a distant bench marches through a field of daisies kicking them in any direction and reciting the rhyme "She loves me . . . she loves me not . . . she loves me . . . she . . . "[58] One can't help but feel that the final answer of the oracle will be "She loves me not."

The most drastic example of a negative end to playing the divination game occurred on 14 October 1980, when Richard Meeker, the son of actress Mary Tyler Moore, shot himself to death. Using a shotgun as a divination device instead of a harmless daisy, he turned the love oracle into a "Game of Death" as the reporter of *Time* magazine so appropriately entitled the short account of Meeker's death. Here is what happened:

> According to Judy Vasquez, 21, who shared a house with him [Meeker, age 24] near the University of Southern California campus, Meeker was chatting with her about his girlfriend, Linda Jason, 21, of Fresno. He casually plucked from the wall over his bed a short-barreled .410 gauge shotgun. Sitting with legs folded in the lotus position, Meeker rested the butt of the gun on his ankles, pointed the barrel at his face and began loading and unloading a shell.
> Asked Vasquez: "Do you think she's in love with you?" Replied Meeker, tilting his head to the right: "She loves me." With a click, he unloaded the gun and tilted his head to the left. Said he: "She loves me not." There was another click as he loaded the gun and said: "She loves me." Click. "She loves me not." Click. Meeker stared intently at Vasquez and shouted: "She loves me!" A blast ripped into Meeker's face, and he fell dead.[59]

This scene appears to be a modified version of Russian roulette and we will never know whether Meeker was just playing a dangerous game or whether he intended to commit suicide. In any case, he obviously attempted to communicate his feelings.

It is communication between the sexes that is needed and where that is missing even the lonely game with a daisy flower can present a danger to a person's emotional stability. The modern teenager or young adult can still fall into the trap this depressing game becomes when it is played in solitude without the joy of playing it with the person one loves. A cartoon from the mid-fifties shows this trap by picturing a young man plucking a daisy instead of asking one of the two women who happen to be walking by whether she really loves him or not. All that the woman can say is "It would never occur to Alvin to ask me!"[60] A similar problem is illustrated in a longer comic strip where two young girls pluck one daisy after another to find out whether Gregory loves one of them. Thank goodness the father finally puts an end to it by asking whether it "wouldn't be more logical if she found out from Gregory" herself.[61] It is in fact more logical to communicate one's feelings but shyness, insecurity, and other apprehensions will lead even today's youngsters into asking the daisy oracle before mustering up the courage for direct communication.

If a person cannot find the nerve to ask someone for a date or simply does not have the opportunity to meet new people, then a computerized service that finds partners for single people offers a new technological game of "She loves me, she loves me not . . . " by matching up people via programmed personality profiles.[62] Whether this modern electronic oracle is any more reliable than the traditional and cheaply available daisy is anybody's guess. An interesting cartoon from 1979 illustrates an old man who obviously missed the love boat somehow. He sadly holds a drooping daisy whose petals fall off without actually being plucked.[63] The German cartoonist Wilhelm Schlote seems to imply that for this man the time of oracles has passed. One could, however, also interpret this scene in a more humorous fashion as showing that the daisy—just another good old daisy of the millions that have already been used for divination purposes—has become so well conditioned that it performs the game of plucking daisy petals by itself. This is certainly the case in a recent comic strip of the "B.C." series by Johnny Hart, where a daisy drops one of its petals to help out a pessimist: "'When there's so much love in the world, why must I be left out?' [asks the pessimist]—'Don't be such a pessimist!' [responds the daisy] 'Here!' [daisy drops a petal]—'She loves me

not . . . ' [says the pessimist]—'Sigh' [daisy].''[64] Not even an animated daisy with the best intentions can help an eternal misanthrope who starts the counting rhyme against every conventional rule with the negative ''She loves me not'' statement. All that the daisy can do is sigh, for even if she were to continue the game and drop her remaining six petals (remember most daisies have an odd number of petals) the rhyme would end negatively.

There are, of course, more humorous cartoons to be found employing the traditional daisy motif. A chic lady in a German cartoon from the thirties somewhat mechanically plucks a daisy and thinks to herself: ''Geht's nicht auf, dann bin ich zu Tode betrübt! Geht's aber auf, dann ist es einfach eine Gemeinheit, daß er nicht da ist!''[65] (If the rhyme doesn't end well, I'll be rather disappointed! If it ends well, however, then I think it's a shame that he's not here!). From the same time is also the delightful cartoon that shows a young woman plucking away at an artificial daisy decorating the hat of an elderly lady. The scene takes place in an overcrowded trolley and the caption appropriately reads "Das Liebesorakel in der Straßenbahn"[66] (The love oracle in the trolley).

If an artificial daisy will do, then there is no reason why an enamoured woman should not also play the divination game by counting her toes in the absence of daisies. An amusing cartoon from 1912 pictures a mother and her daughter after having gone swimming. Perhaps instead of drying herself the daughter seems to use her toes as a love oracle, prompting her mother to ask: "Aber Kind, jetzt zählst du wohl gar an den Zehen ab, ob er dich liebt?"[67] (But child, are you crazy enough to count your toes to see whether he loves you?). When love can lead to such folly, then there is no reason why a modern cartoonist should not go one step further and proclaim in his caption "Der Blumentest ist nicht mehr so poetisch wie früher" (The flower test is not as poetic as in former times). The cartoon pictures a man plucking daisies to determine his sexual fortunes: "'Sie geht mit mir ins Bett!'— 'Sie geht nicht mit mir ins Bett!'—' . . . und jetzt das nächste Blümlein: Sie geht mit mir ins Bett!' . . . "[68] ("She goes to bed with me!"—"She goes not to bed with me!"— ". . . and now the next little flower: She goes to bed with me! . . . ").

But the depoetization of the flower oracle is not altogether a modern phenomenon. As early as 1893 the German artist Adolf Oberländer drew a cartoon entitled "Der Gockel als Gänseblümchen" (The rooster as a daisy) whose caption is composed of the traditional rhyme "Er liebt mich . . . er liebt mich nicht . . . er liebt mich!"[69] (He loves me . . . he loves me not . . . he loves me!). The irony lies in the fact that a woman holds a healthy rooster in her arms instead of a daisy and that she plucks away at the cock's tail feathers as she repeats the rhyme. On one level this might just show a farm woman surrounded by her chickens and somewhat foolishly expressing her appreciation of her flock. One can also look at the plucking of the tail feathers of a rooster as a kind of metaphorical emasculation of a dominating husband perhaps. The chicken imagery is maintained in a contrasting misogynous caricature by the famous satirist Olaf Gulbransson from the year 1956. He illustrates a meek, wall-flower-type young woman plucking a daisy in the left frame of his cartoon, and metamorphoses her into an obese motherly type with four children grouped around her like chicks around the mother hen in the opposing frame. The caption, which reads "Aus einer Feder—können fünf Hühner werden"[70] (Out of one feather—can come five chickens), not only compares the skinny woman to a feather but also alludes to her and her children (all girls!) as a flock of chickens, a "dummes Huhn" (dumb chicken) being an invective against women in German folk speech.

Yet the modern emancipated woman strikes back, as an interesting addition to the divination rhyme on a needlepoint kit shows:

> He loves me
> He loves me not
> 'Tis no matter
> I'm all he's got.[71]

In other words divinations do not matter anymore. This is also the advice that the New England poet John Stevens Wade gives his young son in "Daisies" (1974), a modern poem about daisies and their value as fortune-tellers.

> When it is plucking time for my young son
> and I am *Father William* and wiser than my words,
> I won't tell the boy what I know about honeycombs.
> We'll sit upstairs and talk sex;
> talk of that mysterious thrill
> that leaves each blood cell tall
> as a sunflower. If he should mention
> daisies, I'll say: "Well, there was once
> an ancient theory about such things . . . "
> then my voice will fade as if I had forgotten.
> I won't tell him that saying love-
> me and love-me-not is just one
> way of pulling a daisy apart.
> Let him learn this from some woman
> who will want him to make confetti
> out of every field in sight. I'll just tell him
> that women are wiser than we are
> when it comes to the mystery of loving,
> but of daisies, their knowledge is slight.[72]

And at the same time as Wade published this anti-daisy poem in 1974 Hank Ketcham seems to have illustrated its content to a certain degree in one of his "Dennis, the Menace" cartoons whose caption reads: "Margaret just played 'loves-me-loves-me-not' with a daisy . . . an' I got lucky!"[73] The poem and the cartoon express the difficulties of love relationships that the daisy can't possibly solve.

Until now most of the examples of the modern survival of the daisy divination have followed more or less the traditional use of daisies as a love oracle. But children are known to be inventive in their games, and why shouldn't a little girl pluck a daisy not to ascertain whether a little boy loves her but whether God loves her. In a touching cartoon from the series "The Girls" by Franklin Folger the girl approaches her mother in the kitchen with the upsetting declaration: "God doesn't love me. I know he doesn't—I tried Him with a daisy."[74] Another child at a garden show transfers the daisy game to a large house plant and plucks the last large leaf, triumphantly declaring, "He loves me!" while her embarrassed mother has only eyes for the mutilated plant.[75] These are humorous parodies of an often repeated children's game and certainly reflect common familial experiences.

The naive children's world is, however, quickly changed into a worrisome and problematic view of modern society when adult satirists begin to adapt the daisy divination motif to their needs. They use the fortune-telling abilities of the daisy to express the uncertain future of political, economic, and societal problems. The earliest political employment of the daisy motif that I have been able to find is a 1916 caricature by Olaf Gulbransson, which shows a plain and common mother asking the daisy about whether the escalating First World War might not come to an end soon: "Friede—nicht Friede—Friede— nicht Friede—Friede . . . "[76] (Peace—not peace—peace—not peace —peace . . . ). The devastating war dragged on for more than two years, and the aftereffects can still be felt in another German cartoon from March 1922. In an obvious allusion to Goethe's Gretchen in *Faust*, the caricaturist illustrates a woman plucking the petals of a daisy to find out whether the Americans will take part at the Genoa Conference that took place from 10 April to 19 May 1922 to consider problems with Russia and general questions of world economy. Each daisy petal bears the name of a German newspaper, obviously referring to the different speculations by the press about America's participation, which ultimately did not occur. The caption carries the title "Der Amerikaner" (The American) and underneath is printed the altered rhyme "Das deutsche Gretchen: 'Er kommt nach Genua—er kommt nicht—er kommt—er kommt nicht—'"[77] (The German Gretchen: "He comes to Genoa—he comes not—he comes—he comes not—").

World War II also gave satirists plenty of occasions to utilize the oracle. At the beginning of the war, a German satirist published a caricature in the magazine *Kladderadatsch*, by then controlled by Nazis. The British Prime Minister Neville Chamberlain in a skirt and with high heels is shown plucking a daisy to find out whether Joseph Stalin, who observes from a distant bench, loves him or not: "'Er liebt mich —— . . . —— . . . —— . . . gar nicht!'"[78] ("He loves me . . . not at all!"). It is interesting to note that the German caricaturist deliberately leaves out the intermediate steps of the German rhyme which, as we recall, are "He loves me from the heart, painfully, a little, or not at all," in order to discredit the Western Alliance as directly as possible. About half a year later, in May 1940, there appeared another anti-British cartoon with the title "Orakel" (oracle) by Olaf Gulbransson in the famous satirical magazine *Simplicissimus*. The artist illustrates Neville Chamberlain, Winston Churchill, and a third British politician plucking daisies, wondering how the war is going for Britain: "Wir siegen— ein bißchen—ein wenig—oder gar nicht!"[79] (We are winning—a bit—a little—or not at all!). Again the rhyme in the caption ends with the propagandistic answer "not at all."

Turning to the political arena after the Second World War, we have a cartoon of Harry S. Truman from 1950 wondering about whether certain dissatisfied Democratic elements still love him as much as during the 1948 election when they strongly supported him. With a troubled expression on his face Truman recites the slightly revised oracle rhyme, "They love me, they love me not."[80] A similar cartoon from 1957 depicts the two German political opponents Konrad Adenauer and Erich Ollenhauer, who each pluck daisies to ascertain their popularity in the minds of the people. The cartoon is fittingly entitled "Wahl-Orakel" (Election-oracle), and consistent with the personal attacks of political campaigns, Ollenhauer accuses Adenauer of cheating: "Das war unfair! Jetzt haben Sie zwei auf einmal gezupft!"[81] (That was unfair. Now you've plucked two [petals] at once!). But while the politicians bicker among themselves before the election, some people couldn't care less and wouldn't dream of taking advantage of their right to vote. Instead, a young couple in another cartoon simply packs a picnic and goes to the country to spend a lovely afternoon with each other playing the worry-free traditional oracle game with the daisy. Their conclusion is a clearcut "Auf so eine angenehme Weise habe ich das Wählengehen noch nie versäumt"[82] (I have never before missed the voting at an election in such a pleasant way).

Politicans nevertheless worry about their fortune and future, and satirists delight in depicting their uncertainty. A striking example of a politican not being sure which way to make a decision is a caricature from 1960 depicting Willy Brandt's uncertainty about his stance on atomic energy and weapons in Germany. The cartoon is entitled "Das Atom-Orakel" (The Atom-oracle) and shows Willy Brandt, Konrad Adenauer, and Erich Ollenhauer each plucking the petals of a daisy. But it is Willy Brandt in the foreground who clearly is in a conflict situation, and his indecisiveness is well expressed in the accompanying caption: "Ich mag . . . ein wenig . . . gar nicht . . . vielleicht doch . . . mit Schmerzen . . . nicht ganz von Herzen . . . mit Kopf . . . oder ohne . . . trotz Erich . . . wegen Konrad . . . mit Qual . . . für die Wahl . . . ich mag!"[83] (I want to . . . a little . . . not at all . . . maybe yes . . . painfully . . . not quite from the heart . . . with the head . . . or without . . . in spite of Erich [Ollenhauer] . . . because of Konrad [Adenauer] . . . with agony . . . for the election . . . I want to!). Brandt's oscillations are further underscored by an allusion to the German proverb "Wer die Wahl hat, hat die Qual" (Who has the choice, has the agony) in the altered nursery-rhyme caption. The traditional rhyme is thus intertwined with proverbial elements, politics, and the politicians of the day, making this a satirical and yet also understanding caricature of Brandt's predicament. Such deeply feeling satires are rare. Often they are only superficial illustrations of political situations. This is certainly the case in a recent cartoon where a German politician tries to find out whether a fourth political party might be formed in Germany or not. Dozens of daisies have already been plucked, and the politician seems to continue his destruction of them ad infinitum, reciting his rhyme "Sie kommt—sie kommt nicht"[84] (She [the party] comes—she comes not).

National politics are only one of the new stomping grounds for the daisy divination, for daisies are equally suitable for representing the frustrations of international politics. When German-French relations were not very good, in January 1965, a caricaturist pictured the German chancellor Ludwig Erhard plucking a four-leafed clover, which in itself is a traditional sign of luck. The one leaf still remaining contains an image of Charles de Gaulle and the New Year's wish of Erhard is that de Gaulle will be a reasonable political partner during the coming year: "Er liebt mich! Das wünscht sich für 1965, Louis"[85] (He loves me! That is the wish for 1965 of Louis [i.e. Ludwig Erhard]). But almost half a year later there appeared a front cover cartoon in *Simplicissimus* showing that negotiations about agro-economical matters between the two leaders had broken down. The two politicians have parted company, but a grotesquely drawn, half-naked French woman representing the French nation in need of the economic strength of Germany plucks a daisy and tries to assure the German readers that the French will rejoin negotiations: "Glaub mir doch! Unser Charles wird wiederkommen!"[86] (Please believe me! Our Charles [de Gaulle] will be back!).

As is generally known, Germany experienced a "Wirtschaftswunder" (economic miracle) in the late fifties and sixties, and there were early voices who warned that this economic recovery might be too speedy and be standing on shaky ground. An interesting cartoon shows another almost naked person sitting underneath an overhanging rock plucking a daisy to find out whether the new economic wealth is going to last or not. The innovative rhyme in the caption, "Der goldene Überhang" (The Golden Overhang), clearly expresses these economic worries:

> Es bröckelt, es rieselt.
> Es kriselt nicht, es kriselt,
> es ist kaum zu fassen,
> bei vollen Kassen.
>
> Hält sich das Wunder?
> Oder fällt es 'runter?
> Bleibe ich munter?
> Oder liege ich drunter?[87]
>
> (It crumbles, it trickles.
> It is not a crisis, it is a crisis,
> it is hardly understandable,
> while the cash registers are full.
>
> Will the wonder continue?
> Or is it going to fall down?
> Am I going to be fine?
> Or will I lie underneath [i.e. go down]?)

Economic crises are no rarity any more today, and a typical caricature might well be the following one: The management of an automobile company is plucking away at the leaves of a branch and in the background stand hundreds of unsold cars. The caption says it all: "Wir werden sie los—wir werden sie nicht los . . . "[88] (We will get rid of them—we will not get rid of them . . . ).

Politics and economics seem to dominate modern lives, but then there are also decisions to be made that involve individual lives directly. One of the most complex questions of our society is certainly that of capital punishment. Where does one really stand on this important issue? Are there universal guidelines for the death penalty or are there haphazard differences from state to state? Who is to decide and on what legal and moral principles? A powerful recent cartoon expresses the ambiguities surrounding capital punishment in a grotesque image. The criminal sits on the electric chair awaiting his execution while a hefty judge pulls off daisy petals to the rhyme of "To kill him . . . To kill him not . . . To kill him . . . To kill him not . . . "[89] The old love rhyme has become perverted in a world of crime and crises. Not only the criminal fears for his life. Humanity itself is on the verge of self-destruction through wars, atomic bombs, neutron bombs, and other such death threats. The modern author Elias Canetti summarizes this dangerous human predicament with a one-line aphorism that reduces the old love rhyme to one of existence or non-existence: "Ich bin. Ich bin nicht. Das neue Abzählspiel der Menschheit"[90] (I am. I am not. The new counting game of humanity).

While most of the preceding examples stop with a plucked petal that expresses a depressing negation, there is also the modern world of advertising, which, of course, returns to the more positive meaning of the daisy divination. Here love, beauty, and the right choice dominate, and the daisy motif is used to convince the consumer to pick the right product. The plucked flower petal joined to the positive statement predicts success and perfect happiness, and the dreamworld of the children's rhyme is reaffirmed. For example, a French advertisement for the canned fruit company Libby's had for its slogan the slightly changed divination rhyme: "Je t'aime un peu, beaucoup . . . mais j'aime passionnément Libby's"[91] (I love you a little, much . . . but I love Libby's passionately). The name of the company is placed where the highest degree of love is expressed in the rhyme, and this is supposed to convince French consumers to buy Libby's canned pineapples since other people obviously love them best. The international flower delivery company Fleurop very appropriately chose the headline "Sie liebt mich . . . liebt mich nicht . . . sie liebt mich!"[92] (She loves me . . . loves me not . . . she loves me!) to advertise its service of sending flowers to people in love almost anywhere. Quite similar in its emotional and romantic appeal is an advertisement by the German

national telephone company. The major slogan is " . . . ruf doch mal an!" ( . . . why not call!) but the actual text starts with the traditional formula "Er liebt mich, er liebt mich nicht, er . . . " (He loves me, he loves me not, he . . . ), and the illustration shows a young woman in a pensive pose plucking the petals of a daisy.[93] The implication is obviously that while flower divinations are fine, much more direct and quicker would be a telephone call. And we might wonder whether this attractive German woman was influenced herself by another advertisement, one for Nivea cosmetic cream. The commercial artist had the wonderful idea of using the round container of the Nivea cream as the center of an imaginary daisy to which he simply added some white flower petals. Someone seems to have pulled off two of the petals already, and underneath this obvious daisy divination motif is printed the following altered counting rhyme:

Sie schützt mich.
Sie pflegt mich.
Sie macht mich zart.
Sie macht mich schön.[94]

(It [Nivea] protects me.
It takes care of me.
It makes me soft.
It makes me pretty.)

A bit more direct, although still not employing the actual counting rhyme, is an American advertisement for Dan River sheets. There is an illustration of a woman lying in a bed made up with sheets made by Dan River. She is about to begin pulling the petals off a daisy next to which the word "Prediction" followed by a colon is printed. The conclusion is expressed in the caption, which prophecies "a love affair with Dan River Sheets."[95] As sure as the daisy divination will result in a positive statement of love, so will the consumer fall in love with newly purchased sheets from the Dan River Company.

It is little wonder that jewelry stores in particular return to the daisy oracle to market their products. The Tiffany Company ran an interesting advertisement that illustrates a daisy from which one petal surrounded by a fancy ring is just falling off. Above the petal appears the question "She loves you?" and the male viewer is obviously supposed to answer "Yes, she loves me" and run right out and buy some piece of jewelry for his loved one.[96] And, finally, the jewelers have succeeded in inventing a mechanical daisy divination charm, which will be able to answer the question of love at any time anywhere, no matter whether it is the season for daisies or not. A large advertisement in a 1958 *New York Times Magazine* carried the slogan "He loves me! He loves me not! Spin the Daisy—it tells of love!" Below the illustration of two gold-plated round charms made up of a spinnable daisy and an outer ring with the inscribed rhyme "loves me, a little, much, madly, not at all" the copy explains: "The most unique, refreshing idea yet in jewelry. The Daisy Charm spins round 'n round—stops in the exact degree of his affection. True love or passing fancy—no matter—spinning the Daisy is intriguing fun!"[97] Another store's advertisement describes the "Spin-the-Daisy" charm as its "new conversation-piece gold-plated daisy with simulated ruby that actually spins to answer that most-asked question, 'love me, or love me not?'"[98] And a third very similar advertisement advises people to purchase this "Good Luck in Love" charm in order to "play the 'Roulette of Love,' see how he loves you.

# BEST & CO.
Fifth Ave. at 51 St., New York 22, N. Y.

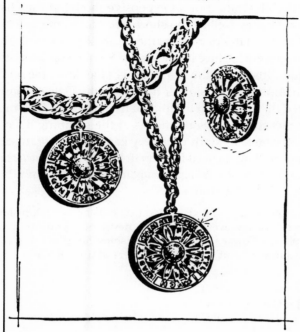

## "Spin-the-Daisy"

*Up in the clouds . . . or due for a fall,*
*This daisy charm will tell you all.*
*"Spin-the-daisy", a game of chance;*
*Your fortune in love . . . seen at a glance!*

Our new conversation-piece gold-plated daisy with
simulated ruby that actually spins to answer
that most-asked question, "love me, or love
me not!" Main Floor

| | |
|---|---|
| Daisy charm. **5.95** | Daisy pin. **5.95** |
| Daisy on bracelet. **7.95** | Daisy on 24" necklace. **7.95** |

Prices plus tax

Mail and phone orders filled — Plaza 9-2000
Please include postage beyond our motor delivery area

**And at all our Branches**

Don't pluck the daisy, spin the new French love roulette charm."[99] This advertisement also prints the traditional rhyme "I love you . . . a little . . . very much . . . passionately . . . with madness . . . not at all" under the illustration of an expensive model of the charm from Paris. This rhyme as well as the shortened "loves me, a little, much, madly, not at all" that is printed on the actual charm reveals the French origin of the gimmick, since it follows the French versions cited earlier in this chapter. Instead of the simple "loves me, loves me not" alternation that an American version of the "Spin-the-Daisy" charm would have resulted in, the French traditional rhyme allows for a much more fascinating measure of love by means of the spinning daisy.

A more affordable modern prophecy game in case of the absence of daisies is reported by Richard Dorson in his study of *American Folklore*. The daisy divination rhyme is once again maintained, but the daisy is replaced by a drinking straw.

> From the many hours whiled away on coke dates, a modern form of "He loves me, he loves me not" has developed, with drinking straws replacing flower petals. Upon finishing her drink, the coed twists the straw around each of her fingers in turn, while repeating:
>
> > He loves me, he don't,
> > He'll marry me, he won't,
> > He would if he could, he could if he would,
> > But he won't.
>
> The line she utters as she reaches the end of the straw gives the prophecy. But there is more to come. A girl friend names the ends of the straw for two boy friends. Betty Coed presses her two index fingers on the middle of the straw and flattens it out toward the ends. The prophecy applies to the boy named for the end of the straw she flattens first. Now she tears the straw in two and forms a cross. She folds the ends over and over, taking a new end each time, until the four last tag ends remain. Then, wishbone fashion, she pulls one of these ends while her friend pulls another, making her wish. If both girls have hold of the same piece, the wish is doomed. If however lover girl pulls free a piece, her wish will come true, provided she places it in her shoe and keeps it there until fulfillment. Many a girl has worn out her piece walking on it in her shoe.[100]

This last example leads us back to our earlier discussion of divination games with cherry stones, apple seeds, plum stones, buttons, blades of grass, and so on. Where daisies to serve as love oracles are missing, other more easily available substitutes will have to do. But there is no doubt that the daisy is much the preferred natural divination flower and that it seems to have a universal appeal to lovers everywhere. As rational adults we might not want to believe in flower oracles anymore, but children and young lovers continue to want to know their fate, and they enjoy the game of plucking flowers, while their parents, as conscious or subconscious carriers of the traditional lore, also react to the modern, manipulated forms of the old daisy motif as it appears in literature, art, caricatures, and advertisements. Who does not think of the "loves me, loves me not" question when confronted with a daisy or with one of the many dichotomies of the modern world? What has happened is that the daisy nursery rhyme has become adapted to the complexities and specificities of today's life, but its traditional form also continues to be present as one of the fundamental questions of mankind. It is, of course, the positive solution to various problems that one looks for in the daisy oracle, and, since chances are very good that the game will end on a positive note, it continues to be a fun occupation for children as this last little poem, "Wishing on a Daisy," from a recent Hallmark greeting card expresses so well:

> Wishing on a daisy
> Is lots of fun to do
> When every little petal
> Holds a special wish for you . . .
> There's one for luck
> and one for cheer
> and one for joy and laughter . . .
> And lots more for the best of health
> and happiness ever after![101]

# 4 The Proverb in the Modern Age

## Old Wisdom in New Clothing

The traditional proverb has been studied in a multitude of ways by folklorists, literary and cultural historians, philologists, social scientists, and many more.[1] Numerous large collections have been published over the centuries for the major national languages and dialects,[2] and there also exists a vast amount of secondary literature on the fascinating subject of proverbs.[3] Yet, we can generalize and claim that most scholarly publications on the proverb have been historically oriented, searching for the origin and dissemination of various proverb texts or looking for the proverbs among so-called primitive tribes. Lately, however, proverb scholars have also become aware of the use and function of traditional proverbs in modern technological and sophisticated societies, and we now have important studies of proverbs in modern literature, in psychological testing, and in the various forms of mass media such as newspapers, magazines, and advertisements.[4]

The following remarks will present a picture of precisely how traditional proverbial wisdom continues to live and function in modern communication. Doubtlessly traditional proverbs still play a signifi-

cant role in today's speech, where they continue to be used to moralize, to instruct, to advise, and to reflect on everyday occurrences. But
perhaps more often than not proverbs now are used in an innovative
way, that is they are changed and twisted until they fit the demands of
our modern age. Changing times and situations require forms of
expression that the traditional proverbs can no longer supply. However, it often suffices to adapt an antiquated proverb to the modern
context. This process of innovation on the basis of tradition becomes
proof of the continuity of such traditional forms as proverbs, and it is
this "constancy in change" that makes modern-oriented proverb studies such a challenging field of investigation for interdisciplinary and
comparatively oriented researchers.

In order to present as complete a picture as possible of the way
proverbs survive in the modern age, we will address four major
aspects of the traditional and innovative use of proverbs: first there will
be a general analysis of proverb illustrations from the Middle Ages to
modern cartoons and caricatures; second we will deal with the more
specific problem of misogynous proverbs and their role in modern
sexual politics; third we will demonstrate ways well-known proverbs
or their critical variations are used in lyrical poetry; and finally and
more specifically we will discuss a case study of one proverb, "Wine,
Women and Song," from its origin to its appearance in modern cartoons and on T-shirts. Throughout the pages of this chapter examples
will be cited from literary sources, art, and the mass media, indicating
that proverbs belong to all types of communication and that they
distinguish themselves through an unlimited adaptability to ever new
contexts. Proverbs in collections might appear to be trite remnants of
the wisdom of times past, but when contextualized in their original
wording or in telling variations they become a most effective verbalization of human and societal concerns.

Turning now to our first concern, proverbs in various forms of art
from medieval times to the present, we will see that proverb illustrations traditionally represent an attempt to depict basic human problems, usually in a satirical and moralistic manner. Proverb pictures can
be traced from the Middle Ages to the twentieth century,[5] but it is
without doubt Pieter Brueghel's celebrated picture "Netherlandic
Proverbs" (1559) that is best known.[6] It has long been established that
Brueghel illustrates proverbial expressions or phrases and not proverbs, but the more than forty extant investigations, ranging from

shorter notes on particular expressions to the book-length studies by Wilhelm Fraenger, Jan Grauls, Franz Roh, and recently Alan Dundes and Claudia Stibbe[7] have not been able to isolate all the expressions in the picture. The entire picture contains about 115 illustrations of standard European and Dutch proverbs and proverbial expressions. A detail of the left bottom corner[8] exemplifies the complexity of this proverbial review of the follies and vices of the world. With great artistic skill Brueghel has been able to illustrate fifteen expressions in this section alone, among them "To bang one's head against the wall," "To bell the cat," and "To be as patient as a lamb." Each individual scene is an intrinsic part of the larger satirical mosaic of everyday life in the sixteenth century.

Surely Brueghel's colorful picture has the greatest artistic value of all proverb pictures, but there were many other pictures that showed multiple proverb scenes before and after him. Franz Hogenberg, for example, made an etching in 1558 that contains twenty-one proverbs,[9] and Jan van Doetinchem followed in 1577 with a series of four etchings depicting eighty-eight proverbs and proverbial expressions.[10] Yet another print from around 1633 by Johannes Galle assembles seventy expressions with captions,[11] attesting that this art form survived well into the baroque age. What differentiates these prints from Brueghel's oil painting is that each proverbial scene has a caption, and it might be added here that these captions have been of great value in determining the proverbial expressions in Brueghel's picture. The proverb illustration together with the proverbial caption satirizes standard human behavior and fulfills a didactic purpose similar to that of much of the popular literature of the sixteenth and seventeenth centuries. While Brueghel's famous picture continues to fascinate viewers in the Berlin art museum or as a reproduction in art books, on posters, or even a large jigsaw puzzle,[12] there are also two modern posters that attempt to continue this tradition of illustrating numerous proverbs and proverbial expressions. In 1975 T. E. Breitenbach published his poster entitled "Proverbidioms,"[13] which is an attempt to illustrate approximately three hundred phrases and idioms. While he depicts a more recent village scene, the picture is definitely a variation of Brueghel's earlier picture. Many of the expressions of the Brueghel picture are included, but there are also illustrations of such newer expressions as "To be off one's rocker," "To have a screw loose," and "To be a self-made man." As in the painting by Brueghel so in this modern poster we find the proverbial expressions interpreted literally, which adds to the humor and satire of the picture. The verbal metaphor is illustrated in a realistic sense thereby giving at times grotesque new meanings to common expressions. Two years earlier William Belder had already printed his similar poster "As the Saying Goes" (1973), which illustrates fifty-one proverbs and sayings with captions.[14] Here the human figures are humorous drawings, and most of the poster basically attempts to translate proverbs such as "A bird in the hand is worth two in the bush" or "Many hands make light work" into literal illustrations. Despite the humor the poster has a definite didactic character and would probably be a good addition to a child's room. The game of identifying the various proverb scenes on these posters has most likely entertained many viewers just as generations of people have been intrigued by the more famous Brueghel picture.

Besides these pictures with multiple proverb scenes—called "Wimmelbilder" or "De blauwe huyck" (The blue cloak) after the central proverb scene in Brueghel's picture depicting the expression "To hang the blue cloak on the husband" (i.e. to commit adultery)—there also developed a tradition of painting twenty to thirty-six individually framed proverb scenes onto one page, each scene carrying a proverbial caption and once again basically illustrating in a satirical manner the shortcomings of the world. Many examples of these prints can be found from the sixteenth to nineteenth centuries, attesting to the popularity of proverb illustrations as a satirical tool. Most of them carry the general title "De verkeerde wereld" (The absurd world, or The world upside-down), a name also given at times to the multiple scene pictures mentioned above. A fine example of such a framed proverb print containing thirty-two illustrations and captions was printed in Amsterdam in the sixteenth century.[15] Another Dutch print with the title "Spreekwoordenprent" (proverb print) from the eighteenth century illustrates thirty similar expressions,[16] while a print with "Gewoonelijke Spreekwoorden in figuren afgebeeld" (common proverbs in pictures) from the beginning of the nineteenth century assembles twenty frames.[17] Toward the end of that century we have a print entitled "De verkeerde wereld" with thirty-six illustrations,[18] showing the popularity of this traditional satirical medium. Many expressions such as "To throw pearls before swine," "To hang one's coat to the wind," and the popular "To shit on the world" appear again and again in these prints as well as in the "Wimmelbilder," indicating a certain stock of about one hundred favored expressions.

Parallelling the two multiple-scene-oriented proverb illustrations there exists a third form of proverb picture where one picture depicts only one proverb or proverbial expression. Of particular interest is a fifteenth century collection of 182 woodcuts, each illustrating a proverb with a French verse caption, appropriately called *Proverbes en rimes* by its two twentieth century editors.[19] Among others we find illustrations of the proverbs "Who keeps company with the wolf must learn to howl,"[20] and "Let sleeping dogs lie,"[21] as well as the proverbial expression "To beat the dog before the lion."[22] In each case the verse caption includes the proverb, whose basic underlying didactic content is enhanced by the satirical and moralistic lines of the verse.

Woodcuts illustrating proverbs can also be found in many books, especially of the sixteenth century, as for example "Das Kind mit dem Bade ausschütten"[23] (To pour the baby out with the bath water) and "Sein Steckenpferd reiten"[24] (To ride one's hobby-horse) in Thomas Murner's *Narrenbeschwörung* (1512), or "Zwischen die Mühlsteine geraten"[25] (To get between two millstones) in Sebastian Brant's *Narrenschiff* (1494). Pieter Brueghel also drew single proverb scenes, especially in the well-known series of twelve round proverb pictures from 1558. In his drawing of the Dutch proverb "With no other guide the two blind men fall into a ditch full of water"[26] it is clear that Brueghel has the biblical proverb "The blind leading the blind" in mind, a motif that he repeated in a more artistic oil picture in 1568.[27] A systematic search through illustrated books and large collections of woodcuts and etchings would yield more examples. They would help to bring to light a definite chain of proverb motifs that have fascinated illustrators over the centuries with their satirical view of the world.

It is especially the modern cartoonists who are keeping the tradition of satirical illustrations alive. Proverbs like "Don't look a gift horse in the mouth," "To buy a pig in a poke," and "Strike while the iron is hot" can, for example, all be traced from the aforementioned French manuscript *Proverbes en rimes* of the fifteenth century to cartoons of the present day. The woodcut illustrating the gift-horse proverb[28] reappeared in 1919 as a caricatuare showing Woodrow Wilson's problems with the Senate of the United States over the conception of the League of Nations.[29] Similarly the woodcut of "To buy a pig in a poke"[30] finds its 1880 counterpart in a caricature satirically commenting on the shady dealings that went into the building of the Canadian Pacific Railway.[31] And the effectiveness of a third woodcut, depicting the proverb "Strike while the iron is hot,"[32] has lost nothing of its satirical and didactic

*To throw out the baby with the bathwater.*

persuasiveness in a modern German caricature, showing former Chancellor Helmut Schmidt as a blacksmith decisively striking the spreading terrorism in Germany with a large hammer.[33]

For the proverbial expression "To bell the cat" we have been able to collect five illustrations ranging from the fifteenth century to the present day. There is first of all a woodcut from 1494 in Sebastian Brant's *Narrenschiff*.[34] Brueghel also included the expression in his "Netherlandic Proverbs" picture.[35] This expression was also very popular on prints with multiple framed proverb illustrations, as for example in the upper left corner of an eighteenth-century proverb print.[36] Changing the expression from a mere "Belling the cat" to a provocative "Who will bell the elephant?" Francisco Goya included in his collection of twenty-two grotesque etchings called *Los Proverbios* from before 1824 one in which several men are trying to fasten bells onto a large elephant.[37] The intriguing illustration brings to mind the military occupation of Spain by Napoleon, and perhaps one could interpret this etching as a precursor of modern political caricatures. Such a political cartoon appeared in *Time* in 1975 showing the former Secretary of State Henry Kissinger as the political cat that needs to be belled.[38] Just as in the Brueghel and Goya pictures this caricature does not need a caption, since it is clear that the roaming political cat should be watched with care.

In modern cartoons, proverbs and proverbial expressions continue to play a significant role.[39] Often the cartoonist simply draws a humorous sketch of the literally interpreted expression, as for example for "To drink like a fish,"[40] "To lose one's marbles,"[41] "To be out of one's gourd,"[42] and "That's the way the ball bounces."[43] But the images and captions of more serious cartoons depict in a satirical tone the wide range of problems of modern life. For example there appeared a cartoon of a customer in a bakery store being forced to ask, "Since when is a baker's dozen eleven?"[44] And the same satirical view of spiraling inflation was expressed in another cartoon with the caption, "It used to be that a fool and his money were soon parted—now it happens to everybody."[45] In another cartoon the proverb "To err is human, to forgive divine" is drastically altered to read "To err is unlikely, to forgive unnecessary"[46] in light of our computer-run lives. Very effective and to the point was a caricature of oil sheiks who summed up their advantageous position in controlling the flow and price of oil with the gloating statement, "Hate to admit it, but I don't think we've a better expression in Arabic than having 'em over a barrel."[47] A sad commentary on today's employment problems is expressed in the next two cartoons and their altered proverb captions: "If at first you don't succeed, you're fired,"[48] and "Now Ted says if we can't beat the unemployment figures we can join them."[49] And to turn to a timely political problem, we have a British cartoon from 1954 about the growing racial hatred and prejudice in South Africa, which carried the appropriate biblical proverb caption "Whatsoever a man soweth,"[50] whose bitter conclusion, "he must reap," we can see in present-day South Africa.

*To buy a pig in a poke.*

Most of the examples presented thus far have rather explicit proverbial captions, either stating the expressions in their original wording or
varying them to fit a certain satirical purpose. Often, however, cartoonists use captions that merely allude to a proverb, but the illustration makes it perfectly clear which proverb is meant. This is the case
with a humorous drawing of some beavers at work with the caption
"Just because we're beavers, I don't see why we can't goof off like
other animals once in a while."[51] Obviously this is an allusion to the
common expression, "To work like a beaver." In the following three
examples the proverbial statement is truly kept to a mere allusion, but
the illustrated birds permit the actual expression to come to the viewer's mind immediately: "It's time you know about the bees and us"[52]
hints at the expression "To know about the birds and the bees," while
the cartoons with the caption "Good Lord! How early do you have to
be around here?"[53] and "Good morning"[54] obviously allude to the
well-known proverb "The early bird catches the worm," especially in
light of the fact that birds and worms are being illustrated.

These final examples show a tendency to return to Brueghel's
famous "Netherlandic Proverbs" picture. The modern cartoonist, just
like Brueghel in the sixteenth century, assumes that the viewer knows
the proverb or proverbial expression that is being illustrated. However, although Brueghel needed no captions for his proverbial scenes,
the modern cartoonist seems to prefer a simple verbal allusion to
insure meaningful communication. At times these proverbial cartoons
are nothing more than humorous play, but more often they become
pointed satirical commentaries on human problems and concerns,
especially with the altered proverb texts as captions. Since metaphorical proverbs could in fact be defined as verbalized pictures it is not
surprising that illustrators since the Middle Ages have felt compelled
to translate the traditional proverb texts into pertinent pictures depicting the values of their time.

That proverbs contain the value system of the time of their origin
leads us to our second point, the traditionally misogynous proverb in
confrontation with the modern concerns of sexual politics. A cursory
glance at any major proverb collection reveals the obvious antifeminism prevalent in proverbs. Almost every proverb that touches upon
women contains a severe negation of the value of women in society.
This is easily illustrated by such proverbs as "A woman is the weaker
vessel," "A woman's answer is never to seek," "A woman's tongue

*"Good morning."*

wags like a lamb's tail," "All women may be won," "Women are as wavering as the wind," "Women naturally deceive, weep, and spin," "Women in state affairs are like monkeys in glass houses," and, of course, the often quoted "Women are necessary evils."[55] These examples amply show that the proverb makers of past centuries were misogynists, who in the bitterness of old age and regret could seemingly think of nothing better to do than to discredit with proverbial invectives the women who most likely had served them very well. Yet these unflattering expressions of folk wisdom have been handed down to us from generation to generation, and it will obviously take time to break down the barriers of tradition in these antifeminist slurs.

These proverbs reflect male chauvinistic ideas in an easily repeatable formulaic structure greatly enhanced by metaphorical images. It is not surprising, therefore, that male artists from the Middle Ages to the present day have drawn on this type of proverb to express their own stereotypical views of women as malicious, deceitful, vain, irritable, and so on. For example, we have an engraving by Pieter Brueghel from the year 1558 that illustrates a variant of the internationally disseminated proverb about the great house plagues, "Three things drive a man out of his house: smoke, rain, and a scolding wife."[56] Brueghel also included several other sketches of antifeminist proverbial expressions in his already mentioned "Netherlandic Proverbs" picture. In addition to the young adultress hanging a blue cloak over her cuckold husband we have, for example, a quarrelsome and cunning woman tying the devil onto a pillow, illustrating the Dutch expression "Zij zou de duivel op het (en) kussen binden"[57] (She would bind the devil himself to a pillow). This expression about a strong and shrewish woman was very popular in the late Middle Ages, as a Flemish misericorde depicting it indicates.[58] Such a woman would, of course, also insist on wearing the breeches (pants) in the house, and there exist many broadsheets of the "De verkeerde wereld" type mentioned above that illustrate such a domineering woman.[59] The remedy for this type of aggressive woman is drastically indicated in a misericorde from the sixteenth century which depicts the most antifeminist proverb of them all, "A good woman must be beaten."[60]

These quarrels between husband and wife are, perhaps not surprisingly, still the subject matter of many modern proverbial cartoons that delight in showing the battle of the sexes. In one caricature, a husband attempts to maintain his special position in the office with the proverbial argument "How many times must I tell you, Mildred? A man's office is his castle!"[61] But in another illustration of the same proverb we can see a liberated wife denying her spouse his lordship in the house, and his proverbial argument, "But, dear, a man's castle is supposed to be his home" does not appear to hold water anymore.[62] Even when the husband might be sick and wants to be waited on, the woman counters with the spiteful answer "Sick my eye . . . you just like the idea of 'feed a cold.'"[63] And in another caricature it is once again the woman who degrades her partner in a sarcastic fashion with the statement "I'll tell you what makes him tick. Booze makes him tick."[64] But is it not surprising for wives to act this way when their husbands throw such proverbial statements as the following at their heads: "In this house, only ONE cook spoils the broth."[65] The woman has stood in the kitchen as usual, and all that the spouse can do is complain or ignore her

*A good woman must be beaten.*

completely, as another delightful but telling caricature shows: A minister and his wife are sitting at the breakfast table. He is reading the newspaper and is pouring his own cup of coffee, while his wife sits there neglected and bored. Her appropriate comment in the caption reads, "Careful, dear, your cup runneth over."[66] But even this biblical comment does not awaken her husband from his morning routine.

The quibbling between spouses also often results from sexually oriented comments, as is the case with a cartoon showing a couple watching the evening news with Harry Reasoner and Barbara Walters. In the caption the wife asks disgustedly: "Can't you just watch the news without speculating on whether he's getting into her pants?"[67] Very typical is without doubt the proverbial scene in which a man observes a beautiful woman at the beach. His wife has just pointed out to him that beauty isn't everything and he snaps, "All right, so you can't judge a book by its cover!"[68] Another wife in a second cartoon reacts to this situation with a similar proverbial remark concerning her husband's weaker moments: "That's Harold for you—other pastures always look greener."[69] That a woman might finally be fed up with her spouse's lack of interest in her is shown in a cartoon where a woman is about to leave her surprised husband with the short proverbial and therefore only too human statement, "To make a long story short, goodbye."[70] In another cartoon it's the husband who has left, as his wife relates to a friend, "And then one day I told him to shape up or ship out, and he shipped out."[71] These scenes from a marriage seem to be final stages, and yet there is always that modern wisdom expressed by a young woman in love with a handsome man, "I've been told, Adam, that two can live as cheaply as one,"[72] which will lead people into marriage and its proverbial quarrels. And altered or unaltered proverbs and proverbial expressions will continue to express such basic sexual household politics in a most telling manner.[73]

But proverbial illustrations of our day are not always reflections of basic human problems. On the contrary, modern cartoonists and commercial advertising artists do their very best (or worst) to continue sexual stereotyping. It is amazing how many advertisements still use proverbial headlines (often altered) with appropriate pictures to keep alive the image of woman as being inferior to man, capable only of cooking and being man's ever-ready pretty little servant and sex object. Taking the well-known proverb "Four things drive a man out of his house: too much smoke, a dripping roof, filthy air, and a scolding wife" as a basis, a plumbing business varied its content but kept the basic structure of the saying for the following chauvinistic customer handout:

> Four Things a Woman Should Know
>    How to look like a girl
>    How to act like a lady
>    How to think like a man
>    And how to work like a dog.[74]

The idea that a woman should work like a dog is also picked up in a disgusting advertisement varying the proverb "A dog is man's best friend." The picture shows a dog and a water softener with the proverbial slogan: "One is man's best friend. The other is a woman's,"[75] which is to say that man and dog belong together while woman and such household chores as dishes and laundry are equally natural friends. And even the postscript, "after diamonds, that is," on the bottom left makes matters only worse, for it hints at the slanderous proverb that "Diamonds are a girl's best friend," which implies that the materialistic value system is inherent in women. Such sexual stereotyping is also obvious in the next two advertisements for Dole bananas: "If the dress no longer fits, peel it,"[76] and "Waist not, want not."[77] Yes, the copywriters have performed impressive linguistic tricks on existing proverbs to create catchy headlines that will most certainly get the reader's attention. Yet why do they address themselves only to women in the illustration? Do men not equally suffer from weight problems so that at least in one example an overweight male might have been included?

The opposite of such stereotyping of female obesity is, of course, the illustration and exploitation of the beautiful female for sales purposes.[78] Why, one asks, are "sexy" women shown in the following advertisements, which clearly address themselves to men: "Winchester separates the men from the boys"[79] is the proverbial headline for a Winchester cigars ad that pictures a cigar-smoking man with an attractive woman; "Smart as a whip"[80] attempts to sell fashionable male shirts and includes a female model with a whip; and "Our suit is known by the company it keeps"[81] is a headline based on a proverb used to sell elegant suits. The man modeling such a suit is accompanied by yet another striking woman. The women are clearly reduced to attention-getting sex objects, which is obviously also the fact with the advertising slogan "Beautiful hindsight"[82] for women's jeans, recalling the proverb "Hindsight is better than foresight."

To get away from the obvious sexist examples we could turn to the seemingly proper biblical proverb "Man does not live by bread alone" (Matthew 4:4) and the interesting piece of graffiti that states "Man cannot live by sex alone."[83] The word "man" is most likely meant to refer to humans of both sexes. Nevertheless, in the advertisement slogan "Traveling man does not live by bed alone"[84] one definitely gets the feeling that the male-dominated advertising world is addressing only male hotel customers. The word "woman" would fit equally well into this headline, and if the copy writers do not want to use the lengthy "man and woman" formula, why don't they simply say "People do not live by bed alone"? The proverbial ring would be kept alive, and we are sure that the effectiveness of the slogan would also be assured. Why talk about "traveling man" when many women are very active in various professions that include travel? That the business world is still very much a man's world is also illustrated by the way Japan Air Lines tried to sell its service with the headline "One man's sushi is another man's steak."[85] Once again we have the basic linguistic problem of the traditional proverb "One man's meat is another man's poison," but is it not nevertheless fair to ask where the woman is in the accompanying picture? And take this advertisement by PPG Industries with the proverbial question "If man believed in leaving well enough alone, where would we be?"[86] This example is clearly chauvinistic because the expression "To leave well enough alone" is in itself absolutely free from any gender identification. But the copywriter chose to stress the man's world. There is no reason whatsoever why this headline could not have read "If people believed in leaving well enough alone, where would we be?"

Problematic also is the popular proverb "Behind every great man, there is a woman," which, to be sure, implies a positive influence of the woman on the man but without placing her on his level of success. A florist's advertisement for national secretaries' week used the modified headline "Behind every great man . . . are the great women who helped you make it,"[87] but one wonders how seriously the statement of "the great women" was meant. Much more realistic perhaps was a caricature showing one of those successful males who tries by shrewd proverbial reasoning to take advantage of just such a hard working and supportive secretary by stating "They say behind every successful man, Miss Ashton, there's a woman. Will you be that woman to me?"[88] However, Pierre Cardin has come out with a new proverbial slogan for its perfume advertisements, namely "Behind every great woman, there's a man."[89] In a modern world that starts to emphasize equality of the sexes, the old proverb "Behind every great man, there is a woman" should most certainly be reversible. Both forms of the proverb, original and variation, stress the teamwork of the sexes and illustrate how a new version of a proverb can complement the old one.

Many other national advertisements attempt to overcome the male-oriented proverb slogan by changing the original proverb ever so slightly. The First National Bank of Boston, for example, chose the headline: "If you're disappointed with your pension plan's performance . . . how do you think Tom, Dick and Mary feel?"[90] The familiar expression "Every Tom, Dick and Harry" is quickly changed to include at least one woman, and good old Mary is even in a picture with the two men. Yet one senses a certain amount of lip-service to the women's liberation movement in this advertisement, for after all, how long will it take until the picture will show two women and only one man? But it is a start, and due to the feminist movement there does in fact seem to be an attack against the traditionally misogynous proverbial wisdom. At least some newer advertisements and cartoons try to rectify false beliefs about women by drawing on traditional proverbs and effectively changing them or even by creating new ones. Already in 1957 the New York Times dared an advertisement like "Their work is never done,"[91] explicitly showing women as professionals and not doing house chores. Twenty years later we find the delightful advertisement "A woman's work is never done,"[92] showing a businesswoman hard at work in a plane while a man is fast asleep next to her. Obviously this woman is taking care of business matters, and perhaps she even uses a briefcase that was advertised with the headline "For women who mind their business,"[93] again meaning professional activities and not the timid role-playing at home. Perhaps she even works for Sears, where "They don't separate the women from the men"[94] in the hiring process, or she might also be employed with an insurance company, for "A woman's place may be with New York Life"[95] and not at home. While the basic structure of the proverb is maintained in these innovative headlines, the small verbal changes create a new slogan that is a true reflection of modern societal needs and concerns.

One of these concerns is the role that the modern woman ought to play on the political scene. Let us return once more to the old proverb "A woman's place is in the home" and notice how it can suddenly take on a very relevant meaning, one that is politically of great importance.

Junior House fashions used the following advertisement: "A woman's place is in the House."[96] A basically chauvinistic proverb is here given an entirely new meaning, by changing the original text from "home" to "house," thereby referring to the White House and House of Representatives. Of course, this country needs more female politicians, and the day will come when a woman will finally occupy the White House itself. In the meantime one can purchase T-shirts with the expanded inscription "A woman's place is in the House . . . and in the Senate!"[97] Because of the effects such advertisements have on all of us, it becomes more and more conceivable that some of the old prejudices will be destroyed and that some of these feminist T-shirt slogans might be the proverbs of tomorrow.

In this regard notice this advertisement for T-shirts with three splendid slogans:

1. A woman's place is in the House . . . and in the Senate!
2. A woman without a man is like a fish without a bicycle.
3. The best man for the job . . . may be a woman.[98]

While the women express their independence and liberation by wearing T-shirts with inscriptions such as "A woman without a man is like a fish without a bicycle"[99] or even "A man's house is his castle—let him clean it,"[100] men perhaps wonder where all of this will lead, although they basically agree that the following proverbial slogan should characterize modern women: "Out of the frying pan and into the future!"[101]

Such examples of "liberated" proverb usage and proverb alteration are still relatively rare. Unfortunately, people are much too quick to continue to accept the stereotypical proverbs as ultimate truths without analyzing their texts properly. Modern mass media helps in keeping many of the one-sided views concerning women alive by not discriminating more carefully in their slogan choice. But by shrewdly varying existing proverbs some advertisers and cartoonists have in fact created proverbial slogans that are more befitting to the modern age. In such a fashion the misogyny of the old proverbial statements is revealed while at the same time effective new expressions of emancipatory ideas and concerns are found, indicating the proverbs' continued relevance even for modern aspects of sexuality and sexual politics. Verbal stereotypes have done and still do much damage to the relationship between the sexes, and much time will still have to pass until all people realize that the proverbial quotation "All men are created equal" should in fact say "All *people* are created equal." In the mean-time we have at least the appropriately transfigured proverb: "A Ms. is as good as a Male."[102]

Modern literary authors have reacted in a more critical fashion to traditional proverbs. While proverbs in older literature usually served didactic and moralistic purposes, they are now often employed for expressions of parody, irony, or satire. Even more important, the texts are manipulated to express novel ideas for which the originals are no longer fitting. The use and function of proverbs in literature have been the subject of numerous scholarly investigations, ranging from collections and interpretative remarks concerning proverbial materials in the works of such world renowned authors as William Shakespeare, François Villon, or Johann Wolfgang von Goethe to analyses of proverbs in lesser known regional writers.[103] Such studies have always concentrated on prose and dramatic literature, while lyrical poetry (including folksongs and ballads) has been neglected for an apparently obvious reason. Somehow lyrical verses seem not to be suitable for bits of prosaic wisdom, and yet there does exist a considerable amount of proverbial poetry, or paremiological verse, to use a more technical term, in Anglo-American,[104] French, German,[105] and other languages.

François Villon's fifteenth century *Ballade des proverbes* is an early French example. Similar didactic proverb poetry was also well established in late medieval England and Germany. John Heywood assembled the largest number of short, rhymed proverb poems (two to forty lines) in his six hundred *Epigrams upon Proverbs* (1556–1562), usually elaborating on a proverb in a didactic and yet at times humorous fashion, as the following two examples make clear:

### Of Wits

So many heads, so many wits: nay, nay!
We see many heads and no wits, some day.[106]

### Praise of a Man above a Horse

A man may well lead a horse to the water
But he cannot make him drink, without he list.
I praise thee above the horse, in this matter;
For I, leading thee to drink, thou hast not missed
Alway to be ready, without resistance,
Both to drink, and be drunk, ere thou were led thence.[107]

The creation of epigrams or short poems around proverbs continued well into the eighteenth century and is occasionally still practiced today. Samuel Taylor Coleridge, for example, did not consider it beneath his dignity to write a poem elaborating on the proverb "love is blind," entitled "Reason for Love's Blindness":

> I have heard of reasons manifold
>     Why Love must needs be blind,
> But this the best of all I hold—
>     His eyes are in his hand.
>
> What outward form and feature are
>     He guesseth but in part;
> But that within is good and fair
>     He seeth with the heart.[108]

Certainly better known and doubtlessly of much greater poetic value is Robert Frost's somewhat longer poem "Mending Wall" (1914) reflecting upon the traditional wisdom expressed in the proverb "Good fences make good neighbors."[109]

A more complex type of proverb poem is represented by those three to seven stanza poems in which the proverb title is repeated at the end of each stanza as a leitmotif. This repetitive use of the proverb is congruous with the unquestioning didactic use of proverbs that we have already observed above. The following anonymous, sixteenth-century, five stanza poem is based on the proverb "Wedding and hanging is destiny," and the proverbial leitmotif becomes an ironic expression of the frustrated husband's all-too-human problems with his wife:

> I am a poor tiler in simple array,
> And get a poor living, but eightpence a day,
> My wife as I get it doth spend it away,
>     And I cannot help it, she saith; wot we why?
>     *For wedding and hanging is destiny.*
>
> I thought, when I wed her, she had been a sheep,
> At board to be friendly, to sleep when I sleep;
> She loves so unkindly, she makes me to weep;
>     But I dare say nothing, God wot! wot ye why?
>     *For wedding and hanging is destiny.*
>
> Besides this unkindness whereof my grief grows,
> I think few tilers are matched with such shrows:
> Before she leaves brawling, she falls to deal blows
>     Which, early and late, doth cause me cry
>     *That wedding and hanging is destiny.*
>
> The more that I please her, the worse she doth like me;
> The more I forbear her, the more she doth strike me;

The more that I get her, the more she doth glike [mock] me;
   Woe worth this ill fortune that maketh me cry
   *That wedding and hanging is destiny.*

If I had been hanged when I had been married,
My torments had ended, though I had miscarried;
If I had been warned, then would I have tarried;
   But now all too lately I feel and cry
   *That wedding and hanging is destiny.*[110]

In the nineteenth century Eliza Cook wrote a wholesome poem interpreting the world as a glorious place since "There's a Silver Lining to Every Cloud," as the title and the end of each of the six stanzas—of which the fourth serves as an example here—declare.

Let us not cast out mercy and truth,
   When guilt is before us in chains and shame.
When passion and vice have cankered youth,
   And age lives on with a branded name;
Something of good may still be there,
   Though its voice may never be heard aloud,
For while black with the vapors of pestilent air,
   "There's a silver lining to every cloud."[111]

Another poet, Alice Cary, quite shrewdly uses the proverb "Hoe your own row" (1849) repeatedly to teach young people the necessity and value of good solid work. Even the slowest learner will have gotten the message that untiring personal effort will lead to a successful life when reaching the seventh and last stanza:

I've known too, a good many
   Idlers, who said,
"I've right to my living,
   The world owes me bread!"
A *right*! lazy lubber!
   A thousand times No!
'Tis his, and his only
   Who hoes his own row.[112]

Equally didactic is the following poem by Vincent Godfrey Burns whose title, "Man Does Not Live by Bread Alone" (1952) makes clear from the start that it is a poetic examination of the basic truth of the biblical proverb (Matthew 4:4). Each of the three stanzas is enclosed by this proverb and this six-time repetition of the same proverb makes the intention of the author very obvious. Between the proverb texts, he explains such spiritual matters as thought, truth, and love, by which man lives in addition to his materialistic need for bread.

Man doth not live by bread alone
But by each elevating thought
By which his ship of life is wrought;
Each harbor light however dim
That makes life's broad sea plain to him
Is like a searchlight from the throne—
Man doth not live by bread alone.

Man doth not live by bread alone
But by those truths which greatly feed
His hungering soul's deep spirit-need,
By inward music sweet and clear
That tunes with joy his inner ear;
Give man the food of soul, not stone—
He doth not live by bread alone.

Man doth not live by bread alone,
He hath a hunger of the heart
And cannot walk from man apart;
No living human long can stand
Without the grasp of friendly hand,
The touch, the fellowship, the voice
That make the lonely heart rejoice;
Love all our sorrows can atone—
Man doth not live by bread alone.[113]

While the poems mentioned thus far function as clear and straight-forward reaffirmations of the basic wisdom of traditional proverbs, there exists also an interesting modern exception to this use of prover-bial leitmotifs. W. H. Auden wrote a poem based on a highly didactic proverb, but he reversed the text from "Look before you leap" to the provocative new title "Leap Before You Look" (1940), thereby pointing to an existential philosophy that entails and accepts danger and chance. The important thing is no longer the careful looking advised by the old proverb, but rather the need for leaping into an active and committed life.

The sense of danger must not disappear:
The way is certainly both short and steep,
However gradual it looks from here;
Look if you like, but you will have to leap.

Tough-minded men get mushy in their sleep
And break the by-laws any fool can keep;
It is not the convention but the fear
That has a tendency to disappear.

The worried efforts of the busy heap,
The dirt, the imprecision, and the beer

Produce a few smart wisecracks every year;
Laugh if you can, but you will have to leap.

The clothes that are considered right to wear
Will not be either sensible or cheap,
So long as we consent to live like sheep
And never mention those who disappear.

Much can be said for social savoir-faire,
But to rejoice when no one else is there
Is even harder than it is to weep;
No one is watching, but you have to leap.

A solitude ten thousand fathoms deep
Sustains the bed on which we lie, my dear:
Although I love you, you will have to leap;
Our dream of safety has to disappear.[114]

Notice also a poem, "I Built Myself a House of Glass" (ca. 1910), by Edward Thomas, who chose the proverb "People in glass houses should not throw stones" to allude to his isolated way of living, which seems to lack the acceptance of risk and danger called for in W. H. Auden's poem.

I built myself a house of glass:
It took me years to make it:
And I was proud. But now, alas!
Would God someone would break it.

But it looks too magnificent.
No neighbour casts a stone
From where he dwells, in tenement
Or palace of glass, alone.[115]

It is this indirect quotation and critical reflection upon standard proverbs that characterizes the use of proverbs in modern lyrical poetry—traits that can also be noticed in the use of proverbs in other forms of literature and in the mass media of advertisements and cartoons as we have discussed above.

Thus far every poem that has been mentioned centers on the interpretation of but one proverb, and the question naturally arises whether there exist also poems in which several proverbs or proverbial expressions are combined to give the resulting poem meaning. François Villon's already mentioned "Ballade des proverbes" merely lists twenty-eight proverbs, and, since they are not contextually linked, it is actually more a small proverb collection than a poem with meaningful content. However, there does exist quite a tradition of poems incorporating numerous expressions. One of the finest examples is the anonymous "Ballad of Old Proverbs" (1707), which contains twenty-seven proverbs and proverbial expressions. The eight stanzas are a humorous and somewhat sarcastic defense of a rebuffed lover, and they gain their effectiveness by the many earthy and partially lewd folk expressions they use, as the following stanza shows:

> Alas, no Enjoyments, nor Comfort I can take,
>   In her that regards not the worth of a Lover;
> A Turd is as good for a Sow, as a Pancake:
>   Swallow that Gudgeon, I'll Fish for another,
> She ne'er regards my aking Heart,
>   Tell a Mare a Tale, she'll let a Fart.[116]

John Gay wrote a similar poem entitled "A New Song of New Similes," which puts dozens of proverbial comparisons into the mouth of another rejected lover, and which most likely was directly influenced by the previous poem. The poem starts with the lover describing the effects of his ill-fated love affair in most vivid comparisons:

> My passion is as mustard strong;
>   I sit, all sober sad;
> Drunk as a piper all day long,
>   Or like a March hare mad.

This lamentation carries over to several stanzas praising the beauty of his love Molly in such phrases as:

> Brisk as a body-louse she trips,
>   Clean as a penny dressed;
> Sweet as a rose her breath and lips,
>   Round as the globe her breast.

And the last stanza paints a gloomy picture of possible death by employing proverbial comparisons:

> Sure as a gun, she'll drop a tear
>   And sigh perhaps, and wish,
> When I am rotten as a pear,
>   And mute as any fish.[117]

This playful manipulation of proverbial expressions also found its way to the United States, where a similar poem dealing with a problematic love affair was published under the title "Yankee Phrases" in 1803. This one stanza suffices to draw the by-now-familiar picture:

But now to my sorrow I find,
   Her heart is as hard as a brick;
To my passion forever unkind,
   Though of love I am full as a tick.[118]

But perhaps more interesting and an even greater tour de force, literally consisting of nothing but proverbs, proverbial expressions, and allusions, is the following poem by the twentieth-century American poet Arthur Guiterman, entitled "A Proverbial Tragedy" (1915):

The Rolling Stone and the Turning Worm
   And the Cat that Looked at a King
Set forth on the Road that Leads to Rome—
   For Youth will have its Fling,
The Goose will lay the Golden Eggs,
   The Dog must have his Day,
And Nobody locks the Stable Door
   Till the Horse is stol'n away.

But the Rolling Stone, that was never known
   To Look before the Leap
Plunged down the hill to the Waters Still
   That run so dark, so deep;
And the leaves were stirred by the Early Bird
   Who sought his breakfast where
He marked the squirm of the Turning Worm—
   And the Cat was Killed by Care![119]

Guiterman succeeds in twisting and changing proverbs in such a fashion that they take on new meanings without becoming unrecognizable by the reader. The proverbial "rolling stone" even becomes a sort of a character whose life path is described in laconic expressions to its tragic end. And his fellow travelers, the equally proverbial worm and cat, also find their destruction in a proverbially predestined fashion. The poem thus mirrors the pessimistic world view inherent in so many proverbs, and on a more philosophical level becomes an expression of the tragic beginning of World War I. The metaphorical apocalypse expressed in the poem is, therefore, much more than a playful linguistic trick.

Proverb poems of such depth are obviously rare and the Guiterman poem most likely will remain the proverb poem par excellence. One need only compare this poem with the following collage text, "Proverbial Ruth" (1974), by the Canadian poet John Robert Colombo, who has done nothing else but take about two dozen proverbs of parallel structure and link them by replacing key words with the name Ruth, in the following manner:

> A good archer is known by his Ruth, not his arrows.
> A good Ruth makes a good ending.
> A good cause makes a stout heart and a strong Ruth.
> A good Ruth makes good company.
> A good Ruth needs never sneak.
> A good Ruth deserves a good bone.
> A good Ruth is the best sermon.
> A good Ruth needs no paint.
> A good fellow lights his Ruth at both ends.
> A good Ruth is one-half of a man's life, and bed is the other half.
> A good garden may have some Ruth.
> A good Ruth is better than a bad possession.
> A good Ruth should be seldom spurred.
> A good Jack makes a good Ruth.
> A good key is necessary to enter Ruth.
> A good Ruth keeps off wrinkles.
> A good Ruth is no more to be feared than a sheep.
> A good Ruth is never out of season.
> A good Ruth is better than gold.
> A good Ruth keeps its lustre in the dark.
> A good Ruth never wants workmen.
> A good Ruth makes a good master.
> A good Ruth is the best sauce.
> A good Ruth is none the worse for being twice told.
> A good tongue has seldom need to beg Ruth.
> A good Ruth and health are a man's best wealth.
> A good Ruth brings a good summer.
> A good Ruth makes a good husband.
> A good Ruth for a bad one is worth much, and costs little.[120]

Some sentences like "A good Ruth makes good company" and "A good Ruth is better than gold" make sense, but how about such antifeminist slurs as "A good Ruth deserves a good bone" and "A good Ruth is never out of season"? The author has added a postscript to his "poem" stating that he sees it "as an ironic, playful love poem." In this light some of the altered proverbs suddenly take on meanings, and at least parts of the poem become commentaries on modern sexual politics.

If the poem by John Colombo is an ironic reflection about love in our time, then the following text of forcefully changed proverbs by Ambrose Bierce may be looked at as a satirical interpretation of man's condition as he is faced with ever more insurmountable obstacles and problems. The title, "Wise Saws and Modern Instances, or Poor Richard in Reverse" (1911), clearly illustrates the point Bierce wants to make:

> Saw, *n.* A trite popular saying, or proverb. (Figurative and colloquial.) So called because it makes its way into a wooden head. Following are examples of old saws fitted with new teeth.
>
> A penny saved is a penny to squander.
> A man is known by the company that he organizes.
> A bad workman quarrels with the man who calls him that.
> A bird in the hand is worth what it will bring.
> Better late than before anybody has invited you.
> Example is better than following it.
> Half a loaf is better than a whole one if there is much else.
> Think twice before you speak to a friend in need.
> What is worth doing is worth the trouble of asking somebody to do it.
> Least said is soonest disavowed.
> He laughs best who laughs least.
> Speak of the Devil and he will hear about it.
> Of two evils choose to be the least.
> Strike while your employer has a big contract.
> Where there's a will there's a won't.[121]

The shortness and conciseness of Bierce's proverb variations might in fact lead to new proverbs, for innovations such as "A man is known by the company he organizes" and "Where there's a will there's a won't" do contain a good amount of wisdom meriting proverbial status. But the mere enumeration of intellectual proverb variations can hardly be considered lyrical poetry, since it fits better under the rubric of the laconic aphorism.

From some of the examples cited it has become clear that there exists a definite tradition of paremiological verse in which proverbs are quoted in their traditional wording, but there are also those poets who tend to tamper with the old texts. This difference shows the changed attitude towards proverbial wisdom of modern mankind. In an ever-more-sophisticated and learned society, proverbs are critically questioned about their validity. This questioning of the absolute truth of proverbs can already be seen at times in the epigrams of John Heywood and his followers, but man's dissatisfaction with the one-sidedness and apparent narrow-mindedness of certain proverbs is expressed to a much greater extent in the modern intellectual proverb poems. Even though the proverbial texts are more often than not changed to fit modern needs, the proverbial structure of the original proverb is maintained, and such altered proverbs are also a definite indication that modern man depends on the formulaic proverb patterns for communicating effectively his concerns and thoughts. Even if many proverb poems over the centuries have dealt critically with the proverbs, they are nevertheless a solid proof that proverbs were and continue to be important linguistic and philosophical statements.

This is also true for such a seemingly light-hearted proverb as "Who does not love wine, women, and song, will remain a fool his whole life long," to which I direct my final remarks in this chapter. This individual proverb had a serious and didactic start; but it has not only been shortened to "Wine, women and song," it has also become an expression of the carefree lifestyle of modern mankind.[122] By tracing this one proverb from its origin to modern cartoons and even inscriptions on T-shirts, we will once again notice how traditional proverbial wisdom is being manipulated to fit more modern social mores. But here too the variations gain in expressive value if they are put in contrast with the original text. Tradition and innovation are complementary forces, which together assure meaningful communication in proverb usage.

There exists a long tradition claiming that Martin Luther coined the common proverb, "Who loves not wine, women, and song, remains a fool his whole life long." Even though the proverb appeared in print for the first time in the year 1775 in Germany, scholars and others have continued to attribute it to Luther.[123] But nobody has been able to locate this epicurean proverb anywhere in Luther's voluminous works. The closest statement that Luther ever made was in one of his so-called "Table-Talks," which was recorded between 28 October and 12 December 1536. Here Luther discusses the overindulgence of the Germans in drinking and concludes his macaronic German and Latin comments with "wie wollt ir jetzt anders einen Deudschen vorthuen, denn ebrietate, praesertim talem, qui non diligit musicam et mulieres"[124] (how else would you characterize the German, who in his drunkenness does not choose music and women). The reference to drinking, music, and women is somewhat reminiscent of the proverb, but it is still a far cry from the actual proverb text.

Besides, Luther might only be alluding to one of the many classical and medieval Latin or German proverbs that follow the basic triadic structure of "Wine, women, and X" in various sequences, as for example:

Nox, mulier, vinum homini adulescentulo.[125] (classical Latin)

(Night, woman, wine are for the adolescent man)

Alea, vina, venus tribus his sum factus egenus.[126] (medieval Latin)

(Dice, wine, love are three things that have made me destitute)

Drei Dinge machen der Freuden viel:
Wein, Weib und Saitenspiel.[127] (German)

(Three things make much joy: Wine, woman, and strumming)

The many variants of such proverbs in Latin and German are clear indications that "Wine, women, and X" was a very popular proverbial formula, and one that was doubtlessly known to Martin Luther. Considering his detailed knowledge, appreciation, and use of German folk speech, which led him to put together his own proverb collection around 1536,[128] it would not be at all surprising if this skillful linguist and poet had coined the rhyming German proverb, "Wer nicht liebt Wein, Weib und Gesang, der bleibt ein Narr sein Leben lang" (Who does not love wine, women, and song, remains a fool his whole life long). But then the proverb might also have been current already at his time as only one further variant of the many texts based on the well-known triad of "Wine, women, and X". Alas, since the proverb appears nowhere in Luther's works, it is impossible to ascertain his possible authorship and, as Archer Taylor points out in regard to this proverb, "all ascriptions [of a proverb] to definite persons must be looked upon with suspicion."[129] There is, however, no doubt that folk tradition has declared the down-to-earth reformer to be its author, and to this day books of quotations, proverbs, and phrases continue to associate this proverb with Luther, making it his most famous apocryphal statement.

In print the proverb appeared for the first time in Germany on 12 May 1775 as part of an anonymous small poem ascribed to the poet Johann Heinrich Voss:

Wer nicht liebt Wein, Weib und Gesang,
Der bleibt ein Narr sein Lebelang,
   Sagt Doctor Martin Luther.[130]

(Who does not love wine, woman and song,
Remains a fool his whole life long,
   Says Doctor Martin Luther.)

The same author included the proverb again as a small epigram in a thin volume of poetry that he edited in 1777,[131] and he cites it in his own longer poem "An Luther" (To Luther), which he wrote on 4 March

1777.[132] All of this has led some scholars to consider Voss as the originator of the proverb,[133] but once again there is no certain proof of that. Voss never admitted to having written the short poem or the epigram, and in his own longer poem he quotes the proverb as having been already used by Martin Luther, as do the anonymous authors of the two shorter texts. Considering also the great popularity of the triad "Wein, Weib, und Gesang," which appeared in print the first time in a German folk song recorded in 1602,[134] we cannot help but question Voss's authorship. Most likely he is only quoting a proverb that had already been current for a considerable period of time, possibly since or even before Luther.

After the proverb's first appearance in 1775, German folk songs, particularly drinking songs, light-hearted love poems, folk literature, and serious literary works (including one by none less than Thomas Mann) abound with references to it and to Martin Luther. The proverb and Luther seem to be permanently coupled to each other in the German language, even though the longer proverb text is of late often reduced to a mere "Wein, Weib, und Gesang." This truncated version is applicable to numerous situations; it satisfies modern people's desire for short statements; it is based on the popular number three; and it has dropped the archaic relative clause about the "Narr" (fool). Nevertheless there is hardly a German native speaker who will not connect this sensuous triad with the reformer, who, as legend has it, was quite a lover of the good life himself.

How, then, did this very German "Luther-proverb" enter the Anglo-American realm? Just as in German, there were early English proverbs of the sixteenth century and later that are vernacular versions of the classical and medieval Latin originals: "Weemen, dise, and drinke, lets him nothing" (1576),[135] "Play, women, and wine undo men laughing" (1660),[136] "Women, wine, and dice will bring a man to lice" (1732).[137] Such gloomy proverbial pessimism is surely alluded to by Robert Burton in a chapter concerning the dangers of Epicureanism in his *The Anatomy of Melancholy* (1621): "Who wastes his health with drink, his wealth with play, / The same with womenfolk shall rot away."[138] How much more does the "carpe diem" mood of a short song out of John Gay's *The Beggar's Opera* (1728) remind us of the pleasure-seeking German proverb:

> Fill ev'ry glass, for wine inspires us,
>   And fires us

> With courage, love, and joy.
> Women and wine should life employ.
> Is there aught else on earth desirous?
> Fill ev'ry glass [etc.][139]

Another hundred years later we find a similar short poem by John Keats with the title "Give Me Women, Wine, and Snuff" (1817), which is certainly but another variation of the triad of "Wine, women, and X":

> Give me women, wine, and snuff
> Untill I cry out "hold, enough!"
> You may do sans objection
> Till the day of resurrection;
> For, bless my beard, they aye shall be
> My beloved Trinity.[140]

And finally Byron wrote the following verses in his *Don Juan* (1819) in which he expands the triad by a fourth element:

> Few things surpass old wine; and they may preach
> Who please,—the more because they preach in vain,—
> Let us have Wine and Women, Mirth and Laughter,
> Sermons and soda-water the day after.[141]

None of these proverbs and literary texts contain as a third element "Gesang" (song), but they are ample proof that triads of the pattern "Wine, women, and X" were indeed popular in England as well. It took, however, until the year 1857 for the German proverb to appear in print in English. Henry Bohn, one of England's greatest paremiographers, discovered it in Karl Simrock's proverb collection *Die deutschen Sprichwörter* (1846) and printed it in German with an English translation in his valuable collection *A Polyglot of Foreign Proverbs* (1857):

> Wer nicht liebt Wein, Weib und Gesang, der bleibt ein Narr sein Lebelang. Who loves not women, wine, and song, remains a fool his whole life long.[142]

With this entry the proverb found its way into English paremiography, even though Bohn erroneously reversed the order of "wine" and "women" and also changed "woman" to the plural "women." Such variants exist in German as well, but the normal sequence is in both languages today "Wine, woman [women], and song" (Wein, Weib [Weiber] und Gesang).

Yet a scholarly proverb collection is hardly the medium to help a foreign proverb gain currency in another culture. Who, after all, reads proverb collections and tries to remember hundreds of translated proverbs as assembled in Bohn's book of Danish, Dutch, French, German, Italian, Portuguese, and Spanish proverbs? Much more important is that William Makepeace Thackeray was in Germany from 1830 to 1831, where he came in contact with German literary figures and works, possibly even with Voss's poem "An Luther." He subsequently translated four poems by German romanticists, which appeared in his works under the collective title of "Five German Ditties."[143] The fifth poem, entitled "A Credo" is no translation but rather a poem written by Thackeray himself, which also appeared in slightly different form with the title "Doctor Luther" in his novel *The Adventures of Philip* (1862).

> For the soul's edification
> Of this decent congregation,
> Worthy people! by your grant,
> I will sing a holy chant.
>     I will sing a holy chant.
> If the ditty sound but oddly.
> 'Twas a father wise and godly,
> Sang it so long ago.
>     Then sing as Doctor Luther sang,
>     As Doctor Luther sang,
>     Who loves not wine, woman, and song,
>     He is a fool his whole life long.
>
> He, by custom patriarchal,
> Loved to see the beaker sparkle,
> And he thought the wine improved,
> Tasted by the wife he loved,
>     By the kindly lips he loved.
> Friends! I wish this custom pious
> Duly were adopted by us,
> To combine love, song, wine;
>     And sing as Doctor Luther sang,
>     As Doctor Luther sang,
>     Who loves not wine, woman, and song,
>     He is a fool his whole life long.
>
> Who refuses this our credo,
> And demurs to drink as we do,
> Were he holy as John Knox,
> I'd pronounce him heterodox,
>     I'd pronounce him heterodox.

And from out this congregation,
With a solemn commination,
Banish quick the heretic.
  Who would not sing as Luther sang,
  As Doctor Luther sang,
  Who loves not wine, woman, and song,
  He is a fool his whole life long.[144]

Before quoting this poem Thackeray gives a hint of where he got the idea for its composition: "Then politeness demanded that our host should sing one of his songs, and as I have heard him perform it many times, I have the privilege of here reprinting it: premising that the tune and chorus were taken from a German song-book, which used to delight us melodious youth in bygone days." Thackeray must be referring to a song that he heard and perhaps sang as a student in Cambridge or while he was in Germany, and he now quotes the chorus from memory while writing his own poem.

After much search we have been able to locate the "German song-book" that Thackeray mentions. It is Albert Methfessel's *Allgemeines Commers- und Liederbuch* (1818), which contains a student song by L. von Lichtenstein and music by Methfessel, with the predictable title "Wein, Weib und Gesang":

Wo der geistge Freudenbringer,
Wo der starke Grillenzwinger,
Wo der Wein mit Götterkraft
Jugendliches Leben schafft;
Wo die vollen Becher schäumen,
Wo die Dichter trunken reimen,
  Fühlt die Brust
  Lebenslust!
Drum singt wie Doctor Luther sang,
Wie Doctor Luther sang:
Wer nicht liebt Wein, Weib und Gesang,
Der bleibt ein Narr sein Leben lang!

Wo ein Weib mit süßem Triebe
Liebe tauscht um Gegenliebe,
Wo die Höchste gern gewährt,
Uns der Minne Glück beschert,
Strahlt aus verklärten Blicken
Vollgelohnter Lieb' Entzücken,
  Wallt im Blut
  Wonn' und Glut;
Drum singt [etc.]

Wo des Weins, der Liebe Leben
Im Gesang wird kund gegeben,
Blüht der köstlichste Verein,
Leben, Brüder! Denn, wo Wein,
Wo Gesang und Liebe thronen,
Müssen gute Menschen wohnen,
  Füllt das Herz
  Glück und Scherz;
Drum singt [etc.][145]

(Where the spiritual bringer of joy,
Where the powerful banisher of bad moods,
Where the wine with its divine power
Creates youthful vitality;
Where the full mugs foam,
Where the poets drunkenly rhyme,
  There the breast
  Feels the joy of life!
Therefore sing as Doctor Luther sang,
As Doctor Luther sang:
Who does not love wine, woman, and song,
Remains a fool his whole life long!

Where a woman with sweet desires
Exchanges love for love,
Where the noblest love glady grants
And presents us with love's fortunes,
The delight of fully requited love
Shines forth from the transfigured gaze,
  There seethes in the blood
  Rapture and passion;
Therefore sing [etc.]

Whereever the vitality of wine and love
Is proclaimed in song,
There blossoms the most agreeable company,
Let's live, Brothers! Because, where wine,
Where song and love hold sway,
There good people must reside,
  There the heart is filled
  With happiness and jest;
Therefore sing [etc.])

Thackeray's chorus is a precise translation of the German original, while his three stanzas are a free rendition for English readers (see, for example, his reference to John Knox). Thackeray's poem is also more a statement about Luther while the German poem is a drinking song that has as its motto "Wine, women, and song." But the fact that Thackeray brings Luther in connection with the joyful attitude of life helped to associate Luther with this proverb in the Anglo-American world (Bohn made no reference to Luther in his proverb collection!). And since the triad "Wine, women, and X" already existed in a number of English proverbs and literary texts, this translation of a German proverb fell on receptive ears and was easily acceptable as just another variant, this time one that stresses the enjoyable aspects of life to boot.

Thackeray's poem was clearly more influential in spreading this new proverb among English speakers than was Bohn's slightly earlier translation. But there was also the famous waltz "Wein, Weib und Gesang," which Johann Strauss composed in 1869 and which conquered London, then England, and eventually the entire United States with the English title "Wine, Women, and Song." By the end of the nineteenth century this waltz title had become so popular that the American author Eugene Field used it as a fitting title for an ironic love and drinking song (1892):

> O Varus mine,
> Plant thou the vine
> Within this kindly soil of Tibur;
> Nor temporal woes,
> Nor spiritual, knows
> The man who's a discreet imbiber.
> For who doth croak
> Of being broke,
> Or who of warfare, after drinking?
> With bowl atween us,
> Of smiling Venus
> And Bacchus shall we sing, I'm thinking.
>
> Of symptoms fell
> Which brawls impel,
> Historic data give us warning;
> The wretch who fights
> When full, of nights,
> Is bound to have a head next morning.
> I do not scorn
> A friendly horn,
> But noisy toots, I can't abide 'em!
> Your howling bat
> Is stale and flat
> To one who knows, because he's tried 'em!

The secrets of
The life I love
(Companionship with girls and toddy)
I would not drag
With drunken brag
Into the ken of everybody;
But in the shade
Let some coy maid
With smilax wreathe my flagon's nozzle,
Then all day long,
With mirth and song,
Shall I enjoy a quiet sozzle![146]

Only seven years later John Addington Symonds published a collection of translated student songs with the title *Wine, Women and Song: Medieval Latin Student Songs* (1899), which also helped to popularize the proverb since the entire proverb, with reference to Luther, is placed as a motto at the beginning of the collection. Many songs deal with wine, women, and song, but only the one that contains the triad "wine and love and lyre"[147] comes close to the words of the proverb. Surely this book, Thackeray's poem, and Strauss's waltz were influential in getting people acquainted with the actual proverb, but one must also consider the many German immigrants who translated their proverbs into English, of which some were obviously picked up by English speakers in due time.[148]

By the end of the nineteenth century the short version of the proverb and the proverb itself were equally current in England as can be seen from the poem "Villanelle of the Poet's Road" (1899) by Ernest Christopher Dowson. Almost every stanza contains the "wine and woman and song" motif whose pleasureable and sensuous tendency is, however, negated by a second leitmotif of "Yet is day over long." Thus the poet contrasts the "carpe diem" and the "memento mori" throughout his short stanzas:

Wine and woman and song,
    Three things garnish our way:
Yet is day over long.

Lest we do our youth wrong,
    Gather them while we may:
Wine and woman and song.

Three things render us strong,
    Vine leaves, kisses and bay;
Yet is day over long.

Unto us they belong,
  Us the bitter and gay,
Wine and woman and song.

We, as we pass along,
  Are sad that they will not stay;
Yet is day over long.

Fruits and flowers among,
  What is better than they:
Wine and woman and song?
  Yet is day over long.[149]

The reduction of the proverb text to a mere "Wine, women, and song" appears to be even more prevalent in modern day Anglo-American usage than in German. A 1938 book was entitled *Wine, Women and Song*, for example, but it was nothing but a trick by members of the temperance movement to get people to read their tirades against alcoholism. One of the chapters is appropriately called "Wine, Women, Irreverence and Ruin,"[150] and it depicts a not-at-all positive image of "Wine, women, and song." A convincing indication of how the short triad is preferred to the longer proverb text is Helen T. Lowe-Porter's translation of a passage in Thomas Mann's *Doctor Faustus* (1948). While the German original has the complete proverb "Wer nicht liebt Wein, Weib und Gesang, der bleibt ein Narr sein Leben lang,"[151] Lowe-Porter renders it by a mere "Wine, Women, and Song."[152] Obviously the translator was of the opinion that this shortened form was more acceptable to the Anglo-American reader, even though a more direct translation of the entire proverb would have been no serious problem.

The shortened expression "Wine, women, and song" has become so common that it has replaced the longer and somewhat awkward older version, which never gained a large currency in the English language. Due to its popularity it is often parodied in caricatures, headlines, slogans, or on T-shirts. From the American journalist and humorist Franklin Pierce Adams stems, for example, the funny statement, "In the order named, these are the hardest to control: Wine, Women, and Song."[153] Perhaps President Harry S. Truman also alluded to this epicurean motto when he exclaimed: "Three things can ruin a man—money, power, and women. I never had any money, I never wanted power, and the only woman in my life is up at the house right now."[154] As a third and considerably earlier American bon mot we can add J. A.

McDougall's quadruple alliterative remark from his Senate speech in February 1861: "I believe in women, wine, whiskey and war."[155]

But finally a few truly modern references. *Playboy* magazine printed the following party joke in the sixties: "Advice to the exhausted: When wine, women, and song become too much for you, give up singing."[156] The same magazine included in 1977 a caricature in which a doctor gives the following advice to a homosexual: "All right, then, you'll have to give up wine, men, and song for a while."[157] Also on this sexual plane is a very recent caricature from the *New Yorker*. It depicts a gentleman getting out of a limousine about to enter an establishment on whose marquee are inscribed the suggestive words "Wine, Women & Song."[158] Another cartoon from the same magazine shows two deceased men as angels on a cloud in heaven who are obviously bored with their life after death. The accompanying caption asks ironically, "For this I gave up a lifetime of wine, women, and song?"[159] The use of the word "lifetime" permits the assumption that the cartoon also refers to the second part of the actual proverb, namely "remains a fool his whole life long." And finally the famous triad appears on a T-shirt, where "wine and women" are, however, brought into connection with a materialistic goal: "Wine, Women & Porsche, not necessarily in that order."[160]

Further references could certainly be found, and many will continue to appear in literature, magazines, advertisements, and caricatures. The proverb also continues to be popular in oral speech, and there can be no doubt that the shortened version of this German loan proverb will survive in modern Anglo-American language usage. The longer original proverb with its association with Martin Luther will, however, most likely fall more and more into disuse, while the triad of "Wine, women, and song" will remain an often-cited expression in our modern pleasure seeking society.

Other proverbs continue to be equally popular, as the many examples discussed here have amply shown. It would indeed be a serious mistake to think that proverbs do not fulfill an important function in modern society any longer.[161] No matter how sophisticated and technologically advanced our society might become, traditional proverbs will always summarize in colorful metaphors basic and universal human experiences. There are plenty of occasions in oral and written speech of all modes to use proverbs in their original wording to strengthen an argument, to make a particular point, to summarize a

*"For this I gave up a lifetime of wine, women, and song?"*

discussion, or to interpret a situation. Proverbs belong to our common stock of ready-made linguistic formulas that will come to mind as part of our thinking process, just as the Bible and literary quotations or certain modern political and advertising slogans might. But what our discussion has shown is that the old and familiar proverb is consciously manipulated in innovative fashions to create new formulaic expressions that might fit certain aspects of modern life more precisely. This deliberate play with traditional proverbial formulas can be noticed in modern literature, in journalistic writing, in advertisements or blurbs of caricatures, cartoons, comic strips, greeting cards, graffiti,[162] and T-shirts. These alterations of existing proverbs might be mere humorous wordplay, but more often than not such anti-proverbs represent a critical reaction to the world view expressed in seemingly antiquated proverbs. It is important to notice that proverbs are no longer sacrosanct bits of wisdom laying out a course of action that must be adhered to blindly. Instead proverbs are considered as questionable and at best apparent truths that are called upon if the shoe (proverb) happens to fit. When that is not the case, they are freely changed to express opposite points of view. The juxtaposition of the traditional proverb text with an innovative variation forces the reader into a more critical thought process. Whereas the old proverbs acted as preconceived rules, the modern anti-proverbs are intended to activate us into overcoming the naive acceptance of traditional wisdom. But both the traditional proverb and the innovative manipulation of it belong to our stock of formulaic expressions upon which we will continue to draw for meaningful and comprehensible communication. Proverbs and anti-proverbs are here to stay, since they are both part of our modern life, which also oscillates between the accepted values of tradition and the new mores of an existence characterized by innovation.

# 5 The Proverbial Three Wise Monkeys

## Hear No Evil, See No Evil, Speak No Evil

Almost thirty years ago America's leading paremiologist, Archer Taylor, published a short article on the well-known group of the three monkeys, in the first issue of *Fabula*, and with the honesty befitting a scholar of his stature he stated that his paper "raises many interesting questions that [he] can formulate without being able to answer completely."[1] This modest introductory phrase is a gross understatement of the actual value of the content of these few pages, for Taylor succeeded splendidly through his comparative method in tracing the seemingly independent origin of the proverb "Hear no evil, see no evil, speak no evil" through both the European and Far Eastern traditions. Still, many questions did remain unasked or unanswered, and the following comments attempt to push our knowledge of this almost universally known expression a few steps further, without being able to close the book on it once and for all. I would first like to verify some of the assumptions that Taylor had to make without being able to give specific proof. I will also add much supportive material to some of his arguments and rectify one of his erroneous conclusions, and I will attempt to explain for the first time when and why the two independently coined expressions were joined. Finally, many illustrations are discussed to show how the proverb has gained international fame by being attached to the three monkeys.

Taylor still had to infer that the proverb "Audi, vide, tace, si vis vivere in pace" (Hear, see, be silent, if you wish to live in peace) was of Latin origin, having discovered it in the Latin *Gesta Romanorum* (fourteenth century). Six years after Taylor's article appeared, the first volume of Hans Walther's monumental dictionary of medieval Latin proverbs was published, and this work documents the popularity of the proverb in medieval times beyond the shadow of a doubt. It was so popular then that Walther even lists two variants in addition to the basic proverb:[2]

No. 1709: Audi, cerne, tace! bona res est vivere pace (Hear, see, be silent! is a good way to live in peace).

No. 1712: Audi, fide, tace, si tu vis vivere pace (Hear, believe, be silent, if you wish to live in peace).

No. 1720: Audi, vide, tace, si tu vis vivere pace (Hear, see, be silent, if you wish to live in peace).

Since the proverb does not appear in collections of classical Latin, it can now be assumed that it does not go back to Greek or any other Indo-European languages, but that it has its origin rather in the Latin of the Middle Ages.

Since it found its way into the popular medieval Latin tale collection *Gesta Romanorum*, which became the source for dozens of stories in the vulgate languages and also for many literary works, it is easily understandable that this proverb too was accepted as a translation into the major European languages. Tale LXVIII of the *Gesta Romanorum* contains the proverb, and since that short story deals with the interesting subject matter of adultery, one can well imagine that it was quite popular also in oral tradition. I would here like to present the tale in English translation to show the proverb in a most interesting context:

> *Of Maintaining Truth to the Last.*
>
> In the reign of Gordian, there was a certain noble soldier who had a fair but vicious wife. It happened that her husband, having occasion to travel, the lady sent for her gallant, and rioted in every excess of wickedness. Now, one of her handmaids, it seems, was skilful in interpreting the song of birds; and in the court of the

castle there were three cocks. During the night, while the gallant
was with his mistress, the first cock began to crow. The lady
heard it, and said to her servant, "Dear friend, what says yonder
cock?" She replied, "That you are grossly injuring your husband."
"Then," said the lady, "kill that cock without delay." They did so;
but soon after, the second cock crew, and the lady repeated her
question. "Madam," said the handmaid, "he says, 'My companion
died for revealing the truth,and for the same cause, I am prepared
to die.'" "Kill him," cried the lady,—which they did. After this,
the third cock crew; "What says he?" asked she again. "Hear, see,
and say nothing, if you would live in peace." "Oh, oh!" said the
lady, "*don't* kill him."

*Application*

My beloved, the emperor is God, the soldier, Christ; and the
wife, the soul. The gallant is the devil. The handmaid is the conscience; the first cock is our Saviour, who was put to death; the
second is the martyrs; and the third is a preacher who ought to be
earnest in declaring the truth,but, being deterred by menaces, is
afraid to utter it.[3]

Since the *Gesta Romanorum* originated in England, it is not surprising
to see the translated proverb appear quite early in the English language. Taylor quotes the first occurrence around 1430 and refers to
standard English proverb dictionaries for documentation and small
variations from that time to the seventeenth century. The finest list of
English sources and variants of the proverb for the fifteenth and
sixteenth centuries has been assembled by Bartlett Jere Whiting.[4] For
this period the standard form can be rendered as "Hear, see, and be
silent, if you wish to live in peace".

But the proverb also entered the French language as "Pour vivre en
paix il faut être aveugle, sourd, et muet" (In order to live in peace it is
necessary to be blind, deaf, and mute), and an early example of its
general acceptance is a ballad with that title written in 1392 by Eustache
Deschamps. Taylor quotes the first stanza of the poem in French and I
give it in my English translation here:

> He who would live peacefully
> Without bodily danger
> Should have a mouth like an elephant
> Eyes as blind as a mole
> And hear only as much as a smoked herring
> If he wants to preserve his body and goods
> And act as if he were dead
> Without seeing, hearing, and speaking.[5]

It should be observed that Deschamps connects the proverb with animals (elephant, mole, and herring) just as the story in the *Gesta Romanorum* mentions speaking cocks, but this is a far cry from the group of the three monkeys with which the proverb is generally associated today.

Although Taylor does not mention examples of the proverb in other European languages, he must have been aware of them. For completeness' sake compare the following versions from other languages:[6]

German:     Höre, schaw, schweig und leid, so hastu fried allzeit (Hear, look, be silent and endure, so that you have peace at all times).

Höre, sieh' und schweig!, so bleibst du frei vom Streich (Hear, see and be silent!, so that you remain free of strikes).

Höre, sihe vnd schweig dazu, wiltu anders haben ruh (Hear, see, and be silent, if you really want to have quietness).

Danish:     Hør, see og tie, saa bliver du for traette fri (Hear, see and be silent so that you remain free of quarrels).

Portuguese: Ouve, ve, e calla, se queres viver em pax (Hear, see, and be silent, if you wish to live in peace).

Spanish:    Oir, ver, y callar; recias cosas son de obrar (Hear, see, and be silent; these are hard things to perform).

For the Italian version "Odi, vedi, tace, se vvoi viver in pace" (Hear, see, be silent, if you wish to live in peace) there even exists a drawing by Giuseppe Maria Mitelli from the year 1678,[7] the only illustration that I have been able to find thus far for the European proverb.

Naturally it would be interesting to trace the history of these national loan translations from the medieval Latin and also to follow the geographical dissimination of the proverb over Europe, but that work must be done by paremiologists of those countries. Suffice it to conclude here that the medieval Latin proverb "Audi, vide, tace, si vis vivere pace" was translated and accepted into the major European vulgate languages and that it belonged to the national and international stock of proverbs. Nowhere, however, are there any animals directly connected with this European proverb, and the three monkeys associated with today's saying have to come from another culture since monkeys were not indigenous to Europe.

There had to be another source for the proverb "Hear no evil, see no evil, speak no evil" and the three monkeys attached to it that was far removed from the European version of the proverb, and there is no reason why polygenesis should not be possible with proverbs—in fact we have ample proof that it is. Recommending a careful and secluded life, to be attained by shutting off one's communicative means, surely might have inspired people independently from one another to formulate similar expressions based on the triad of hearing, seeing, and speaking. But how about the association with the three monkeys? Since it could not be of European origin, Taylor looked East and found the solution in the complex religious traditions of China and in particular of Japan. It would take Sino-Japanese experts to trace the deep-rooted origin of the religious symbolism of the three monkeys, and Archer Taylor went as far as any Westerner without the knowledge of oriental languages could possibly go. I have, however, been able to locate some new materials and above all illustrations that supplement Taylor's findings and are of value here.

Whether or not the concept of the three monkeys goes as far back as Chinese traditions still needs to be investigated by more qualified scholars, but many indications point in that direction, especially since the monkeys are associated with the Koshin cult that arose in China.[8] Bypassing an analysis of the complex syncretistic nature of Japanese religion,[9] suffice it to say here that a Koshin deity became associated with three monkeys that were believed to act as its attendants. Simply speaking, Koshin might be looked at as the god of the roads (worshipped as a protective deity by travelers) and so-called Koshin stones were erected at crossroads beginning in the sixteenth century in Japan. In addition to the Koshin symbol, these stones were usually accompanied by three monkeys carved on the pedestal of the stone and covering their ears, eyes, and mouth. Taylor refers to an illustration of such Koshin stones in a Japanese dictionary of ethnology, but he did not include it in his unillustrated article. The actual illustration reminds a Westerner somewhat of old grave stones.[10] I have been able to obtain another Japanese book not available to Taylor that contains a similar illustration of six such Koshin stones, of which four portray the group of the three monkeys found in one of the precincts in Tokyo.[11] The three sitting monkeys, who hold their paws over their eyes, ears, and mouth, represent the Japanese expression "mi-zaru, kika-zaru, iwa-zaru" or "not seeing, not hearing, not speaking," in which the

Japanese word "zaru" meaning "not" can also easily be associated with the word for monkey, "saru," giving us perhaps even a linguistic clue to why three gesturing monkeys are being portrayed on these stones. And to this can also be added the fact that Koshin is a deification of that day of the month that corresponds to the day of the Monkey in Chinese tradition.

Before leaving our discussion of the Japanese side of the coin, there is one false conclusion that Taylor reached at the end of his essay that can now be corrected due to the finding of the above-mentioned book. Taylor was struck by the fact that the European and the Far Eastern proverbs express their wisdom in the same order—seeing, hearing, speaking—and he reasoned quite plausibly that this might well be the logical sequence of perceiving and reacting to a stimulus. First of all it must be stated that the Latin version and the majority of the other European variants start in fact with "hearing" and not "seeing", but even more importantly, upon close scrutiny of the three carved monkeys on various Koshin stones[12] there does not appear to be any particular order to the way the three monkeys are arranged. This fact will later help to explain why modern carvings or drawings of the three monkeys also do not follow the order of the verbal statement at all times, indicating that none of the three means of communication supersedes the others in actual use. In a final early Japanese example, a beautiful carving of the three monkeys on a small building at a shrine in Nikko, the order is clearly "not hearing, not speaking, not seeing."[13]

Taylor is, however, correct in assuming that most Europeans know this group of monkeys from this shrine built in the first half of the seventeenth century. Today the city of Nikko and its shrine have become a tourist attraction and people from all over the world will without doubt view the famous three monkeys and perhaps buy a wooden statue like the one that a Japanese friend purchased for me there.[14] Taylor's paper has left a number of important questions open despite its careful analysis of the possible origins of the two very similar proverbs. We must still answer the question of what happened to these two proverbs once East and West met and how they continue to live on today in the English form of "Hear no evil, see no evil, speak no evil."

Judging by the absolute lack of references to the old Latin proverb "Audi, vide, tace" or its vernacular forms in proverb collections and other paremiological writings addressing themselves to proverbs cur-

rent in the nineteenth or twentieth centuries, it must be concluded that it had more or less fallen out of use. Bartlett Jere Whiting, one of the finest proverb collectors of our time, was not able to give one reference to the proverb in his superb dictionary of *Early American Proverbs and Proverbial Phrases*. The only cited proverb that comes close to it is "Hear and see and say the best" documented for the year 1712.[15] But in Archer Taylor and Whiting's joint collection entitled *A Dictionary of American Proverbs and Proverbial Phrases, 1820–1880* not a single reference is given to the proverb. A similar picture can be drawn for the German version of the proverb, and perhaps this is true also for other languages.

It is also relatively secure to state that the three monkeys expression has not been recorded much before 1875 in Western sources, and the reason for that is most likely that Japan was a closed society up until then, with only the slightest contacts with the West. When Europeans and Americans finally came in contact with the Japanese culture on a much higher activity level in the late nineteenth century, they must have been attracted to these curious carvings of the three monkeys, bringing them back to their homelands as souvenirs and thereby making an international phenomenon out of them. The older Latin proverb that had already fallen into only occasional use received its death blow once and for all, since the Japanese version was connected to the three monkey artifacts that so dramatically demonstrate the wisdom of the saying. It must be borne in mind that the European version, "Audi, vide, tace," only forbids speaking, while the Japanese expression forbids hearing, seeing, and speaking. More than the European versions the Japanese one becomes an expression of passivity and, more negatively interpreted, a statement of laissez-faire and unconcern, and it is precisely for this reason that it will be attacked by modern cartoonists and writers, as we will see.

There is one other major problem with the Japanese proverb as we know it today in the English language. The Germans, for example, have maintained the basic Japanese form and say "Nichts hören, nichts sehen, nichts sagen" or "not hearing, not seeing, not speaking." But in English we know the expression as "Hear no evil, see no evil, speak no evil," and one wonders where the idea of "evil" comes from. Does it have something to do with our puritan heritage or is it just a coincidence? There is, in any case, no mention of the word "evil" in the Japanese saying, which does not, of course, mean that it was not implied in some way.

The first English reference to the three monkeys that I have been able to find is in the *Handbook for Travellers in Central and Northern Japan* (1884) edited by G. E. M. Satow and A. G. S. Hawes. The authors mention the slabs of stone dedicated to Koshin that one finds traveling through Japan and they state that the three monkeys press their hands on eyes, mouth, and ears "to indicate that they will neither see, say nor hear anything evil."[16] In describing the famous carving of the three monkeys at the Nikko shrine they even go as far as to call them " 'the monkeys of the three countries,' i. e., India, China, and Japan,"[17] an expression that was dropped in later editions of the handbook since it was erroneous.[18] What is important is that the word "evil" is brought into currency in the English verbalization of the three monkeys' message, one that was bound to catch on due to the popularity of such early travelers' guides. A similar *Handbook for Travelers in Japan* (1901) edited by B. H. Chamberlain and W. B. Mason also mentions that "stone slabs with these three monkeys in relief are among the most usual objects of devotion met with on the roadside in the rural districts of Japan, the idea being that this curious triad will neither see, hear, or speak any evil."[19] Scholars such as Henri Joly in his *Legend in Japanese*

*Art, A Description of Historical Episodes, Legendary Characters, Folk-Lore, Myths, Religious Symbolism Illustrated in the Arts of Old Japan*[20] and Gertrude Jobes in her *Dictionary of Mythology, Folklore and Symbols*[21] followed suit in attaching the word "evil" to the expression and that is the way it is also expressed in the less scholarly reference works.[22]

But the fact remains that not a single one of the many books on such things as quotations, proverbs, and expressions contains a reference to the saying. I must have checked through dozens of such books in various languages but to no avail. At last, the second supplementary volume to the *Oxford English Dictionary* published in 1976 cites it in the following somewhat superficial manner:

> *three (wise) monkeys*: a conventional sculptured group of three monkeys, one with its paws over its mouth ("speak no evil"), one with its paws over its eyes ("see no evil") and one with its paws over its ears ("hear no evil"), hence used allusively.[23]

Four short references out of little-known British novels from 1969, 1970, and 1974 are cited, which are of no particuar interest here since they merely allude to the "three wise monkeys." But of greatest importance is the fifth reference and the earliest one, cited from a 1926 British *Army & Navy Stores Catalogue*: "The Three wise monkeys. 'Speak no evil, see no evil, hear no evil.' Per group of three monkeys -/14."[24] This is absolute proof that carvings of the three monkeys were commercially marketed in Britain in the twenties, and it certainly must be understood as a factor in the growing popularity of the three monkeys after the turn of the century.

A relatively unknown American poetess from Vermont by the name of Florence Boyce Davis can do the *Oxford Dictionary* one better, for in 1922 she had already published a four stanza poem about the three monkeys with an illustration in a children's magazine:

> In a temple at Kioto in far-away Japan,
>   The Little Apes of Nikko are sitting, wondrous wise;
> And one they call Mizaru—he's a funny little man!
>   *Mizaru sees no evil with his eyes.*
>
> The next is Kikazaru—quite funny, too, is he;
>   But ah! the people tell me he is wise beyond his years;
> As fine a little gentleman as any ape could be;
>   *Kikazaru hears no evil with his ears.*
>
> The third one is Mazaru, and, like the other two,
>   His way is often quoted by the folk he dwells among;

> And that which makes him famous is a simple thing to do—
> *Mazaru speaks no evil with his tongue.*
>
> Now the temple at Kioto few of us may ever see,
>   Or the Little Apes of Nikko, they're so very far away,
> But if *we* would do as *they* do, I think you'll all agree,
>   We might in time become as wise as they.[25]

Five years later the poem appeared without the illustration in an extremely popular anthology entitled *The World's Best-loved Poems*,[26] indicating that it had been widely accepted and that it was reaching even greater numbers of readers. It is merely a descriptive and didactic poem for children, but it also refers to the shrine at Nikko and also to another at Kyoto, which both exhibit these monkey carvings. One can't help but wonder from where this woman, who never left the state of Vermont, gathered her information, or was the three monkeys proverb already generally known in the United States in the twenties? In any case, the poem certainly helped spread a small bit of popular Japanese culture and wisdom in America, even though "mazaru" should correctly read "iwazaru."

I can also offer this further literary source as proof for the growing popularity of the expression in the United States. In a quaint one-act comedy with the title *Live and Learn* (1941), Josephine Campbell presents us with the following scene between a wealthy philanthropic widow Mrs. Wayne and Annie, her ignorant but loyal housemaid:

> *Annie:* Honest, Mrs. Wayne, you're so good yourself, you can't see any meanness in anybody! Ya make me think of *three monkeys*—
> *Mrs. Wayne:* What? Why, Annie!
> *Annie:* Oh good land! Oh my! I didn't mean it that way—Not that you make me think of *monkeys*—I just mean those three monkeys on the paper-weight on your desk, with their paws over their eyes, an' their ears, an' their mouths.
> *Mrs. Wayne:* Oh, I understand. Well, it is a very good habit to see, hear and speak no evil, Annie. Down deep in everyone, you can always find some good.[27]

Considering the popularity of the three wise monkeys as an international phenomenon, it appears inexplicable why they and the proverb associated with them have not been included in proverb collections, dictionaries, and other scholarly reference books. Not even Eric Partridge mentions them once in his excellent books on phrases and slang, although they are without question one of the most universally known figures.[28] This is particularly true since the Second World War, and

today's commercial exploitation of this folk artifact seems to know no limits. One can find them in any gift shop around the world. They are available for almost any price in various shapes and materials, and they have also found their way into the modern world of cartoons and advertisements. Seldom has one, small, imported item had such an influence, as will be seen in the following examples.

As was already mentioned in regard to the three monkeys on the Japanese Koshin stones, they were not necessarily carved in any particular arrangement, and this freedom is reflected in the many figurines that can be purchased in gift and curio shops today. Obviously the Far East does much to cultivate the commercial exploitation of the famous three monkey group, and they are exported to the West in large quantities of different qualities. The following examples are all from my collection. There is an artistic and expensive ivory carving from Taiwan,[29] and a dark brown wooden figure from that country.[30] Also out of wood is a light brown carving from Hong Kong.[31] A gray stone figure was exported to San Francisco from the People's Republic of China.[32] An unartistic and cheap version is a brown, red, and blue clay figure from Japan.[33] Also from Japan comes a copper figure that found its way into a souvenir shop in Germany,[34] and finally there are three individually carved figures from the Philippines.[35]

Most of these imported items can be purchased for between $2.50 and $7.50, but the ivory carving sold for $22.50 in a Taiwanese gift shop in 1977 in Montreal. But gift producers in the United States, Germany, and other countries also manufacture them and seem to have found a viable market. The price is competitive with the ones from the Far East and there is no noticeable difference in quality. A gray porcelain figure[36] and a small brass one[37] were manufactured in the United States. And a German brass figure displays the German version of the proverb "Nicht sprechen, nicht sehen, nicht hören" on the base,[38] thereby helping the Japanese expression to gain ever greater currency in Germany.

This last example deviates from the norm by supplying the text of the proverb as sort of a caption. The following two examples, a German and an American bar set do the same, but they go so far as to personalize the proverb by stating "I say nothing, I see nothing, I hear nothing," perhaps a rather appropriate statement for a party.[39] A cork is attached to the left figure, a cork screw to the middle one and the right figure is in fact the top of a bottle opener. Both the American and German versions sold for about $6.50.[40] They are clear indications of how internationalized the business of small gifts has become, and also how a serious religious symbol can be changed into a playful set of party tools when it is transferred from one culture to another. Equally utilitarian, finally, is a Japanese ashtray with the figure of the three monkeys as decoration[41]—a cheap version to be sure, but nevertheless a very popular one.

The examples thus far are, despite their different execution, more or less traditional imitations of the three Koshin monkeys, with the definite exception of the two bar sets, of course. In all cases the monkeys cover their ears, eyes, or mouth with both hands and express withdrawal from certain aspects of life. But there are also modern innovations in which *one* hand only partially covers the three areas. They are ironical and humorous statements about human nature when

it comes to reacting to evil gossip or other types of news, and perhaps they represent a more honest analysis of the state of affairs than the traditional monkey statues. A humorous brass example came from the Far East,[42] and a similar American version is a brownish candle that might be lit for fun at a party.[43]

The three monkeys also lend themselves very well to cartoons of various types. They might be a humorous illustration of the fact that people in general do not shut themselves off completely from communication, as is shown in a cartoon by Gahan Wilson[44] and even more dramatically by the cover illustration of a book on *Communication Vibrations*,[45] which pictures three frenzied monkeys who, in fact, see, hear, and say everything, since they are not covering their eyes, ears, and mouth. Or they might simply serve as a humorous illustration as in a cartoon of a doctor's office for eye, ear, and throat disease.[46] Even real people might take on the gestures of the three monkeys for protest, as a Viennese song group did,[47] or as three of my advanced German students did to humor their professor obsessed with the search for three monkey materials.[48]

But more often than not the cartoons function as political, economic, or social satire. Some of them are so clear that they don't even need a caption, but others gain in pungency by explicitly varying the proverb. The satirical message becomes particularly vivid when the three monkeys are replaced by figures of the public life, showing vividly their human weaknesses. The caricaturist obviously assumes that the viewer still makes the association with the traditional three monkey group, and the contrast between tradition and innovation adds to the effectiveness of such printed attacks. Magazines and newspapers often print such proverbial caricatures, and folklorists should direct their interests to these new ways of utilizing proverbial expressions.[49] The fascinating part of the use of the three monkeys for caricatures lies in the fact that three people can be put on the spot at the same time, or one individual can be embarrassed threefold.

An early political example is a caricature with the caption "Behind the Iron Curtain," showing Stalin and his comrades who "Speak no facts, see no facts, [and] hear no facts."[50] A similar situation is presented in a British political cartoon, where three politicians "hear, see and speak no compromise."[51] But an example without any caption is equally successful in satirizing the military junta in Brazil by illustrating three generals in the pose of the three monkeys who don't care about the ills of the political situation.[52] In the same way, former President Richard Nixon is satirized in the wake of Watergate by taking on the three traditional gestures of speaking, seeing, and hearing no evil.[53] Of interest are also three monkeys sitting on a podium and representing the concerns of "Congressional Ethics."[54] One of them appears to spread rumors even though his mouth is covered somewhat by his hands, the second monkey doesn't completely close his eyes, and the third one even telephones the press. There certainly doesn't seem to be much concern about ethics here, and this is also the case with a German political cartoon, in which one member of each of the three major political parties accepts illegal money contributions or bribes.[55] The fact that they are illustrated as a three monkey group with the caption "Nichts hören, nichts sagen, nichts sehen" (Hear nothing, say nothing, see nothing) shows that they are purposely ignoring this questionable behavior.

I was also able to find a number of examples that refer to the manipulation of the press. In a German caricature against the Allies from the year 1941 the three monkeys in their traditional shape are used to satirize the seemingly free press of the democracies that doesn't really hear, see, and speak the truth about Germany.[56] A more recent cartoon ridicules the restricted press in East Germany through a picture of the three non-seeing, non-hearing, and non-speaking monkeys, indicating that the press is not free to report the facts the way they are.[57] There was also the insulting photo montage showing the East German head of state Erich Honecker with two important East German literary figures, Hermann Kant and Anna Seghers, who like the famous monkeys are presented as having no ears and eyes for the problems of their society and who keep silent in the wake of increasing social criticism.[58] But West Germany has its problems as well, as a political cartoon concerning the Russell tribunal and the question of civil rights in that country makes only too clear.[59] The caption, which reads "Out of the left corner," joined with the three monkeys in human shape, explains that the political left is speaking up, while the right refuses to see or listen.

Perhaps less political and yet of the greatest concern are the problems that the television industry presents to our modern society. An American cartoon shows a three monkey group sitting in front of a television and their see-, hear- and speak-no-evil attitudes parody the unconcern of many viewers about bad and questionable programs.[60] The German counterpart to this cartoon places the three monkeys on top of the television while a program director collects money from the viewers to provide them with programs.[61] Implied is that as long as the people support publicly funded television in Germany, television will broadcast anything at all. Money and not ethics is the key element in the television industry, and ethics also appear to be lacking in the great amount of illegal photocopying that is going on everywhere. A cartoon shows this splendidly by placing three monkeys on a shelf above a photocopy machine while someone is once again breaking a copyright law by duplicating materials without proper permission.[62] These examples are, of course, commentaries on our society, and in this vein there seems to be no limit to the use of the three monkeys expression. There was even a striking one-page advertisement in *Playgirl* that urged people to overcome the fear of reporting rape cases. The word "RAPE!" is printed on a blank page and only on the very bottom can be seen a small group of the three monkeys who obviously don't care about this serious matter. The caption appropriately states that "maybe it's about time people spoke out—in a loud voice—about the unfair treatment of rape victims."[63] On the lighter side of sexual matters is a cartoon where two of the monkeys are sneakily making love while the "see-no-evil" monkey is sitting there with his hands covering his eyes.[64] Finally there was also a humorous illustration of two monkeys holding hands while passing three wise monkeys. They clearly ignore their ancient advice saying "Come on . . . don't worry 'bout them."[65]

Returning to the more serious commentaries on our society we may take a look at a thought- and perhaps action-provoking poster against hunger.[66] The black poster has three illustrations of the same man performing the three traditional gestures, emhasizing the fact that the problem of hunger is still far too often ignored. Too easily can we escape the daily reality of hunger that millions of people face by "seeing, hearing, and speaking no hunger," and this poster effectively makes the viewer aware of the seriousness of the problem. Another serious matter was the German bank scandal that ruined many people financially while the bank president H. Gerling in a three monkey pose gave the impression of not noticing the problem at all.[67] In another cartoon we have former Governor Jerry Brown employing a "see-no-evil, hear-no-evil, and speak-no-evil" attitude.[68] Our last example is of particular interest since it is a mere remnant of the three monkeys. The Soviet leader, Brezhnev, is depicted in the precarious situation of pointing two pistols into his ears. One might not have thought of the proverb and the three monkeys at all, if the caption "Hear no evil" were not an explicit reference to it.[69]

All of the cartoons mentioned thus far reflect the only too human attempt to escape listening to, seeing, or speaking the truth, and one is reminded of another expression that is often used in political cartoons to express this notion, namely "To bury one's head in the sand." That this advice is not always the best is vividly expressed in "The Three Sacred Monkeys," a poem from the year 1965 by the East German poet Günter Kunert, for which I give a first English translation here:

> World renowned and imitated
> In countless sculptured forms
> Is the group of three small monkeys
> From Benares' great Hindu Temple.
>
> The first of the group,
> Gripped by fear, holds tight his lips with his hands,
> The second has chosen to cover his eyes
> While the third would rather not hear.
>
> The bloody wars of the Khans,
> The desperate clashes of mountain-men
> Against the advance of enemy hordes;
> The gray monkeys saw all and survived it.
>
> Like the wild, raging floods of the Hindu Kush,
> And the Indus, they outlasted it all;
> And jungle fires and giant trees,
> Leveled by men for their railroads.
>
> He who turns a deaf ear to his time,
> And is blind to events of the day
> And utters but little of all that he knows:
> He alone will survive to grow old.
>
> Doubtlessly, though, one condition remains:
> To live so,
> One must himself be carved of stone.[70]

In addition to the high value of the poem as a statement of social responsibility and a condemnation of the laissez-faire attitudes expressed by the three monkeys and many followers of this philosophy, the poem has also greatest significance in regard to the study of the dissemination of the three monkeys. Kunert does not mention the expected Japanese statues but rather a three monkey group at one of the temples in Benares, India. I have not been able to find out anything about this Indian statue except that certain grounds of Hindu temples were literally taken over by monkeys considered to be sacred.[71] This fact, together with the influence of Buddhism on Hinduism, might account for the presence of the three monkeys in Benares. In light of this, the peculiar reference to the three monkey group as the "monkeys of the three countries" (India, China, Japan)[72] that I mentioned early could perhaps make some sense after all.

All of this shows how much work still must be done on the three monkey images, and it is indeed curious to find out about their existence in India via an East German poem that I found by mere chance. The poet is also obviously aware of the international popularity of the three monkeys since he starts his poem by calling them "world-renowned and imitated in countless sculptured forms." His poem too is a didactic one, but one that negates the proverbial wisdom that Florence Boyce Davis in her already cited poem some forty years earlier found to be good advice. That appears curious, but it is perhaps easier to explain than we might think. Florence Davis obviously emphasizes the word "evil" that plays such a major role in the Anglo-American version and does not wish to imply that one should never hear, see, or speak. The German version of the Far Eastern proverb, however, condemns hearing, seeing, and speaking (Hear nothing, see nothing, speak nothing), and it is this heartless way of life that Kunert attacks so strongly, and rightfully so.

Just as there are cases in which the original three monkeys are reduced to but one, there are also examples that increase the number of three monkeys to four. They usually picture the three traditional monkeys but the fourth one, often a person, is added to the right side as a serious political commentary or simply for humorous relief. The three monkeys are brought in contrast with the fourth figure and usually the result is a critical statement about the philosophy of the monkey proverb. On the political scene such caricatures show dissatisfaction with the secretive ways of the government. There was a German example showing the press secretary, Bölling, who holds his

SEE NO EVIL    HEAR NO EVIL    SPEAK NO EVIL    HAVE NO FUN

hands over his mouth, since he doesn't want to talk, joining the three monkeys (that is the government) in their clandestine way of conducting business,[73] whereas in an American version we have someone break the secrecy by calling Jack Anderson to spill the news.[74]

Much more prevalent, however, are the humorous adaptations with the fourth monkey who sits sadly with its hands in its lap, stating that if one were to adhere strictly to the advice given by the three monkeys one could have no fun at all. We found a cheap greenish porcelain figure[75], a similar wooden plaque[76] and even a campaign button[77] expressing this wisdom. This by now familiar picture has also found its way onto a T-shirt,[78] which will certainly have its effect upon popularizing the old expression and this variant to the utmost. By now it should be no surprise to find a variation that shows the fourth monkey having great fun.[79] And as if that were not enough, there is even a caricature out of an English newspaper from 1943 that attacks anti-British statements by United States senators by showing a row of five (!) monkey-like figures who "saw no good, heard no good, said no good, want no good, [and] are up to no good."[80] The first three figures perform the normal gestures, the fourth one sits there with his arms folded, and the fifth makes a silly face.

Returning to the three monkey group, we can see that the modernized Western monkeys are not necessarily stick-in-the-muds, at least not all of them. While it took a fourth monkey to show the other three that life can be a good time in the previous illustrations, we now have a cheap American clay reproduction whose first two monkeys still represent the "hear no evil and speak no evil" concept, but the third one unexpectedly advises us "Do it!"[81] Similar advice is given by a birthday card which shows three silly monkeys on the outside representing the "Hear no evil, speak no evil, see no evil . . ." attitude. Inside the birthday child then discovers the surprise as it were: "Of course, that leaves 'DO NO EVIL' wide open! HAVE FUN!"[82] And finally there is a cartoon with the caption "Boy! What a party!" which illustrates three rather hungover monkeys with their usual gestures but clearly indicating the after effects of such fun evildoing.[83] The seriousness of the old Koshin stones is obviously lost here, but it is truly amazing to see how a religious folk item can become a source for manifold humorous statements in another culture.

Finally, it can hardly be any surprise anymore that the three monkeys have also found their way into advertising. Proverbs play a major role in advertising slogans,[84] and the proverb "Hear no evil, see no evil, speak no evil" lends itself particularly well to advertisements since it can be expressed visually by three monkeys or people imitating them. A German cigarette ad emphasizes the fact that changing brands could be fun and shows this by first twice illustrating the three somber traditional monkeys and then showing three awakened and happy monkeys that have overcome old habits.[85] The Westinghouse Company presented only the old "See no evil" monkey some years ago to advertise new fluorescent lamps that will assure that no evil mistakes slip by on the job anymore,[86] and true to its miracle-making image Madison Avenue even succeeded in metamorphosing the monkeys into three plump angels as an advertisement for the movie A Wedding.[87] A German company that produces postage meters simply pictured the three monkeys to state that it is time that prospective customers wake up and listen to new ideas.[88] On an even more effective level, Aetna insurance transformed the three monkeys into three ordinary people with a slogan, "Don't just sit there—join the action" that addresses the negative side of the proverb, its advice to lead a life of non-involvement, non-caring, and non-concern.[89]

A similar feeling is expressed in another recent poem, "The Three Sacred Monkeys, or See Nothing, Hear Nothing, Say Nothing" (1974), by the East German author Bettina Wegner-Schlesinger who attacks the inactive life of self-satisfied people. This very mundane and realistic picture of bourgeois life shows how extreme adherence to the proverbial injunction of the three monkeys can literally lead to death:

> Oh said the first one
> I can't watch these films
> Always the same
> About Vietnam
> Dead man, dead child . . .
> And became blind.

> Oh said the second
> I always turn it off
> I want some peace
> In my own house
> Went to the radio, wiped off some dust
> And became deaf.

> Oh said the third one
> I've nothing to add
> To make this decision
> Is too much for me
> Went to the sofa, turned around
> And became mute.

> We've blessed their gifts
> And buried them together.[90]

This poetic negation will, of course, not prevent the ever-increasing popularity of the three monkeys in any shape or form on an ever expanding international basis. The three sacred and wise little monkeys have lost their innocence and have become almost a negative symbol—perhaps one of the most fascinating expressions of life's ambivalence. It is appropriate, then, that our last example, which shows the three monkeys as a book mark from Pennsylvania,[91] is almost an entire reversal of the old Japanese wisdom, perhaps even a return to the English variant from the year 1623: "Heare all, see all, and hold thee still / If peace desirest with thy will." This version is also known as "Hear all, see all, say now't."[92] We might well have a case here where the European proverb of selfishness is attached to an altered version of the three monkeys from Japan, a truly fascinating mixture of the folk speech, thought, and art of various cultures and times.

# 6 History and Interpretation of a Proverb About Human Nature
## Big Fish Eat Little Fish

Paremiology or the study of proverbs is an international science based on synchronic and diachronic research methods. Nowhere is this more obvious than in the investigation of the origin, history, dissemination, function, and meaning of an individual proverb such as "Big fish eat little fish." What at first glance might appear to be only another trite piece of traditional wisdom in the language of a particular region or country quickly proves to have roots that extend back to the beginning of civilization. Just like individual basic words, certain proverbs can be traced back to the first written records of antiquity, and in some cases it can be shown that such a proverb was transmitted from one century and tongue to another so that it is now found throughout virtually all the world.

Even though one cannot completely rule out polygenesis for such internationally disseminated proverbs, it is usually possible to prove through painstaking comparative research that such proverbs go back to classical antiquity or even to the earlier Sumerian proverbs that were recorded on extant cuneiform tablets.[1] We can thus state that at least some proverbs have definite Indo-European origins and that they were transmitted orally and in writing over centuries to a multitude of national languages and their dialects.[2] The fact that such proverbs might also be found in non-Indo-European languages adds to the complexity of the picture, since linguistic and cultural borrowing might have taken place. But the possibility of an independent origin must be taken into consideration, since a basic phenomenon, observation, or experience could well result in similar or even identical verbalizations in different places of the world that caught on and became proverbs.

Thus it is not clear whether the Chinese proverb, "The large fish eat the small; the small fish eat the water insects; the water insects eat water plants and mud"[3] or its slight variations, "The big fish eat the little fish, the little fish eat the water-insects, and the water-insects eat the weeds and the mud"[4] and "The big fish eat the little ones, the little ones eat the shrimps, and the shrimps are forced to eat mud"[5] is related to our shorter fish proverb. The Indo-European proverb does not contain this tripartite structure; in fact it emphasizes only the basic observation that the larger and stronger will devour (i.e. conquer) the smaller and weaker. These longer Chinese variants might therefore be indigenous to this area of the world, or, of course, there is a chance that the shorter proverb of our civilization was lengthened in China. To determine what happened, the history of the Chinese proverb needs to be studied in great detail, something that goes beyond the limited scholarly abilities of most Westerners. The fact that the American author Carl Sandburg used a proverb in his epic poem *The People, Yes* (1936) that is very similar to the third Chinese variant cited above does not help to resolve this issue either. Sandburg states that "The big fish eat the little fish, the little fish eat shrimps and the shrimps eat mud,"[6] and this proverb is followed by many more proverbial utterances and idioms. Since this literary work reflects the immigrant language and mentality of Sandburg's Chicago and its melting pot of people, it seems safe to assume that he is quoting the English translation of a Chinese proverb without identifying it as such. This text might in fact be current among the American Chinese population, and perhaps it has gained some currency among bilingual American people in English as well. However, it does not enjoy wider currency in this country and is definitely a loan translation from the Chinese. A scholar could well have concluded that Sandburg was simply adding his own thought to the standard proverb "The big fish eat the little fish" when in fact he is citing the English version of a popular Chinese proverb. These are the pitfalls of proverb research that is not based on international and multi-cultural considerations.

There is also the problem of the Turkish proverb "The large fish eats the little fish"[7] which, except for its singular use of the noun, is identical to the standard Western proverb. And yet Turkish belongs to the Altaic language family and is far removed from the Indo-European language group. In this case we have to consider the possibility of polygenesis until someone traces the history of the Turkish text. Perhaps we are not far from the truth if we suspect a loan translation of the proverb into Turkish at a time when Turks came in close contact with the Indo-Europeans, something that occurred a great deal during the history of the Turkish people. A third example of a non-Indo-European proverb is this Hausa text from Africa: "Fish, be ashamed as you do not become fat except by eating the flesh of your kin."[8] This text is quite different in that it seems to explain the phenomenon of big fish eating little fish in a moralistic fashion. There is a good chance that this text did originate independently in Africa. Missionaries or colonists who would have brought the Western proverb with them would doubtlessly have disseminated their much shorter text. It appears safe to assume a separate origin of the proverb until it can be proven otherwise.

When we turn to the Indo-European side of the issue, it immediately becomes clear that there must be some common origin for the numerous parallel proverbs in the many languages and dialects. In his recent polyglot proverb collection Jerzy Gluski lists six equivalent texts for such major languages as English, French, German, Italian, Spanish, and Russian:

English: The great fish eat up the small.
French: Les gros poissons mangent les petits.
German: Die grossen Fische fressen die kleinen.
Italian: I pesci grossi mangiano i piccini.
Spanish: Los peces grandes se comen a los chicos.
Russian: Bol'shaia ryba malen'kuiu tselikom glotaet.[9]

And in an appendix of Latin proverbs he also cites "Piscem vorat maior minorem"[10] (The larger fish eats the smaller fish), indicating this as a common source for these proverbs. The major proverb dictionary for the Germanic and Romance languages lists thirty texts including Danish, Icelandic, Norwegian, Swedish, and many others.[11] The Danish proverb, "De store Fiske aede de smaa, Saa ligge de under, som mindst formaae" (The big fish eat the little, thus they succumb who are the least capable), once again goes beyond the basic proverb by adding an explanatory comment. This addition is doubtlessly Danish in origin and helps to clarify the universal meaning of the basic proverb text, which is today usually quoted by itself.

There is no room here to trace the history of the proverb in every national language and its dialects. We will limit ourselves to establishing the development of the English proverb from ancient times to its survival in the modern age and leave the rest to scholars elsewhere in the world. What this limited survey entails was already indirectly expressed by the nineteenth century French paremiologist Pierre-Marie Quitard who in 1842 quoted the French proverb with the following explanation as to its meaning and history:

POISSON—*Les gros poissons mangent les petits.*

Les puissants oppriment les faibles.—Ce proverbe, commun à presque toutes les langues modernes, tant la vérité qu'il exprime est généralement reconnue, était très usité parmi les Grecs et les Latins, qui disaient encore: *Vivre en poisson,* pour signifier n'avoir d'autre loi que celle du plus fort; mais il n'avait pas pris naissance chez ces peuples; il est probable qu'il leur était venu des Indiens, car il se trouve dans l'*Histoire du poisson,* épisode du Mahabharata, poëme épique sanscrit qui doit compter trente-huit siècles d'existence d'après les calculs du savant Wilkins, et qui n'en peut compter moins de trente d'apres l'opinion la plus circonspecte.[12]

(FISH—*The big fish eat the little.*

The powerful oppress the weak.—This proverb, common to almost all modern languages, whose truth is generally recognized, was very much in use among the Greeks and Romans, who also said: *To live like fish,* to indicate having no other law but that of the strongest; but it did not originate among these people; it is likely that it came to them from the Indian people, for it is found in the *History of Fish,* an episode in the Sanskrit epic poem of the *Mahabharata,* which according to the calculations of the scholar Wilkins must be thirty-eight centuries old, and which according to the most cautious opinion cannot be less than thirty centuries old.)

This statement indicates that, although we will have to look far beyond the Latin origin of the proverb suggested by Jerzy Gluski, the

Latin language was instrumental in the dissemination of the proverb into the vernacular Western European languages. Some tracing of roots was done in a short but superb philological article "'Lest Men, Like Fishes'" by Wilfrid Parsons in 1945.[13] He was able to show that the sources of the proverb go back to ancient Sanskrit, Greek, and Hebrew sources, and we will present some of the most important steps here by borrowing from Parsons' findings and adding to them.

The earliest recorded allusion to the proverb "Big fish eat little fish" is to be found in the didactic poem *Works and Days* by the Greek writer Hesiod of the eighth century B.C. In a chapter called "An Exhortation to Justice" he states that while animals live in violent and lawless disorder, men have laws and justice to create an orderly society:

> For this law is allotted to men by Zeus, son of Kronos:
> fish and beasts of the wild and birds that fly in the air
> eat one another, since Justice has no dwelling among them;
> but to men he gives Justice, which is the greatest of blessings.
> If one is willing to speak what he sees to be justice, what he
> knows is the right thing, far-seeing Zeus grants him a blessed life.
> But if he witnesses falsely and willfully perjures himself,
> being a liar, a harmer of Justice, incurably blind,
> he is leaving his family a gloomier future existence.
> He who swears truly creates for his family future prosperity.[14]

The necessity of justice and the need for a responsible form of government also led the unknown author (Vyasa?) of the Sanskrit epic *Mahabharata* (600 B.C.–200 A.D.) to a comparison of the unruly animal world with that of a kingdom ruled and protected by a good king. Anarchy is considered the greatest evil, and only solid government with a king can prevent such chaos:

> For these reasons the gods created kings for protecting the people.
> If there were no king on Earth for wielding the rod of chastise-
> ment, the strong would then have preyed on the weak after the
> manner of fishes in the water. It hath been heard by us that men,
> in days of old, in consequence of anarchy, met with destruction,
> devouring one another like stronger fishes devouring the weaker
> ones in the water.[15]

About two pages later the author explains this statement further, returning several times to the thought of the strong devouring the weak as the basic meaning of the fish metaphor:

> The duties of all men, O thou of great wisdom, may be seen to
> have their root in the king. It is through fear of the king only that

men do not devour one another. It is the king that brings peace on Earth, through due observation of duties, by checking all disregard for wholesome restraints and all kinds of lust. Achieving this, he shines in glory. As, O king, all creatures become unable to see one another and sink in utter darkness if the sun and the moon do not rise, as fishes in shallow water and birds in a spot safe from danger dart and rove as they please (for a time) and repeatedly attack and grind one another with force and then meet with certain destruction, even so men sink in utter darkness and meet with destruction if they have no king to protect them, like a herd of cattle without the herdsman to look after them. If the king did not exercise the duty of protection, the strong would forcibly appropriate the possessions of the weak, and if the latter refuse to surrender them with ease, their very lives would be taken.[16]

In a fascinating article on "The Hindu Theory of the State" Benoy Kumar Sarkar points out that Hindu political thinkers differentiated the state from the non-state, the latter being absolute anarchy or "mâtsya-nyâya" (the logic of the fish). Without the control of the government, unequal strengths will appear everywhere and "when the one can overpower the other, there is generated a field for the operation of the logic of the fish and the survival of the fittest."[17]

The same thought is also expressed by the Hebrew prophet Habakkuk of the seventh century B.C. in the Old Testament. He too saw violence and destruction all around him, since law and order were missing among the nations and their people. In Habakkuk 1:13–14 the prophet calls in despair upon his God to explain this logic of the fish so rampant among mankind:

> Thou who are of purer eyes than to behold evil
>     and canst not look on wrong,
> why dost thou look on faithless men,
>     and art silent when the wicked swallows up
>     the man more righteous than he?
> For thou makest men like the fish of the sea,
>     like crawling things that have no ruler.

And in the tractate *Abodah Zarah* (strange worship, idolatry) from about 450 B.C. in the Babylonian Talmud we have a fascinating explanation of this Biblical reference:

> Rab Judah says in the name of Samuel: Why is it written, *And Thou makest man as the fishes of the sea, and as the creeping things, that have no ruler over them?* Why is man here compared to the fishes of the sea? To tell you, just as the fishes of the sea, as soon as they

come on to dry land, die, so also man, as soon as he abandons the Torah and the precepts [incurs destruction]. Another explanation: Just as the fishes of the sea, as soon as the sun scorches them, die; so man, when struck by the sun, dies. This can be applied to the present world, or to the future world. . . . Another explanation: Just as among fish of the sea, the greater swallow up the smaller ones, so with men, were it not for fear of the government, men would swallow each other alive. This is just what we learnt: R. Hanina, the Deputy High Priest, said, Pray for the welfare of the government, for were it not for the fear thereof, men would swallow each other alive.[18]

The knowledgable translator and editor of the Talmud, Rabbi I. Epstein, adds in a footnote William Shakespeare's lines spoken by Marcius in *Coriolanus*, Act I, Scene 1:

> What's the matter,
> That in these several places of the city
> You cry against the noble senate, who,
> Under the gods, keep you in awe, which else
> Would feed on one another?

Even though Shakespeare might have been aware of the Talmud passage, Epstein hastens to add that he is perhaps alluding to yet another biblical verse, Psalm 124:2–3, which, though not mentioning the fish metaphor either, clearly seems to be a reference to it:

> If it had not been the Lord who was for us,
> When men rose up against us,
> Then they had swallowed us up alive,
> When their wrath was kindled against us.

From these early textual references it becomes obvious that this fish metaphor is part of a common tradition of the Indo-European people. While the references from the Sanskrit writings had little influence on the Western tongues, the uses of the metaphor in the Old Testament, the Talmud, and in Greek literature were of great consequence, even though the religious writings do not quote the idea of the logic of the fish in the form of a bona fide proverb as yet. This step from a vivid metaphor to a precise metaphorical proverb must have taken place when people wanted to express its basic meaning without contextualizing it. The idea that the strong devour the weak or that the rich exploit the poor was a commonplace one, and the proverb "Big fish eat little fish" could represent the entire realm of what Charles Darwin later called the survival of the fittest, be it in the animal or the human world.

In Greek literature Aristotle quotes the proverb without the political implications that were expressed in the references cited thus far:

> The basse and the grey mullet are bitter enemies, but they swarm together at certain times; for at times not only do fishes of the same species swarm together, but also those whose feeding-grounds are identical or adjacent, if the food-supply be abundant. The grey mullet is often found alive with its tail lopped off, and the conger with all that part of its body removed that lies to the rear of the vent; in the case of the mullet the injury is wrought by the basse, in that of the conger-eel by the muraena. There is war between the larger and the lesser fishes: for the big fishes prey on the little ones.[19]

More than a century later the Greek historian Polybius writes in a more contextualized fashion of people in general, "They deserve to be said to live like fishes, among which, they say, although they are of the same kind, the destruction of the lesser becomes the sustenance and life of the greater."[20] This social interpretation with an underlying moralistic tone is also expressed in the first century B.C. by the Roman scholar and writer Varro: "Qui pote, plus urget, piscis ut saepe minutas magna comest"[21] (He who is strongest oppresses, as the great fish often eats the lesser). Eventually the common Latin text became "Piscem vorat maior minorem"[22] (The larger fish eats the smaller fish). It survived in this standard form until the Latin of the Middle Ages, though such minor variants as "Grandibus exigui sunt pisces piscibus esca" (Small fish are food for large fish) and "Pisces maiores constat glutire minores: Sic homo maioris sepe fit esca minor"[23] (It is evident that larger fish eat smaller ones: Thus a smaller man may often be food for a larger one) also appear, the latter drawing once again a parallel between animal and human behavior.

In addition to the appearance of Greek and Latin references to the proverb in secular literature and in medieval Latin proverb collections, we must also take into account the considerable influence the early church fathers had in helping to spread the knowledge of this proverbial metaphor and proverb through their Greek and Latin treatises. Eventually much of their wisdom filtered down into the vernacular and became current among larger groups of the population. Add to this the great importance of the Bible with its Habakkuk passage, and we can see how this often used Greek and Latin phrase was accepted in translation by people speaking the developing European languages. Wilfrid Parsons and recently also Manfred Bambeck[24] have assembled an impressive number of such patristic references to the proverb, of which a few examples must suffice here. It will become clear that these texts continue the social, political, and moralistic interpretations we found in the very early Sanskrit, Greek, and Hebrew quotations.

The second century Christian philosopher Athenagoras vehemently chastised illicit sexual behavior using the fish metaphor in a drastic way:

> These adulterers and pederasts defame the eunuchs and the once-married, while they themselves live like fishes; for these swallow up whatever falls in their way, and the stronger pursues the weaker. Indeed, this is to feed on human flesh, to do violence to the very laws which you and your ancestors, with due care for all that is fair and right, have enacted.[25]

St. Basil (330?–379?) shows in his writings that men act like fish, one preying on the other so that life is reduced to repeated sequences of the larger devouring the smaller. The biggest vice in all of this seems to be avarice or greed, coupled with the lust for power, something that we will later see in more modern texts and pictorial representations as well.

> The greater number of the fishes devour one another and the smaller among them is the food of the greater. And if it ever happens that one which has overcome a lesser becomes the prey of a still greater, then both go into the belly of the last one. What else do we men do in tyrannizing over (καταδυναστεία) inferiors? And how does he differ from the last fish, who out of insatiable greed for wealth hides the weak within the unslaked bounds of his avarice?[26]

Another Greek church father, St. John Chrysostom (345?–407) also comments on this constant power struggle, arguing with reference to Habakkuk that a government with a king is necessary to control such animalistic behavior.

> Because of our depravity there was need of government. . . .
> There is a king that we may not be like reptiles; a king that like fishes we may not devour one another.[27]

From the Western church fathers writing in Latin let us quote at least two passages, one from St. Ambrose (340–397) and one from St.

Augustine (354–430). The commentary by St. Ambrose is very similar to that of St. Basil since he refers to the same place in the hexaemeron (the six-day period of the Biblical creation) that St. Basil did:

> But there are those who devour each other and feed on their own flesh. The lesser among them is the food of the greater, and again this greater is attacked by a stronger and in turn the attacker of one becomes the food of still another. Thus it happens that when he has devoured one, he is devoured by another and both come into the one belly, the devourer and his prey, and there is in the same insides a meeting of the prey and its punishment. . . . Because they are given for man's use, they are also a sign that in them we may see our vicious behavior, and may take warning from the example of them, lest anyone stronger oppress the lesser, and thus afford an example for injustice to a still stronger.[28]

And St. Augustine also echoes this thought of a continuous chain devouring each other:

> The sea is said to be the world, bitter with salt, tossed by tempests, where men through their perverse and evil lusts become like the fishes devouring each other . . . and when one bigger fish has devoured a lesser, he is also devoured by a bigger still. . . . O piscis male, praedam vis de parvo, praeda efficieris magno [O wicked fish, you take from the small so that you may become large].[29]

And finally, to bring us closer to the beginning of the appearance of the proverb in the English language, let us notice Archbishop Heriveus of Reims's early tenth-century commentary on the vanished Carolingean empire and the socio-political misery that came from it:

> You see before you the anger of the Lord. . . . Towns have been depopulated, monasteries ruined or burnt, the fields turned into deserts. . . . As the first men lived without law, they were kept from evil doing by no fear . . . so now, abandoning all fear of human and divine laws, they despise the commands of the Bishops, and each one does what he wills: the stronger oppresses the weaker, and men are like the fish of the sea which everywhere are devoured by each other.[30]

Here the old Hindu logic of the fish appears again, and the proverb is used to express violence and anarchy in an unmistaken image.

In addition to Greek and Latin secular or patristic writings containing references of the proverb, there is a third type of written tradition to be considered that will be of consequence for the final appearance of the proverb in so many vernacular languages. This is the incredibly

popular pseudo-scientific work commonly called *Physiologus*. It originated around 200 A.D. in Alexandria, and the Greek original was
translated into Latin in the fourth century. The work contains about
fifty descriptions of animals, and since their life habits are interpreted
as allegories of scriptural passages, it was translated into just about
every European vernacular language. The manuscript tradition of the
*Physiologus* or "Bestiary" as it is often referred to is extremely complex
and is of no consequence here.[31] We present the story of the whale
(aspidoceleon or asp-turtle) from one of the most complete fourth or
fifth century Latin manuscripts, in an English translation. It will be
seen that the whale is described as the big fish eating the little fish:

> Physiologus spoke of a certain whale in the sea called the aspi-
> doceleon that is exceedingly large like an island, heavier than
> sand, and is a figure of the devil. Ignorant sailors tie their ships to
> the beast as to an island and plant their anchors and stakes in it.
> They light their cooking fires on the whale but, when he feels the
> heat, he urinates and plunges into the depths, sinking all the
> ships. You also, O man, if you fix and bind yourself to the hope
> of the devil, he will plunge you along with himself into hell-fire.
>     The whale has another nature: when he grows hungry he opens
> his mouth very wide and many a good fragrance comes out of his
> mouth. Tiny little fish, catching the scent, follow it and gather
> together in the mouth of that huge whale, who closes his mouth
> when it is full and swallows all those tiny little fish, by which is
> meant those small in faith. We do not find the larger and perfect
> fish approaching the whale, for the perfect ones have achieved the
> highest degree. Indeed, Paul said, "We are not ignorant of his
> cunning" [II Cor. 2:11]. Job is a most perfect fish as are Moses and
> the other prophets. Joseph fled the huge whale, that is, the wife
> of the prince of the cooks, as is written in Genesis [Gen. 39]. Like-
> wise, Thecla fled Thamyridus, Susanna the two wicked old men of
> Babylon, Esther and Judith fled Artaxerxes and Holofernes. The
> three boys fled the King Nebuchadnezzar, the huge whale [Dan.
> 3], and Sara the daughter of Raguelis fled Nasmodeus (as in To-
> bia). Physiologus, therefore, spoke well of the aspidoceleon, the
> great whale.[32]

In addition to the popular tale of the whale being mistaken for an
island and then taking ship and sailors to their doom at the bottom of
the sea,[33] there is a second comment on the nature of the whale.
Obviously he is the biggest fish of them all; he is seen to be evil, and he
tricks the smaller fish (here perhaps the sinners) by his sweet breath
(evil cunning) into his mouth (damnation or even death). Thus the fish

appear to be swimming voluntarily into the beast's (devil's) mouth since they are attracted to the sweet-smelling monster.

This interpretation is also obvious from the earliest illustrations of the "Big fish eat little fish" motif. In his splendid book *Animals in Art and Thought to the End of the Middle Ages*, Francis Klingender includes three such drawings of the dual tale about the whale as an island and as an eater of small fish, which he found in Latin *Physiologus* manuscripts from the twelfth century. While one of the illustrations shows the ship and the fire on the whale with the whale devouring several fish, the other illustration presents the whale swallowing up many small fish head first while at the same time starting to capsize the ship.[34] Even to the present day we will continue to see small fish entering the big fish's mouth head first, which might be interpreted as a sign of deception. Other small fish will definitely be pursued by the big fish, symbolizing their involuntary capture by an aggressive and stronger rival.

The evil whale becomes the devil and hell in the earliest Old English *Physiologus* dating from the second half of the eighth century, for which I cite James Pitman's excellent poetic translation of "The Whale (Asp Turtle)":

> Another trait he has,
> This proud sea-swimmer, still more marvelous.
> When hunger grips the monster on the deep,
> Making him long for food, his gaping mouth
> The ocean-warder opens, stretching wide
> His monstrous lips; and from his cavernous maw
> Sends an entrancing odor. This sweet scent,
> Deceiving other fishes, lures them on
> In swiftly moving schools toward that fell place
> Whence comes the perfume. There, unwary host,
> They enter in, until the yawning mouth
> Is filled to overflowing, when, at once,
> Trapping their prey, the fearful jaws snap shut.
>   So, in this fleeting earthly time, each man
> Who orders heedlessly his mortal life
> Lets a sweet odor, some beguiling wish,
> Entice him, so that in the eyes of God,
> The King of glory, his iniquities
> Make him abhorrent. After death for him
> The all-accursed devil opens hell—
> Opens for all who in their folly here
> Let pleasures of the body overcome
> Their spirits' guidance. When the wily fiend

Into his hold beside the fiery lake
With evil craft has led those erring ones
Who cleave to him, sore laden with their sins,
Those who in earthly life have hearkened well
To his instruction, after death close shut
He snaps those woful jaws, the gates of hell.
Whoever enters there has no relief,
Nor may he any more escape his doom
And thence depart, then can the swimming fish
Elude the monster.
           Therefore it is [best
And] altogether [right for each of us
To serve and honor God,] the Lord of lords,
And always in our every word and deed
To combat devils, that we may at last
Behold the King of glory. In this time
Of transitory things, then, let us seek
Peace and salvation from him, that we may
Rejoice for ever in so dear a Lord,
And praise his glory everlastingly.[35]

Here the old *Physiologus* text has become a moral and religious lesson, where bad people are swallowed up by ultimate evil, somewhat reminiscent of our earlier references indicating the evil logic of the fish where anarchy rules.

Other Old English bestiaries carried on this vivid scene of the whale eating up little fish,[36] yet nowhere was I able to find a vernacular English rendering of the Latin proverb "Piscem vorat maior minorem." Since it does not appear in the Latin original of the *Physiologus* either, the scribes must not have felt free to include its early English text. Or had the Latin proverb not yet become current in the developing language? Had no monk at a monastic school included the Latin proverb as a translation exercise for his pupils? We know that many Latin proverbs entered the vernacular languages in that fashion.[37] Whenever this occurred for the proverb of the fish (and we rule out polygenesis in this case), it was able to catch on quickly since its underlying metaphor was known through the Old Testament and the bestiaries and to the educated clergy through the treatises of the church fathers. Its basic meaning of the larger and stronger having control to the point of destruction over the smaller and weaker was obvious, and its metaphor comprehensible to everyone who looked at nature with open eyes. Just as occurred with the other European vernacular languages, the Latin proverb must have been translated into English in the early Middle Ages where it eventually gained some currency and began to appear in written documents.

For the English language the earliest written version of the proverb was located by Bartlett Jere Whiting, whose untiring paremiographic work based on historical principles has made him the greatest proverb collector of the Anglo-American language. Any scholar dealing with the origin and history of English proverbs will find Whiting's proverb dictionaries absolutely invaluable. I owe some of the following references from English and American works to him and to some others.[38] Whiting found the first English quotation of the proverb in an Old English homily on St. Andrew from the twelfth century. It is interesting to note that the scribe first quotes a variant of the Latin proverb and then gives his English translation: "Item: in mari pisces maiores deuorant minores. Est—sone þe more fishes in þe se eten þe lasse." This is probably a clear indication that the proverb of "Big fish eating little fish" came into the English language via a loan translation from the medieval Latin. The religious writer of this homily interprets the meaning of the proverb in the fashion of the earlier religious writings by the prophets and church fathers mentioned above, with a particular emphasis on the dichotomy of rich and poor, as the following excerpt in modern English shows:

> And on account of such flowing and such ebbing the prophet calleth this world a sea, thus saying, *Mirabiles elationes maris, &c.* Marvellous are the 'out-sendings' of the sea, and wonderful is our Lord in virtue. *Item: in mare pisces majores devorant minores.* Again, the greater fishes in the sea eat the smaller and live on them. So in this world do the rich who are lords, destroy the poor men who are underlings, and moreover live on them and obtain from their labour hounds and hawks and horses and weapons and spotted and grey (fur) and dainty meats and drinks, and all that they possess they have from their common labours.[39]

It should also be noted here that the big fish as the rich and the small fish as the poor later gave rise to a variant of the fish proverb in the form of "The rich eate the poore" dating from 1593.[40] This proverb, however, has not competed favorably with the more metaphorical and universal "Big fish eat little fish."

The next appearance of the proverb is in the epic poem *Kyng Alisaunder* from about the year 1300, depicting the life of Alexander the Great in much detail. Here the king makes a straightforward observation on the sea and includes a slight variant of the proverb. In fact, since the

editor of the epic has published two manuscripts in parallel arrangement, we can quote two wordings of the proverb:

> He say þe ekeris wonynge
> And þe fysches lotynge
> How eueriche oþer mette
> And þe more þe lasse frete

> He seiȝ þe jkeres woniynge
> And þe fisshes lotyinge,
> Hou euery oþer gan mete,
> And þe more þe lesse gan frete.[41]

> (He speaks of the waiting sea-monster
> And the lurking fish
> How everyone meets the other
> And the greater eats the lesser.)

What we see here is that a proverb, and certainly one translated from a
foreign language, does not immediately take on an absolutely rigid
form. It takes time until the proper proverbial wording is found. The
proverb to this day is usually cited in one of the following slight
variants: "The great fish eat the small," "The great fish eat up the
small," "The great fish devour the less," and perhaps the two most
popular, "Great fish eat little fish" and "Big fish eat little fish," where
the parallel structure prevalent in so many proverbs is at its best.

Other variants continued to appear as "fischis fretes of þe lesse"[42]
(Fish devour the smaller) in a fourteenth century poem and "þe more
fishes swelewen þe lasse"[43] (The larger fish swallow the smaller) in a
sermon about evil and sin by John Wycliffe (ca. 1320–1384). But in a
religious tract from about 1415 entitled *The Lantern of Light*, which
spells out the principal tenets of Wycliffe's followers, we find the
proverb yet again in another wording:

> þe fisches þat swymmen in þis see. ben alle þe peple þat lyuen in
> þis world / boþe good & yuel of euery degree. of iche staate tem-
> perel or spirituel / But as þe greet fisches eeten þe smale. so miȝti
> riche men of þis world / deuouren þe pore to her bare boon. eet-
> ing þe moselles þat hem beest likeþ / as þe wise man seiþ.[44]

> (The fish that swim in the sea are all the people that live in this
> world, both good and evil of every degree, of each state temporal
> or spiritual. But as the great fish eat the small, so mighty rich men
> of this world devour the poor to their bare bone, eating the mor-
> sels that they like best, as the wise man says.)

This moralistic treatise on good and evil uses the proverb "þe greet
fisches eeten þe smale" once again to explain the injustice of the world.

Habakkuk's description of man being like fish is quoted later on, and the rich are scolded for treating the poor in such an unfair, beast-like manner. Such early uses of the proverb are clear indications of its original religious and moralistic meaning, even while it was being used to bring about more social justice.

No wonder that in the anonymous morality play *The Castell of Perseverance* (ca. 1425) death can quote the identical proverb to characterize people. They live like fish, they are proud and go after riches, while they forget death who will certainly come as surely as bigger fish will appear:

> but now al-most I am for-ʒete;
>     men, of deth, holde no tale;
> in coveytyse here good þey gete;
>     þe gretë fyschys ete þe smale;
> but whane I dele my dernë dette,
>     þo prowdë men I shal a-vale:
> hem schal helpyn, noþer mel nor mete,
>     tyl þey be drewyn to dethys dale:
>         my lawë þei schul lerne.
>     þer ne is peny nor pownde
>     þat any of ʒou schal sauë sownde;
>     tyl ʒe be grauyn vndyr grownde,
>         þer may no man me werne.[45]

> (but now I [death] am almost forgotten;
> men take no account of death;
> through greed they acquire goods on earth;
> the great fish eat the small;
> but when I collect my last debt,
> I shall humble proud men:
> I shall help them neither with meal or meat,
> till they be drawn to death's dale:
> my law they shall learn.
> There is not penny or pound
> that shall soundly save any of you;
> till you be buried under ground,
> where no man may refuse me.)

The same picture of the evil world is also presented in a minisermon by a bishop in yet another anonymous morality play appropriately called *Pride of Life* (ca. 1450). Here the fear of God has vanished, truth has disappeared, oaths are false, lechery and gluttony are everywhere, and the rich are once again particularly evil and blind to the plight of the poor:

Paraventur men halt me a fol
　　To sig þat sot tal;
þai farit as fiscis in a pol
　　þe gret eteit þe smal.

Ric men spart for noþing
　　To do þe por wrong;
þai þingit not on hir ending
　　Ne on Det þat is so strong.[46]

(Perhaps men consider me a fool
To say this silly thing;
They move like fish in a pool
The great eat the small.

Rich men stop at nothing
To do wrong to the poor;
They do not think about their end
Nor about death that is so strong.)

While such memento mori descriptions are appropriate to the religious undertones of these early works, John Lydgate's repeated use of the proverb is more secular. Even though he deviates in wording from the by now common form "The great fish eat the little" due to such poetic considerations as rhyme, he is nevertheless clearly cognizant of the proverb. In his long poem "A Disputation between a Horse, a Sheepe and a Goose for Superioritie (ca. 1440) he speaks explicitly of the oppression that occurs among animals and mankind:

Fortunes cours dyversly is dressid
　　Bi liknessis of many othir tale;
Man, best, & fowle & fisshis been oppressid
　　In ther natur bi female or bi male;
　　Of grettest fissh devourid been the smale,
Which in natur is a ful straunge guyse,
　　To seen a Kokkow mordre a Nityngale,
An innocent brid of hattreede to despise.[47]

Basically the same rendering of the proverb also appears in Lydgate's poetic fable "The Tale of the Hownde and the Shepe groundyd ayen periune & false wytnes founde by Isopus" (ca. 1449). Here he tells of the wolf, dog, and kite preying on the sheep just as the poor people are devoured by the rich. In fact, we can also see here the beginning of the later proverb "The rich eat the poor," which in this form stems from 1593, as cited above:

The sheepe thus deyd, his body al to-rent,
　　The ravenous wolf the kareyne did assaile;

The hound recouered his par by iugement;
  The false kyte cast hym nat to faile,
  To have a repast vpon his adventaile.
Thus in this world by extorcion veriliche
Poore folk be devoured alwey by the riche.

By examples, in stewes long and large,
  Of grete fissh devoured bien the smale.
Hardy is the bote that stryvith agenst the barge.
  To ouerpress a pore man the riche set no tale.
  A cloth sakke stuffid, shame it is to pike a male.
What nedith the see to borwe of smale rivers,
Or a grete barne to borow of strait garners?[48]

And in a similar rewriting of an Aesopic fable "The Tale of the Wolfe and the Lambe" (ca. 1449), Lydgate starts once again with a version of the proverb changed slightly due to rhyme considerations and then explains via the example of the wolf devouring the sheep:

Grete pykes, þat swymme in large stewes,
  Smaller fysshe most felly þey deuour.
Who haþe most myght, þe febler gladly sewes:
  The pore haþe few hys party to socour.
  The rauenous wolf open þe lambe doþe lour;
Of whyche Isopus in hys booke
Fully notably thys example he toke.[49]

Obviously reminiscent of two Aesopic fables and perhaps even influenced by this rendering from Lydgate are the following verses in the chapter "Of ryches vnprofytable" in Alexander Barclay's The Ship of Fools (1509), which is a freely translated adaptation of Sebastian Brant's Narrenschiff (1494). Barclay addresses the conflict between rich and poor and compares the greed of the rich to the way the wolf eats sheep. This unfair behavior also brings to mind our proverb in duplicate form as "The wolfe etes the shepe, the great fysshe the small":

The ryche are rewarded with gyftis of dyuerse sorte
With Capons and Conyes delycious of sent
But the pore caytyf abydeth without confort
Though he moste nede haue: none doth hym present
The fat pygge is baast, the lene cony is brent
He that nought hathe, shall so alway byde pore
But he that ouer moche hath, yet shall haue more
The wolfe etis the shepe, the great fysshe the small
The hare with the houndes vexed ar and frayde
he that hath halfe nedes wyll haue all
The ryche mannes pleasour can nat be denayde

Be the pore wroth, or be he well apayde
Fere causeth hym sende vnto the ryches hous
His mete from his owne mouth, if it be delycious

And yet is this ryche caytyf nat content
Though he haue all yet wolde he haue more.[50]

Barclay used the proverb one more time in his third "Ecloge of the misery and behauiour of Court and Courtiers" (ca. 1513–14) in which the simple shepherd Coridon sums up the lord (rich) and servant (poor) relationship with the statement:

But this hath bene sene forsooth and euer shall,
That the greater fishe deuoureth vp the small[51]

The fact that Coridon uses an introductory formula to state his wisdom can be taken as an indication that "The great fish eats (devours) the small" was definitely considered to be a proverb by the end of the fifteenth century.

We would thus expect the proverb to appear in sixteenth century proverb collections, but it does not yet appear in John Heywood's collection *A Dialogue of Proverbs* (1546).[52] About thirty years later, however, it is included in John Florio's Italian-English *Florio. His firste Fruites: which yeelde familiar speech, merie Prouerbes, wittie Sentences, and golden sayings* (1578) in the juxtaposition: "El pesce grande, mangia el piccolo.—The great fishe eateth the little."[53] Obviously the Latin proverb remained in the Italian language, and the fact that Florio lists the English equivalent shows again that it had long been accepted into the English vernacular as well. It is strange, however, that Randle Cotgrave in his *Dictionarie of the French and English Tongves* (1611) cites only the French version of the proverb without giving the English parallel as he does for others: "Les gros poissons mangent les petis: . . . Justly applyed to the vniust world, wherein the rich deuoure the poore, the strong the weake, the mightie the meane."[54] Our guess is that the English proverb was inadvertently omitted, for judging by the comments interpreting the proverb it is hard to imagine that Cotgrave did not know it. But all these matters are certainly solved by the first truly polyglot assembly of "Big fish eat little fish" proverbs in Thomas Draxe's erudite *Bibliotheca Scholastica Instrvctissima. Or, A Treasurie of ancient Adagies, and sententious Prouerbes, selected out of the English, Greeke, Latine, French, Italian and Spanish* (1616). Among the variants and equivalents that fit our discussion are, in the order in which they appear by Draxe:

The pleasures of the mightie, are the teares of the poore.
Serpens nisi serpentem edit, non fit Draco.
The noble man, the Spider; and the countryman, the Flie.
The great fish eateth up the small.
Piscem minorem, major piscis devorat.[55]

We can easily add such proverbs as "The little cannot be great unless he devours many," "There would be no great ones if there were no little ones," "The rich devour the poor, the strong the weak" (already cited above), "A serpent must eat another serpent before it can become a dragon" (see Latin version above), and "Great trees keep under the little ones" for the English language alone,[56] but each of these has a history of its own and simply couches the same idea of the strong oppressing the weak in another metaphor.

But let us make at least a small comment on the "serpent" proverb, which is also quoted by Draxe, since it also goes back to classical antiquity, was known in medieval Latin, and was then translated into vernacular languages. Erasmus of Rotterdam's famous *Adagia* (1500ff.) included it in Greek and Latin. This great humanistic scholar obviously also alluded to our beastly fish in his commentary on the viperous dragon:

> [A]    *Serpens Ni Edat Serpentem, Draco Non Fiet*
> Potentes aliorum damnis crescunt, et optimatum fortunae non in tantum augerentur, nisi essent quos exugerent. [B] Quemadmodum inter pisces et beluas maiores viuunt laniatu minorum. [C] Quanquam mihi quidem et hoc dictum fecem vulgi videtur olere.[57]
>
> ([A]    *Unless a serpent eat a serpent, it will not become*
>             *a dragon*
> They [people] become powerful by hurting others, and their fortunes will not be as great as desired unless they drain those [people] whom they would be. [B] Just as among the fish and the beasts the larger live by mangling of the smaller. [C] Although to me in truth this dictum in general seems to smell of feces.)

The inclusion of the snake proverb with an allusion to our fish-proverb in this extremely important proverb collection of the sixteenth century played a significant role in spreading both proverbs into the vernacular languages. We would conjecture that the English proverb "The little cannot be great, unlesse he devoure many,"[58] which George Herbert included in his *Outlandish Proverbs* (1640) is but a watered down version of the serpent proverb brought into connection with "Big fish eat little fish." The serpent-dragon could even be interpreted as the sea-monster (whale) of the old *Physiologus*, which becomes more threatening by devouring more and more small creatures. In fact, Morris Palmer Tilley, another great scholar of the English proverb, lists the variant "Rich men are like Whales, for they grow great by the ruine of others" (1659) under his many entries concerning the proverb "A serpent must eat another serpent before it can become a dragon."[59]

Having traced the proverb "Big fish eat little fish" well into the seventeenth century, let us now turn to additional early iconographic representations of the proverb. The reader will recall the two whale illustrations from the twelfth and thirteenth centuries discussed above, and it should be no surprise to find this motif toward the beginning of the fifteenth century in British misericordes. Wood carvers who were supposed to decorate choir benches with religious motifs frequently interspersed their carvings with secular matters. Often they used fable motifs, proverbs, or proverbial expressions. In the case of a misericorde at Lakenheath, Suffolk, one such artist illustrated a large whale swallowing up a smaller fish. Another carving from Earl Soham, Suffolk, shows yet another whale with a fish stuck in its gigantic mouth. In both misericordes the victim enters the big fish head first, most probably signifying that it enters into the trap by deception and cunning on the part of the whale. We are thus reminded of the *Physiologus* tale of the whale and the fish. Arthur Gardner, who identified the large fish in the misericordes as whales, refers to the scene as belonging to this bestiary tale: "In these small examples it [the whale] is swallowing a smaller fish, a symbol of sinners engulfed by the Devil."[60] We had already interpreted the tale in this fashion, and judging by the popularity of the *Physiologus* and its stories, we can assume that the carvers were in fact illustrating the whale story.

Later in the fifteenth century Hieronymus Bosch illustrated the "big fish eat little fish" motif in small scenes of three of his grotesque pictures. Bosch is known for juxtaposing religious and secular themes, and he was clearly aware of the evil symbolism of the large fish. In the center panel of his *Garden of Earthly Delights* he has a large fish (whale) swallowing up a smaller one head first.[61] Art historian Peter Glum has identified many of the scenes in this painting as iconographical presentations of the *Physiologus* bestiary,[62] and we can interpret this particular scene in context of the entire picture as showing that the epicurean small fish (the sinner searching for earthly pleasures) will be damned and go to the hell of the devil represented by the whale. At least as grotesque is another fish scene that Bosch included in the left panel of his famous *The Temptations of Saint Anthony*. Here the giant fish has grasshopper legs, a church seems to ride on its back, and it even seems to have a wheel in the form of a shield (symbolizing war) for propulsion. Since this beast is also swallowing a fish, we can perhaps interpret this scene as indicating the devilish greed of the world, including the rapacity of the church, which will clearly move toward war, devastation, and anarchy as the early church fathers have predicted it.[63] A third scene in the right panel of Bosch's *The Hay Wain* is even more direct in its social satire. The entire picture illustrates the Biblical proverb "All flesh is hay," showing the transitory nature of life. Once again we have a fish-like monster, but this time it has human legs, and a man is being devoured head first, while a snake, the ultimate symbol of evil, witnesses the incorporation of this sinner into the bowels of human hell.[64] In this scene men are indeed, as Habakkuk has observed, "like the fish of the sea." This surrealistic illustration shows the self-destruction of humanity through deception, greed, and sin. It can certainly be concluded from these three scenes that Bosch was preoccupied with interpreting the proverb "Big fish eat little fish" and that he widened the written interpretation of this piece of wisdom of the prophets and philosophers of the past through his artistic visions of inhumanity.

The artist who continued Bosch's satirical view of the world in the sixteenth century was Pieter Brueghel, who included a simple realistic scene of a big fish eating a little fish in his celebrated picture *The Netherlandic Proverbs* from 1559. The illustration is very similar to the misericorde at Earl Soham and the fish in Bosch's *The Temptation of Saint Anthony*, and we may assume that Brueghel was influenced by Bosch in this scene. Once again the smaller fish enters the larger one head first.[65] We should interpret this scene as belonging to the patristic and *Physiologus* tradition, meaning that evil and, in the case of this picture, foolish deeds in an upside-down world will lead to literal destruction. Man as the "swimming" sinner without any religious or moral direction will wind up in the mouth of the big fish, that is in hell, or more secularly expressed, in anarchy. Alan Dundes and Claudia Stibbe in their superb study of this fascinating picture add further interpretative possibilities to this particular scene, but unaware of the

*Physiologus* tradition, they have difficulty in coming to terms with why the little fish seems to have "voluntarily" swum into the open trap:

> Big fish eat little fish. This popular proverb was also represented by Bruegel in a separate drawing (1556) devoted to it. The proverb suggests that the strong and powerful inevitably incorporate—literally—the weak and powerless. The placement of the proverb scene in the painting may hint at a contrast between eating as an act of incorporation and defecation as an act in which something leaves the body. In this context, it is noteworthy that the small fish being swallowed is entering the large fish headfirst. The mouth or face of the large fish is thereby contrasted with the tail of the small one. Possibly the implication is that the small fish was foolish. It could at least have tried to swim away from the large one.[66]

Another illustration of a stranded dead whale with a fish in its mouth appears as a small detail in Brueghel's *The Triumph of Death* (ca. 1562).[67] Here death is the final winner as we have seen in some of the early English literary texts. The evil big fish, who this time seems to hold the smaller fish by its tail, is finally overcome, bringing an end to the mighty or rich who have oppressed their weak or poor fellow men for such a long time. In this picture we sense a true power struggle between the powerful and the weak, but in the end the typical motif of the memento mori makes clear the futility of the strife.

We have a much more important and influential drawing from Pieter Brueghel executed in pen and gray ink in 1556 and reproduced in 1557 as a mirror image copperplate engraving by Pieter van der Heyden with the addition of Latin and Dutch captions: "Grandibvs exigvi svnt pisces piscibvs esca. Siet sone dit hebbe ick zeer langhe ghiweten dat die groote bissen de clejne"[68] (The small fish are eaten by the big fish. See son, this I have known for a very long time, that the great [fish] bite the small). The publisher Jerome Cock most likely added the signature "Hieronymus Bos. inventor" in the lower left corner to help with the sales of this print since Bosch was the better known artist at the time. The word "Ecce" (Behold! See there!) above the rowboat was added by van der Heyden and it seems to be uttered by the old and wise man in the boat who wants the viewer to take a closer look at the follies and vices of the world. For his satirical vision of mankind Brueghel chose as his main theme the proverb "Big fish eat little fish", but he also includes scenes illustrating other Dutch expressions, such as "Little fish lure the big," "One fish is caught by means of another," "Fish are

·GRANDIBVS   EXIGVI   SVNT   PISCES   PISCIBVS   ESCA·

hooked through fish," and "They hang by their own gills" (that is, they are caught by their own weakness or vulnerability).[69]

The picture shows the world upside-down, as can be seen immediately from the soldier-like figure in the center, which is sawing open the large stranded fish by holding the grotesque saw upside-down. Smaller fish are being devoured everywhere, indicating that the world knows no law and order, and that anarchy rules supreme. The absolute chaos is also shown by the fact that the fish are being swallowed head first, sideways (an impossibility), and tail first. It is a world of violence, threat, doom, and death. Each wants to live, prosper, and exert power over the other, including even the fantastic fish-like monster flying through the skies with a gaping mouth. The oppressor who victimizes the small, weak, and poor becomes the victim, and this unceasing chain reaction is splendidly illustrated in a small scene of the right bottom corner, where a big fish has by its tail a smaller one, which in turn has clasped his jaws around a smaller fish yet. It is surprising that this little fish does not appear to have its mouth open as well in order to seek a tiny victim before being swallowed up. The fact that these fish are being incorporated from the rear means that this is an involuntary act, the stronger simply overcoming the weaker. But right below that scene is a fish devouring another head first which, as we have seen, goes back to the *Physiologus* tale, the small fish falling prey to the bigger one through its own vulnerability or stupidity. Such contradictions are as inconsistent as life itself. The purpose of the entire review of the human condition through proverbial fish scenes seems to be to educate people by using a fantastic and didactic visualization of its vices and follies.

About fifty years later we have Brueghel's popular fish engraving once again reversed, on a broadsheet from the year 1619. The Latin version of "Big fish eat little fish" is included on the left top, while the slightly changed Dutch text, "Siet sone dit heb' ick seer lange gheweten / Dat die groote Vissen die cleyne eten" (See, son, this I have known for a very long time, that the large fish eat the small), stands at the bottom. However, the big fish has the inscription "Barnevelsche Monster" and some of the fish to be devoured carry the names "Mörßberg," "Grotius," "Hogerbets," "Vorstius," "Ledenberg," "Cornhart," and "Joris." The use of these names shows that this is a political illustration in which these small "fish" and the big "fish" Johann von Oldenbarnevelt are being satirized. The man cutting the big fish open is Moritz von Oranien, who won the early power struggle over the Northern provinces in the Netherlands that is being illustrated by having Oldenbarnevelt executed.[70] The caricature, one of the very early proverbial and political cartoons, changes the universal meaning of Brueghel's print to apply it to a political issue of the day. Oldenbarnevelt is effectively demonized in this illustration, and Moritz appears on the side of justice as the positive hero.

A third reproduction of Brueghel's 1556 drawing is an engraving executed by Johannes Galle around 1640 in Antwerp. It is basically the same as the 1619 engraving, but Galle added three identical Latin, French, and Dutch inscriptions and their source (Iacob. 2:6) to the top:

Oppressio pavpervm
Divites per potentiam
Opprimunt vos.[71]

(Oppression of the poor. The rich oppress you with force.)

This printer addresses the old rich-poor dichotomy and once again intends to educate people through his satirical depiction of the world, executed at the end of the Thirty Years' War that had brought a great deal of oppression and destruction.

One further copper engraving, from about 1600, contains a reproduction of Brueghel's illustration in the left bottom corner.[72] But this artist makes Brueghel's big fish only part of his grotesque illustration of the proverb "Big fish eat little fish." In the center of this print the big fish sit around a table eating little fish. Everywhere else in the picture we have scenes of fish eating others. The major exception is the large fish in the bottom right corner, which has human-like creatures inside its stomach. Brueghel's fish scene and this one face each other and are placed in striking juxtaposition, obviously as a statement that men live like fish and that the stronger will subdue the weaker. Explanatory didactic Dutch texts are scattered throughout the picture, making it an effective statement on how the strong and rich take advantage of the weak and poor. The humans who are included in the stomach of the big fish or whale in the bottom right corner most likely refer to the idea that these sinners wind up in hell, as we have seen from the texts of the *Physiologus*. On the top of the print we read the inscription, "Siet vrinden dit heeftmen veel iaren geweten / dat de groote vissen de cleynen eeten" (Look friends, people have known this for many years, that big fish eat the little), which almost repeats the title of the print from 1557. "Sone" (son) is replaced by "vrinden" (friends), however, since in this picture it is not just an old man (father) explaining the world to a young man (son) but the artist showing everybody willing to look and learn how men are like fish in the sea. The fact that the fish are on land acting out human roles makes the satire even more obvious. The result of leaving their natural habitat will surely be death, and that is what will happen if mankind continues to behave like fish.

Certainly the Dutch author Jacob Cats must have had such a Brueghel print in mind when in 1632 he wrote his didactic poem in fifteen rhymed couplets telling the reader that the big fish eat the little ones everywhere one looks. The poem has the title "Siet kint, dit heb ick langh geweten / Dat groote vissen de kleyne eten"[73] (See child, this I have known for a long time / That big fish eat the little ones). His subtitle to the poem points indirectly to one of the proverb prints discussed above, for the reader is encouraged to imagine a fisherman who is explaining to a child how big fish eat little fish.

While it is strange that Cats did not include an illustration with this poem in his otherwise richly illustrated *Spiegel van den ouden en nieuwen tijdt* (1632), we do not have to look far to find literature and art joining forces in the emblematic publications of the early seventeenth century. The German Joachim Camerarius included in his *Symbolorvm et emblematvmex aqvatilibvs et reptilibvs* (1604) a round emblem showing a fish eating a smaller one of its own kind. The Latin text reads "Propriis non pareit alvmnis. Lucius in proprium ut sua viscera congerit aluum, sic ipsi sese conficiunt homines"[74] (He doesn't spare his own children. As the pike incorporates its children into its stomach, thus humans torture each other). The fact that the smaller fish is devoured with the head first adds to the cruelty involved when one member of the species kills an innocent member of the same species. From Spain we have Sebastián de Covarrubias Orozco's emblem collection *Emblemas morales* (1660), which includes an illustration of a giant fish swallowing up a smaller one head first. Another large fish with a wide open mouth is ready to do the same, and some smaller fish seem to be swimming straight into the danger presented by the sea monster. The title of the emblem reads befittingly "Maiora minoribvs obsvnt"[75] (The large hunts the small) and the eight-line Latin commentary argues that fish will even devour others while death is upon them since their greed knows no bounds. Another German emblem is Peter Isselburg's *Emblemata Politica* (1617), which again shows a sea monster or whale-like creature devouring a fish head first. The Latin motto reads "Minor esca maioris"[76] (The smaller is food of the larger). A good fifty years later (ca. 1670) we find a similar fish-monster preying on a smaller fish as part of a wall decoration at Ludwigsburg, Germany. The Latin inscription is identical to the one just cited, pointing out once again that the weak and meek will be conquered by the mighty.[77]

It is little wonder that this motif of "Big fish eat little fish" gained such popularity in the seventeenth century. War, might, and oppression were rampant, and we are justified in looking at these emblems as political statements. They are satirical caricatures of sorts without attacking any person in particular. The proverb and its emblematic

Minor esca
maioris

illustration permitted the artists to express their interpretation of the human condition in an indirect but still comprehensible fashion. Such indirect criticism of the politics of the day couched in the language of natural phenomena most certainly was an effective way to vent frustrations and moralize and teach at the same time. This can be seen from an Italian drawing from 1678 by Giuseppe Maria Mitelli, who illustrated the proverb "Il pesce grosso mangia il minuto"[78] (The big fish eats the little). Just as in the Brueghel picture an old man is teaching a young boy about the nature of things. But while the fish in the emblems show the inevitability of their fate by swimming towards the monster, in this picture the smaller fish try to swim away, that is they try to flee from the stronger, who is temporarily hampered in its cruel ways by having caught a fish sideways. Too much greed does have its trouble too, and even the big fish is not always absolutely successful in its evil schemes.

Realizing that the print from 1557 with its many reproductions as well as newer, more inclusive illustrations of the mighty swallowing up the weak from about 1600 were popular satirical and didactic prints, we wonder whether Shakespeare might not have had a copy of one of them in front of him when he wrote the following lines in act 2, scene 1 of *Pericles* (1608):

> *Third Fisherman:* Master, I marvel how the fishes live in the sea.
> *First Fisherman:* Why, as men do a-land,—the great ones eat up the little ones: I can compare our rich misers to nothing so fitly as to a whale; 'a plays and tumbles, driving the poor fry before him, and at last devours them all at a mouthful: such whales have I heard on o' the land, who never leave gaping till they've swallowed the whole parish, church, steeple, bells, and all.
> *Pericles: [aside]* A pretty moral.
>
> . . .
>
> *Pericles: [aside]* How from the finny subject of the sea
> These fishers tell th' infirmities of men;
> And from their watery empire recollect
> All that may men approve or men detect!—

A very similar exchange using the proverb takes place between Emilia and her page Ioculo in John Day's play *Law-Trickes or, who vvould have thovght it* (1608).

> *Ioculo:* ... but Madam, doe you remember what a multitude of fishes we saw at Sea? and I doe wonder how they can all liue by one another.
> *Emilia:* Why foole, as men do on the Land, the great ones eate

vp the little ones, but *Ioculo*, I am great, passing great, and
readie to lye downe.[79]

Both plays appeared in the same year, and clearly someone is copying
the other just as Brueghel's illustration was copied. Since Shakespeare
was the more popular of the two authors and since *Pericles* was most
likely performed before 1608, we may assume that Day heard the lines
and used them for his own end. In any case, of importance in both
references is that the life of fish is compared to that of men. Both the
animal and the human world are governed by the same lack of order,
respect, and fairness.

This view is splendidly expressed in the play *The Roaving Girle or Moll
Cut-Purse* (1611) by Thomas Middleton and Thomas Dekker, where a
sergeant by the name of Curtleax makes his comparison of fish and
men:

> We are as other men are, sir; I cannot see but he who makes a
> show of honesty and religion, if his claws can fasten to his liking,
> he draws blood: all that live in the world are but great fish and
> little fish, and feed upon one another; some eat up whole men, a
> sergeant cares but for the shoulder of a man. They call us knaves
> and curs; but many times he that sets us on worries more lambs
> one year than we do in seven.[80]

This rogue of sorts finds a good counterpart in the 1630 English
translation of Mateo Alemán's Spanish novel *The Rogve: or, The Life of
Gvzman de Alfarache* (1599). Alemán returns to the whale imagery and
the intepretation of the whale as the devil, and he presents strong
social criticism of the rich who grow large by the oppression of others:

> In all my travels, I haue ever observed, that these great rich
> men, and powerfull persons, are like vnto Whales, who opening
> wide the mouth & jawes of their covetousnesse, swallow vp all
> that comes in their vvay, to the end that their houses may be well
> provided for and their revenues increased, without casting any
> eye of compassion vpon the poore young Orphane; or lending an
> eare to the cry of the distressed Damsell; or affording his shoul-
> ders for to vphold the feeble and the vveake; or opening his char-
> itable hands to relieue the sicke, and him that is in neede: but
> rather vnder the name of good government, every man so gov-
> ernes himselfe, that he does the best he can, to draw all the vvater
> to his owne Mill. They publish good desires; but they exercise
> bad actions. Their pretensions are faire; but their practise starke
> naught. They would seeme to bee Gods Lambes, innocent and
> harmelesse soules, but the Devill onely makes profit of them: they

fall wholly to his share; he, and none but he reapes the fruit of them: God hath the name indeede, but the Devill hath the shearing of them.[81]

And in Shakespeare's *All's Well that Ends Well* (1593/1603?) we find yet another rogue in the character of Paroles who alludes to the proverb of "The big fish eat little fish" in act 4, scene 3:

My meaning in't, I protest, was very honest in the behalf of the maid; for I knew the young count to be a dangerous and lascivious boy, who is a whale to virginity, and devours up all the fry it finds.

But that is Shakespeare who with his craftsmanship is capable of going beyond the more traditional statement of the proverb and meaning, taking it even on the sexual level. He also has Falstaff in act 3, scene 2 of *King Henry IV, Part 2* (1597) state the proverb only in a very indirect manner:

Well, I'll be acquainted with him, if I return; and it shall go hard but I'll make him a philosopher's two stones to me: if the young dace be a bait for the old pike, I see no reason, in the law of nature, but I may snap at him. Let time shape, and there an end.

What was referred to as the "logic of the fish" earlier is now called "the law of nature," and that law is represented by our proverb. Notice, though, how freely Shakespeare incorporates the proverb into the dramatic dialogue. He really doesn't quote the text at all, but he illustrates it verbally. We thus have proverbial language without the actual proverb, and it is this masterful twisting and changing of traditional proverbs that make Shakespeare one of the truly outstanding employers of proverbial wisdom.[82]

Shakespeare's references to proverbs become integral parts of the speech of the characters, and the didacticism of the big fish proverb that we have noticed so much barely plays a role. But that is the Shakespearean exception, for Roger Williams, the founder of Rhode Island, presents us in his fascinating early book on the American Indian languages entitled *A Key into the Language of America: or, An help to the Language of the Natives in that part of America, called New-England* (1643) with an interpretation of the proverb that goes right back to the prophet Habakkuk.

*The general* Observation *of Fish.*
How many thousands of Millions of those under water, sea-Inhabitants, in all Coasts of the world, preach to the sonnes of

men on shore, to adore their glorious Maker by presenting themselves to Him as themselves (in a manner) present their lives from
the wild Ocean, to the very doores of men, their fellow creatures
in *New England*.

> *More Particular.*
>
> *What* Habacuck *once spake, mine eyes*
>     *Have often seene most true,*
> *The greater fishes devoure the lesse,*
>     *And cruelly pursue.*
>
> *Forcing them through Coves and Creekes,*
>     *To leape on driest sand,*
> *To gaspe on earthie element, or die*
>     *By wildest* Indians *hand.*
>
> *Christs little ones must hunted be*
>     *Devour'd; yet rise as Hee.*
> *And eate up those which now a while*
>     *Their fierce devourers be.*[83]

The same early American colonist returned one year later in his *The
Blovdy Tenent, of Persecution, for Cause of Conscience, discussed in A
Conference betweene Trvth and Peace* (1644) to Habakkuk's Old Testament
statement. He argues for the necessity of civil government

> for the preservation of Mankinde in *civill order* and *peace*, (the
> *World* otherwise would bee like the *Sea*, wherein Men, like *Fishes*
> would hunt and devoure each other, and the greater devoure the
> lesse.)[84]

And a few pages later "Truth" exclaims how good it would be if
everybody were free from the persecutions of the fish, who clearly
represent a chaotic political situation:

> Deare *Peace*, Habacucks Fishes keep their constant bloody game of
> *Persecutions* in the Worlds mighty *Ocean*; the greater taking, plun-
> dring, swallowing up the lesser: O happy he whose portion is the
> *God* of *Iacob!* who hath nothing to lose under the *Sun*, but hath a
> *State*, a *House*, an *Inheritance*, a *Name*, a *Crowne*, a *Life*, past all the
> *Plunderers, Ravishers, Murtherers* reach and furie![85]

Such political considerations are echoed some fifty years later in
William Penn's *Essay Towards the Present and Future Peace of Europe*
(1693), in which he outlines a sort of confederation among the national
entities that might finally bring an end to their strifes and wars:

> They [the sovereigns] remain as sovereign at home as ever they
> were. Neither their power over their people nor the usual revenue

they pay them is diminished; it may be the war establishment may be reduced, which will indeed of course follow, or be better employed to the advantage of the public. So that the sovereignties are as they were, for none of them have now any sovereignty over one another; and if this be called a lessening of their power, it must be only because the great fish can no longer eat up the little ones and that each sovereignty is equally defended from injuries and disabled from committing them.[86]

Judging by subsequent European history, the rivalry among the kingdoms and principalities did not cease, because mankind's fish nature continued to lead it into persecutions and wars. As Algernon Sidney explained in his late seventeenth century *Discourses on Government* (published 1698), "men lived like fishes, the great ones devoured the small,"[87] which was already the case in Hesiod's and Habakkuk's times, and which continued to Sidney's days and to ours.

Such wars do not only occur among nations, they also take place in the artistic world due to envy, rivalry, and distrust. Jonathan Swift in his lengthy satirical poem "On Poetry: A Rhapsody" (1733) gives a convincing picture of such problems, and he expands the fish metaphor to include the frog, wolf, and flea. We are, in fact, reminded of Alexander Barclay's earlier "The wolfe etis the shepe, the great fysshe the small." And yet there is a big difference here, because the "big fish" poet for once is not doing the biting; in the artistic world it is the smaller talents who do the snapping, all the way up from the smallest light to the biggest. We thus have a very innovative reversal of our motif, and we can call Swift's parody the first modern reinterpretation of the classical proverb.

> *Hobbes* clearly proves that ev'ry Creature
> Lives in a State of War by Nature.
> The Greater for the Smallest watch,
> But meddle seldom with their Match.
> A Whale of moderate Size will draw
> A Shole of Herrings down his Maw.
> A Fox with Geese his Belly crams;
> A Wolf destroys a thousand Lambs.
> But search among the rhiming Race,
> The Brave are worried by the Base.
> If, on *Parnassus'* Top you sit,
> You rarely bite, are always bit:
> Each Poet of inferior Size
> On you shall rail and criticize;

And strive to tear you Limb from Limb,
While others do as much for him.

   The Vermin only teaze and pinch
Their Foes superior by an Inch.
So, Nat'ralists observe, a Flea
Hath smaller Fleas on him prey,
And these have smaller Fleas to bite 'em,
And so proceed *ad infinitum:*
Thus ev'ry Poet in his Kind,
Is bit by him that comes behind;
Who, tho' too little to be seen,
Can teaze, and gall, and give the Spleen.[88]

But such a variation is very much the exception until almost the middle of the present century. The proverb and its wisdom continued to be taken very seriously for about two hundred more years. In addition to political interpretations we also find more and more applications of the proverb to economic situations, a use that has become very prevalent today. A couple of years before Swift's poem we find a treatise entitled *Money the Sinews of Trade* (1731), published anonymously in Boston, which emphasizes right at the beginning the need for a good money policy in the colonies, stating:

> The distress and perplexity attending the Trade of the Province in general; but more especially this Town, in which is carried on so much business, is now become the common talk of all People: and if something be not done to supply the Place with a Medium to pass from man to man in the way of Commerce, in a little time the Trade will be all a Barter, or exchanging one Commodity for another, and it is easy to foresee the vast Inconveniences and Mischiefs such a Trade will be attended with. Men will live by preying upon one another; like the Fish in the sea, the greater will devour the less; the whole Trade will get into a few Hands in a short time, and the middling sort of People who are the chief Support of any Place, will soon come (many of 'em) to Poverty, and instead of Supporting Church and State, will become a burden to both.[89]

A few years later we have another such anonymous Boston publication entitled *A Letter Relating to a Medium of Trade* (1740), which attempts to find ways of overcoming the evil of usury in the province of the Massachusetts-Bay:

> 'Tis propos'd, That the abovesaid Silver and Gold, as it comes in, be let out upon good Security, at Six per Cent. per Annum,

special Regard to be had in letting the same to such Persons thro'
the Province, as may be in Danger of Oppression by the Extortion
of excessive Usury or otherwise; from such, who may delight in
the Pleasure which their Brethren the great Fish of the Sea, take in
devouring the less. And due Care being also taken to call in the
Silver so let, before the Year 1760, by which Means the Sum in the
Treasury may be very considerably increased.[90]

And John Adams wrote in a letter dated 12 December 1785 that he was
very distressed by avarice in lending money, expressing himself in a
way that makes us think of our more modern term loan shark:

While such Interest can be obtained, much Property will be di-
verted from Trade. But this must have an End. The great Fish will
have eaten all the little ones, and then they must look out for
other Prey. The Multiplicity of Law Suits, is much like what I remember after the Peace of 1763, but when a certain Quantity of
Property had shifted hands they diminished. It is generally agreed
that our People have been imprudent and extravagant, but I hope
that Profligacy and want of Principle have not taken any deep
root.[91]

His wife Abigail Adams had already written to him on 27 November
1775 in a more general political sense that the nature of mankind has
barely evolved from that of the fish world:

I am more and more convinced that Man is a dangerous creature, and that power whether vested in many or few is ever grasp-
ing, and like the grave cries give, give. The great fish swallow up
the small, and he who is most strenuous for the Rights of the people, when vested with power, is as eager after the perogatives of
Government. You tell me of degrees of perfection to which Humane Nature is capable of arriving, and I believe it, but at the
same time lament that our admiration should arise from the scar-
city of the instances.[92]

Things were indeed not perfect in this young country at the time of
the revolution, as a newspaper account from 16 September 1775 in the
*Constitutional Gazette* so vividly shows. We sense a touch of irony in
this passage, and the inclusion of the proverb "set a rogue to catch a
rogue" reminds us of the parallel fish proverbs "Let (venture) a herring
(sprat) to catch a whale" or simply "Venture a small fish to catch a great
one" that we mentioned earlier:

General Gage, it is said, has hanged three of the provincials, for
breaking open and plundering some of the houses in Boston
evacuated by the inhabitants; so that the great thieves, it seems,

begin to hang the little ones. O! glorious times indeed! But what then? Why, then the fate of these petty rogues is, in some respects, like that of the little fish that are occasionally devoured to fatten and keep alive the larger ones. Besides, administration have herein verified the ancient aphorism, viz.: *set a rogue to catch a rogue*. Well, what next? Why the next thing is, a short but fervent petition, that Jack Ketch, Esq., might go forward in the business of hanging with despatch, till the world is filled with great thieves as well as little ones.[93]

The somewhat fatalistic view that the logic of the fish will always be here continued into the nineteenth century and beyond. In a lengthy American poem entitled "The Shade of Plato; or, A Defense of Religion, Morality and Government" (1806) by David Hitchcock, it is even argued that all of this might belong to the greater scheme of God himself. Who, after all, are men to question the justice of God until they have reached his supreme wisdom? Such theodicy seems alien to us, but it belongs to the process of rationalizing the evil forces around us. If anything can diminish such natural laws, then it is a strong morality, belief in God and the establishment of a controlling and just government. Notice in the following lines, though, the many questions that plague mankind to this day:

> Although by man unrealiz'd,
> Each plan is best that Heaven devis'd:
> And this was one among the rest,
> That pleas'd superior wisdom best.
> Then why should man his Maker blame
> Ere he can comprehend his aim?
>   Would man thus hastily impeach
> Whate'er his reason cannot reach;
> Then let him God's last end express,
> Why the great fish destroy the less?
> Why wolves, because they have the pow'r,
> The harmless lambkins may devour?
> Why each ferocious beast of prey,
> May take inferior lives away?
> Any why, with unreserv'd controul,
> Man has deathwarrants for the whole![94]

A bit more realistic is a Thanksgiving Day sermon preached in Boston on 28 November 1850 by Theodore Parker. Entitling his remarks "The State of the Nation," Parker argues for morality, solid work ethics, and, of course, a fair and just government to prevent the young American nation from falling prey to stronger fish in the ocean of civilization. He conjures up Rome as an example and thus uses the fish proverb once again in a didactic and political fashion. One senses the word "Ecce" of the earlier Brueghel prints behind this lesson. In this effective role as a cautionary example the proverb is bound to have been used over the centuries innumerable times. Parker's remarks may stand as a typical example for the nineteenth century uses of the proverb, and they will allow us to move on into the twentieth century in this review of a universal proverb about human nature.

> Do you know how empires find their end? Yes, the great States eat up the little. As with fish, so with nations. Aye, but how do the great States come to an end? By their own injustice, and no other cause. They would make unrighteousness their law, and God wills not that it be so. Thus they fall; thus they die. Look at these ancient States, the queenliest queens of earth. There is Rome, the widow of two civilizations,—the Pagan and the Catholic. They both had her, and unto both she bore daughters and fair sons. But, the Niobe of Nations, she boasted that her children were holier and more fair than all the pure ideas of justice, truth, and love, the offspring of the eternal God. And now she sits there, transformed into stone, amid the ruins of her children's bones.[95]

One wonders how the minister Theodore Parker would have reacted to an article with the identical title, "The State of the Nation," by E. P. Thompson, which appeared, ironically, in a British magazine called *New Society* on 6 December 1979. Certainly Great Britain (or the great United States) has not been swallowed up, but the large aquarium with its fish is still governed by the dichotomy of "anarchy and culture" as the subtitle explains. Nor is there much hope of cleaning up the mess, for society appears to be so entangled in the scheme of the big fish eating the small ones that its sudden end would surely bring about the demise of the state.

> If a private citizen tries to peer into the state today, it seems like nothing so much a huge aquarium, filled with inky water and flourishing weeds. The weeds are the Official Secrets Acts, and the water is dark with "confidential matter." The aquarium is populated only with shadows. Some little fish flick past in schools, but they are anxious about the great predators which lie upon the mud or which, like permanent secretaries, dart from the shadows of a ministry to the tangled shelter of private industry. Big fish eat little fish, and the great fish eat the big. But all fish have a common interest in the dirty water and the weeds. The water is

the sink of ideological legitimation in which alone they can survive and maintain their predatory style of life. The weeds protect them from public scrutiny or account. Clean up the tank and put them in water of a clear constitution and they would not live.[96]

Considering this state of affairs one is indeed inclined to agree with Peter Udell's lyrics to the music of Gary Geld in the popular song "Big Fish, Little Fish" (1969):

> That's the way it goes
> Ev'rybody knows
> That's the way it's always been
> 'n' how it's gotta be!
>
> Big fish eat little little fish.
> Little little fish eat littler fish.
> Littler fish eat the littlest fish.
> And that's the way it goes.
>
> Big birds peck little little birds.
> Little little birds peck littler birds.
> Littler birds peck the littlest birds.
> For any seed that grows.
>
> Big bugs eat little little bugs.
> Little little bugs eat littler bugs.
> Littler bugs eat the littlest bugs.
> The winner gets the rose.
>
> That's the way it goes
> Ev'rybody knows
> That's the way it's always been
> 'n' how it's gotta be!
>
> Ours is not to question why
> Or to reason why.
> The Lord creates the order
> and we just live and die.
>
> That's the way it's always been.
> For ev'rything that grows.
> 'n' how it's gotta be.
> Now why do you suppose?[97]

It is exactly the nagging question of why life has to be like this that characterizes the many appearances of the proverb in our time. For the most part written or pictorial uses of it continue the fatalistic tradition that the bigger and stronger will always take advantage of the smaller and weaker. In a modern alienating satirical text entitled "If the Sharks were Humans" (1930) Bertolt Brecht showed this belief by writing indirectly about Germany's move towards fascism. He clearly states that sharks as men would be much worse than normal sharks since they would go about their destructive business of annihilating others in an ordered and carefully planned way: welfare, education, politics, culture, and religion would all be structured so as to be in absolute control of a few big fish. The entire society would consist of a carefully orchestrated process of creating small and meek fish that could easily be controlled or devoured if they were to step out of line. Brecht wrote his apocalyptic text in the subjunctive, but history showed that Germany under Nazi rule lived by the logic of the fish, and the proverb, which is never directly stated by Brecht, fits precisely his description of a dictatorship of fear, oppression, and cruelty.

> If the sharks were humans, they would [teach] little fish how to swim into the jaws of the sharks. . . . If the sharks were humans, they would of course carry on wars with one another. . . . If the sharks were humans, they would of course also have art. There would be beautiful pictures which would show the teeth of the sharks in splendid colors and their jaws as pure gardens of delight in which one could beautifully play. The theaters on the ocean's floor would show how courageous little fish would swim enthusiastically into the jaws of the sharks, and the music would be so wonderful that the little fish would rush dreamily into the jaws of the sharks. There would also be a religion, if the sharks were humans. It would teach that the little fish would only begin to live properly in the bellies of the sharks. Moreover, there would also be an end to equality of all the little fish if the sharks were humans. Some of them would receive offices and would be placed above the others. Those who were a bit larger would even be allowed to devour the smaller ones. That would of course be pleasant for the sharks since they themselves would then get larger pieces to devour. . . . In short, there would only be something like culture in the ocean if the sharks were humans.[98]

And how are things in the socio-political situation of the world today? Has Brecht's prophetic vision become obsolete? Judging from illustrations of various interpretations of the proverb in mass media caricatures and advertisements, one certainly gets the feeling that it is still very much a world where "Big fish eat little fish." In the following remarks we have divided our rich materials into five groups: (1) one large fish randomly pursuing several smaller ones; (2) a big fish just planning to devour one individual small fish; (3) a sequence of three or more fish trying to swallow each other up; (4) the vicious circle of fish of the same size trying to incorporate each other; and (5) the attempt of many small fish to gang up on the larger one. Our references come from American, English, German, and Russian newspapers and magazines, a cultural spread that proves that such reinterpretations of a classical proverb are an international phenomenon. The illustrations and their texts vary in quality, taste, and significance, but all of them show mankind's reaction to a life in which the big fish eat little fish. Some are extremely satirical and cynical, others are full of irony or even humor, but such are the reactions of us moderns who so much would like to break out of this endless chain reaction of rapacity of all kinds. They are therefore also highly moralistic expressions following the trend of the early philosophers, prophets, church fathers, and literary as well as political authors, intended to make this world a more human place.

Let us now turn to a few caricatures using the motif of one large fish randomly pursuing several smaller ones. It is important to notice that the little fish are always swimming away, meaning that they are clearly aware of the danger of the perpetrator and that they are trying to flee. In the *New Yorker* appeared a cartoon that illustrates without any specific applicability and with much black humor two big fish in their traditional role of pursuing little fish. They both have smirking faces and with a disgusting feeling of superiority they quote the old and true proverb to each other: " 'Big fish eat little fish.' I like that."[99] A German newspaper article is more specific adding to the headline "Kampf der Konzerne"[100] (Battle of the Companies) an illustration of a big fish symbolizing a large company trying to buy up smaller ones whether they like it or not. The same idea was the subject of a Soviet caricature from *Pravda* showing the large fish of "Big Monopolies" in America ravaging and absorbing smaller businesses.[101] The illustration contains an interesting variation in that the big fish has already caught the little ones in a net, meaning that big business is in fact ruling supreme. A 1974 Soviet cartoon from *Pravda* is even more direct, for in this illustration opposing the colossal amounts of money the capitalist member-states of N.A.T.O. are expending for the arms race the fish are clearly labelled: The big fish is the military budget, which is pursuing the smaller budgets of such "fish" as schools, medicine, science, pensions, and social benefits.[102] And then there is also a cartoon that pictures a super-boss or, as slang would have it, a "big fish" in a restaurant to whom dozens of waiters are carrying plates with fish on them.[103] There

Drawing by Joseph Farris; © 1979 The New Yorker Magazine, Inc.

*" 'Big fish eat little fish.' I like that."*

is no caption, and the cartoonist seems to imply that this big fish does not even need to chase after the small ones. His power and control are so vast that all the small fish cater to him. He is obviously so rich and mighty that there is no escaping him, as the dead fish on the plates signify.

The aggressive nature of the big fish is perhaps even more pronounced in our second group of caricatures and advertisements, in which the beast is trying to devour one specific victim. The juxtaposition of large and small leaves no doubt of the outcome of this unfair situation. Utilizing the "fish" of the actual proverb "Big fish eat little fish" a British cartoon from 1961 from the satirical magazine *Punch* pictures the small "Sam's Fish Shop" which is about to be devoured by the much larger "Suprema Fisheries Corporation."[104] Realizing what has happened to small grocery stores and other shops, we know that the big fish illustrated in the sign of the Suprema Company will in fact put Sam's shop out of business. In the corporate world there is always the danger of the larger company swallowing up the smaller, and Avis car rental used this idea for an effective advertisement with the headline "When you're No. 2, you try harder. Or else." Below this familiar slogan one can see a small fish (Avis) being chased by a bigger one (Hertz), and the explanatory copy of the advertisement starts with the following observation: "Little fish have to keep moving all of the time. The big ones never stop picking on them. Avis knows all about the problems of little fish. We're only No. 2 in rent-a-cars. We'd be swallowed up if we didn't try harder. There's no rest for us."[105] Leave it to Madison Avenue to turn the old proverb with its negative connotation into a positive advertising campaign. What Avis as the smaller fish wants to do, of course, is to bite a piece out of the larger market corner of the Hertz company. Another advertising firm used exactly this idea to create a most colorful advertisement for AT&T illustrating a small fish trying to bite off a piece of the tail of a contented big fish with its mouth closed for once. This time the headline reads "How the Competition is Planning to Steal Your Customers." The copy doesn't need to mention fish since the effective illustration speaks for itself. Instead it alludes to the Bible, saying that "now the ambitious David is stealing the efficient Goliath's customers."[106] And, of course, it is AT&T that can help the Goliath company to modernize its high tech systems so that those nasty little fish (competitors) will not get a bite out of them.

One thing is sure, though, no matter how wide the little fish in the advertisement stretches its jaws, it cannot really endanger the business monopoly by itself. For once the monopoly realizes the small threat, it will awaken from its feeling of security and like a giant shark attack the one who dared to question its giant share of the market. An anti-American caricature from *Pravda* illustrates this situation precisely, by having a shark (monopolies) pursue a small fish (small business). The appropriate caption reads "The Foundation of 'Healthy' Competition."[107] A second Soviet caricature shows a little fish (wages) swimming right toward the open jaws of a large fish (prices). The caption reads "These fish are the same age, they've just grown differently. It all depends on the feeding." The additional commentary that so often is placed on top of Soviet cartoons for propagandistic reasons reads, "Price increases in capitalist countries have greatly outstripped the increase of wages for blue- and white-collar workers."[108] This is indeed an effective political-economic caricature, and the fact that the small fish faces the larger one very cleverly shows that this discrepancy between wages and prices can only get worse. It is interesting to note though that we have not been able to find such "Big fish eat little fish" cartoons reacting to Soviet problems. Using the proverb for internal situations would too drastically expose shortcomings of the system, and that could hardly be tolerated. But it certainly lends itself beautifully to showing the ills of other societies. Just imagine the following caricature, which appeared in 1983 in an American newspaper, getting to the Soviet Union: no caption or comment, but simply a monstrous fish (u.s.s.r.) chasing a little fish (Afghanistan).[109] Soviet citizens know the proverb very well, and they certainly would understand this satirical view of what their government is doing to a small sovereign country. Perhaps they have thought of this parallel already, but of course it will never appear in print as a form of self-criticism. One thing is clear, though, these illustrations with a big fish pursuing just one defenseless smaller one are potent statements no matter for what intentions they are used.

The third group of modern iconographical uses of the proverb is based on a sequence of three or more fish trying to swallow each other up. Each fish is always bigger than the one immediately before it, and this chain of successive incorporations indicates the strategy of the survival of the fittest in clear images. Often the proverbial three fish suffice to show how our entire dealings seem to be based on this logic of the fish, that is that people are no better than fish who live by devouring each other. We are reminded of the tripartite Chinese proverb "The large fish eat the small; the small fish eat the water-insects; the water-insects eat water plants and mud," which we quoted at the beginning and which expresses in words what the following illustrations show visually. We have already observed that the proverb is often employed to reflect on economic matters. It can in fact be said that "Big fish eat little fish" has become something of a leitmotif in caricatures that deal with the so-called merger mania rampant in this country. Several recent newspapers and magazines reported on this phenomenon. As early as 1978 an article in *Esquire* carried the headline "Merger Mania Runs Amok" together with an illustration of three realistically drawn fish in pursuit of each other.[110] *The Boston Globe* summarized the business affairs of an entire year with an article entitled "1981: A rush to merge"[111] and again an illustrator drew three fish devouring each other. A major article in *Time* even used the headline "Swallowing Up One Another. A new megawave of mergers washes over corporate America"[112] and added two facing strings of four fish, each trying to swallow each other. The double presentation of the idea of the proverb in this context is meant to show how uncontrolled and vicious this merger obsession has become, when one greedy open mouth is confronted by another. The absurdity of this entire merger craze was finally ridiculed in a recent cartoon in which an infinite number of fish swallow each other up. Each fish lives in constant fear of the next larger one, and even the largest one is afraid that still a bigger one is coming from somewhere. No wonder then that the last and biggest fish in this line-up can say to the one it is about to devour: "You're nervous!! Ted Turner and Rupert Murdoch [two of the most blatant merger maniacs] are right behind me!"[113]

Staying with economics for a moment we also have a fascinating cartoon from the German artist Horst Haitzinger entitled "usw. usw. 1971"[114] (etc. etc. 1971). It repeats in a multiple sequence the problem of "Lohn" (wages) being eaten up by "Preis" (prices), which we already saw in one of the Soviet caricatures. This situation is so bad that an angler (an employee) who finally had a good wage on the hook is pulled into the water by this telescopic monster. In other words, the ever-increasing spiral of wages and prices has gone out of control. For a while inflation also seemed to be out of control, and this was splendidly characterized by one-, two-, five-, and ten-dollar bills with added body parts of fish eating each other.[115] Everybody could certainly understand what was meant here. This was also the case with a small brochure that was sent out by the Life Insurance Companies in America with an illustration of fish-like humans preying on each other and the slogan "Inflation. Let's self-control it."[116] Taxes, of course, are another vicious problem, and a report on how personal taxes have gone up between 1965 and 1984 and projected to the year 2000 used the big fish eating little fish as an illustrative model with the appropriate title "A Bigger Bite: How Your Tax Bite Has Grown."[117] And finally there are the economics of the car industry and the threat of foreign imports. A German caricature summarized this problem simply with yet another triadic structure: A small car representing the Common Market (E.G.) car manufacturers is placed into the open car mouth of the U.S. companies and both fit comfortably into the gigantic jaws of a Japanese car.[118] Indeed a very telling picture of today's automobile market situation.

Turning to political uses of the sequential illustrations of fish of various sizes, we have a second cartoon by Horst Haitzinger from 1979: Cambodia is being devoured by Vietnam, and Vietnam in turn by China, but following this threesome is the mean-looking u.s.s.r. fish with its jaws closed but ever ready to snap if the right moment presents itself.[119] A more recent German cartoon entitled "Killersatelliten" has three killer satellites, which look like killer sharks, going after a basic satellite, their sequence being "Killersatellit, Antikillersatellit, Anti-antikillersatellit."[120] This terminology by itself suffices to express the absurdity of space weapons. There is also a very telling caricature from 1985 entitled "Lebanese Cookbook." From the left we have four fish as usual attempting to destroy each other. The Moslems are preying on the Christians, they on the p.l.o., and the p.l.o. on an unidentified small fish (perhaps other factions in Lebanon). These fish are however swimming directly into the jaws of the Syrian fish whom a much bigger fish, namely a grotesquely drawn Soviet general, holds in a frying pan.[121] This cartoon unmistakably wants to show that the Lebanese factions are bringing about their own demise by letting the logic of the fish lead them to ruin and control by Syria and the Soviet Union.

Social concerns can also be well expressed by using the fish sequence in various sizes. The Life Insurance Companies in America used the idea again, this time showing fish-like creatures with human heads in an advertisement that addresses the problem of waste and misuse of resources in our society. The headline reads "Will History Remember Us As the Consumers who Consumed Themselves?"[122] The word "consume(r)" parallels the idea of incorporation (the actual placing into the body) very well. Pollution is another big problem that faces modern civilization, and if we do not watch out we will lose more and more of our marine life. Sure, big fish eat little fish, as a cartoon shows realistically, but the biggest fish is suddenly followed by a giant oil tanker whose bow has opened wide and is spilling thousands of barrels of crude oil.[123]

Another continuous social concern is the class structure and the various levels that people tend to group others into. A fascinating German cartoon depicts this very vividly with five simply drawn fish each wearing a hat. The biggest fish models a formal top hat, which represents the richest capitalists; the next wears a homburg and might represent the upper middle class; the fedora signifies the burgher class; the cap the workers; and the last fish, the truly poor, has no hat at all.[124] For a clothes-conscious society this is an absolutely revealing social

satire. One of those capitalist executive types was depicted in the *New Yorker* sitting behind a large office desk, and behind him on the wall is a giant picture with a sequence of four fish devouring each other.[125] One gets a clear feeling of how this particular person at least got into the position where he is now the biggest fish of them all. Such a person doubtlessly would subscribe to the philosophy expressed in yet another very telling cartoon from the *Saturday Review*. Here four fish in increasing sizes are lined up, and each in turn asks one of the following questions: "Why me Lord?" "Why him Lord?" "Why them Lord?" "Why not?"[126] And of course he can also agree with the following cartoon, which lines up three fish with the following thoughts: "There is no justice in the world." "There is some justice in the world." "The world is just."[127] Since the biggest fish has arrived at the ultimate "top" by devouring smaller fish left and right, the world might in fact seem just to him since it appears to be in his control. But even a person like that with absolute power and great riches would do well to take a look into the old *Physiologus*, where the whale, the biggest sea animal of all, represents the place where he might wind up, namely hell, through which he has put so many people in order to get to the position he is in now.

One wonders whether there is ever a chance of throwing a monkey-wrench into this seemingly natural sequence of events. Well, over thirty years ago *Punch* magazine printed a cartoon in which the fish second to the largest one at the end of a long chain of big fish eating little fish all of a sudden declares: "I just don't seem to be hungry."[128] We can interpret this as saying that it wants to step out of the normal and expected course of events. In another cartoon of a string of fish, the smallest one, in front of a door with the inscription "Assertiveness Training," has turned around and faces the whole school of fish with their jaws wide open.[129] It takes courage and guts really to break out of the line-up as it were. Another color drawing by the German artist Hans Ticha illustrates the same idea. Four fish in metallic colors are for once not drawn horizontally but vertically with the biggest fish on the top and the smallest one on the bottom. This part of the illustration looks almost like a grotesque power drill with the smallest fish being the bit and the biggest one being the tool itself. A yellow arrow facing down next to the four fish intensifies the powerful drive downwards. And there, on the bottom, is a fifth fish, the smallest one, which lies there sideways, probably alluding to the German proverbial expression "jemandem in die Quere kommen" (to get into somebody's way) or simply "sich schräg stellen" (to deviate from the expected norm).[130] It is an attempt to overcome the logic of the fish, and the title of the drawing is "Erkenntnisse" (recognition or enlightened thoughts), which seems to imply that we should recognize the necessity of over-coming the natural law of big fish eating little fish. But can an individual really break through this powerful chain, or are what we have seen in the last three cartoons only isolated cases? Must we always live by the old proverbial wisdom of "Big fish eat little fish," as a realistic illustration of the proverb shows it ad infinitum,[131] where the sequence of fish eating fish simply doesn't stop? Is there no hope at all of overcoming this fatalistic proverb?

Judging by the fourth group of our examples, which illustrate the

vicious circle of fish of the same size trying to incorporate each other, the aggressive behavior is not about to stop. Yet another article on a "Four-Way Takeover" was accompanied by an illustration showing four equal-sized sharks chasing each other around.[132] It reminds us of a dog chasing its tail without ever quite getting it. Perhaps the circular motion shows the futility of all of this and our inability to stop it. This certainly is the case in an older *New Yorker* cartoon that reduces all of life to such a crazy circle of fish. Each fish has its individual label, such as: "Chauvinism," "Taxes," "Ambition," "Nixon," "Facts," "Time," "Space," "Noise," and "Truth."[133] One would think that such fish of equal size could stop the "incorporation" process, but it appears to be human nature to be satisfied only if aggression takes place. Such illustrations also show simply that one thing leads to another, and that this is part of the human condition.

Turning to our fifth and last group of modern references and reinterpretations of the proverb, we have the attempt of many small fish to gang up on the larger one. What the isolated individual fish was not able to achieve can perhaps be accomplished if the small fish show some solidarity against the large perpetrators. This is no new idea, for the famous German paremiographer Karl Friedrich Wilhelm Wander wrote as early as 1858 in his political diary of comments on proverbs the following thought: "'Große Fische fressen die kleinen,' wenigstens dann, wenn diese sich fressen lassen, und so lange bis sie auf den Gedanken kommen, sich zu sammeln und—die großen zu fressen."[134] ("Big fish eat little," at least as long as the latter let themselves be eaten, and until they come up with the idea of joining together and eating the large ones).

This thought process was beautifully illustrated in four watercolor pictures by Leo Lionni in his children's book *Swimmy* (1963). The first picture shows a big fish chasing many little red fish and a small black fish called Swimmy. The simple text states "One bad day a tuna fish, swift, fierce and very hungry came darting through the waves. In one gulp he swallowed all the little red fish. Only Swimmy escaped." The next picture shows how Swimmy "taught them [a new group of small fish] to swim close together, each in his own place." The third illustration contains a big fish formed by the little red fish with Swimmy being the black eye: "When they had learned to swim like one giant fish, he said, 'I'll be the eye!'" And predictably, the fourth picture has the little fish turned big fish chase a couple of large tunas away: "And so they swam in the cool morning water and in the midday sun and chased the big fish away."[135] What a wonderful way of teaching young children the value of assertiveness and solidarity.

But cartoonists have also used the same idea to show adults how to overcome the ever-present threat of the big fish. In 1975 Ken Sprague drew a two sequence cartoon that first shows the normal state of affairs of a big fish chasing several small ones and then the small fish in their consolidated big-fish shape ready to devour this aggressor.[136] A similar symbolic inversion is presented in Basilios Mitropoulos' cartoon from 1975 with the title "Little fish eats big fish." A big fish composed of many little fish with another "Swimmy" as its eye swims along calmly and self-assuredly while the formerly large fish is pursuing it in a perplexed fashion.[137] In two recent political and economical caricatures this new motif is repeated. In a flier distributed in the German university town of Göttingen in 1983 we have once again a two-sequence illustration. In the first frame it is Uncle Sam in the shape of a large fish wearing his customary top hat who wants to eat the small Nicaraguan fish. But in the second frame the unified Nicaraguans are chasing the American intruder away.[138] Another caricature has the strong united "Lobbyists" pursue President Reagan's fish symbolizing his "Tax Reform," showing clearly the power of such groups to influence positively or negatively any change in government policy.[139]

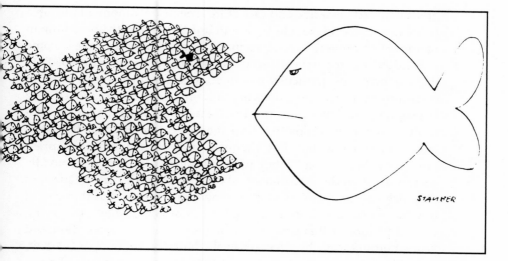

STAUBER

Two final cartoons without any captions can wind up this modern survey. A Swiss illustration shows a large fish with its mouth closed opposite a "Swimmy" type fish of equal size with its mouth gaping open.[140] The other and our last cartoon returns to the earlier way of illustrating a chain of three fish about to devour each other, but this time the largest fish is our solidarity fish made up of many little ones.[141] What are we to think of these final examples? Certainly the consolidated big fish has its positive sides in checking the rapacity of individual large fish. The "Swimmy" fish might even be considered to represent yet another classical proverb going way back to Homer, namely "In union (or concord) is strength."[142] But what if this strength is not used in the controlled manner we see in some of our final examples? Then the entire solidarity effort becomes only another element in the law of nature that holds that big fish will always eat little fish. Unfortunately this also means that humans will continue to be ruled by the logic of the fish and that there is no escape from it. Good unified intentions will bring about a temporary improvement, but then the vices of greed and aggression take over again.

We can thus conclude our detailed survey of the fatalistic proverb "Big fish eat little fish" from ancient times to the present day with the observation that in general it contains wisdom that has been recognized by the world for many centuries and still holds true today. Even the symbolic inversion of this proverbial law in aphoristic writing, graffiti, advertisements, and caricatures seems only momentarily able to liberate mankind from its basic and unfortunate truth about human nature. Such proverb inversions in the form of parodies have become very popular in recent years, since people are questioning the absolute value of proverbs, particularly in modern technological societies.[143] In certain contexts such negations of traditional proverbs are indeed very appropriate, but that does not invalidate such proverbs for the majority of other situations to which they might be applied. Basic human nature really has not changed, and since proverbs express "monumenta humana"[144] they will continue to comment most vividly on universal modes of behavior. We might all wish that the proverb "Big fish eat little fish" would be rendered obsolete, but that would require mankind to become more human at last. Judging by the recorded history of this proverb, which spans almost three thousand years, nothing really has changed at all. Rapacity is as rampant as ever, and although the large perpetrators might take on ever new shapes, the metaphorical proverb "Big fish eat little fish" will always be a most fitting description of this unfortunate situation.

# Notes

## Introduction
(pages ix–xx)

1. For the text of the poem see *Goethes Werke*, ed. by Erich Trunz. Hamburg: Christian Wegner, 7th ed. 1964, vol. 1, pp. 247–248.
2. See especially Edward B. Tylor, *Primitive Culture*. 2 vols. New York: H. Holt, 1874.
3. Concerning such views of "tradition" see Hermann Bausinger, *Volkskultur in der technischen Welt*. Stuttgart: Kohlhammer, 1961, pp. 98–100, 108–113, and 117–121; Jan Harold Brunvand, *The Study of American Folklore*. New York: W. W. Norton, 1968; 2d ed. 1978, pp. 1–8; and Alan Dundes, "The Devolutionary Premise in Folklore Theory," *Journal of the Folklore Institute*, 6 (1969), 5–19.
4. See Hans Moser, "Gedanken zur heutigen Volkskunde: Ihre Situation, ihre Problematik, ihre Aufgaben," *Bayerisches Jahrbuch für Volkskunde*, no volume (1954), 228.
5. The German word is "Umstilisierungsprozesse." See Kurt Ranke, "Volkskunde und Kulturgeschichte," *Zeitschrift für deutsche Philologie*, 74 (1955), 347.
6. Jaromir Jech, "Variabilität und Stabilität in den einzelnen Kategorien der Volksprosa," *Fabula*, 9 (1967), 55.
7. Ingeborg Weber-Kellermann, *Deutsche Volkskunde zwischen Germanistik und Sozialwissenschaften*. Stuttgart: Metzler, 1969, p. 93.
8. Hermann Bausinger, *Volkskunde: Von der Altertumsforschung zur Kulturanalyse*. Darmstadt: Carl Habel, 1971, p. 84.
9. Gerhard Heilfurth, "Volkskunde," in *Komplexe Forschungsansätze*, (Volume 4 in *Handbuch der empirischen Sozialforschung*), ed. by René König. Stuttgart: Ferdinand Enke, 1974, p. 175.
10. Günter Wiegelmann, "Theorien und Methoden," in *Volkskunde: Eine Einführung*, ed. by G. Wiegelmann, Matthias Zender and Gerhard Heilfurth. Berlin: Erich Schmidt, 1977, p. 50.
11. See Richard Dorson's famous lecture "Folklore in the Modern World," which he delivered in 1973 at Indiana University in Bloomington and which was published in Dorson's significant volume *Folklore and Fakelore: Essays toward a Discipline of Folk Studies*. Cambridge, Massachusetts: Harvard University Press, 1976, p. 48.

12. The lectures were published as *Tradition und Ursprünglichkeit: Akten des III. Internationalen Germanistenkongresses 1965 in Amsterdam*, ed. by Werner Kohlschmidt and Herman Meyer. Bern: Francke, 1966. Of particular interest are the papers of Herman Meyer, "Tradition und Ursprünglichkeit in Sprache und Literatur" (pp. 18–25); Emil Staiger, "Dialektik der Begriffe Nachahmung und Originalität" (pp. 29–38); and Harold Jantz, "Kontrafaktur, Montage, Parodie: Tradition und symbolische Erweiterung" (pp. 53–65).

13. Hermann Bausinger and Wolfgang Brückner (eds.), *Kontinuität? Geschichtlichkeit und Dauer als volkskundliches Problem*. Berlin: Erich Schmidt, 1969.

14. See Hermann Bausinger, "Zur Algebra der Kontinuität" (note 13), pp. 26–27. See also Karl-Sigismund Kramer, "Umweltverflechtung und Kontinuität" (note 13), pp. 85–86.

15. See the superb article by Lutz Röhrich, "Das Kontinuitätsproblem bei der Erforschung der Volksprosa" (note 13), pp. 117–133.

16. See Nils-Arvid Bringéus, "Das Studium der Innovation," *Zeitschrift für Volkskunde*, 64 (1968), 161–185.

17. On the use of folklore in tourism and other commercial purposes see Hans Moser, "Vom Folklorismus in unserer Zeit," *Zeitschrift für Volkskunde*, 58 (1962), 177–209; and Vilmos Voigt, "Folklore and 'Folklorism' Today," in *Folklore Studies in the Twentieth Century*, ed. by Venetia Newall. Woodbridge, United Kingdom: D. S. Brewer, 1978, pp. 419–424.

## Chapter 1. Grim Variations
## (pages 1–44)

1. For an excellent survey of this research see Max Lüthi, *Märchen*. Stuttgart: Metzler, 1962; 7th ed. 1969. Much bibliographical information for individual fairy tales can be found in Walter Scherf, *Lexikon der Zaubermärchen*. Stuttgart: Alfred Kröner, 1982.

2. An inclusive overview of the Brothers' Grimm various research interests with detailed bibliographical references is provided by Ludwig Denecke, *Jacob Grimm und sein Bruder Wilhelm*. Stuttgart: Metzler, 1971.

3. See Bruno Bettelheim, *The Uses of Enchantment: The Meaning and Importance of Fairy Tales*. New York: A. Knopf, 1976. See also the various psychological interpretations in Wilhelm Laiblin (ed.), *Märchenforschung und Tiefenpsychologie*. Darmstadt: Wissenschaftliche Buchgesellschaft, 1969.

4. Regarding Ernst Bloch's philosophical view of fairy tales see the chapter "The Utopian Function of Fairy Tales and Fantasy: Ernst Bloch the Marxist and J. R. R. Tolkien the Catholic" in Jack Zipes, *Breaking the Magic Spell: Radical Theories of Folk & Fairy Tales*. Austin, Texas: University of Texas Press, 1979, pp. 129–159. See also his fascinating book *Fairy Tales and the Art of Subversion: The Classical Genre for Children and the Process of Civilization*. New York: Wildman Press, 1983.

5. See Waltraut Woeller, *Der soziale Gehalt und die soziale Funktion der deutschen Volksmärchen*. Berlin: Akademie Verlag, 1955; and Christa Bürger, "Die soziale Funktion volkstümlicher Erzählformen—Sage und Märchen," in Heinz Ide (ed.), *Projekt Deutschunterricht 1: Kritisches Lesen: Märchen, Sage, Fabel, Volksbuch*. Stuttgart: Metzler, 1971, pp. 25–56.

6. See Johannes Bolte and Georg Polívka, *Anmerkungen zu den Kinder- und Hausmärchen der Brüder Grimm*. 5 vols. Leipzig: Dieterich, 1913–1932; rpt. Hildesheim: Georg Olms, 1963.

7. Heinz Rölleke (ed.), *Brüder Grimm: Kinder- und Hausmärchen*. 3 vols. Stuttgart: Reclam, 1980 (esp. vol. 3); and H. Rölleke, *"Wo das Wünschen noch geholfen hat": Gesammelte Aufsätze zu den "Kinder- und Hausmärchen" der Brüder Grimm*. Bonn: Bouvier, 1985.

8. Of particular importance among Max Lüthi's numerous studies are *Das europäische Volksmärchen. Form und Wesen*. Bern: Francke, 1947; 3d ed. 1968; and *Das Volksmärchen als Dichtung: Ästhetik und Anthropologie*. Köln: Diederichs, 1975.

9. Vladimir Propp, *Morphology of the Folktale*, ed. by Louis Wagner and Alan Dundes. Austin, Texas: University of Texas Press, 2d ed. 1968.

10. See especially Lutz Röhrich, *Märchen und Wirklichkeit*. Wiesbaden: Franz Steiner, 1956; 3d ed. 1974; and L. Röhrich, *Sage und Märchen: Erzählforschung heute*. Freiburg: Herder, 1976.

11. Jack Zipes (see note 4).

12. See the numerous essays on various aspects of fairy tales in Felix Karlinger (ed.), *Wege der Märchenforschung*. Darmstadt: Wissenschaftliche Buchgesellschaft, 1973; Helmut Brackert (ed.), *"Und wenn sie nicht gestorben sind . . ." Perspektiven auf das Märchen*. Frankfurt: Suhrkamp, 1980; and Michael M. Metzger and Katharina Mommsen (eds.), *Fairy Tales as Ways of Knowing: Essays on Märchen in Psychology, Society and Literature*. Bern: Peter Lang, 1984. See also the eighteen studies on the fairy tale of *Cinderella* alone that Alan Dundes edited in the volume *Cinderella: A Folklore Casebook*. New York: Garland Publishing, 1982.

13. For these remarkable studies see Ernst Böklen, *Schneewittchenstudien*. 2 vols. Leipzig: J. C. Hinrichs, 1910 and 1915; Anna Birgitta Rooth, *The Cinderella Cycle*. Lund: C. W. K. Gleerup, 1951; Marianne Rumpf, *Rotkäppchen: Eine vergleichende Untersuchung*. Diss. Göttingen, 1951; Michael Belgrader, *Das Märchen von dem Machandelboom (KHM 47): Der Märchentypus AT 720: My Mother Slew Me, My Father Ate Me*. Bern: Peter Lang, 1980.

14. See in this regard Joseph Rysan's pioneering article "Folklore and Mass-Lore," *South Atlantic Bulletin*, 36 (1971), 3–9, in which he argued that "there is no reason why the Finnish method employed so successfully in the field of folktales could not be applied to the study of the transmission and migration of modern mass-lore rumors" (p. 9). We propose that the Finnish method be used to study the dissemination of modern texts and allusions to certain fairy tales in the mass media on an international basis.

15. Regarding "Little Red Riding Hood" see Hans Ritz (pseud. Ulrich Erckenbrecht), *Die Geschichte vom Rotkäppchen: Ursprünge, Analysen, Parodien eines Märchens*. Göttingen: Muriverlag, 1981; 3d ed. 1983; Jack Zipes, *The Trials and Tribulations of Little Red Riding Hood: Versions of the Tale in Socio-Cultural Context*. London: Heinemann, 1982; in German translation with the title *Rotkäppchens Lust und Leid: Biographie eines europäischen Märchens*. Köln: Diederichs, 1982; Wolfgang Mieder, "Survival Forms of 'Little Red Riding Hood' in Modern Society," *International Folklore Review*, 2 (1982), 23–40. The two lengthy articles in magazines and newspapers are Rolf Käppeli, "Rotkäppchen darf nicht sterben: Über die Ursprünge einer Kindergeschichte und wie diese im Lauf der Zeit und im Dienst der Herrschenden und Unterdrückten ständig verfremdet wurde," *Tages-Anzeiger Magazin*, no. 38 (22 September 1984), 44–47 and 49–50; and Erwin Brunner, "Die Affäre Rotkäppchen: Der ungeklärte Grimminalfall im Märchenwald: War der Wolf unschuldig? Hat das Mädchen ihn verführt?" *Die Zeit*, no. 52 (28 December 1984), 15–18 (American edition).

Additional texts and illustrations for this fairy tale also by Lutz Röhrich, *Gebärde-Metapher-Parodie: Studien zur Sprache und Volksdichtung*. Düsseldorf: Pädagogischer Verlag Schwann, 1967, pp. 130–152; Wolfgang Mieder (ed.), *Grimms Märchen—modern: Prosa, Gedichte, Karikaturen*. Stuttgart: Reclam, 1979, pp. 79–99; W. Mieder (ed.), *Mädchen, pfeif auf den Prinzen! Märchengedichte von Günter Grass bis Sarah Kirsch*. Köln: Eugen Diederichs, 1983; 2d ed. 1984, pp. 69–72; and W. Mieder (ed.), *Disenchantments: An Anthology of Modern Fairy Tale Poetry*. Hanover, New Hampshire: University Press of New England, 1985, pp. 93–114.

16. See Hermann Bausinger, "Möglichkeiten des Märchens in der Gegenwart," in *Märchen, Mythos, Dichtung: Festschrift zum 90. Geburtstag Friedrich von der Leyens*, ed. by Hugo Kuhn and Kurt Schier. München: C. H. Beck, 1963, pp. 15–30 (esp. pp. 19–23).

17. See Max Lüthi, *The European Folktale: Form and Nature*, trans. John D. Niles. Philadelphia: Institute for the Study of Human Issues, 1982, p. 86.

18. See Zipes, *Breaking the Magic Spell* (note 4), p. 18.

19. See Röhrich, *Märchen und Wirklichkeit* (note 10), p. v.

20. See Lüthi (note 17), p. 125.

21. See Lüthi, *Das Volksmärchen als Dichtung* (note 8), p. 184.

22. The term "Antimärchen" (anti-fairy tale) was first used by André Jolles, *Einfache Formen*. Halle: Max Niemeyer, 1930; rpt. Tübingen: Max Niemeyer, 3d ed. 1965, p. 242. See also Lüthi (note 17), p. 87.

23. The survey was commissioned by the *Bunte* magazine and reported by Wilfried Ahrens, "Grimms Märchen—sagenhaft!" *Bunte*, No. 14 (28 March, 1985), 132–133.

24. Regarding these movies see Kay F. Stone, "Fairy Tales for Adults: Walt Disney's Americanization of the 'Märchen,'" in *Folklore on Two Continents: Essays in Honor of Linda Dégh*, ed. by Nikolai Burlakoff and Carl Lindahl. Bloomington, Indiana: Trickster Press, 1980, pp. 40–48.

25. See Linda Dégh and Andrew Vázsonyi, "Magic for Sale: Märchen and Legend in TV Advertising," *Fabula*, 20 (1979), 47–68 (esp. p. 57).

26. The poem is included in Mieder, *Disenchantments* (note 15), p. 5. All other poems cited in this chapter are taken from this book.

27. *New Yorker* (6 December 1977), p. 177.

28. *New Yorker* (24 January 1977), p. 37.

29. *Good Housekeeping* (February 1979), p. 237.

30. *Burlington Free Press* (11 November 1983), p. 9D.

31. *Burlington Free Press* (5 April 1978), p. 7D.

32. *Simplicissimus*, no. 39 (27 December 1926), p. 527.

33. *Bloomington Sunday Herald-Times* (25 December 1981), no pp. given.

34. *Saturday Review* (14 February 1953), p. 18.

35. *Brattleboro Reformer* (13 May 1981), p. 18.

36. *Los Angeles Times* (29 October 1979), part IV, p. 17.

37. *Punch* (22 July 1981), p. 157.

38. *New Yorker* (14 June 1982), p. 53.

39. *San Francisco Chronicle* (7 March 1979), p. 23.

40. Reprinted in Mieder (note 26), pp. 4–5.

41. *Fortune* (June 1935), p. 29. For studies on folklore and advertising see Otto Görner, "Reklame und Volkskunde," *Mitteldeutsche Blätter für Volkskunde*, 6 (1931), 109–126; Julian Mason, "Some Uses of Folklore in Advertising,"

*Tennessee Folklore Society Bulletin*, 20, no. 3 (1954), 58–61; Alan Dundes, "Advertising and Folklore," *New York Folklore Quarterly*, 19 (1963), 143–151; and Lutz Röhrich, "Folklore and Advertising," in *Folklore Studies in the Twentieth Century*, ed. by Venetia J. Newall. Woodbridge, United Kingdom: D. S. Brewer, 1978, pp. 114–115.

42. Chas Addams, *Es war einmal . . . Addams und Eva*. München: Deutscher Taschenbuchverlag, 1971; 4th ed. 1973, no pp. given.

43. *Playboy* (December 1977), p. 304.

44. *New Yorker* (4 January 1964), p. 58.

45. *Simplicissimus*, no. 52 (26 December 1959), p. 828.

46. For three earlier interpretations of this fairy tale see Lutz Röhrich, "Der Froschkönig und seine Wandlungen," *Fabula*, 20 (1979), 170–192; Wolfgang Mieder, "Modern Anglo-American Variants of 'The Frog Prince' (AT 440)," *New York Folklore*, 6 (1980, published 1982), 111–135; and Walter Blair, "The Funny Fondled Fairytale Frog," *Studies in American Humor*, 1 (1982), 17–23. For additional German texts and cartoons see W. Mieder, *Grimms Märchen—modern* (note 15), pp. 105–118.

47. *Burlington Free Press* (25 August 1982), p. 8D.

48. *Good Housekeeping* (September 1984), p. 198.

49. *Ladies' Home Journal* (November 1974), p. 204.

50. *Punch* (16 January 1980), p. 113.

51. *Punch* (16 November 1966), p. 759.

52. See the excellent papers by Katalin Horn, "Märchenmotive und gezeichneter Witz: Einige Möglichkeiten der Adaption," *Österreichische Zeitschrift Für Volkskunde*, 86, new series 37 (1983), 209–237; and K. Horn, "Grimmsche Märchen als Quellen für Metaphern und Vergleiche in der Sprache der Werbung, des Journalismus und der Literatur," *Muttersprache*, 91 (1981), 106–115.

53. Reprinted in Mieder (note 26), pp. 38–39.

54. *Better Homes & Gardens* (February 1979), p. 200.

55. *New Yorker* (6 August 1984), p. 33.

56. *Playboy* (1976, unidentified issue).

57. Reprinted in Mieder (note 26), p. 27.

58. *Die Weltwoche*, no. 27 (7 June 1982), p. 43.

59. *Punch* (14 February 1958), p. 246.

60. *Punch* (29 October 1969), p. 713.

61. Chas Addams (note 42), no pp. given.

62. *New Yorker* (5 February 1966), p. 46.

63. *Cosmopolitan* (November 1982), p. 318.

64. *Playboy* (August 1977), p. 152.

65. Reprinted in Mieder (note 26), pp. 30–31.

66. See for example the *Adult Erotica Catalog* published by Diverse Industries in California. The Spring Catalog 1978 contained advertisements for such films with appropriate illustrations on p. 10, each film costing $12.95.

67. *Punch* (29 June 1966), p. 958.

68. *Penthouse* (November 1977), p. 178.

69. *Penthouse* (April 1976), p. 40.

70. Reprinted in Mieder (note 26), p. 28.

71. *Audubon*, vol. 87, no. 4 (July 1985), p. 20.

72. *Field & Stream* (April 1979), p. 188.

73. Reprinted in Mieder (note 26), p. 41.
74. *Punch* (25 April 1973), p. 563.
75. *Penthouse* (December 1978), p. 222.
76. *Boston Globe* (30 April 1985), comic section, no pp. given. For an introduction to folklore materials in comic strips see Rolf Wilhelm Brednich, "Die Comic Strips als Gegenstand der Erzählforschung." Paper distributed at the *VIth Congress of the International Society for Folk-Narrative Research* (Helsinki, June 16–21, 1974) 19 pp. Compare also the earlier paper by Grace Partridge Smith, "The Plight of the Folktale in the Comics," *Southern Folklore Quarterly*, 16 (1952), 124–127.
77. *Playgirl* (August 1976), p. 111.
78. *Punch* (21/28 December 1983), p. 41.
79. Horst Haitzinger, *Archetypen*. München: Bruckmann, 1979, p. 47.
80. *Punch* (30 July 1969), p. 181.
81. *Good Housekeeping* (January 1980), p. 196.
82. *New Woman* (September 1982), p. 60.
83. *Brattleboro Reformer* (29 June 1978), p. 4.
84. *Saturday Review* (29 May 1976), p. 38.
85. *New York Times* (2 August 1981), p. 3E.
86. *Newsweek* (12 November 1979), p. 85.
87. *Saturday Review* (2 November 1963), p. 13.
88. *Los Angeles Times* (10 November 1983), section II, p. 7.
89. *Burlington Free Press* (25 March 1981), p. 14A.
90. *Burlington Free Press* (26 January 1984), p. 8A.
91. For some earlier studies see Priscilla Denby, "Folklore in the Mass Media," *Folklore Forum*, 4, no. 5 (1971), 113–125; and Donald Allport Bird, "A Theory for Folklore in Mass Media: Traditional Patterns in the Mass Media," *Southern Folklore Quarterly*, 40 (1976), 285–305.
92. Card by American Greetings Company (purchased in Burlington, Vermont, in January 1982).
93. Hallmark Contemporary Cards (purchased in Burlington, Vermont, in March 1979).
94. Card by Hallmark Company (purchased in Burlington, Vermont, in February 1980).
95. Reprinted in Mieder (note 26), p. 159.
96. For an earlier essay on cartoons using Grimm fairy tale motifs, see John T. Flanagan, "Grim Stories: Folklore in Cartoons," *Midwestern Journal of Language and Folklore*, 1 (1975) 20–26.
97. *New Yorker* (27 July 1957), p. 69.
98. *New Yorker* (2 October 1965), p. 53.
99. *New Yorker* (10 December 1984), p. 54.
100. *New Yorker* (27 March 1965), p. 42.
101. *New Yorker* (2 January 1965), p. 26.
102. *Cosmopolitan* (October 1981), p. 274.
103. *New Yorker* (23 July 1979), p. 61.
104. *New Yorker* (16 February 1963), p. 35.
105. *Burlington Free Press* (11 December 1978), p. 10A.
106. *Photo Play* (January 1975), p. 1.
107. *Time* (6 March 1978), p. 54.
108. *Punch* (29 December 1965), p. 959.

109. *New Yorker* (8 January 1966), p. 34.
110. *Playboy* (December 1978), p. 315. For an obscene female counterpart to this sexual cartoon see *Hustler* (February 1979), p. 84.
111. *Saturday Review/World* (18 December 1973), p. 49.
112. Herbert Block, *Herblock Special Report*. New York: Norton, 1974, p. 54. The cartoon dates from January 2, 1960.
113. *Der Spiegel*, no. 28 (7 July 1975), p. 70.
114. *The Economist* (14 June 1985), cover page.
115. *Burlington Free Press* (23 June 1983), p. 7D.
116. *Nebelspalter*, no. 31 (29 July 1980), p. 29.
117. *New Yorker* (15 March 1982), p. 44.
118. *Bloomington Herald-Telephone* (9 February 1982), p. 26.
119. Reprinted in Mieder (note 26), p. 157.
120. *The New York Times* (5 April 1979), p. D24.
121. Reprinted in Mieder (note 26), pp. 153–154.
122. *Playboy* (September 1979), p. 179.
123. *Playboy* (April 1977), p. 129.
124. See Horst Haitzinger (note 79), p. 43. Other sexual cartoons can be found in *Playboy* (August 1977), p. 150; *Penthouse* (December 1977), p. 214; *Playgirl* (January 1984), p. 94. See also the obscene joke that parallels these visual interpretations in *Playboy* (March 1982), p. 132.
125. *Pardon: Vom Besten*. Frankfurt: Pardon Verlagsgesellschaft, 1977, p. 84. The cartoon was published in the *Pardon* magazine in 1975. A similar cartoon is to be found in Lutz Röhrich, *Der Witz: Figuren, Formen, Funktionen*. Stuttgart: Metzler, 1977, p. 72a.
126. Mike Peters, *Win one for the Geezer: The Cartoons*. New York: Bantam Books, 1982, p. 17.
127. *Mad* (December 1974), p. 28.
128. *Vermont Cynic* (23 February 1978), p. 8.
129. *Punch* (1 July 1970), p. 33.
130. Mike Peters, *The Nixon Chronicles*. Dayton, Ohio: Lorenz Press, 1976, p. 92.
131. *Monterey Peninsula Herald* (22 July 1983), p. 22.
132. *Burlington Free Press* (9 April 1984), p. 5A.
133. The poem is printed in *Deutsche Gedichte 1930–1960*, ed. by Hans Bender. Stuttgart: Reclam, 1983, pp. 106–107.
134. See Bettelheim (note 3), p. 161.
135. *The New Yorker: Album of Drawings 1925–1975*. New York: Viking Press, 1975, no pp. given.
136. *Ladies' Home Journal* (November 1977), p. 96.
137. *Punch* (13 June 1979), p. 1048.
138. *Mad* (December 1974), p. 28.
139. *Punch* (6 April 1983), p. 38.
140. *Playboy* (August 1969), p. 133.
141. *Die Weltwoche* (3 November 1982), p. 41.
142. *New Yorker* (20 October 1975), p. 45.
143. *New Yorker* (26 December 1977), p. 31.
144. *Better Homes & Gardens* (March 1977), p. 194.
145. *National Lampoon* (October 1976), p. 81.
146. *New Yorker* (13 June 1977), p. 39.

147. *Punch* (6 December 1978), p. 1008.
148. *Punch* (2 December 1981), p. 1014.
149. *Punch* (24 March 1982), p. 465.
150. *Punch* (22 December 1971), p. 881.
151. *Punch* (21 September 1966), p. 441.
152. *Punch* (15 December 1982), p. 1011.
153. *San Francisco Chronicle* (21 March 1980), p. 5.
154. Reprinted in Mieder (note 26), p. 66.
155. Mieder, *Grimms Märchen—modern* (note 15), p. 24. For a much longer prose version in which a retarded Hansel becomes the murderer of his mother see Andra Diefenthaler's short story "Hansel" in *The Best Short Stories of 1932*, ed. by Edward J. O'Brien. New York: Dodd, Mead and Company, 1932, pp. 101–107.
156. Reprinted in Mieder (note 26), p. 68.
157. Quoted from *Midland Humor*, ed. by Jack Conroy. New York: Current Books, 1947, pp. 353–356.
158. Reprinted in Mieder (note 26), p. 70.
159. *The Economist* (11–17 August 1984), cover page.
160. *Burlington Free Press* (4 December 1982), p. 11A.
161. *Der Spiegel*, no. 18 (30 April 1973), p. 54.
162. *Nebelspalter*, no. 38 (21 September 1982), p. 8.
163. Reprinted in Mieder (note 26), p. 60.
164. *Burlington Free Press* (11 April 1981), p. 8A.
165. Peters (note 126), p. 79.
166. *The Buffalo News* (28 July 1985), comics section, no pp. given.
167. See Metzger (note 12), p. 7.
168. See Werner Psaar and Manfred Klein, *Wer hat Angst vor der bösen Geiß? Zur Märchendidaktik und Märchenrezeption*. Braunschweig: Georg Westermann, 1976; 2d ed. 1980, p. 63.
169. See Lüthi, *Das europäische Volksmärchen* (note 8), p. 69. For the English translation of this significant book by John D. Niles see Lüthi (note 17), p. 74.
170. Lüthi (note 17), p. 80.

## Chapter 2. The Pied Piper of Hamelin
## (pages 45–83)

1. See the twelve-page essay by Christoph Friedrich Fein, *Die entlarvte Fabel vom Ausgange der Hämelschen Kinder: Eine nähere Entdekkung der dahinter verborgenen wahren Geschichte*. Hannover: Johan Christoph Richter, 1749.
2. Two of the significant older studies are Franz Jostes, *Der Rattenfänger von Hameln: Ein Beitrag zur Sagenkunde*. Bonn: P. Hanstein, 1895; and Friedrich Meißel, *Die Sage vom Rattenfänger von Hameln*. Hameln: L. Warneson, 4th ed. 1924.
3. See Willy Krogmann, *Der Rattenfänger von Hameln: Eine Untersuchung über das Werden der Sage*. Berlin: Emil Ebering, 1934; rpt. Nendeln, Liechtenstein: Kraus Reprints, 1967; Wolfgang Wann, *Die Lösung der Hamelner Rattenfängersage: Ein Symbol des Abendlandes*. Diss. Würzburg, 1949; Heinrich Spanuth, *Der Rattenfänger von Hameln*. Diss. Göttingen, 1951; Heinrich Spanuth, *Der Rattenfänger von Hameln: Vom Werden und Sinn einer alten Sage*. Hameln: C. W. Niemeyer, 1951, 2d ed. 1969; and Hans Dobbertin, *Quellensammlung zur Hamel-*

*ner Rattenfängersage*. Göttingen: Otto Schwarz, 1970. Dobbertin's book contains the best bibliography for this legend on pp. 133–148. See also the following significant papers not mentioned in subsequent footnotes of this chapter: Waltraud Woeller, "Zur Sage vom Rattenfänger von Hameln," *Wissenschaftliche Zeitschrift der Humboldt-Universität zu Berlin, Gesellschafts- und sprachwissenschaftliche Reihe*, 6 (1956), 135–146; Otto Lauffer, "Altertumskundliche Beiträge zur Erklärung der Sage von den Hämelschen Kindern," in *Vom Geist der Dichtung: Gedächtnisschrift für Robert Petsch*, ed. Fritz Martini. Hamburg: Hoffmann und Campe, 1949, pp. 306–315; Hans Dobbertin, "Berichtigungen und Ergänzungen zur Hamelner Kinderausfahrt (1284)," *Niedersächsisches Jahrbuch für Landesgeschichte*, 49 (1977), 315–320; Hans Dobbertin, *Beiträge zur Hamelner Kinderausfahrt (1284)*. Springe: Selbstverlag, 1978; Bernard Queenan, "The Evolution of the Pied Piper," *Children's Literature*, 7 (1978), 104–114; and Helmut Krohne, "Der Rattenfänger von Hameln," *Magazin für Abenteuer-, Reise- und Unterhaltungsliteratur*, no. 26 (1980), 34–40.

4. See Hans Dobbertin, "Neues zur Hamelner Rattenfängersage," *Fabula*, 1 (1957), 144–155; and Hans Dobbertin, "Die Hamelner Glasbildinschrift als Hauptquelle der Rattenfängersage," *Zeitschrift für Volkskunde*, 62 (1966), 29–42.

5. Dobbertin, *Quellensammlung* (note 3), pp. 15–16 (ill. 5). The English translation is from my student Barbara Sporzynski Gifford and it is included in her unpublished Master's Thesis entitled *The Pied Piper and His Followers: A Study of a Legend and Its Descendants*. M. A. Thesis University of Vermont, 1980, p. 15. This 278-page thesis is based on my materials on the Pied Piper legend and contains chapters on the origin of the legend, folk legends and songs related to it, the Pied Piper in poetry, prose and drama, the Pied Piper in children's literature, thematic materials in art and music, short allusions to the Pied Piper in cartoons and advertisements, and the impact of tourism on the legend. Regarding the "Lüneburg Manuscript" see also Heino Gehrts, "Zur Rattenfängerfrage," *Zeitschrift für deutsche Philologie*, 74 (1955), 191–204.

6. Dobbertin, *Quellensammlung* (note 3), p. 21. The English translation is from Barbara S. Gifford. Zeitlos probably wrote this account down in June 1553, when he spent several days in Hamelin. The year "1283" goes back to an erroneous source in a Hamelin chronicle.

7. Spanuth, *Der Rattenfänger von Hameln: Vom Werden und Sinn einer alten Sage* (note 3), p. 29. The translation is from Barbara S. Gifford.

8. Ibid, p. 32. A better illustration of the stone is in Dobbertin, *Quellensammlung* (note 3), ill. 10.

9. Ibid, p. 34a (ill. 3; Rattenfängerhaus) and p. 34b (ill. 4: part of the inscription).

10. Ibid, p. 34b (ill. 4). See also Heinrich Spanuth, *Baudenkmäler und historische Stätten in Hameln: Ein Führer durch die Rattenfängerstadt*. Hameln: C. W. Niemeyer, 1950; 5th ed. 1976. For an earlier essay see Martin Waehler, "Denkmale als Ausgangspunkt für Sagen: Zur Entstehung der Rattenfänger-Sage," *Volkswerk: Jahrbuch des Städtischen Museums für deutsche Volkskunde*, 8 (1943), 99–114.

11. See James P. O'Donnell, "Der Rattenfänger von Hameln," *Der Monat. Eine internationale Zeitschrift*, no. 93 (1956), 54–61. See also the similar English version of this paper "What Happened to These Children?" *The Saturday Evening Post* (24 December 1955), pp. 26–27 and 54–55. The books mentioned in note 3 all refer to various theories. But see also Waltraud Woeller, "Zur

Entstehung und Entwicklung der Sage vom Rattenfänger von Hameln," *Zeitschrift für deutsche Philologie*, 80 (1961), 180–206.

12. Notably C. F. Fein tried to link the legend with this tragic battle (note 1). Franz Jostes (note 2) also adhered to this theory.

13. See for example Willy Krogmann (note 3), pp. 40–43.

14. For a medical discussion of this theory see D. Wolfers, "A Plaguey Piper," *The Lancet* (3 April 1965), 756–757. Wolfers also mentions the "Totentanz" (Dance of Death) in connection with the legend.

15. See Sabine Baring-Gould, "The Pied Piper of Hamelin," in S. Baring-Gould, *Curious Myths of the Middle Ages*. London: Rivingtons, 1873, pp. 417–446; Heinrich Lessmann, *Der deutsche Volksmund im Lichte der Sage*. Berlin: Herbert Stubenrauch, 1937, pp. 254–273; Gerhard Goebel, "Apoll in Hameln: Ein Nachtrag zu den 'Göttern im Exil,'" *Germanisch-Romanische Monatsschrift*, 63, New Series 32 (1982), 286–299.

16. See Wolfgang Wann and Heinrich Spanuth (note 3). See also Hans Dobbertin, *Wohin zogen die Hämelschen Kinder (1284)?* Hildesheim: August Lax, 1955 (*Niedersächsisches Jahrbuch für Landesgeschichte* 27 [1955], 45–122); Alfred Cammann, "Rattenfängersage und Ostsiedlung nach dem derzeitigen Stande der Forschung," *Heimat und Volkstum: Jahrbuch für bremische, niedersächsische Volkskunde*, no volume (1957), 66–76; Hans Dobbertin, "Der Ausgang der Hämelschen Kinder: Ein Vermißtenschicksal der Kolonisationszeit wurde zur Volkssage," *Jahrbuch für Volkskunde der Heimatvertriebenen*, 4 (1958), 35–68; Lotte Weinerth, *Was hat die Rattenfängersage von Hameln mit Olmütz zu tun?* Steinheim, Main: Diwisch, 1971.

17. Dobbertin, *Quellensammlung* (note 3), pp. 24–25. The translation is by Barbara S. Gifford.

18. Ibid, pp. 121–131.

19. See Leander Petzoldt, *Historische Sagen*. München: C. H. Beck, 1977, vol. 2, pp. 66–69; and Leander Petzoldt, *Deutsche Volkssagen*. München: C. H. Beck, 1978, pp. 48–49. For some English examples see Mary Claire Randolph, "Rat Satires and the Pied Piper of Hamelin Legend," *Southern Folklore Quarterly*, 5 (1941), 81–100.

20. Spanuth, *Der Rattenfänger von Hameln* (note 3), p. 166 (ill. 2).

21. Petzoldt, *Historische Sagen* (note 19), vol. 2, p. 67.

22. Dobbertin, *Quellensammlung* (note 3), pp. 46–47 (ill. 17). The translation is my own.

23. See the detailed remarks by Manfred Brauneck, "Der Rattenfänger von Hameln: Ein Beitrag zur Sagenbehandlung auf der Unterstufe," *Der Deutschunterricht*, 20, no. 6 (1968), 28–41.

24. The rhymed version is printed in Dobbertin, *Quellensammlung* (note 3), pp. 67–69 (ill. 23). The illustration together with the detail is also found in Spanuth, *Der Rattenfänger von Hameln* (note 3), p. 64a (ill. 5).

25. See Donald Ward, *The German Legends of the Brothers Grimm*. Philadelphia: Institute for the Study of Human Issues, 1981, vol. 1, p. 393. There is, however, an unpublished English translation from 1980 in Barbara S. Gifford's study (note 5), pp. 6–8.

26. Dobbertin, *Quellensammlung* (note 3) pp. 118–120; and Ward (note 25), pp. 207–208.

27. See Richard Verstegan, *A Restitution of Decayed Intelligence in Antiquities.* Antwerp: Robert Bruney, 1605; London: John Norton, 1634, pp. 85–87. Also

printed in Dobbertin, *Quellensammlung* (note 3), pp. 57–59. For another early English version in the form of a letter dated 1 October 1643, see James Howell, *Epistolae Ho-Elianae: Familiar Letters, Domestick and Foreign*. London: J. Darey, 9th ed. 1726. Also printed in Dobbertin, *Quellensammlung* (note 3), p. 84.

28. See Andrew Lang, *The Red Fairy Book*. London: Longmans, Green and Co., 1890; rpt. New York: Dover, 1966, pp. 208–214. For a short discussion of French versions see Jean-Luc Busset, "Les sources du 'Joueur de Flûte' de Mérimée: La légende du preneur de rats de Hameln," *Revue de littérature comparée*, 53 (1979), 17–26.

29. Quoted from Arthur Dickson, "Browning's Source for the 'Pied Piper of Hamelin,'" *Studies in Philology*, 23 (1926), 329 (the whole article on pp. 327–336). For some additional scholarship on Browning and the Pied Piper see George Willis Cook, *A Guide-Book to the Poetic and Dramatic Works of Robert Browning*. Boston: Houghton, Mifflin & Co., 1891, pp. 291–294; William Clyde DeVane, *A Browning Handbook*. New York: Appleton-Century-Crofts, 1955, pp. 127–131; J. L. Winter, "Browning's Piper," *Notes and Queries*, new series 13 (October 1967), 373; and Jack W. Herring, *The Pied Piper of Hamelin in the Armstrong Browning Library, Baylor University, Waco, Texas*. Waco, Texas: Baylor University Browning Interests, 1969.

30. For a short discussion of this poem as well as its complete text see William Hall Griffin, "Robert Browning the Elder," *The Bookman*, 248 (May 1912), 66–70.

31. See *The Complete Works of Robert Browning*, ed. Roma A. King. Athens, Ohio: Ohio University Press, 1971, vol. 3, pp. 252–253. For a modern parody of this poem depicting problems of homosexuality in California see Sean Kelly and Michel Choquette, "The Pied Piper of Burbank," *National Lampoon* (March 1971), pp. 58–61.

32. *Complete Works of Robert Browning* (note 31), p. 259.

33. A few recent examples of children's books dealing with the Pied Piper are Kurt Baumann, *The Pied Piper of Hamelin*. New York: Methuen, 1978; Kay Brown, *The Pied Piper of Hamelin*. New York: Derrydale, 1978; Tony Ross, *The Pied Piper of Hamelin*. New York: Lothrop, Lee & Shepard, 1978; and Donna Diamond, *The Pied Piper of Hamelin*. New York: Holiday House, 1981.

34. *The Pied Piper of Hamelin*, by Robert Browning, with thirty-five illustrations by Kate Greenaway, engraved and printed in colours by Edmund Evans. London: Frederick Warne, 1888. The small reprint was published in 1983 by the Merrimack Publishing Corporation in New York.

35. Walter Ruhm, *Der Rattenfänger von Hameln nach dem Gedicht von Robert Browning*. Hameln: C. W. Niemeyer, 1967.

36. For a discussion of these texts and more see Spanuth, *Der Rattenfänger von Hameln* (note 3), pp. 70–81; and Gifford (note 5), pp. 62–119. Here will be listed only a few dramatic and musical adaptations not included in Spanuth's or Gifford's studies: Carl August Görner, *Der Rattenfänger von Hameln: Märchen-Komödie mit Gesang in 10 Bildern*. Altona: A Prinz, ca. 1880; Adolf Neuendorff, *Rattenfänger von Hameln: The Rat-Charmer of Hamelin: Comic Opera in Four Acts*. New York: E. Schuberth, 1881; Walter H. Aiken, *The Pied Piper of Hamelin: Operetta for Treble Voices*. Cincinnati, Ohio: Willis Music Co., 1917; Joseph W. Clokey, *The Pied Piper of Hamelin: Opera in Three Acts*. Boston: C. C. Birchard, 1923; Agnes Curren Hamm, *Robert Browning's "Pied Piper of Hamelin" Arranged as a Choral Drama*: Milwaukee, Wisconsin: The Tower Press, 1942; Melvin

Bernhardt, *The Pied Piper of Hamelin.* Chicago: The Coach House Press, 1963; William Glennon, *The Pied Piper.* Chicago: The Coach House Press, 1968; and Peter Wilson, *The Pied Piper of Hamelin: An Assembly-Length Musical.* Elgin, Illinois: Performance Publishing, 1981.

37. Quoted from Achim von Arnim and Clemens Brentano, *Des Knaben Wunderhorn*, ed. Arthur Henkel. München: Deutscher Taschenbuch Verlag, 1963, vol. 1, p. 27.

38. *The Poems of Goethe*, translated by E. A. Bowring, et al. New York: Lovell Coryell, 1882, pp. 108–109.

39. Johann Wolfgang von Goethe, *Faust*, ed. Erich Trunz. Hamburg: Christian Wegner, 1963, p. 117 (line 3699).

40. See Morris Palmer Tilley, *A Dictionary of the Proverbs in England in the Sixteenth and Seventeenth Centuries.* Ann Arbor, Michigan: University of Michigan Press, 1950, p. 541; Vincent Stuckey Lean, *Lean's Collectanea: Proverbs (English & Foreign), Folk Lore, and Superstitions, Also Compilations towards Dictionaries of Proverbial Phrases and Words, Old and Disused.* ed. by T. W. Williams. Bristol: J. W. Arrowsmith, 1903; rpt. Detroit: Gale Research Co., 1969, vol. 3, p. 494; G. L. Apperson, *English Proverbs and Proverbial Phrases: A Historical Dictionary.* London: J. M. Dent, 1929; rpt. Detroit: Gale Research Co., 1969, p. 487; F. P. Wilson, *The Oxford Dictionary of Proverbs.* Oxford: Clarendon Press, 1970, p. 615.

41. Wilson (note 40), p. 615.

42. See for example Archer Taylor and Bartlett Jere Whiting, *A Dictionary of American Proverbs and Proverbial Phrases, 1820–1880.* Cambridge, Massachusetts: Harvard University Press, 1958, p. 131.

43. See A C. Mounsey, "England must pay the piper," *Notes and Queries*, 6th series, 9 (March 29, 1884), pp. 248–249. Brewer repeated his claim in *The Reader's Handbook.* Philadelphia: J. P. Lippincott, 1893, p. 766.

44. See *Brewer's Dictionary of Phrase and Fable*, revised by Ivor H. Evans. New York: Harper & Row, 1970, pp. 812 and 832–833.

45. Albert M. Hyamson, *A Dictionary of English Phrases.* New York: E. P. Dutton, 1922; rpt. Detroit: Gale Research Co., 1970, p. 274.

46. Charles N. Lurie, *Everyday Sayings: Their Meanings Explained: Their Origins Given.* New York: G. P. Putnam's Sons, 1928; rpt. Detroit: Gale Research Co., 1968, pp. 259–260.

47. Laurence Urdang and Nancy LaRoche, *Picturesque Expressions: A Thematic Dictionary.* Detroit: Gale Research Co., 1980, p. 53.

48. See Lurie (note 46), p. 259.

49. *The Random House Dictionary of the English Language*, ed. by Jess Stein. New York: Random House, 1967, p. 1090.

50. *Webster's Third New International Dictionary of the English Language*, ed. by Philip Babcock Gove. Springfield, Massachusetts: Merriam, 1971, p. 1712.

51. *The World Book Dictionary*, ed. by Clarence and Robert Barnhart. Chicago: World Book, 1976, vol. 2, p. 1578. It is interesting to note that the figurative meaning is not yet included in *The Oxford English Dictionary.* Oxford: Clarendon Press, 1933; rpt. 1961, vol. 7, p. 896.

52. *The Collected Works of Ambrose Bierce.* New York: Neale Publishing Co., 1910, vol. 4, p. 257.

53. *Der wahre Jakob*, no. 519 (12 June 1906), p. 5077.

54. *Kladderadatsch*, no. 20 (19 May 1929), p. 15.

55. *Kladderadatsch*, no. 8 (19 February 1933), p. 15.
56. *Kladderadatsch*, no. 44 (31 October 1937), p. 4.
57. *Kladderadatsch*, no. 3 (16 January 1944), p. 4.
58. *Saturday Review* (30 August 1947), p. 14.
59. Erich Weinert, *Gedichte 1941–1953*, ed. by Edith Zenker. Berlin: Aufbau, 1976, p. 27.
60. Bertolt Brecht, *Gesammelte Werke*, ed. by Elisabeth Hauptmann, Frankfurt: Suhrkamp, 1967, vol. 9, pp. 802–803.
61. *The New York Times* (4 February 1934), section 4, p. 2E. Also printed in Ernst Hanfstaengl, *Hitler in der Karikatur der Welt: Tat gegen Tinte*. Berlin: Braune Verlag, 1934, p. 48.
62. *Time* (15 March 1943), inside front cover. Also in *Fortune* (May 1943), inside back cover.
63. *Der Spiegel*, no. 37 (8 September 1969), p. 31.
64. *Schwarzwälder Bote* (17 February 1979), p. 1.
65. *Nebelspalter*, no. 49 (4 December 1979), p. 11.
66. *Pravda* (9 July 1978). I owe this reference to my colleague Kevin McKenna. For an informative analysis of the reworkings of the legend in the Soviet Union see Günther Wytrzens, *Eine russische dichterische Gestaltung der Sage vom Hamelner Rattenfänger*. Wien: Verlag der Österreichischen Akademie der Wissenschaften, 1981.
67. The caricature was reprinted in the *World Press Review* (November 1981), p. 46.
68. *Time* (18 December 1974), p. 36.
69. *Burlington Free Press* (8 January 1977), p. 6A.
70. *Die Zeit*, no. 49 (8 December 1978), p. 1.
71. *New Yorker* (11 October 1958), p. 35.
72. *Die Weltwoche*, no. 31 (30 July 1980), p. 4.
73. *New Yorker* (22 December 1980), p. 39.
74. *Saturday Review* (13 January 1962), p. 71.
75. *Playboy* (June 1976), pp. 150–151.
76. *Saturday Review* (22 September 1962), p. 21.
77. *Vermont Cynic* (17 March 1977), p. 7.
78. *Burlington Free Press* (6 September 1981), p. 7D.
79. Merchandise bag, found in April 1978 in St. Armands Key, Florida.
80. Poster distributed on the University of Vermont (Burlington, Vermont) campus in April 1979.
81. *Punch* (17 June 1970), p. 925.
82. *Punch* (14 May 1980), p. 735.
83. *New Yorker* (25 November 1961), p. 47.
84. *Punch* (21 February 1979), p. 301.
85. Baltimore Yellow Pages (1977). I owe this reference to my former student Barbara Schermerhorn.
86. See James Gould and Clifford Morgan, "Hearing in the Rat at High Frequencies," *Science*, 94 (15 August 1941), p. 168.
87. *Burlington Free Press* (11 January 1978), p. 1A. A shorter version of this report also appeared in *Time* (29 August 1977), p. 32.
88. S. B. Hustvedt and Archer Taylor, "The Pied Piper of Hamelin," *California Folklore Quarterly*, 3 (1944), 150–151. For a short comment on this "dramatization" of the ancient legend see Wayland Hand, "From Folk Legend to Folk

Custom: The Shift from Narrative to Dramatic Contexts," *Midwestern Journal of Language and Folklore*, 2 (1976), 14–15 (the whole article on pp. 10–19).

89. Hand (note 88), p. 15.

90. *Bild und Funk* (20 January 1984), p. 5.

91. *New Yorker* (27 September 1982), p. 42.

92. *Good Housekeeping* (July 1981), p. 224.

93. *New Yorker* (12 November 1979), p. 54.

94. *Better Homes and Gardens* (September 1979), p. 164.

95. Charles M. Schulz, *Go Fly a Kite, Charlie Brown: A Peanuts Book*. New York: Holt, Rinehart & Winston, 1960, no pp. given.

96. *New Yorker* (14 August 1965), p. 29.

97. *Kansas Quarterly*, 4, no. 1 (1971/1972), p. 41.

98. Mac Hammond, *The Horse Opera and Other Poems*. Columbus, Ohio: Ohio State University Press, 1950, 2d ed. 1966, p. 85.

99. *Penthouse* (March 1975), p. 53.

100. *New Yorker* (3 July 1978), p. 31.

101. *Punch* (7 November 1979), p. 813.

102. Gwendolyn MacEwen, *Magic Animals: Selected Poems Old and New*. Toronto: Macmillan, 1974, p. 26.

103. David Curry, *Here (Poems, 1965–1969)*. New York: New Rivers Press, 1970, p. 70.

104. John Ashberry, *Some Trees*. New York: Corinth Books, 1970, p. 69.

105. Ingeborg Engelhardt, *Der Ruf des Spielmanns*. Stuttgart: K. Thienemann, 1977; rpt. München: Deutscher Taschenbuch Verlag, 1982.

106. Carl Zuckmayer, *Der Rattenfänger: Eine Fabel*. Frankfurt: Fischer, 1975. There is also a longer protest ballad by Hannes Wader that interprets the legend as class struggle and generation conflict. It is included in Ingrid Röbbelen, "'Fast jeder weiß, was in Hameln geschah / vor tausend und einem Jahr . . . ' Hannes Wader: 'Der Rattenfänger,'" *Praxis Deutsch*, no. 35 (May 1979), 51–54.

107. Gloria Skurzynski, *What Happened in Hamelin*. New York: Four Winds Press, 1979. For a long poetic retelling of the basic legend see *The Collected Poems of Wilbert Snow*. Middletown, Connecticut: Wesleyan University Press, 1960, pp. 266–267.

108. The unpublished "Rattenfängerspiel" (Pied Piper Play) consists of six typed manuscript pages.

109. See the many postcards and pamphlets that can be purchased at almost every corner and store in Hamelin.

110. Such puzzles are produced by the Playskool Company and by H. G. Toys.

111. The Wible Language Institute produced a tape with thirty color slides of the legend for the teaching of elementary German in the United States (ca. 1975). These educational materials can be purchased from the Wible Language Institute, 24 South Eighth Street, Allentown, Pennsylvania, 18105.

112. Hallmark Story Lines. Greeting card purchased in Burlington, Vermont (September 1982).

113. Nikolaus Cybinski, *Werden wir je so klug sein, den Schaden zu beheben, durch den wir es wurden? Aphorismen*. Lörrach: Waldemar Lutz, 1979, p. 37.

114. This colorful caricature by Adolph Born is entitled "Winter in Hameln" and appeared in the Swiss satirical magazine *Nebelspalter*, no. 7 (15 February 1983), p. 8.

115. Sigbert Latzel, *Stichhaltiges: Aphorismen*. St. Michael: J. G. Bläschke, 1983, p. 30.

## Chapter 3. Modern Variants of the Daisy Oracle (pages 84–117)

Originally published in *Midwestern Journal of Language and Folklore*, 11 (1985), 65–115 (with 66 illustrations).

1 See for example Iona and Peter Opie, *The Oxford Dictionary of Nursery Rhymes*. Oxford: Clarendon Press, 1951, pp. 331–332 and 404–405.

2. The entire poem is quoted in *Walther von der Vogelweide: Sprüche—Lieder—Der Leich*, ed. by Paul Stapf. Berlin: Tempel, 1963, p. 336.

3. The translation is taken from William Wells Newell, *Games and Songs of American Children*. New York: Harper, 1883; rpt. New York: Dover, 1963, p. 105. It is also quoted in Opie (note 1), p. 332.

4. See Ignaz Zingerle, *Das deutsche Kinderspiel im Mittelalter*. Innsbruck: Wagner, 1873, p. 32. This English translation as well as all the others in this chapter are mine.

5. Ibid., p. 32.

6. See the excellent discussion of the treatment of daisies in English literature in Vernon Rendall, *Wild Flowers in Literature*. London: The Scholartis Press, 1934, pp. 204–239 (Chaucer and Shakespeare pp. 206–208). Of interest also are Frederick G. Savage, *The Flora and Folk Lore of Shakespeare*. Cheltenham: J. Burrow, 1923, pp. 21–24; and Henry N. Ellacombe, *The Plant-Lore and Garden-Craft of Shakespeare*. London: W. Satchell, 1884, pp. 361–378.

7. The manuscript was edited by Carl Haltaus, *Liederbuch der Clara Hätzlerin*. Leipzig: Gottfried Basse, 1840, p. 173. The book is primarily a collection of folk songs, but on pp. 171–173 Hätzlerin gives short explanations of the meaning and uses of certain plants and flowers. I owe this reference to Wilhelm Wackernagel, "Die Farben- und Blumensprache des Mittelalters," in W. Wackernagel, *Kleinere Schriften: Abhandlungen zur deutschen Alterthumskunde und Kunstgeschichte*. Leipzig: S. Hirzel, 1872, vol. 1, pp. 231–232. The Brothers Grimm cite a reference similar to the one by Clara Hätzlerin and state in a footnote that it refers to the well-known game of plucking a flower as a love oracle. See Brüder Grimm, *Altdeutsche Wälder*. Cassel: Thurmeissen, 1813; rpt. Darmstadt: Wissenschaftliche Buchgesellschaft, 1966, vol. 1, p. 152.

8. For a detailed discussion of various names of the daisy in German folk speech see Heinrich Marzell, "Wie heißt die Marguerite im Volksmund?" *Volkskundliche Gaben: John Meier zum siebzigsten Geburtstage dargebracht*, ed. by Harry Schewe. Berlin: Walter de Gruyter, 1934, pp. 130–137. Even more names (literally dozens of them) are listed in Heinrich Marzell, "Chrysanthemum Leucanthemum L.—Wucherblume," *Wörterbuch der deutschen Pflanzennamen*. Leipzig: S. Hirzel, 1943, vol. 1, cols. 956–972. See also Heinrich Marzell, "Maßliebchen" and "Wucherblume" in *Handwörterbuch des deutschen Aberglaubens*, ed. by Eduard Hoffmann-Krayer and Hanns Bächtold-Stäubli. Berlin: Walter de Gruyter, 1932/33 and 1938/41, vol. 5, cols. 1861–1863 and vol. 9, cols. 817–820. A more recent encyclopedic article on the folklore of flowers makes no mention of the daisy oracle. See Gertraud Meinel, "Blume" in *Enzyklopädie des Märchens*, ed. by Kurt Ranke et al. Berlin: Walter de Gruyer, 1979, vol. 2, cols. 483–495.

9. G. F. Northall, *English Folk-Rhymes: A Collection of Traditional Verses Relating to Places and Persons, Customs, Superstitions, etc.* London: Kegan Paul, Trench, Trübner & Co., 1892, rpt. Detroit: Singing Tree Press, 1968, p. 543.

10. James T. R. Ritchie, *Golden City*. Edinburgh: Oliver & Boyd, 1965, p. 23.

11. Carl Withers, *A Rocket in My Pocket: The Rhymes and Chants of Young Americans*. New York: Holt, Rinehart and Winston, 1948, p. 177. The illustration is by Suzanne Suba.

12. *Brigitte* (October 1956), p. 8. Located by Mrs. Kate Olschki.

13. Iona and Peter Opie, *The Lore and Language of Schoolchildren*. Oxford: Clarendon Press, 1959, pp. 338–339.

14. Doreen Gullen, *Traditional Number Rhymes and Games*. London: University of London Press, 1950, p. 19.

15. See for example Henry Carrington Bolton, *The Counting-Out Rhymes of Children*. New York: Appleton, 1888; rpt. Detroit: Singing Tree Press, 1969, p. 6.

16. A. A. Milne, *Now we Are Six*. New York: E. P. Dutton, 1927; rpt. 1961, pp. 20–23. The illustrations are by Ernest H. Shepard.

17. Alan Patrick Herbert, *"Tinker, Tailor": A Child's Guide to the Professions*. Garden City, New Jersey: Doubleday, Page & Co., 1923, pp. 7–8.

18. For a detailed bibliography on this divination rhyme see Roger D. Abrahams, *Jump-Rope Rhymes: A Dictionary*. Austin, Texas: University of Texas Press, 1969, pp. 39 and 168–169. See also Roger D. Abrahams and Lois Rankin, *Counting-Out Rhymes: A Dictionary*. Austin, Texas: University of Texas Press, 1980, pp. 197–198. Three longer variants are listed in Iona and Peter Opie (note 13), p. 339; Alison Utley, *Country Things*. London: Faber and Faber, 1946, pp. 63–64; and Patricia Evans, *Rimbles: A Book of Children's Classic Games, Rhymes, Songs, and Sayings*. Garden City, New York: Doubleday, 1961, pp. 24–25.

19. Leslie Daiken, *Out Goes She: Dublin Street Rhymes*. Dublin: The Dolmen Press, 1963, p. 26.

20. John Le Carré, *Tinker, Tailor, Soldier, Spy*. New York: Alfred A. Knopf, 1974, p. 273.

21. *New Yorker* (29 September 1980), p. 122.

22. For references see above all Iona and Peter Opie (note 1), pp. 404–405; and William Wells Newell (note 3), pp. 105–107. Newell also cites several examples from Switzerland, Austria, and France.

23. Franz Magnus Böhme (ed.), *Deutsches Kinderlied und Kinderspiel*. Leipzig: Breitkopf & Härtel, 1924, p. 185.

24. Ernst Ludwig Rochholz, *Alemannisches Kinderlied und Kinderspiel aus der Schweiz*. Leipzig: J. J. Weber, 1857, p. 173.

25. Ibid., p. 172.

26. Ibid., p. 173.

27. Iona and Peter Opie (note 1), p. 331. With an illustration of a girl plucking a daisy in Kathleen Lines, *Lavender's Blue: A Book of Nursery Rhymes*. New York: Franklin Watts, 1954, p. 118.

28. Lillian Morrison, *Touch Blue: Signs and Spells—Love Charms and Chants—Auguries and Old Beliefs—in Rhyme*. New York: Thomas Y. Crowell, 1958, p. 15. With an illustration of a girl plucking a daisy in Maud and Miska Petersham, *The Rooster Crows: A Book of American Rhymes and Jingles*. New York: McMillan, 15th ed. 1966, no. pp. given.

29. Personal communication from Dr. Jane Beck (State Folklorist of Ver-

mont) in a letter of 23 October 1980. A similar sequel can be found in William Wells Newell (see note 3), p. 109:

Thirteen wishes,
Fourteen kisses,
All the rest little witches.

30. Iona and Peter Opie (note 13), p. 336.

31. This variant is recorded in Iona and Peter Opie (note 1), p. 331. Lillian Morrison (note 28), p. 11, also prints this version with another variant and includes a daisy illustration by Doris Lee:

Hate her,
Have her,
This year,
Next year,
Sometime,
Never.

Both versions are also recorded in William and Ceil Baring-Gould, *The Annotated Mother Goose*. New York: Bramhall House, 1962, pp. 206–207.

32. See Felix Liebrecht, "Ein Volksvers [He loves me, he loves me not]," *Germania*, 33 (1888), 179–180. For a discussion of German variants see Wolfgang Mieder, "Moderne Varianten des Blumenorakels: 'Er (sie) liebt mich, er (sie) liebt mich nicht,'" in *Festschrift für Lutz Röhrich zum 60. Geburtstag*, ed. by Rolf Wilhelm Brednich and Jürgen Dittmar. Berlin: Erich Schmidt, 1982, pp. 335–345 (*Jahrbuch für Volksliedforschung*, 27/28 (1982/83).

33. See for example in Wayland D. Hand (ed.), *Popular Beliefs and Superstitions from North Carolina (Frank C. Brown Collection of North Carolina Folklore*, vol. 6). Durham, North Carolina: Duke University Press, 1961, p. 623.

34. For references see T. F. Thiselton-Dyer, *The Folk-Lore of Plants*. New York: D. Appleton, 1889, p. 95; and Lizzie Deas, *Flower Favourites: Their Legends, Symbolism and Significance*. London: George Allen, 1898, pp. 130–131.

35. For these and many more variants see Eugène Rolland, *Flore populaire ou histoire naturelle des plants dans leurs rapports avec la linguistique et le folklore*. Paris: Jean Maisonneuve, 1908, vol. 7, pp. 52–54.

36. Concerning the dozens of names for the daisy see Heinrich Marzell (note 8), and Martha Egli, *Benennungsmotive bei Pflanzen an schweizerischen Pflanzennamen untersucht*. Diss. Zürich, 1930, pp. 49–52.

37. See for example E. K. Blümml and A. J. Rott, "Die Verwendung der Pflanzen durch die Kinder in Deutschböhmen und Niederösterreich," *Zeitschrift des Vereins für Volkskunde*, 11 (1901) p. 63. It might be of interest to note that Wolfgang Amadeus Mozart used the divination rhyme in a letter to his father on 22 November 1777. At the end he expresses greetings to his sister in the following manner: "und meine schwester . . . umarme ich von herzen, mit schmerzen, ein wenig, oder gar nicht." (and my sister I embrace with all my heart, painfully, a little, or not at all). See Wilhelm A. Bauer and Otto Erich Deutsch (eds.), *Mozart: Briefe und Aufzeichnungen*. Kassel: Bärenreiter, 1972, vol. 2, p. 139.

38. John Ruskin, *Proserpina: Studies of Wayside Flowers*. New York: John W. Lovell, 1885, vol. 1, p. 103.

39. Friedrich August Moritz Retzsch, *Umrisse zu Goethe's Faust: Erster und zweiter Teil.* Stuttgart: J. G. Cotta, 1840, plate 16. Another illustration can be found in *Faust: Eine Tragödie von Goethe mit 163 Federzeichnungen von Franz Stassen.* Berlin: Verlagsanstalt für Vaterländische Geschichte und Kunst, 1920, p. 130.

40. *Goethes Faust,* ed. by Erich Trunz. Hamburg: Christian Wegner, 1963, pp. 101–102, lines 3179–3186.

41. The English translation is quoted from Charles E. Passage, *Johann Wolfgang von Goethe: Faust: Part One & Part Two.* Indianapolis, Indiana: Bobbs-Merrill, 1975, pp. 111–112.

42. The poem is cited in T. F. Thiselton-Dyer (note 34), p. 96; and in Miss Carruthers, *Flower Lore: The Teachings of Flowers.* Belfast: McCaw, Stevenson & Orr, 1879; rpt. Detroit: Singing Tree Press, 1972, p. 48. I was unable to locate the poem in *Poetical Works of Letitia Elizabeth Landon,* 2 vols. London: Longman, 1855.

43. *The Complete Poetical Works of James Russell Lowell.* Boston: Houghton Mifflin, 1897, p. 5. I owe this reference to Miss Carruthers (note 42), p. 49.

44. *Sonnets from the Portuguese.* By Elizabeth Barret Browning. Illustrated by Ludvig Sandöe Ipsen. Boston: Ticknor, 1886, no pp. given. This edition labels the sonnet as number 42, although it is usually referred to as number 43. My colleague David Scrase helped me in identifying the illustrated flower as the Passion Flower.

45. Marianne Bernhard (ed.), *Grandville: Die Seele der Blumen: Les fleurs animées.* Dortmund: Die bibliophilen Taschenbücher, 1978, p. 29.

46. *Das Ludwig Richter Album: Sämtliche Holzschnitte,* ed. by Wolf Stubbe. München: Rogner & Bernhardt, 1974, vol. 1, p. 666.

47. *Ibid.,* vol. 1, p. 171.

48. Postcard from around 1900. Located by Ms. Marilyn Jorgensen.

49. Valentine card produced by the Merrimack Publishing Corporation in New York around 1900. Located by Ms. Marilyn Jorgensen.

50. Valentine card from 1907. Located by Mrs. Lucille Busker.

51. Valentine card produced by the P. F. Volland Company in Chicago in 1913. Located by Mrs. Helen Walvoord.

52. Jane Waiman, *He Loves Me, He Loves Me Not.* Rouses Point, New York: Globe Publishing Corporation, 1979. Located by Ms. Francine Page.

53. Thomas S. Buechner, *Norman Rockwell: Artist and Illustrator.* New York: Harry N. Abrams, 1970, plate 441.

54. Robert Keeshan, *She Loves Me . . . She Loves Me Not.* New York: Harper & Row, 1963. The illustrations are by Maurice Sendak.

55. *Fliegende Blätter,* vol. 151, issue 6, no. 3863 (1919), p. 63.

56. *Nebelspalter,* no. 17 (28 April 1981), p. 46.

57. *Austin-American Statesman* (4 October 1980), p. 6D. Located by Ms. Marilyn Jorgensen.

58. *Punch* (21 March 1979), front cover.

59. See "A Game With Death: Actress Mary Tyler Moore Loses Her Son." *Time* (27 October 1980), p. 33.

60. *San Francisco Chronicle* (20 July 1954), no page reference.

61. *San Francisco Chronicle* (15 May 1966), no page reference.

62. *The German Tribune* (26 August 1969), no page reference.

63. Postcard published by the Wolf Weitsdörffer Company in Cologne,

West Germany. The cartoon was drawn by Wilhelm Schlote in 1979. Located by my student Ms. Christine Reimers.

64. *Oakland Tribune* (29 February 1980), no page reference. Located by Ms. Karen Hurwitz.

65. *Simplicissimus*, vol. 40, no. 11 (9 June 1935), p. 129.

66. *Fliegende Blätter*, vol. 190, issue 13, no. 4887 (30 March 1939), p. 198.

67. *Simplicissimus*, vol. 17, no. 17 (22 July 1912), p. 263.

68. *Schweizer Illustrierte*, no. 18 (29 April 1974), p. 11.

69. See Eduard Fuchs, *Die Frau in der Karikatur*. München: Verlag für Literatur und Kunst, 1907, p. 40. The cartoon stems from Adolf Oberländer and appeared first in the satirical German magazine *Fliegende Blätter* in 1893.

70. *Simplicissimus*, no. 11 (17 March 1956), p. 163.

71. See the needlepoint catalogue *The Stitchery* (Wellesley, Massachusetts, 1981), p. 2. Located by Mrs. Lucille Busker and Dr. Barbara Mieder.

72. John Stevens Wade, *Well Water and Daisies*. La Crosse, Wisconsin: Juniper Books, 1974, p. 1. Also printed in Michael McMahon, *Flowering after Frost: The Anthology of Contemporary New England Poetry*. Boston: Branden Press, 1975, pp. 44–45. The "Father William" in the second line of the poem is an allusion to the well-known poem by Lewis Carroll that starts " 'You are old, Father William,' the young man said." See Lewis Carroll, *Alice's Adventures in Wonderland and Through the Looking-Glass*. New York: The New American Library, 1960, pp. 48–51.

73. *San Francisco Chronicle* (11 May 1974), no page reference. Located by Mrs. Kate Olschki.

74. *San Francisco Chronicle* (11 December 1960), no page reference. Located by Mrs. Kate Olschki.

75. *San Francisco Chronicle* (18 July 1960), no page reference. Located by Mrs. Kate Olschki.

76. *Simplicissimus*, vol. 20, no. 47 (22 February 1916), p. 555.

77. *Kladderadatsch*, no. 13 (26 March 1922), cover page. Located by my student Ms. Trixie Stinebring.

78. *Kladderadatsch*, no. 42 (15 October 1939), p. 11. Located by my student Ms. Trixie Stinebring.

79. *Simplicissimus*, vol. 45, no. 20 (19 May 1940), p. 232.

80. *Saturday Review* (30 September 1950), p. 11. Located by Mrs. Kate Olschki.

81. *Simplicissimus*, no. 35 (31 August 1957), p. 549.

82. *Simplicissimus*, no. 36 (7 September 1957), p. 565.

83. *Simplicissimus*, no. 50 (10 December 1960), p. 790.

84. *Frankfurter Allgemeine Zeitung* (26 October 1978), p. 3.

85. *Simplicissimus*, no. 1 (2 January 1965), p. 3.

86. *Simplicissimus*, no. 16 (31 July 1965), p. 241.

87. *Simplicissimus*, no. 24 (13 June 1959), p. 373.

88. *Der Spiegel*, no. 35 (21 August 1967), p. 62.

89. *Burlington Free Press* (26 May 1979), p. 4A. Located by Dr. Barbara Mieder.

90. See Elias Canetti, *Die Provinz des Menschen: Aufzeichnungen 1942–1972*. München: Carl Hanser, 1973, p. 294.

91. *Sélections du Reader's Digest* (August 1956), p. viii. Located by Mrs. Kate Olschki.

92. *Die Zeit* (26 September 1967), no page reference. Located by Mrs. Kate Olschki.
93. *Stern*, no. 9 (23 February 1978), p. 47.
94. *Hör zu*, no. 45 (10 October 1979), p. 162.
95. *Vogue* (November 1962), no page reference. Located by Mrs. Kate Olschki.
96. *Wall Street Journal* (1 June 1966), no page reference. Located by Mrs. Kate Olschki.
97. *New York Times Magazine* (2 March 1958), p. 54. Located by Mrs. Kate Olschki.
98. *New York Sunday Times* (9 March 1958), no page reference. Located by Mrs. Kate Olschki.
99. *New York Times* (8 February 1959), no page reference. Located by Mrs. Kate Olschki.
100. Richard Dorson, *American Folklore*. Chicago: University of Chicago Press, 1959; 10th ed. 1978, p. 264.
101. Greeting card from the Hallmark Company, purchased in April 1980 in Burlington, Vermont.

## Chapter 4. The Proverb in the Modern Age
## (pages 118–156)

1. See for example the representative essay collection edited by Wolfgang Mieder and Alan Dundes, *The Wisdom of Many: Essays on the Proverb*. New York: Garland Publishing, 1981. Other such essay volumes include W. Mieder (ed.), *Ergebnisse der Sprichwörterforschung*. Bern: Peter Lang, 1978; François Suard and Claude Buridant (eds.), *Richesse du proverbe*, 2 vols. Lille: Université de Lille III, 1984; Naiade Anido (ed.), *Des proverbes . . . à l'affût*. Paris: Publications Langues'O, 1983; and Peter Grzybek and Wolfgang Eismann (eds.), *Semiotische Studien zum Sprichwort: Simple Forms Reconsidered I*. Tübingen: Gunter Narr, 1984.

2. See above all the two bibliographies by Wilfrid Bonser, *Proverb Literature: A Bibliography of Works Relating to Proverbs*. London: William Glaisher, 1930; rpt. Nendeln, Liechtenstein: Kraus Reprint, 1967; and Otto Moll, *Sprichwörterbibliographie*. Frankfurt: Vittorio Klostermann, 1958.

3. Over two thousand books, dissertations and articles are critically evaluated in Wolfgang Mieder, *International Proverb Scholarship: An Annotated Bibliography*. New York: Garland Publishing, 1982. See also the many bibliographical references in Lutz Röhrich and W. Mieder, *Sprichwort*. Stuttgart: Metzler, 1977; as well as the yearly bibliographical updates prepared by W. Mieder in *Proverbium: Yearbook of International Proverb Scholarship*.

4. For the German proverb see Wolfgang Mieder, *Das Sprichwort in unserer Zeit*. Frauenfeld: Huber, 1975; W. Mieder, *Deutsche Sprichwörter in Literatur, Politik, Presse und Werbung*. Hamburg: Helmut Buske, 1983; and W. Mieder, *Sprichwort, Redensart, Zitat: Tradierte Formelsprache in der Moderne*. Bern: Peter Lang, 1985. See also the two large collections of modern proverb variations edited by W. Mieder, *Antisprichwörter*, 2 vols. Wiesbaden: Verlag für deutsche Sprache, 1982 and 1985.

5. For a bibliographical review of the scholarship on proverbs in art see Wolfgang Mieder, "Bibliographischer Abriß zur bildlichen Darstellung von

Sprichwörtern und Redensarten," *Forschungen und Berichte zur Volkskunde in Baden-Württemberg 1974–1977*, ed. by Irmgard Hampp and Peter Assion. Stuttgart: Müller & Gräff, 1977, vol. 3, pp. 229–239.

6. A good reproduction of the picture is included in Christopher Brown, *Bruegel*. New York: Crescent Books, 1975, p. 11.

7. See Wilhelm Fraenger, *Der Bauern-Bruegel und das deutsche Sprichwort*. Erlenbach-Zürich: Eugen Rentsch, 1923; Jan Grauls, *Volkstaal en volksleven in het werk van Pieter Bruegel*. Antwerpen: N. V. Standaard-Boekhandel, 1957; Franz Roh, *Pieter Bruegel d. Ä. Die niederländischen Sprichwörter*. Stuttgart: Philipp Reclam, 1960; and Alan Dundes and Claudia A. Stibbe, *The Art of Mixing Metaphors: A Folkloristic Interpretation of the "Netherlandish Proverbs" by Pieter Bruegel the Elder*. Helsinki: Suomalainen Tiedeakatemia, 1981.

8. For this detail see Timothy Foote, *The World of Bruegel, c. 1525–1569*. New York: Time-Life Books, 1968, pp. 154–155.

9. Louis Lebeer, "De blauwe huyck," *Gentsche Bijdragen tot de Kunstgeschiedenis*, 6 (1939/1940), 167 (the entire article pp. 161–229).

10. Maurits de Meyer, "'De Blauwe Huyck' van Jan van Doetinchem, 1577," *Volkskunde*, 71 (1970), 334–343. In French translation published as "'De Blauwe Huyck': La Cape Bleue de Jean van Doetinchem, datée 1577," *Proverbium*, 16 (1971), 564–575.

11. See Lebeer (note 9), p. 176.

12. The German Ravensburger Puzzle Company produced a large puzzle with three thousand pieces of this picture with a list of the proverbial expressions.

13. The poster "Proverbidioms" by T. E. Breitenbach appeared in 1975 in Altamont, New York. We found it in 1985 in a bookstore in Cambridge, Massachusetts.

14. The poster "As the Saying Goes" by William Belder was published in 1973 by the James Galt Company in London. My student Lori Greener located it in a Boston bookstore.

15. See Maurits de Meyer, *De volks- en kinderprent in de Nederlanden van de 15e tot de 20e eeuw*. Antwerpen: Standaard Boekhandel, 1962, p. 32 (ill. 12). See also pp. 427–432 and 440–451 for other prints.

16. Ibid., p. 444 (ill. 135).

17. Ibid., p. 94 (ill. 40).

18. Ibid., p. 426 (ill. 131).

19. Grace Frank and Dorothy Miner, *Proverbes en rimes: Text and Illustrations of the Fifteenth Century from a French Manuscript in the Walters Art Gallery, Baltimore*. Baltimore, Maryland: The Johns Hopkins Press, 1937.

20. Ibid. plate 48.

21. Ibid. plate 135.

22. Ibid., plate 162.

23. The woodcut is reprinted in Lutz Röhrich, *Lexikon der sprichwörtlichen Redensarten*. Freiburg: Herder, 1973, vol. 1, p. 91.

24. Ibid., vol. 2, p. 1001.

25. Ibid., p. 1011.

26. Jacques Lavalleye, *Pieter Bruegel the Elder and Lucas van Leyden: The Complete Engravings, Etchings, and Woodcuts*. New York: Harry N. Abrams, 1967 plate 158. See also Jozef de Coo, "Twaalf spreuken op borden van Pieter Bruegel de Oude," *Bulletin des Musées royaux des Beaux-Arts*, 14 (1965), 83–104.

27. Brown (note 6), p. 92.

28. Frank and Miner (note 19), plate 34.

29. See A. T. Reid, *Selections of the Current Cartoons drawn by Albert T. Reid bearing upon issues of the day 1919*. New York: W. A. Grant, 1920, no pp. given.

30. Frank and Miner (note 19), plate 2.

31. J. W. Bengough, *A Caricature History of Canadian Politics*. Toronto: Grip Printing Co., 1886; rpt. Toronto: Peter Martin, 1974, p. 231.

32. Frank and Miner (note 19), plate 109.

33. *Die Zeit*, no. 19 (9 May 1975), p. 1. All references from this German weekly newspaper refer to the American edition.

34. Röhrich (note 23), vol. 1, p. 496.

35. Ibid.

36. Louis Maeterlinck, *Le Genre satirique dans la sculpture flamande et wallone*. Paris: Jean Schemit, 1910, p. 289 (ill. 196).

37. Enrique Lafuente Ferrari, *Goya: His Complete Etchings, Aquatints, and Lithographs*. New York: Harry N. Abrams, 1962, p. 236. See also George Levitine, "The Elephant of Goya," *Art Journal*, 20 (1961), 145–147.

38. *Time* (1 December 1975), pp. 8–9.

39. See the excellent paper with many examples by Lutz Röhrich, "Die Bildwelt von Sprichwort und Redensart in der Sprache der politischen Karikatur," *Kontakte und Grenzen: Probleme der Volks-, Kultur- und Sozialforschung: Festschrift für Gerhard Heilfurth*, ed. by Hans Friedrich Foltin. Göttingen: Otto Schwarz, 1969, pp. 175–207.

40. *Playboy* (July 1974), p. 165.

41. *Playboy* (November 1974), p. 176.

42. *Playboy* (October 1974), p. 172.

43. *New Yorker* (6 July 1957), p. 65.

44. *New Yorker* (28 April 1975), p. 46.

45. *St. Louis Post-Dispatch* (19 January 1975), p. 12D.

46. *New Yorker* (14 August 1965), p. 24.

47. *Punch* (2 May 1973), p. 602.

48. *St. Louis Post-Dispatch* (31 January 1975), p. 12D.

49. *Punch* (3 November 1971), p. 589.

50. Michael Wynn Jones, *The Cartoon History of Britain*. New York: Macmillan, 1971, p. 270.

51. *New Yorker* (21 July 1962), p. 18.

52. *New Yorker* (16 May 1959), p. 39.

53. *New Yorker* (20 June 1964), p. 39.

54. *New Yorker* (3 May 1958), p. 43.

55. See for example *The Oxford Dictionary of English Proverbs*, ed. by F. P. Wilson. Oxford: Clarendon Press, 3d ed. 1970; and Wolfgang Mieder, *The Prentice-Hall Encyclopedia of World Proverbs*. Englewood Cliffs, New Jersey: Prentice Hall, 1986.

56. Lavalleye (note 26), plate 151. See also the international study of this proverb by Archer Taylor, "'Sunt tria damna domus,'" *Hessische Blätter für Volkskunde*, 24 (1926), 130–146; reprinted in *Selected Writings on Proverbs by Archer Taylor*, ed. by Wolfgang Mieder. Helsinki: Suomalainen Tiedeakatemia, 1975, pp. 133–151.

57. A detail in Röhrich (note 23), vol. 2, p. 1072.

58. Maeterlinck (note 36), p. 255 (ill. 164).

59. For a detail illustration from about 1700 see Röhrich (note 23), vol. 1, p. 440.

60. Maeterlinck (note 36), p. 201 (ill. 123).

61. *New Yorker* (30 March 1963), p. 34.

62. *New Yorker* (15 November 1958), p. 59.

63. *St. Louis Post-Dispatch* (22 August 1974), p. 9D.

64. *New Yorker* (18 November 1974), 47.

65. *St. Louis Post-Dispatch* (29 November 1975), p. 4B.

66. *New Yorker* (17 March 1956), p. 37.

67. *Playboy* (January 1978), p. 279. For sexual matters in proverbs see also Wolfgang Mieder, "Sexual Content of German Wellerisms," *Maledicta*, 6 (1982), 215–223.

68. *New Yorker* (27 August 1960), p. 45.

69. *New Yorker* (21 March 1959), p. 45.

70. *New Woman* (November/December 1977), p. 26.

71. *New Yorker* (21 July 1975), p. 33.

72. *New Yorker* (12 December 1964), p. 235.

73. See the fascinating paper by Frank A. Salamone on how proverbs are used in a traditional society to solve marriage problems, "The Arrow and the Bird: Proverbs in the Solution of Hausa Conjugal-Conflicts," *Journal of Anthropological Research*, 32 (1976), 358–371. See also Martine Segalen, "Le mariage, l'amour et les femmes dans les proverbes populaires français," *Ethnologie Française*, 5 (1975), 119–160 and 6 (1976), 33–88.

74. *Ms.* (May 1976), p. 91.

75. *New Yorker* (26 September 1964), p. 35.

76. *Woman's Day* (May 1975), p. 57. The actual proverb is, of course, "If the shoe fits, wear it."

77. *Better Homes and Gardens* (April 1977), p. 165.

78. For the use of proverbs in advertising see Barbara and Wolfgang Mieder, "Tradition and Innovation: Proverbs in Advertising," *Journal of Popular Culture*, 11 (1977), 308–319; reprinted in Mieder and Dundes (note 1), pp. 309–322.

79. *Playboy* (September 1973), p. 48.

80. *Penthouse* (April 1975), p. 99.

81. *New York Times Magazine* (19 September 1976), p. 13.

82. *Playgirl* (October 1977), p. 3.

83. *Punch* (17 November 1971), p. 684.

84. *Flightime* (June 1978), p. 51.

85. *Gourmet* (September 1974), p. 69.

86. *Time* (25 November 1974), p. 76.

87. *Time* (25 April 1977), p. 5.

88. Included in *The New Yorker: Album of Drawings 1925–1975*. New York: Viking Press, 1975, no pp. given.

89. *New Yorker* (20 September 1976), p. 58.

90. *Financial Executive* (April 1974), p. 87. See also Archer Taylor, "'Tom, Dick, and Harry,'" *Names*, 6 (1958), 51–54.

91. *New Yorker* (20 July 1957), p. 47.

92. *Ms.* (May 1977), p. 49.

93. *New Yorker* (4 October 1976), p. 21.

94. *Ms.* (February 1975), p. 1.

95. *Time* (5 December 1947), p. 35.

96. *New York Times Magazine* (22 September 1974), p. 34.

97. *Ms.* (March 1976), p. 119.

98. *Ms.* (October 1977), p. 109.

99. *Ms.* (March 1978), p. 101.

100. *Ms.* (March 1978), p. 100.

101. *Ms.* (June 1976), p. 46.

102. Bob Abel (ed.), *The American Cartoon Album*. New York: Dodd, Mead, & Co., 1974, no pp. given.

103. See Wolfgang Mieder, *Proverbs in Literature: An International Bibliography*. Bern: Peter Lang, 1978.

104. This part of the present chapter was previously published as "Traditional and Innovative Proverb Use in Lyric Poetry" in *Proverbium Paratum*, 1 (1980), 16–27; a longer version with the title "A Sampler of Anglo-American Proverb Poetry" appeared in *Folklore Forum*, 13 (1980), 39–53.

105. See Wolfgang Mieder, "Moderne deutsche Sprichwortgedichte," *Fabula*, 21 (1980), 247–260; reprinted in Mieder, *Sprichwort, Redensart, Zitat* (note 4), pp. 73–90.

106. John S. Farmer (ed.), *The Proverbs, Epigrams, and Miscellanies of John Heywood*. London: Early English Drama Society, 1906; rpt. New York: Barnes & Noble, 1966, p. 168.

107. Farmer, p. 175.

108. E. H. Coleridge (ed.), *The Poems of Samuel Taylor Coleridge*. London: Oxford University Press, 1912, p. 418.

109. See George Monteiro, "'Good Fences Make Good Neighbors.' A Proverb and a Poem," *Revista de Etnografia*, 16, no. 31 (1972), 83–88.

110. Robert Whitney Bolwell (ed.), *The Renaissance*. New York: Charles Scribner's Sons, 1920, pp. 269–270.

111. Phineas Garrett (ed.), *One Hundred Choice Selections, No. 9*. Freeport, New York: Books for Libraries Press, 1874, pp. 53–54.

112. Alice and Phoebe Cary, *Ballads for Little Folk*, ed. by Mary Clemmer Ames. Freeport, New York: Books for Libraries Press, 1873, pp. 81–83. A similar poem in this collection is "Keep a Stiff Upper Lip," pp. 174–175.

113. Vincent Godfrey Burns, *Redwood and other Poems*. Washington D.C.: New World Books, 1952, p. 114. See also a similar poem entitled "By Bread Alone" by Edna Jaques, *The Best of Edna Jaques*. Saskatoon, Saskatchewan: Modern Press, 1966, p. 50.

114. W. H. Auden, *The Collected Poems of W. H. Auden*. New York: Random House, 1941, pp. 123–124.

115. Harold Monro (ed.), *Twentieth Century Poetry*. London: Chatto, 1950, p. 79.

116. See Charles Clay Doyle, "On Some Paremiological Verses," *Proverbium*, 25 (1975), 979–982.

117. Kingsley Amis (ed.), *The New Oxford Book of English Light Verse*. New York: Oxford University Press, 1978, pp. 33–35.

118. Quoted from Bartlett Jere Whiting, *Early American Proverbs and Proverbial Phrases*. Cambridge, Massachusetts: Harvard University Press, 1977, pp. 511–512.

119. Arthur Guiterman, *The Laughing Muse*. New York: Harper & Brothers, 1915, p. 16.

120. John Robert Colombo, *Translations from the English*. Toronto: Peter Martin, 1974, p. 27.

121. Robert P. Falk (ed.), *American Literature in Parody*. New York: Twayne Publishers, 1955, p. 27.

122. This section has previously been published with the title "'Wine, Women and Song': From Martin Luther to American T-Shirts," *Kentucky Folklore Record*, 29 (1983), 89–101.

123. For a review of the German literature on this proverb see Wolfgang Mieder, "'Wer nicht liebt Wein, Weib und Gesang, der bleibt ein Narr sein Leben lang': Zur Herkunft, Überlieferung und Verwendung eines angeblichen Luther-Spruches," *Muttersprache*, 94 (special issue, 1983–1984), 68–103. See also W. Mieder, "'Wine, Women and Song': Zur anglo-amerikanischen Über-lieferung eines angeblichen Lutherspruches," *Germanisch-Romanische Monats-schrift*, 65, new series 34 (1984), 385–403.

124. Ernst Kroker (ed.), *D. Martin Luthers Werke: Kritische Gesamtausgabe*. Weimar: Hermann Böhlau, 1914. *Tischreden*, vol. 3, p. 344 (no. 3476).

125. August Otto, *Die Sprichwörter und sprichwörtlichen Redensarten der Rö-mer*. Leipzig: Teubner, 1890; rpt. Hildesheim: Georg Olms, 1971, p. 372. With further examples of proverbs based on the triad "nox, amor, vinum."

126. Hans Walther, *Proverbia Sententiaeque Latinitatis Medii Aevi: Lateinische Sprichwörter und Sentenzen des Mittelalters*. Göttingen: Vandenhoeck & Rup-recht, 1965, vol. 1, p. 88 (no. 72). See also nos. 64, 71, and 73.

127. Karl Friedrich Wilhelm Wander, *Deutsches Sprichwörter-Lexikon*. Leip-zig: F. A. Brockhaus, 1867; rpt. Darmstadt: Wissenschaftliche Buchgesell-schaft, 1964, vol. 1, col. 616 (no. 322). Wander lists literally dozens of such proverbs attesting to the popularity of expanding the alliterative binary for-mula of "wine and woman" by a third element, many of them also starting with a *w*.

128. For a critical edition of this proverb collection see *Luthers Sprichwörter-sammlung: Nach seiner Handschrift herausgegeben und mit Anmerkungen versehen*, ed. by Ernst Thiele. Weimar: Hermann Böhlau, 1900.

129. See Archer Taylor, *The Proverb*. Cambridge, Massachusetts: Harvard University Press, 1931; rpt. Hatboro, Pennsylvania: Folklore Associates, 1962, rpt. with an introduction and bibliography by Wolfgang Mieder, Bern: Peter Lang, 1985, p. 38.

130. Matthias Claudius (ed.), *Wandsbecker Bothe* (Friday, 12 May 1775), no. 75.

131. Johann Heinrich Voss (ed.), *Musen Almanach für 1777*. Hamburg: L. E. Böhn, 1777, p. 107.

132. Johann Heinrich Voss, *Sämtliche Gedichte*. Königsberg: Friedrich Nico-lovius, 1802; rpt. Bern: Peter Lang, 1969, vol. 4, pp. 58–60.

133. See for example Bernard Darwin, *The Oxford Dictionary of Quotations*. Oxford: Oxford University Press, 1953, p. 321; Burton Stevenson, *The Macmil-lan Book of Proverbs, Maxims, and Famous Phrases*. New York: Macmillan, 1948; 7th ed. 1968, p. 2526 (no. 4); and John Bartlett, *Familiar Quotations*. Boston: Little, Brown and Co., 15th ed. 1980, p. 399.

134. The song is included in *Herders sämtliche Werke*, ed. by Carl Redlich. Berlin: Weidmann, 1885, vol. 25, pp. 21–22.

135. Wilson (note 55), p. 296.

136. Morris Palmer Tilley, *Elizabethan Proverb Lore in Lyly's "Euphues" and in Pettie's "Petite Pallace" with Parallels from Shakespeare*. New York: Macmillan, 1926, p. 248 (no. 491).

137. G. L. Apperson, *English Proverbs and Proverbial Phrases: A Historical*

*Dictionary*. London: J. M. Dent, 1929, rpt. Detroit: Gale Research Co., 1969, p. 706 (no. 43).

138. Robert Burton, *The Anatomy of Melancholy*, ed. by Holbrook Jackson. London: J. M. Dent, 1972, p. 291.

139. John Gay, *The Beggar's Opera*, ed. by Edgar V. Roberts. Lincoln, Nebraska: University of Nebraska Press, 1969, p. 32.

140. *The Poems of John Keats*, ed. by Jack Stillinger. Cambridge, Massachusetts: Harvard University Press, 1978, p. 47.

141. *The Works of Lord Byron*, ed. by Ernest Hartley Coleridge. London: John Murray, 1903, vol. 6, p. 132, verse 178.

142. Henry G. Bohn, *A Polyglot of Foreign Proverbs*. London: Henry G. Bohn, 1857; rpt. Detroit: Gale Research Co., 1968, p. 184.

143. See *The Complete Works of William Makepeace Thackeray*. Boston: Houghton, Mifflin and Co., 1895, vol. 20, pp. 297–299. None of the editions gives a date for these translations.

144. Ibid., vol. 17, part 1, pp. 199–200.

145. Albert Methfessel, *Allgemeines Commers- und Liederbuch enthaltend ältere und neuere Burschenlieder, Trinklieder, Vaterlandsgesänge, Volks- und Kriegslieder, mit mehrstimmigen Melodien und beigefügter Klavierbegleitung*. Rudolstadt: Hof-, Buch- und Kunsthandlung, 1818; 3d ed. 1823, pp. 102–104. The translation is my own.

146. *The Poems of Eugene Field*. New York: Charles Scribner's Sons, 1912, pp. 390–391.

147. See John Addington Symonds, *Wine, Women and Song: Medieval Latin Student Songs. Now First Translated into English Verse with an Essay*. Portland, Maine: Thomas B. Mosher, 1899, pp. 147–148.

148. See as an example Wolfgang Mieder, "'Der Apfel fällt weit von Deutschland': Zur amerikanischen Entlehnung eines deutschen Sprichwortes," *Der Sprachdienst*, 25 (1981), 89–93.

149. *The Poems of Ernest Christopher Dowson*, ed. by Mark Longaker. Philadelphia: University of Pennsylvania Press, 1962, p. 110. A villanelle is a short poem of French origin consisting usually of five stanzas of three lines each and a final stanza of four lines. It has only two rhymes throughout.

150. See Sam Morris, *Wine, Women and Song*. Del Rio, Texas: William McNitzy, 1938, pp. 58–69.

151. See Thomas Mann, *Doktor Faustus*. Frankfurt: S. Fischer, 1947, p. 149.

152. See Thomas Mann, *Doctor Faustus*, translated from the German by Helen T. Lowe-Porter. New York: Alfred A. Knopf, 1948, p. 97.

153. Franklin Pierce Adams, *Book of Quotations*. New York: Funk & Wagnalls, 1952, p. 848.

154. Leo Rosten, *Infinite Riches: Gems from a Lifetime of Reading*. New York: McGraw-Hill, 1979, p. 510.

155. See H. L. Mencken, *A New Dictionary of Quotations on Historical Principles from Ancient and Modern Sources*. New York: Alfred A. Knopf, 1942; 2d ed. 1960, p. 1303.

156. Quoted from A. K. Adams, *The House Book of Humorous Quotations*. New York: Dodd, Mead & Co., 1969, p. 331.

157. *Playboy* (September 1977), p. 234.

158. *New Yorker* (8 August 1983), p. 62. I owe this reference to my graduate student Leesa Guay.

159. *New Yorker* (4 February 1980), p. 58.

160. *Der Stern*, no. 39 (17 September 1981), p. 142.

161. Some scholars have attempted to argue that proverbs have little use if any in complex cultures with rapid social change. See for example William Albig, "Proverbs and Social Control," *Sociology and Social Research*, 15 (1931), 527–535.

162 See Jess Nierenberg, "Proverbs in Graffiti: Taunting Traditional Wisdom," *Maledicta*, 7 (1983), 41–58.

## Chapter 5. The Proverbial Three Wise Monkeys (pages 157–177)

Originally published in *Midwestern Journal of Language and Folklore*, 7 (1981), 5–38 (with 65 illustrations).

1. See Archer Taylor, "'Audi, Vide, Tace,' and the Three Monkeys," *Fabula*, 1 (1957), 26 (the entire article on pp. 26–31). The paper has been reprinted in Wolfgang Mieder (ed.), *Selected Writings on Proverbs by Archer Taylor*. Helsinki: Suomalainen Tiedeakatemia, 1975, pp. 165–171. For a German treatise of the three-monkey proverb see Wolfgang Mieder, "Die drei weisen Affen und das Sprichwort 'Nichts sehen, nichts hören, nichts sagen,'" *Muttersprache*, 90 (1980), 167–178.

2. See Hans Walther, *Proverbia Sententiaque Latinitatis Medii Aevi: Lateinische Sprichwörter und Sentenzen des Mittelalters*. Göttingen: Vandenhoeck & Ruprecht, 1963, vol. 1, pp. 194–195.

3. See *Gesta Romanorum: or, Entertaining Moral Stories*, translated and edited by Rev. Charles Swan. London: C. and J. Rivington, 1824, vol. 1, pp. 238–240.

4. See Bartlett Jere Whiting, *Proverbs, Sentences, and Proverbial Phrases from English Writings Mainly before 1500*. Cambridge, Massachusetts: Harvard University Press, 1968, p. 275. See also Morris Palmer Tilley, *A Dictionary of the Proverbs in England in the Sixteenth and Seventeenth Centuries*. Ann Arbor, Michigan: University of Michigan Press, 1950, p. 504.

5. See *Oeuvres Complètes de Eustache Deschamps*, ed. Marquis de Queux de Saint-Hilaire. Paris: Firmin Didot, 1878, vol. 1, pp. 186–187.

6. See Karl Friedrich Wilhelm Wander, *Deutsches Sprichwörter-Lexikon*. Leipzig: F. A. Brockhaus, 1870; rpt. Darmstadt: Wissenschaftliche Buchgesellschaft, 1964, vol. 2, col. 777, nos. 23–25.

7. *Proverbi Figurati de Giuseppe Maria Mitelli*, ed. by Lorenzo Marinese and Alberto Manfredi. Milano: Casa Editrice Cerastico, 1963, ill. 4.

8. See E. Dale Saunders, "Koshin: An Example of Taoist Ideas in Japan," in *Religion in the Japanese Experience*, ed. by H. Byron Earhart. Encino, California: Dickenson, 1974, pp. 76–80.

9. See the superb article on the religious implications of the three-monkey symbol by André Wedemeyer, "Das japanische Drei-Affen- Symbol und der Koshin-Tag," *Jahrbuch des Museums für Völkerkunde zu Leipzig*, 16 (1957, published 1959), 28–56. Wedemeyer, independently from Archer Taylor, brings much evidence for the fact that the three monkeys originated in Japan and not in China and that they are associated beyond doubt with the Koshin cult.

10. *Nihon shakai minzoku jiten* (Dictionary of Japanese Sociology and Ethnology). Tokyo: Seibundo Shinkosha, 1952, vol. 1, p. 385.

11. Miwa Zennosuke, *Koshin-machi to Koshin-to*. Tokyo, 1935, plate 7.

12. Ibid., plates 1 and 4, showing five drawing reproductions of Koshin stones.

13. My colleague Robert Dean gave me a tourist slide of the three-monkey decoration at the Toshugu Shrine in Nikko, Japan.

14. Dark wooden figure from Nikko, Japan. Gift from Mr. Toshio Konno.

15. See Bartlett Jere Whiting, *Early American Proverbs and Proverbial Phrases.* Cambridge, Massachusetts: Harvard University Press, 1977, p. 206.

16. Quoted from Wedemeyer (note 9), p. 30.

17. Ibid., p. 30.

18. Ibid., p. 30.

19. Ibid., p. 28.

20. See Henri Joly, *Legend in Japanese Art: A Description of Historical Episodes, Legendary Characters, Folk-Lore, Myths, Religious Symbolism: Illustrated in the Arts of Old Japan.* London: John Lane, 1908; rpt. Rutland, Vermont: Charles Tuttle, 1967.

21. Gertrude Jobes, *Dictionary of Mythology, Folklore and Symbols.* New York: The Scarecrow Press, 1961.

22. See for example R. Brasch, *How Did It Begin? Customs and Superstitions and Their Romantic Origins.* New York: David McKay, 1965, pp. 167–168; and Webb Garrisson, *How It Started.* Nashville, Tennessee: Abingdon Press, 1972, p. 80.

23. *A Supplement to The Oxford English Dictionary,* ed. by R. W. Burchfield. Oxford: Clarendon Press, 1976, vol. 2, p. 1011.

24. Ibid., p. 1011.

25. *St. Nicholas: An Illustrated Magazine for Boys and Girls,* 49, no. 6 (April 1922), p. 579.

26. See *The World's Best-Loved Poems,* ed. by James Gilchrist Lawson. New York: Harper & Brothers, 1927, pp. 67–68. One of my Vermont students remembers having read the poem in high school in the early 1970s.

27. See Josephine Campbell, *Live and Learn.* Kansas City, Missouri: Heuer Publishing, 1941.

28. There is also no mention of the three monkeys in Alan Dundes' article on "The Number Three in American Culture," in which he has assembled dozens of examples for traditional triads. See *Every Man His Way,* ed. by Alan Dundes. Englewood Cliffs, New Jersey: Prentice-Hall, 1968, pp. 401–424.

29. Ivory carving from Taiwan, purchased in November 1977 in a Montreal gift shop for $22.50.

30. Dark brown wooden figure from Taiwan, purchased in December 1978 in Detroit. Gift from Mr. and Mrs. Goerge Schumm.

31. Wood carving from Hong Kong, purchased in January 1978 in a gift shop at O'Hare Airport, Chicago, for $7.50.

32. Gray stone figure from the People's Republic of China, purchased in August 1978 in China Town in San Francisco for $4.00. Gift from my student Ms. Trixie Stinebring.

33. Painted clay figure (brown, red, blue) from Japan, purchased in August 1978 at a Flea Market in South Burlington, Vermont, for $2.00. Gift from my student Ms. Marianna Holzer. I also found a similar brown ceramic figure from Japan, owned by the Special Book Collection Department of the Bailey/Howe Library at the University of Vermont.

34. Copper figure made in Japan, purchased in July 1978 in Lübeck, West Germany, for $3.50.

35. Handmade wood carvings from the Philippines, purchased in August 1978 in San Francisco for $4.00. Gift from my student Ms. Trixie Stinebring.

36. Gray porcelain figure of unknown origin, purchased in December 1978 in Detroit. Gift from Mr. and Mrs. George Schumm.

37. Brass figure of unknown origin, purchased in December 1978 in Burlington, Vermont. Gift from my student Mr. Daniel Page.

38. Brass figure from West Germany, purchased in July 1978 in the Europa-Center in West Berlin for $3.50.

39. Wood figures from West Germany, purchased in August 1978 in Lübeck, West Germany, for $6.00. Gift from Mr. and Mrs. Horst Mieder.

40. Wood figures from the United States, purchased in December 1978 in Detroit. Gift from Mr. and Mrs. George Schumm.

41. Brownish porcelain ashtray from Japan, purchased in April 1979 in Columbus, Ohio. Gift from Mr. George Schumm.

42. Brass figure from the Far East, purchased in July 1978 in Lübeck, West Germany, for $7.50.

43. Brownish candle from the United States, purchased in December 1978 in Detroit. Gift from Mr. and Mrs. Thomas Schumm.

44. Gahan Wilson, *The Man in the Cannibal Pot*. Garden City, New Jersey: Doubleday, 1967, p. 63.

45. *Communications Vibrations*, ed. by Larry L. Barker. Englewood Cliffs, New Jersey: Prentice-Hall, 1974, cover illustration.

46. *New Yorker* (7 May 1979), p. 34. Located by my student Ms. Leesa Haas.

47. *Der Spiegel*, no. 19 (7 May 1979), p.232.

48. The picture was taken in May 1979 on the campus of the University of Vermont and included Ms. Leesa Guay, Ms. Trixie Stinebring, and Mr. Thomas Chaplin.

49. See Lutz Röhrich, "Die Bildwelt von Sprichwort und Redensart in der Sprache der politischen Karikatur," in *Kontakte und Grenzen: Festschrift für Gerhard Heilfurth*, ed. by Hans Friedrich Foltin. Göttingen: Otto Schwarz, 1969, pp. 175–207; and Wolfgang Mieder, *Deutsche Sprichwörter und Redensarten*. Stuttgart: Reclam, 1979, pp. 97–125.

50. *Saturday Review* (25 February 1950), p. 10.

51. *Punch* (8 June 1966), p. 827. Located by my student Mr. Keith Monley.

52. *Time* (18 November 1974), p. 51.

53. Mike Peters, *The Nixon Chronicles*. Dayton, Ohio: Lorenz Press, 1976, p. 81.

54. *U.S. News and World Report* (26 May 1979), p. 28.

55. *Der Stern*, no. 6 (1 February 1979), p. 148.

56. *Kladderadatsch* (23 March 1941), p. 3. Located by my student Ms. Christine Reimers.

57. *Badische Zeitung* (19 April 1979), p. 4. Located by Prof. Lutz Röhrich.

58. *Die Zeit*, no. 23 (8 June 1979), p. 16. All references from this newspaper come out of the American edition.

59. *Die Zeit*, no. 15 (14 April 1978), p. 3.

60. *Esquire* (November 1977), p. 53.

61. Karl Hoche, *Das Hoche Lied: Satiren und Parodien*. München: Knaur, 1978, p. 226.

62. *American Libraries* (May 1977), p. 254.

63. *Playgirl* (August 1978), p. 9.

64. *Penthouse* (April 1979), p. 88.

65. Saturday Review (18 April 1953), p. 26. Located by my student Ms. Christine Reimers.

66. Hunger awareness poster produced by World Vision International, found in a church lobby in Breckenridge, Michigan. Located by Mr. and Mrs. Thomas Schumm.

67. Der Spiegel, no. 14 (31 March 1975), p. 118.

68. People Weekly (3 September 1979), p. 13.

69. Punch (4 February 1970), p. 165. Located by my student Mr. Keith Monley.

70. Günter Kunert, Der ungebetene Gast: Gedichte. Berlin: Aufbau Verlag, 1965, p. 15. I thank my student Mr. Howard Fitzpatrick for helping me with the translation.

71. See Mathew Atmore Sherring, Benares: The Sacred City of the Hindus. London: Trübner, 1868; rpt. Delhi, India: B. R. Publishing Corporation, 1975, pp. 158–159.

72. See Joly (note 20), p. 351. See also We Japanese: Being Descriptions of Many of the Customs, Manners, Ceremonies, Festivals, Arts and Crafts of the Japanese, ed. Fujiya Hotel. Yokohama, Japan: Yamagata Press, 1934; rpt. 1950, p. 103.

73. Die Zeit, no. 41 (7 October 1977), p. 4.

74. New Yorker (2 August 1976), p. 19.

75. Green porcelain figure from the United States, purchased in December 1978 in Muskegon, Michigan. Gift from Mr. and Mrs. Walter Busker.

76. Wooden plaque from the United States, purchased in November 1978 in Salt Lake City, Utah, for $1.75.

77. Green slogan button obtained in the summer of 1979 on the University of Vermont campus, Burlington, Vermont.

78. T-shirt worn by my student Ms. Leesa Haas in September 1978 on the University of Vermont campus.

79. The Harvard Lampoon Centennial Celebration 1876–1973, ed. by Martin Kaplan. Boston: Little, Brown & Co., 1973, p. 233.

80. Time (25 October 1943), p. 29. Located by my student Ms. Trixie Stinebring.

81. White clay figure from the United States. Gift from my student Mr. Eric Stinebring.

82. Hallmark Card, purchased in April 1978 in Chicago. Located by Mr. and Mrs. Walter Busker.

83. Punch (15 December 1971), p. 822. Located by my student Mr. Keith Monley.

84. See Barbara and Wolfgang Mieder, "Tradition and Innovation: Proverbs in Advertising," Journal of Popular Culture, 11 (1977), 308–319. Reprinted in The Wisdom of Many: Essays on the Proverb, ed. by W. Mieder and Alan Dundes. New York: Garland Publishing, 1981, pp. 309–322.

85. Der Spiegel, no. 19 (May 7, 1979), back cover.

86. Time (11 August 1941), p. 50.

87. The Salt Lake City Tribune (14 October 1978), p. 17A.

88. Der Spiegel, no. 6 (6 February 1976), p. 87.

89. Time (2 December 1974), p. 24.

90. See Auswahl 74: Neue Lyrik—Neue Namen, ed. by Bernd Jentzsch, Holger J. Schubert, and Wolfgang Trampe. Berlin: Verlag Neues Leben, 1974, p. 151. Once again I thank my student Howard Fitzpatrick for helping me with the translation.

91. Bookmark from the United States, purchased at the Four Winds Gallery in November 1978 in Ferrisburg, Vermont, for $1.00.

92. Quoted by Taylor (note 1), p. 67. For discussions of the modern questioning of proverbial wisdom, see Wolfgang Mieder, *Das Sprichwort in unserer Zeit*. Frauenfeld: Huber, 1975; W. Mieder, *Deutsche Sprichwörter in Literatur, Politik, Presse und Werbung*. Hamburg: Helmut Buske, 1983; and W. Mieder, *Sprichwort, Redensart, Zitat: Tradierte Formelsprache in der Moderne*. Bern: Peter Lang, 1985.

## Chapter 6. History and Interpretation of a Proverb about Human Nature
(pages 178–228)

1. See for example Edmund I. Gordon, *Sumerian Proverbs: Glimpses of Everyday Life in Ancient Mesopotamia*. New York: Greenwood, 1968.

2. Such a study is presented by Matti Kuusi, *Regen bei Sonnenschein: Zur Weltgeschichte einer Redensart*. Helsinki: Suomalainen Tiedeakatemia, 1957.

3. Arthur H. Smith, *Proverbs and Common Sayings from the Chinese*. Shanghai: American Presbyterian Mission Press, 1914; rpt. New York: Paragon and Dover, 1965, p. 16. Smith mentions that this saying "contains a compendious and accurate description of the relation between the higher officials, the lower officials, and the people of China."

4. Henry H. Hart, *Seven Hundred Chinese Proverbs*. Palo Alto, California: Stanford University Press, 1937; 3d ed. 1940, p. 24 (no. 205).

5. Robert Christy, *Proverbs, Maxims, and Phrases of All Ages*. New York: G. P. Putnam's Sons, 1887, p. 352. The author explains that this proverb is "applied to the classes of society paying taxes."

6. Carl Sandburg, *The People, Yes*. New York: Harcourt, Brace and Co., 1936, p. 234. See also Wolfgang Mieder, "Proverbs in Carl Sandburg's Poem 'The People, Yes,'" *Southern Folklore Quarterly*, 37 (1973), 15–36.

7. Semahat Senaltan, *Studien zur sprachlichen Gestalt der deutschen und türkischen Sprichwörter*. Diss. Marburg, 1968. Marburg: Erich Mauersberger, 1968, p. 152 (no. 115).

8. C. F. J. Whitting, *Hausa and Fulani Proverbs*. Lagos: Government Printer, 1940, p. 41.

9. See Jerzy Gluski, *Proverbs: A Comparative Book of English, French, German, Italian, Spanish and Russian Proverbs with a Latin Appendix*. New York: Elsevier, 1971, p. 157 (section 29, no. 12).

10. Ibid., p. 440 (section 29, no. 12).

11. Ida von Düringsfeld und Otto von Reinsberg-Düringsfeld, *Sprichwörter der germanischen und romanischen Sprachen vergleichend zusammengestellt*. Leipzig: Hermann Fries, 1872; rpt. Hildesheim: Georg Olms, 1973, vol. 1, p. 332 (no. 640). See also Henry G. Bohn, *A Polyglot of Foreign Proverbs, Comprising French, Italian, German, Dutch, Spanish, Portuguese, and Danish with English Translations*. London: Henry G. Bohn, 1867; rpt. Detroit: Gale Research Co., 1968, pp. 34 and 103; and Karl Friedrich Wilhelm Wander, *Deutsches Sprichwörterlexikon*. Leipzig: F. A. Brockhaus, 1867; rpt. Darmstadt: Wissenschaftliche Buchgesellschaft, 1964, vol. 1, col. 1033, "Fisch" (no. 117).

12. Pierre-Marie Quitard, *Dictionnaire étymologique, historique et anecdotique*

*des proverbes et des locutions proverbiales de la langue française.* Paris: P. Bertrand, 1842; rpt. Genève: Slatkine Reprints, 1968, p. 604.

13. See Wilfrid Parsons, "'Lest Men, Like Fishes . . . ,'" *Traditio*, 3 (1945), 380–388. Two addenda with the same titles were published by Bruce Dickins in *Traditio*, 6 (1946), 356–357, and by William Elton in *Traditio*, 18 (1962), 421–422. They include some early English references and mention in passing that the proverb also appears in pictorial form in Pieter Brueghel and Hieronymus Bosch.

14. R. M. Frazer, *The Poems of Hesiod*. Norman, Oklahoma: University of Oklahoma Press, 1983, p. 110 (lines 276–285).

15. *The Mahabharata of Kirshna-Dwaipayana Vyasa*, translated into English prose from the original Sanskrit text by Pratap Chandra Roy. Calcutta: Oriental Publishing Co., 1955, vol. 8 (Santi Parva, part 1), section 67, p. 151.

16. Ibid., section 68, p. 153.

17. See Benoy Kumar Sarkar, "The Hindu Theory of State," *Political Science Quarterly*, 36 (1921), 82. See also pp. 80–81 with references to the *Mahabharata* and the *Ramayana*. The entire article on pp. 79–90.

18. *The Babylonian Talmud: Seder Nezikin*, ed. by Rabbi Dr. I. Epstein. London: The Soncino Press, 1961, vol. 4, pp. 11–12.

19. *The Works of Aristotle*, vol. 4: *Historia Animalium*, translated and edited by D'Arcy Wentworth Thompson. Oxford: Clarendon Press, 1910, Book 9, Chapter 2 (S. 610[b]).

20. Polybius, *Historiae* 15, 20, 3. Cited in English by Parsons (note 13), p. 388. See also August Otto, *Die Sprichwörter und sprichwörtlichen Redensarten der Römer*. Leipzig: Teubner, 1890; rpt. Hildesheim: Georg Olms, 1971, p. 281 (piscis, no. 3); and Carl Sylvio Köhler, *Das Tierleben im Sprichwort der Griechen und Römer*. Leipzig: Fernau, 1881; rpt. Hildesheim: Georg Olms, 1967, p. 49 (no. 9).

21. Varro, *Saturae Menippeae*, 289. Cited in English by Parsons (note 13), p. 388. The Latin text also in Otto (note 20), p. 281 (piscis, no. 3). For more Latin references see Reinhard Häussler (ed.), *Nachträge zu A. Otto, Sprichwörter und sprichwörtliche Redensarten der Römer*. Hildesheim: Georg Olms, 1968, p. 115 (piscis, no. 3).

22. Walter Gottschalk, *Die bildhaften Sprichwörter der Romanen*. Heidelberg: Carl Winter, 1935, vol. 1, p. 251 ("Fische").

23. Hans Walther, *Proverbia Sententiaque Latinitatis Medii Aevi: Lateinische Sprichwörter und Sentenzen des Mittelalters*. Göttingen: Vandenhoeck & Ruprecht, 1964/65, vol. 2, p. 80 (no. 81) and vol. 3, p. 826 (nos. 08f and 12).

24. See Parsons (note 13) and Manfred Bambeck, "'Die großen Fische fressen die kleinen': Bemerkungen zu einem patristischen Traditionshintergrund für Hieronymus Bosch und Pieter Bruegel d. Ä.," *Neuphilologische Mitteilungen*, 82 (1981), 262–268. Bambeck does not refer to Parsons' earlier publication and repeats many of the references contained in that paper while at the same time adding others.

25. Athenagoras, *Legat. pro Christianis*, 34. Cited in English by Parsons (note 13), p. 380.

26. Basil, *In Hexaemeron Hom.*, 7, 3. Cited in English by Parsons (note 13), p. 381.

27. Chrysostom, *Sermo in Gen.*, 4, 2. Cited in English by Parsons (note 13), p. 381.

28. Ambrose, *Exameron*, 5, 5, 13. Cited in English by Parsons (note 13), p. 382.

29. Augustine, *In Ps.* LXIV. Cited in English by Parsons (note 13), p. 382.

30. Quoted from *Concil. Trosl.*, praef. Cited in English by Parsons (note 13), p. 383.

31. See Albert S. Cook (ed.), *The Old English Elene, Phoenix, and Physiologus*. New Haven, Connecticut: Yale University Press, 1919.

32. *Physiologus*, translated by Michael J. Curley. Austin, Texas: University of Texas Press, 1979, pp. 45–46. For the Latin original see Francis J. Carmody, *Physiologus Latinus Versio Y*. Berkeley: University of California Press, 1941, p. 125 (no. 30). (*University of California Publications in Classical Philology*, 12, no. 7 [1941]).

33. For a fascinating study of the origin and dissemination of this tale see Cornelia Catlin Coulter, "The 'Great Fish' in Ancient and Medieval Story," *Transactions and Proceedings of the American Philological Association*, 57 (1926), 32–50. See also Rudolf Schenda, "Walfisch-Lore und Walfisch-Literatur," *Laographia*, 22 (1965), 431–448 as well as Schenda's superb survey of fish lore entitled "Fisch, Fischen, Fischer" in *Enzyklopädie des Märchens*, ed. by Kurt Ranke et al. Berlin: Walter de Gruyter, 1984, vol. 4, cols. 1196–1211.

34. See Francis Klingender, *Animals in Art and Thought to the End of the Middle Ages*. Cambridge, Massachusetts: The MIT Press, 1971, p. 386, ill. 218c and p. 385, ill. 218a. The third illustration on p. 386 (ill. 218b) is very similar to ill. 218c. See also Florence McCulloch, *Medieval Latin and French Bestiaries*. Chapel Hill, North Carolina: University of North Carolina Press, 1960, pp. 75–76, 91–92, 194 and plate 2, ills. 1a and 1b. Both illustrations are only pen and ink reproductions, ill. 1a being identical with ill. 218a, and ill. 1b being a small reproduction of a drawing found in a thirteenth century bestiary of the Anglo-Norman poet Philippe de Thaon. For yet another illustration just showing the whale as an island see Helen Woodruff, "The Physiologus of Bern: A Survival of Alexandrian Style in a Ninth Century Manuscript," *The Art Bulletin*, 12 (1930), 226–253 (esp. p. 232 [fig. 11] and p. 245). I owe the reference to the excellent illustrations in Klingender to my colleague Malcolm Jones.

35. See *The Old English Physiologus*, text and prose translation by Albert Stanburrough Cook, verse translation by James Hall Pitman. New Haven, Connecticut: Yale University Press, 1922, pp. 17, 19 and 21. The entire section on "The Whale (Asp-Turtle)" on pp. 12–21, also including the island tale.

36. See for example the thirteenth century Old English miscellany "Natura cetegrandie" in J. A. W. Bennett and G. V. Smithers, *Early Middle English Verse and Prose*. Oxford: Clarendon Press, 1966, pp. 171–173; and Richard H. Randall, *A Cloisters Bestiary*. New York: The Metropolitan Museum of Art, 1960; 2d ed. 1965, p. 48. I wish to thank my colleague George B. Bryan for his help in locating Old English bestiaries.

37. A good description of this can be found in Friedrich Seiler, *Deutsche Sprichwörterkunde*. München: C. H. Beck, 1922; rpt., 1967, pp. 77–81.

38. See in historical order Vincent Stuckey Lean, *Lean's Collectanea. Proverbs (English & Foreign), Folk Lore, and Superstitions, Also Compilations towards Dictionaries of Proverbial Phrases and Words, Old and Disused*, ed. by T. W. Williams. Bristol: J. W. Arrowsmith, 1903/04, vol. 3, p. 476 and vol. 4, pp. 124–125; G. L. Apperson, *English Proverbs and Proverbial Phrases: A Historical Dictionary*. London: J. M. Dent, 1929; rpt. Detroit: Gale Research Co., 1969, p. 271; Bartlett Jere

Whiting, *Proverbs in the Earlier English Drama*. Cambridge, Massachusetts: Harvard University Press, 1938; rpt. New York: Octagon Books, 1969, pp. 67 and 72; Burton Stevenson, *The Macmillan Book of Proverbs, Maxims and Famous Phrases*. New York: Macmillan, 1948; 7th ed. 1968, p. 1034 (Great and Small, no. 5); Morris Palmer Tilley, *A Dictionary of the Proverbs in England in the Sixteenth and Seventeenth Centuries*. Ann Arbor, Michigan: University of Michigan Press, 1950, p. 218 (F 311); Bartlett Jere Whiting, *Proverbs, Sentences, and Proverbial Phrases from English Writings Mainly Before 1500*. Cambridge, Massachusetts: Harvard University Press, 1968, pp. 185–186 (F 232), p. 252 (G 444), p. 657 (W 473); F. P. Wilson, *The Oxford Dictionary of English Proverbs*, 3d ed. Oxford: Clarendon Press, 1970, p. 333; Bartlett Jere Whiting, *Early American Proverbs and Proverbial Phrases*. Cambridge, Massachusetts: Harvard University Press, 1977, p. 154 (F 146); R. W. Dent, *Shakespeare's Proverbial Language: An Index*. Berkeley: University of California Press, 1981, p. 111 (F 311); J. A. Simpson, *The Concise Oxford Dictionary of Proverbs*. Oxford: Oxford University Press, 1982, p. 18; R. W. Dent, *Proverbial Language in English Drama Exclusive of Shakespeare, 1495–1616: An Index*. Berekely: University of California Press, 1984, p. 343 (F 311). Many other English language proverb collections were checked, but the ones listed here are the most scholarly and useful for historical references.

39. Quoted from *Old English Homilies of the Twelfth Century*, ed. and trans. by Rev. R. Morris. London: N. Trübner, 1873, pp. 176 and 178. The entire section (29) on "St. Andrew" with parallel Old English and modern English texts takes up pp. 172–185 and contains many other references to the sea and its symbol for human life.

40. See Tilley (note 38), p. 570 (R 102).

41. *Kyng Alisander*, ed. by G. V. Smithers. London: Oxford University Press, 1952, p. 328 (lines 4926–4929) and p. 329 (lines 6192–6195).

42. Quoted from Dickins (note 13), p. 357.

43. See *Select English Works of John Wyclif*, ed. by Thomas Arnold. Oxford: Clarendon Press, 1869, p. 70 (Sermon 27 on pp. 68–70).

44. *The Lantern of Light*, ed. by Lilian M. Swinburn. London: Kegan Paul, Trench, Trübner & Co., 1917, pp. 45–46. An almost identical variant appeared about 1320 as "And gret fisches etes the smale" in a homily reprinted in *English Metrical Homilies from Manuscripts of the Fourteenth Century*, ed. by John Small. Edinburgh: William Paterson, 1862, p. 136 (line 2).

45. *The Macro Plays*, ed. by F. J. Furnivall and Alfred W. Pollard. London: Kegan Paul, Trench, Trübner & Co., 1904, p. 161 (lines 2818–2830). The translation is by George B. Bryan and me.

46. *The Non-Cycle Mystery Plays together with The Croxton Play of the Sacrament and The Pride of Life*, ed. by Osborn Waterhouse. London: Kegan Paul, Trench, Trübner & Co., 1909, pp. 99–100 (lines 359–366). The translation is by George B. Bryan and me.

47. *The Minor Poems of John Lydgate*, ed. by Henry Noble MacCracken. London: Oxford University Press, 1934, vol. 2, pp. 563–564 (lines 588–595). See the entire poem on pp. 539–566.

48. Ibid., p. 588 (lines 631–644). The entire poem (Fable 4) on pp. 584–591.

49. Ibid., p. 575 (lines 239–245). The entire poem (Fable 2) on pp. 574–578.

50. *The Ship of Fools*, translated by Alexander Barclay. Edinburgh: William Paterson, 1874, pp. 100–101. The entire section "Of ryches vnprofytable" on pp. 98–102. Bartlett Jere Whiting goes so far as to consider the entire statement "The wolfe etis the shepe, the great fysshe the small" a separate proverb in his

*Proverbs, Sentences, and Proverbial Phrases* (note 38), p. 657 (W 473). However, he only cites Barclay as a source, and until other references are found, we are more inclined to look at this as a mere extension of the proverb and not as a separate proverb text. It should also be noted that Barclay greatly expanded Brant's original German chapter "Von unnützem Reichtum" and that the fish proverb does not appear there at all. See Sebastian Brant, *Das Narrenschiff*, ed. by Hans-Joachim Mähl. Stuttgart: Reclam, 1964, pp. 67–69.

51. *The Eclogues of Alexander Barclay*, ed. by Beatrice White. London: Oxford University Press, 1928, p. 120 (lines 357–358). See also the lines "Euery daye well mayst thou se / That the grete doth ete the small" in Barclay's English translation of Pierre Gringoire's *The Castell of Labour [1506]*. Edinburgh: Roxburghe Club, 1905, p. Eij[a].

52. *The Proverbs of John Heywood*, ed. by Julian Sharman. London: George Bell, 1874, p. 118. The editor cites the proverb "The bigger wyll eate the Been" from the year 1525.

53. John Florio, *His Firste Fruites* (London 1578). Rpt. New York: Da Capo Press, 1969, p. 29[b]. See also "Novella CCI: Madonna Cecchina da Modena, essendo rubata, con uno pesce grasso e uno piccolo, e uno suo figlioletto, sonando la campanella" in *Le Novelle di Franco Sacchetti [ca. 1330–1400]*. Firenze: Felice Le Monnier, 1861, vol. 2, pp. 190–193. In this story a widow purchases a small and a large fish, places the small one into the mouth of the larger one, and walks through the streets of Modena exclaiming "The large fish devour the small" as a sign of protest against unfair treatment she had received from richer citizens.

54. Randle Cotgrave, *A Dictionarie of the French and English Tongue*. London: A. Islip, 1611. Rpt. New York: Da Capo Press, 1971, no pp. given (see under "POI"). For early French references of the proverb see in particular James Woodrow Hassell, *Middle French Proverbs, Sentences, and Proverbial Phrases*. Toronto: Pontifical Institute of Mediaeval Studies, 1982, p. 205 (P 229).

55. Thomas Draxe, *Bibliotheca Scholastica Instrvctissima*, London: J. Bill, 1616. Rpt. Norwood, New Jersey: Walter J. Johnson, 1976, p. 143.

56. For historical references see Tilley (note 38), p. 386 (L 354), p. 515 (O 64), p. 570 (R 102), p. 592 (S 228), and p. 682 (T 507). We also refer to the proverbial expressions "To set a herring to catch a whale," "To throw a sprat to catch a whale," and "To venture a small fish to catch a great one," which are certainly comments on the big fish eating little fish as well; here of course with the intent of catching the greedy larger animal. For historical references see for example Apperson (note 38), pp. 299, 580 and 597–598.

57. *Opera Omnia, Desiderii Erasmi Roterodami*, ed. by C. M. Bruehl and C. Reedijk. Amsterdam: North-Holland Publishing Company, 1981, vol. 2, part 5, p. 220 (no. 2261). For medieval Latin texts see Walther (note 23), vol. 4, p. 817 (nos. 28 and 28a). For English variants see Tilley (note 38), p. 592 (S 228). I would like to thank my colleague George B. Bryan for his help with some of the Latin translations.

58. Quoted from *The Works of George Herbert*, ed. by F. E. Hutchinson. Oxford: Clarendon Press, 1941, p. 351 (no. 922).

59. See Tilley (note 38), p. 592 (S 228).

60. Arthur Gardner, *Minor English Wood Sculpture 1400–1550*. London: Alec Tiranti, 1958, pp. 35–36 and ills. 152 and 154. I owe this valuable reference to Malcolm Jones. See also G. L. Remnant, *A Catalogue of Misericords in Great Britain*. Oxford: Clarendon Press, 1969, p. xxxvi (without ill.).

61. For a detail of this picture see Carl Linfert, *Hieronymus Bosch*. New York: Harry N. Abrams, 1971, p. 109.

62. See Peter Glum, "Divine Judgment in Bosch's 'Garden of Earthly Delights,'" *The Art Bulletin*, 58 (1976), 45–57 (esp. p. 52 [note 65]).

63. For a detail see Linfert (note 61), p. 75. See also Charles D. Cuttler, "The Lisbon 'Temptations of St. Anthony' by Jerome Bosch," *The Art Bulletin*, 39 (1957), 109–126 (esp. pp. 113–114); and D. Bax, *Hieronymus Bosch: His Picture-Writing Deciphered*. Rotterdam: A. A. Balkema, 1979, pp. 34–35.

64. For a detail see Linfert (note 61), p. 63.

65. For a detail see Wilhelm Fraenger, *Der Bauern-Bruegel und das deutsche Sprichwort*. Erlenbach-Zürich: Eugen Rentsch, 1923, ill. 19. A very similar scene of a big fish swallowing a smaller one head first can be found in a large proverb picture by Sebastian Vrancx (1573–1647); see Jan Grauls, "Het spreekwoordenschilderij van Sebastian Vrancx," *Bulletin des Musées royaux des Beaux-Arts de Bruxelles*, 9 (1960), 107–164 (esp. p. 125, no. 43; ill. p. 126). Vrancx illustrates about two hundred proverbs and proverbial expressions and was definitely influenced by Brueghel. For a survey of proverbs in art see Wolfgang Mieder, "Bibliographischer Abriß zur bildlichen Darstellung von Sprichwörtern und Redensarten," in *Forschungen und Berichte zur Volkskunde in Baden-Württemberg 1974–1977*, ed. by Irmgard Hampp and Peter Assion. Stuttgart: Müller & Gräff, 1977, vol. 3, pp. 229–239.

66. Alan Dundes and Claudia A. Stibbe, *The Art of Mixing Metaphors: A Folkloristic Interpretation of the "Netherlandish Proverbs" by Pieter Bruegel the Elder*. Helsinki: Suomalainen Tiedeakatemia, 1981, p. 38 (no. 53). See also Fraenger (note 65), p. 154 (no. 68); and above all Jan Grauls, *Volkstaal en Volksleven in het werk van Pieter Bruegel*. Antwerpen: N. V. Standaard-Boekhandel, 1957, p. 106 (no. 54).

67. The picture can be found in Christopher Brown, *Bruegel: Gemälde, Zeichnungen und Druckgraphik*. Wiesbaden: Ebeling, 1976, ill. 10.

68. For illustrations of both the drawing and the engraving see Charles de Tolnay, *The Drawings of Pieter Bruegel the Elder. With a Critical Catalogue*. New York: The Twin Editions, 1953, plate 24, ill. 44; and Gerhard Langemeyer, Gerd Unverfehrt, Herwig Guratzsch and Christoph Stölzl, *Bild als Waffe: Mittel und Motive der Karikatur in fünf Jahrhunderten*. München: Prestel, 1984, p. 268, ill. 194.

69. For short explanations of the 1557 engraving see Tolnay (note 68), pp. 137–138; Georg Piltz, *Geschichte der europäischen Karikatur*. Berlin: VEB Deutscher Verlag der Wissenschaften, 1980, p. 49; and Lutz Röhrich, *Lexikon der sprichwörtlichen Redensarten*. Freiburg: Herder, 1973, vol. 1, p. 277. Longer excellent discussions of this picture and a few others including modern cartoons are included in Gerd Unverfehrt, "'Große Fische fressen kleine': Zu Entstehung und Gebrauch eines satirischen Motivs," in Langemeyer et al. (note 68), pp. 402–414; and G. Unverfehrt, "Christliches Exempel und profane Allegorie: Zum Verhältnis von Wort und Bild in der Graphik der Boschnachfolge," in Herman Vekeman and Justus Müller Hofstede (eds.), *Wort und Bild in der niederländischen Kunst und Literatur des 16. und 17. Jahrhunderts*. Erfstadt: Lukassen, 1984, pp. 221–241 (esp. pp. 229–234). I gratefully acknowledge Gerd Unverfehrt's superb scholarship and the benefit I had from locating his two essays shortly before completing this manuscript.

70. For an illustration of this print see Unverfehrt (note 69), p. 409, ill. 16.

For an illustration with a German rhymed explanation of these political events see Wolfgang Harms et al., *Illustrierte Flugblätter des Barock*. Tübingen: Max Niemeyer, 1983, pp. 84–85; and Wolfgang Harms (ed.), *Deutsche illustrierte Flugblätter des 16. und 17. Jahrhunderts*. Nendeln, Liechtenstein: Kraus International Publications, 1980, vol. 2, pp. 240–241. An excellent interpretation also by Unverfehrt (note 69), pp. 409–411.

71. A reproduction can be found in Unverfehrt, "Große Fische" (note 69), p. 409, ill. 15.

72. The engraving is reproduced in Langemeyer (note 68), p. 269, ill. 195. For interpretations see Wolfgang Harms (ed.), *Illustrierte Flugblätter aus den Jahrhunderten der Reformation und der Glaubenskämpfe*. Coburg: Kunstsammlung der Veste Coburg, 1983, pp. 296–297; and Unverfehrt, "Große Fische" (note 69), pp. 407–408.

73. Jacob Cats, *Sinne- en Minnebeelden [1618] en Spiegel van den ouden en nieuwen tijdt [1632]* (Amsterdam 1665). Rpt. Den Haag: Van Goor Zonen, 1977, p. 103. Cats also adds an impressive list of variants of the "Big fish eat little fish" proverb from the major European languages on pp. 103–104.

74. The emblem and its text are included in Arthur Henkel and Albrecht Schöne (eds.), *Emblemata: Handbuch zur Sinnbildkunst des XVI. und XVII. Jahrhunderts*. Stuttgart: Metzler, 1967, col. 698.

75. For the text and the emblem see Henkel and Schöne (note 74), cols. 678–679.

76. The emblem is included in Michael Schilling, "Die literarischen Vorbilder der Ludwigsburger und Gaarzer Embleme," in *Außerliterarische Wirkungen barocker Emblembücher: Emblematik in Ludwigsburg, Gaarz and Rommsfelden*, ed. by Wolfgang Harms and Hartmut Freytag. München: Wilhelm Fink, 1975, ill. 36.

77. Ibid., ill. 38.

78. See *Proverbi Figurati di Giuseppe Maria Mitelli*, ed. by Lorenso Mariense and Alberto Manfredi. Milano: Casa Editrice Cerastico, 1963, ill. 15.

79. John Day, *Law-Trickes or, who vvould have thovght it* (London 1608). Rpt. Oxford: Oxford University Press, 1963, p. B3 (lines 274–279).

80. A. H. Bullen (ed.), *The Works of Thomas Middleton*. New York: AMS Press, 1964, vol. 4, p. 86 (lines 145–152). In a footnote (no. 2) Bullen refers to the reference in the two plays by Shakespeare and Day which we have discussed above.

81. Matheo Alemán, *The Rogve: or, The Life of Gvzman de Alfarache*. Oxford: William Tvrner, 1630, vol. 1, p. 34.

82. For the many investigations of Shakespeare's use of proverbs see Wolfgang Mieder, *Proverbs in Literature: An International Bibliography*. Bern: Peter Lang, 1978, pp. 119–123 (nos. 971–1021); and W. Mieder, *International Proverb Scholarship: An Annotated Bibliography*. New York: Garland Publishing, 1982, p. 537 (index).

83. *The Complete Writings of Roger Williams*, ed. by Perry Miller et al. New York: Russel & Russell, 1963, vol. 1, p. 142.

84. Ibid., vol. 3, p. 398.

85. Ibid., p. 424.

86. Quoted from *The Witness of William Penn*, ed. by Frederick B. Tolles and E. Gordon Alderfer. New York: Macmillan, 1957, p. 152.

87. Algernon Sidney, *Discourses on Government*. New York: Richard Lee, 1805, vol. 2, p. 156.

88. *The Poems of Jonathan Swift*, ed. by Harold Williams. Oxford: Clarendon Press, 1937. vol. 2, p. 651 (lines 319–344). The entire poem on pp. 639–659.

89. Quoted from *Colonial Currency Reprints 1682–1751*, ed. by Andrew McFarland Davis. New York: Augustus M. Kelley, 1964, vol. 2, p. 432. The entire treatise on pp. 432–452.

90. Ibid., vol. 4, p. 11. The entire treatise on pp. 1–26.

91. *Warren-Adams Letters, Being Chiefly a Correspondence among John Adams, Samuel Adams, and James Warren*, ed. by Henry Cabot Lodge et al. Boston: The Massachusetts Historical Society, 1925, vol. 2, p. 269.

92. *Adams Family Correspondence*, ed. by L. H. Butterfield. Cambridge, Massachusetts: Harvard University Press, 1963, vol. 1, p. 329.

93. *Diary of the American Revolution from Newspapers and Original Documents*, ed. by Frank Moore. New York: Charles Scribner, 1855, vol. 1, p. 135.

94. *The Poetical Works of David Hitchcock*. Boston: Etheridge and Bliss, 1806, pp. 34–35. The entire poem on pp. 17–115.

95. Theodore Parker, *Speeches, Addresses, and Occasional Sermons*. Boston: Ticknor and Fields, 1861, p. 225.

96. See E. P. Thompson, "The State of the Nation: Anarchy and Culture," *New Society* (6 December 1979), p. 557. The entire article on pp. 557–558.

97. The song is included in Peter Udell and Gary Geld, *"Purlie": Vocal Selections*. New York: Mourbar Music Corp., 1969, pp. 7–9.

98. Bertolt Brecht, "Wenn die Haifische Menschen wären," in *Gesammelte Werke in 20 Bänden*, ed. by Elisabeth Hauptmann. Frankfurt: Suhrkamp, 1967, vol. 12, pp. 394–396. The translation from the German is my own.

99. *New Yorker* (3 September 1979), p. 25.

100. *Die Zeit*, no. 22 (2 June 1978), p. 11 (all references to this newspaper come from the American edition).

101. *Pravda* (12 August 1975), no pp. I owe this reference to my colleague Kevin McKenna.

102. *Pravda* (13 December 1974), no pp. I owe this reference to my student Peter Christiansen.

103. *Saturday Review* (2 February 1980), p. 42.

104. *Punch* (8 February 1961), p. 235.

105. *Saturday Review* (2 May 1964), p. 3.

106. *Time* (22 April 1985), pp. 45–46. I owe this reference to my colleague Veronica Richel.

107. *Pravda* (22 June 1979), no pp. I owe this reference to my colleague Kevin McKenna.

108. *Pravda* (19 April 1973), p. 5. I owe this reference to my student Peter Christiansen.

109. Originally from the *Fort Worth Star-Telegram* (1983). I owe this reference to my student Ardyce Masters who located it in the *Billings* (Montana) *Gazette* (27 June 1983), no pp. The artist is Etta Hulme.

110. *Esquire* (9 May 1978), p. 13.

111. *The Boston Globe* (3 January 1982), p. 41.

112. *Time* (6 February 1984), pp. 46–47. I owe this reference to Dr. Barbara Mieder.

113. *Burlington Free Press* (1 April 1985), p. 6A.

114. Langemeyer (see note 68), p. 270, ill. 196.

115. *New Yorker* (9 May 1977), p. 41. I owe this reference to my student Melissa Brown.

116. John Hancock Life Insurance brochure (mailed out in February 1980).

117. *Financial Security Alert* (May 1985), p. 7. I owe this reference to my colleagues Beatrice and Jared Wood.

118. *Spiegel*, no. 24 (8 June 1981), p. 59. I owe this reference to my colleague Lutz Röhrich.

119. Unverfehrt (note 69), p. 402, ill. 2.

120. Ibid., p. 414, ill. 28.

121. *U.S. News & World Report* (10 June 1985), p. 13. I owe this reference to my colleague Veronica Richel.

122. *Time* (22 October 1979), pp. 50–51. I owe this reference to Dr. Barbara Mieder.

123. *Chicago Tribune* (28 December 1976), p. 11.

124. Unverfehrt, "Große Fische" (note 69), p. 413, ill. 26.

125. *New Yorker* (16 August 1976), p. 88.

126. *Saturday Review* (5 January 1980), p. 7.

127. *New Yorker* (2 February 1981), p. 32.

128. *The Best Cartoons from Punch*, ed. by M. Rosenberg and W. Cole. New York: Simon & Schuster, 1952, no pp. given.

129. *Saturday Review* (November 1980), p. 77.

130. Peter Tille and Hans Ticha, *Sommersprossen: 666 aphoristische Gesichtspunkte*. Halle: Mitteldeutscher Verlag, 1983, p. 109.

131. *Kölsche Sprichwörter*, ed. by Benedikt Linden and "Odysseus." Köln: J. P. Bachem, 1984, no pp. given.

132. *The Wall Street Journal* (24 September 1982), p. 37.

133. *The New Yorker: Album of Drawings 1925–1975*. New York: The New Yorker, 1975, no pp. given.

134. Karl Friedrich Wilhelm Wander (pseud. N. R. Dove), *Politisches Sprichwörterbrevier. Tagebuch eines Patrioten der fünfziger Jahre, zur Charakteristik jener Zeit*. Leipzig: Otto Wigand, 1872, p. 40 (no. 155). Wander kept this diary between 1 January 1857 and the end of 1862, but published it only ten years later for political reasons.

135. Leo Lionni, *Swimmy*. New York: Knopf, 1963, pp. 6–7, 26–27, 28–29, and 30–31. I owe this reference to Ann and Dick Park.

136. Illustrated in David Kunzle, "World Upside-Down: The Iconography of a European Broadsheet Type," in *The Reversible World: Symbolic Inversion in Art and Society*, ed. by Barbara A. Babcock. Ithaca, New York: Cornell University Press, 1978, p. 70

137. Unverfehrt, "Große Fische" (note 69), p. 412, ill. 21.

138. Ibid., p. 413, ills. 24 and 25.

139. *Burlington Free Press* (1 December 1984), p. 10A. About half a year later the same cartoon appeared in a German newspaper with the English inscriptions of the fish translated into the German "Lobbyisten" and "Steuerreform." This is another indication of the major role that mass media plays in disseminating such innovative interpretations of traditional lore. For this illustration see *Die Zeit*, no. 24 (14 June 1985), p. 8.

140. *Nebelspalter*, no. 38 (22 September 1981), p. 16.

141. *San Francisco Chronicle* (1980). No better bibliographical information available at this time. I owe this reference to my colleague Alan Dundes.

142. For some historical references to this proverb see Wilson (note 38), p. 854.

143. For a collection of three thousand such proverb parodies see Wolfgang

Mieder, *Antisprichwörter*, 2 vols. Wiesbaden: Verlag für deutsche Sprache, 1982 and 1985.

144. Matti Kuusi, *Parömiologische Betrachtungen.* Helsinki: Suomalainen Tiedeakatemia, 1957, p. 52.

# Bibliography

This bibliography registers only secondary literature. References to primary literature are included in the footnotes of each chapter.

Abrahams, Roger D. *Jump-Rope Rhymes: A Dictionary.* Austin, Texas: University of Texas Press, 1969.

Abrahams, Roger D., and Lois Rankin. *Counting-Out Rhymes: A Dictionary.* Austin, Texas: University of Texas Press, 1980.

Adams, A. K. *The House Book of Humorous Quotations.* New York: Dodd, Mead & Co., 1969.

Adams, Franklin Pierce. *Book of Quotations.* New York: Funk & Wagnalls, 1952.

Ahrens, Wilfried. "Grimms Märchen—sagenhaft!" *Bunte,* no. 14 (28 March 1985), 132–133.

Albig, William. "Proverbs and Social Control." *Sociology and Social Research,* 15 (1931), 527–535.

Anido, Naiade (ed.). *Des proverbes . . . à l'affût.* Paris: Publications Langues'O, 1983 (*Cahiers de Littérature Orale,* no. 13).

Apperson, G. L. *English Proverbs and Proverbial Phrases: A Historical Dictionary.* London: J. M. Dent, 1929; rpt. Detroit: Gale Research Co., 1969.

Bambeck, Manfred. "'Die großen Fische fressen die kleinen': Bemerkungen zu einem patristischen Traditionshintergrund für Hieronymus Bosch und Pieter Bruegel d. Ä." *Neuphilologische Mitteilungen,* 82 (1981), 262–268.

Baring-Gould, Sabine. "The Pied Piper of Hamelin." In S. Baring-Gould, *Curious Myths of the Middle Ages.* London: Rivingtons, 1873, pp. 417–446.

Baring-Gould, William and Ceil. *The Annotated Mother Goose.* New York: Bramhall House, 1962.

Bartlett, John. *Familiar Quotations.* Boston: Little, Brown and Co., 15th ed. 1980.

Bausinger, Hermann. "Möglichkeiten des Märchens in der Gegenwart." In *Märchen, Mythos, Dichtung: Festschrift zum 90. Geburtstag Friedrich von der Leyens,* ed. by Hugo Kuhn and Kurt Schier. München: C. H. Beck, 1963, pp. 15–30.

Bausinger, Hermann. *Volkskultur in der technischen Welt.* Stuttgart: Kohlhammer, 1961.

270   Bibliography

Bausinger, Hermann. *Volkskunde: Von der Altertumsforschung zur Kulturanalyse.* Darmstadt: Carl Habel, 1971.

Bausinger, Hermann. "Zur Algebra der Kontinuität." In *Kontinuität? Geschichtlichkeit und Dauer als volkskundliches Problem,* ed. by H. Bausinger and Wolfgang Brückner. Berlin: Erich Schmidt, 1969, pp. 9–30.

Bausinger, Hermann, and Wolfgang Brückner (eds.). *Kontinuität? Geschichtlichkeit und Dauer als volkskundliches Problem.* Berlin: Erich Schmidt, 1969.

Bax, D. *Hieronymus Bosch: His Picture-Writing Deciphered.* Rotterdam: A. A. Balkema, 1979.

Belgrader, Michael. *Das Märchen von dem Machandelboom (KHM 47). Der Märchentypus AT 720: My Mother Slew Me, My Father Ate Me.* Bern: Peter Lang, 1980.

Bettelheim, Bruno. *The Uses of Enchantment: The Meaning and Importance of Fairy Tales.* New York: A. Knopf, 1976.

Bird, Donald Allport. "A Theory for Folklore in Mass Media: Traditional Patterns in the Mass Media." *Southern Folklore Quarterly,* 40 (1976), 285–305.

Blair, Walter. "The Funny Fondled Fairytale Frog." *Studies in American Humor,* 1 (1982), 17–23.

Blümml, E. K., and A. J. Rott. "Die Verwendung der Pflanzen durch die Kinder in Deutschböhmen und Niederösterreich." *Zeitschrift des Vereins für Volkskunde,* 11 (1901), 49–64.

Böhme, Franz Magnus (ed.). *Deutsches Kinderlied und Kinderspiel.* Leipzig: Breitkopf & Härtel, 1924.

Bohn, Henry G. *A Polyglot of Foreign Proverbs, Comprising French, Italian, German, Dutch, Spanish, Portugese and Danish with English Translations.* London: Henry G. Bohn, 1857; rpt. Detroit: Gale Research Co., 1968.

Böklen, Ernst. *Schneewittchenstudien.* 2 vols. Leipzig: J. C. Hinrichs, 1910 and 1915.

Bolte, Johannes, and Georg Polívka. *Anmerkungen zu den Kinder-und Hausmärchen der Brüder Grimm.* 5 vols. Leipzig: Dieterich, 1913–1932; rpt. Hildesheim: Georg Olms, 1963.

Bolton, Henry Carrington. *The Counting-Out Rhymes of Children.* New York: Appleton, 1888; rpt. Detroit: Singing Tree Press, 1969.

Bonser, Wilfrid. *Proverb Literature: A Bibliography of Works Relating to Proverbs.* London: William Glaisher, 1930; rpt. Nendeln, Liechtenstein: Kraus Reprint, 1967.

Brackert, Helmut (ed.). *"Und wenn sie nicht gestorben sind . . . " Perspektiven auf das Märchen.* Frankfurt: Suhrkamp, 1980.

Brasch, R. *How Did It Begin? Customs and Superstitions and Their Romantic Origins.* New York: David McKay, 1965.

Brauneck, Manfred. "Der Rattenfänger von Hameln: Ein Beitrag zur Sagenbehandlung auf der Unterstufe." *Der Deutschunterricht,* 20, no. 6 (1968), 28–41.

Brednich, Rolf Wilhelm. "Die Comic Strips als Gegenstand der Erzählforschung." Paper distributed at the VIth Congress of the International Society for Folk-Narrative Research (Helsinki, 16–21 June 1974), 19 pp.

Brewer, Ebenezer Cobham. *Brewer's Dictionary of Phrase and Fable.* New York: Harper & Row, 1870; Centenary edition revised by Ivor H. Evans, 1970.

Bringéus, Nils-Arvid. "Das Studium der Innovation." *Zeitschrift für Volkskunde,* 64 (1968), 161–185.

Brown, Christopher. *Bruegel: Gemälde, Zeichnungen und Druckgraphik.* Wiesbaden: Ebeling, 1976.

Brunner, Erwin. "Die Affäre Rotkäppchen: Der ungeklärte Grimminalfall im Märchenwald: War der Wolf unschuldig? Hat das Mädchen ihn verführt?" *Die Zeit*, no. 52 (28 December 1984), 15–18 (American edition).

Brunvand, Jan Harold. *The Study of American Folklore*. New York: W. W. Norton, 1968; 2d ed. 1978.

Bürger, Christa. "Die soziale Funktion volkstümlicher Erzählformen—Sage und Märchen." In *Projekt Deutschunterricht 1: Kritisches Lesen: Märchen, Sage, Fabel, Volksbuch*, ed. by Heinz Ide. Stuttgart: Metzler, 1971, pp. 25–56.

Busset, Jean-Luc. "Les sources du 'Joueur de Flûte' de Mérimée: La légende du preneur de rats de Hameln." *Revue de littérature comparée*, 53 (1979), 17–26.

Cammann, Alfred. "Rattenfängersage und Ostsiedlung nach dem derzeitigen Stande der Forschung." *Heimat und Volkstum: Jahrbuch für bremische, niedersächsische Volkskunde*, no. vol. (1957), 66–76.

Carruthers, Miss. *Flower Lore: The Teachings of Flowers*. Belfast: McCaw, Stevenson & Orr, 1879.

Christy, Robert. *Proverbs, Maxims and Phrases of All Ages*. New York: G. P. Putnam's Sons, 1887; rpt. Norwood, Pennsylvania: Norwood Editions, 1977.

Coo, Josef de. "Twaalf spreuken op borden van Pieter Bruegel de Oude." *Bulletin des Musées royaux des Beaux-Arts*, 14 (1965), 83–104.

Cook, George Willis. *A Guide-Book to the Poetic and Dramatic Works of Robert Browning*. Boston: Houghton, Mifflin & Co., 1891.

Cotgrave, Randle. *A Dictionarie of the French and English Tongue*. London: A. Islip, 1611; rpt. New York: Da Capo Press, 1971.

Coulter, Cornelia Catlin. "The 'Great Fish' in Ancient and Medieval Story." *Transactions and Proceedings of the American Philological Association*, 57 (1926), 32–50.

Cuttler, Charles D. "The Lisbon 'Temptations of St. Anthony' by Jerome Bosch." *The Art Bulletin*, 39 (1957), 109–126.

Daiken, Leslie. *Out Goes She: Dublin Street Rhymes*. Dublin: The Dolmen Press, 1963.

Darwin, Bernard. *The Oxford Dictionary of Quotations*. Oxford: Oxford University Press, 1953.

Deas, Lizzie. *Flower Favourites: Their Legend, Symbolism and Significance*. London: George Allen, 1898.

Dégh, Linda and Andrew Vázsonyi. "Magic for Sale: Märchen and Legend in TV Advertising." *Fabula*, 20 (1979), 47–68.

Denby, Priscilla. "Folklore in the Mass Media." *Folklore Forum*, 4, no. 5 (1971), 113–125.

Denecke, Ludwig. *Jacob Grimm und sein Bruder Wilhelm*. Stuttgart: Metzler, 1971.

Dent, Robert W. *Proverbial Language in English Drama Exclusive of Shakespeare, 1495–1616: An Index*. Berkeley: University of California Press, 1984.

Dent, Robert W. *Shakespeare's Proverbial Language: An Index*. Berkeley: University of California Press, 1981.

DeVane, William Clyde. *A Browning Handbook*. New York: Appleton-Century-Crofts, 1955.

Dickins, Bruce. "Addendum to 'Lest men, like fishes . . . '" *Traditio*, 6 (1946), 356–357.

Dickson, Arthur. "Browning's Source for the 'Pied Piper of Hamelin.'" *Studies in Philology*, 23 (1926), 327–336.

Dobbertin, Hans. "Der Auszug der Hämelschen Kinder.: Ein Vermißtenschicksal der Kolonisationszeit wurde zur Volkssage." *Jahrbuch für
Volkskunde der Heimatvertriebenen*, 4 (1958), 35–68.

Dobbertin, Hans. *Beiträge zur Hamelner Kinderausfahrt (1284)*. Springe: Selbstverlag, 1978.

Dobbertin, Hans. "Berichtigungen und Ergänzungen zur Hamelner Kinderausfahrt (1284)." *Niedersächsisches Jahrbuch für Landesgeschichte*, 49 (1977),
315–320.

Dobbertin, Hans. "Die Hamelner Glasbildinschrift als Hauptquelle der Rattenfängersage." *Zeitschrift für Volkskunde*, 62 (1966), 29–42.

Dobbertin, Hans. "Neues zur Hamelner Rattenfängersage." *Fabula*, 1 (1957),
144–155.

Dobbertin, Hans. *Quellensammlung zur Hamelner Rattenfängersage*. Göttingen:
Otto Schwarz, 1970.

Dobbertin, Hans. *Wohin zogen die Hämelschen Kinder (1284)?* Hildesheim: August Lax, 1955 (*Niedersächsisches Jahrbuch für Landesgeschichte*, 27 [1955], 45–
122).

Dorson, Richard. *American Folklore*. Chicago: University of Chicago Press,
1959; 10th ed. 1973.

Dorson, Richard. "Folklore in the Modern World." In R. Dorson, *Folklore and
Fakelore: Essays toward a Discipline of Folk Studies*. Cambridge, Massachusetts:
Harvard University Press, 1976, pp. 33–73.

Dorson, Richard (ed.). *Handbook of American Folklore*. Bloomington, Indiana:
Indiana University Press, 1983.

Doyle, Charles Clay. "On Some Paremiological Verses." *Proverbium*, 25 (1975),
979–982.

Draxe, Thomas. *Bibliotheca Scholastica Instrvctissima*. London: J. Bill, 1616; rpt.
Norwood, New Jersey: Walter J. Johnson, 1976.

Dundes, Alan. "Advertising and Folklore." *New York Folklore Quarterly*, 19
(1963), 143–151.

Dundes, Alan (ed.). *Cinderella: A Folklore Casebook*. New York: Garland Publishing, 1982.

Dundes, Alan. "The Devolutionary Premise in Folklore Theory." *Journal of the
Folklore Institute*, 6 (1969), 5–19.

Dundes, Alan. "The Number Three in American Culture." In A. Dundes
(ed.)., *Every Man His Way*. Englewood Cliffs, New Jersey: Prentice-Hall,
1968, pp. 401–424.

Dundes, Alan, and Claudia A. Stibbe. *The Art of Mixing Metaphors: A Folkloristic
Interpretation of the "Netherlandish Proverbs" by Pieter Bruegel the Elder*. Helsinki: Suomalainen Tiedeakatemia, 1981.

Düringsfeld, Ida von, and Otto von Reinsberg-Düringsfeld. *Sprichwörter der
germanischen und romanischen Sprachen vergleichend zusammengestellt*. 2 vols.
Leipzig: Hermann Fries, 1872 and 1875; rpt. Hildesheim: Georg Olms, 1973.

Egli, Martha. *Benennungsmotive bei Pflanzen an schweizerischen Pflanzennamen
untersucht*. Diss. Zürich, 1930.

Ellacombe, Henry N. *The Plant-Lore and Garden-Craft of Shakespeare*. London:
W. Satchell, 1884.

Elton, William. "Addendum: 'Lest men, like fishes.'" *Traditio*, 18 (1962),
421–422.

Evans, Patricia. *Rimbles: A Book of Children's Classic Games, Rhymes, Songs, and
Sayings*. Garden City, New York: Doubleday, 1961.

Farmer, John S. (ed.). *The Proverbs, Epigrams, and Miscellanies of John Heywood.* London: Early English Drama Society, 1906; rpt. New York: Barnes & Noble, 1966.

Fein, Christoph Friedrich. *Die entlarvte Fabel vom Ausgange der Hämelschen Kinder: Eine nähere Entdekkung der dahinter verborgenen wahren Geschichte.* Hannover: Johann Christoph Richter, 1749.

Ferrari, Enrique Lafuente. *Goya: His Complete Etchings, Aquatints, and Lithographs.* New York: Harry N. Abrams, 1962.

Flanagan, John T. "Grim Stories: Folklore in Cartoons." *Midwestern Journal of Language and Folklore,* 1 (1975), 20–26.

Florio, John. *His Firste Fruites.* London: Thomas Dawson, 1578; rpt. New York: Da Capo Press, 1969.

Foote, Timothy. *The World of Bruegel, c. 1525–1569.* New York: Time-Life Books, 1968.

Fraenger, Wilhelm. *Der Bauern-Bruegel und das deutsche Sprichwort.* Erlenbach-Zürich: Eugen Rentsch, 1923.

Frank, Grace and Dorothy Miner. *Proverbes en rimes: Text and Illustrations of the Fifteenth Century from a French Manuscript in the Walters Art Gallery, Baltimore.* Baltimore, Maryland: The Johns Hopkins Press, 1937.

Gardner, Arthur. *Minor English Wood Sculpture 1400–1550.* London: Alec Tiranti, 1958.

Garrisson, Webb. *How It Started.* Nashville, Tennessee: Abingdon Press, 1972.

Gehrts, Heino. "Zur Rattenfängerfrage." *Zeitschrift für deutsche Philologie,* 74 (1955), 191–204.

Gifford, Barbara Sporzynski. *The Pied Piper and His Followers: A Study of a Legend and Its Descendants.* M. A. Thesis, University of Vermont, 1980.

Glum, Peter. "Divine Judgment in Bosch's 'Garden of Earthly Delights.'" *The Art Bulletin,* 58 (1976), 45–57.

Gluski, Jerzy. *Proverbs: A Comparative Book of English, French, German, Italian, Spanish and Russian Proverbs with a Latin Appendix.* New York: Elsevier Publishing Co., 1971.

Goebel, Gerhard. "Apoll in Hameln: Ein Nachtrag zu den 'Göttern im Exil.'" *Germanisch-Romanische Monatsschrift,* 63, new series 32 (1982), 286–299.

Gordon, Edmund I. *Sumerian Proverbs: Glimpses of Everyday Life in Ancient Mesopotamia.* New York: Greenwood, 1968.

Görner, Otto. "Reklame und Volkskunde." *Mitteldeutsche Blätter für Volkskunde,* 6 (1931), 109–126.

Gottschalk, Walter. *Die bildhaften Sprichwörter der Romanen.* 3 vols. Heidelberg: Carl Winter, 1935–1938.

Gould, James and Clifford Morgan. "Hearing in the Rat at High Frequencies." *Science,* 94 (15 August 1941), 168.

Grauls, Jan. "Het spreekwoordenschilderij van Sebastian Vrancx." *Bulletin des Musées royaux des Beaux-Arts de Bruxelles,* 9 (1960), 107–164.

Grauls, Jan. *Volkstaal en volksleven in het werk van Pieter Bruegel.* Antwerpen: N. V. Standaard-Boekhandel, 1957.

Griffin, William Hall. "Robert Browning the Elder." *The Bookman,* 248 (May 1912), 66–70.

Grimm, Jacob. "Bedeutung der Blumen und Blätter." In *Altdeutsche Blätter,* ed. by the Brothers Grimm. Cassel: Thurmeissen, 1813, vol. 1, pp. 131–160. Rpt. with an introduction by Wilhelm Schoof. Darmstadt: Wissenschaftliche Buchgesellschaft, 1966.

Grzybek, Peter and Wolfgang Eismann (eds.). *Semiotische Studien zum Sprichwort: Simple Forms Reconsidered I.* Tübingen: Gunter Narr, 1984. Also published as *Kodikas/Code: Ars Semeiotica*, 7, nos. 3/4 (1984), 193–456.

Gullen, Doreen. *Traditional Number Rhymes and Games.* London: University of London Press, 1950.

Haltaus, Carl (ed.). *Liederbuch der Clara Hätzlerin.* Leipzig: Gottfried Basse, 1840.

Hand, Wayland D. "From Folk Legends to Folk Custom: The Shift from Narrative to Dramatic Contents." *Midwestern Journal of Language and Folklore*, 2 (1976), 10–19.

Hand, Wayland D. (ed.). *Popular Beliefs and Superstitions from North Carolina (The Frank C. Brown Collection of North Carolina Folklore*, vol. 6). Durham, North Carolina: Duke University Press, 1961.

Hanfstaengl, Ernst. *Hitler in der Karikatur der Welt: Tat gegen Tinte.* Berlin: Braune Verlag, 1934.

Harms, Wolfgang (ed.). *Deutsche illustrierte Flugblätter des 16. und 17. Jahrhunderts.* Nendeln, Liechtenstein: Kraus International Publications, 1980.

Harms, Wolfgang (ed.). *Illustrierte Flugblätter aus den Jahrhunderten der Reformation und der Glaubenskämpfe.* Coburg: Kunstsammlung der Veste Coburg, 1983.

Harms, Wolfgang, John Roger Paas, Michael Schilling, and Andreas Wang. *Illustrierte Flugblätter des Barock.* Tübingen: Max Niemeyer, 1983.

Hart, Henry H. *Seven Hundred Chinese Proverbs.* Palo Alto, California: Stanford University Press, 1937.

Hassell, James Woodrow. *Middle French Proverbs, Sentences, and Proverbial Phrases.* Toronto: Pontifical Institute of Mediaeval Studies, 1982.

Häussler, Reinhard (ed.). *Nachträge zu A. Otto, Sprichwörter und sprichwörtliche Redensarten der Römer.* Hildesheim: Georg Olms, 1968.

Heilfurth, Gerhard. "Volkskunde." In *Komplexe Forschungsansätze (Handbuch der empirischen Sozialforschung*, vol. 4), ed. by René König. Stuttgart: Ferdinand Enke, 1962; 3d ed. 1974, pp. 162–225.

Henkel, Arthur, and Albrecht Schöne (eds.). *Emblemata: Handbuch zur Sinnbildkunst des XVI. und XVII. Jahrhunderts.* Stuttgart: Metzler, 1967.

Herring, Jack W. *The Pied Piper of Hamelin in the Armstrong Browning Library, Baylor University, Waco, Texas.* Waco, Texas: Baylor University Browning Interests, 1969.

Horn, Katalin. "Grimmsche Märchen als Quellen für Metaphern und Vergleiche in der Sprache der Werbung, des Journalismus und der Literatur." *Muttersprache*, 91 (1981), 106–115.

Horn, Katalin. "Märchenmotive und gezeichneter Witz: Einige Möglichkeiten der Adaption." *Österreichische Zeitschrift für Volkskunde*, 86, new series 27 (1983), 209–237.

Hustvedt, S. B., and Archer Taylor. "The Pied Piper of Hamelin." *California Folklore Quarterly*, 3 (1944), 150–151.

Hyamson, Albert M. *A Dictionary of English Phrases.* New York: E. P. Dutton, 1922; rpt. Detroit: Gale Research Co., 1970.

Jantz, Harold. "Kontrafaktur, Montage, Parodie: Tradition und symbolische Erweiterung." In *Tradition und Ursprünglichkeit: Akten des III. Internationalen Germanistenkongresses 1965 in Amsterdam*, ed. by Werner Kohlschmidt and Herman Meyer. Bern: Francke, 1966, pp. 53–65.

Jech, Jaromir. "Variabilität und Stabilität in den einzelnen Kategorien der Volksprosa." *Fabula*, 9 (1967), 55–62.

Jobes, Gertrude. *Dictionary of Mythology, Folklore and Symbols*. New York: The Scarecrow Press, 1961.

Jolles, André. *Einfache Formen*. Halle: Max Niemeyer, 1930; rpt. 3d ed. Tübingen: Max Niemeyer, 1965.

Joly, Henri L. *Legend in Japanese Art: A Description of Historical Episodes, Legendary Characters, Folk-Lore, Myths, Religious Symbolism: Illustrated in the Arts of Old Japan*. London: John Lane, 1908; rpt. Rutland, Vermont: Charles F. Tuttle, 1967.

Jostes, Franz. *Der Rattenfänger von Hameln: Ein Beitrag zur Sagenkunde*. Bonn: P. Hanstein, 1895.

Käppeli, Rolf. "Rotkäppchen darf nicht sterben: Über die Ursprünge einer Kindergeschichte und wie diese im Lauf der Zeit und im Dienst der Herrschenden und Unterdrückten ständig verfremdet wurde." *Tages-Anzeiger Magazin*, no. 38 (22 September 1984), 44–47 and 49–50.

Karlinger, Felix (ed.). *Wege der Märchenforschung*. Darmstadt: Wissenschaftliche Buchgessellschaft, 1973.

Klingender, Francis. *Animals in Art and Thought to the End of the Middle Ages*. Cambridge, Massachusetts: The MIT Press, 1971.

Köhler, Carl Sylvio. *Das Tierleben im Sprichwort der Griechen und Römer*. Leipzig: Fernau, 1881; rpt. Hildesheim: Georg Olms, 1967.

Kohlschmidt, Werner and Herman Meyer (eds.). *Tradition und Ursprünglichkeit. Akten des III. Internationalen Germanistenkongresses 1965 in Amsterdam*. Bern: Francke, 1966.

Kramer, Karl-Sigismund. "Umweltverflechtung und Kontinuität." In *Kontinuität? Geschichtlichkeit und Dauer als volkskundliches Problem*, ed. by Hermann Bausinger and Wolfgang Brückner. Berlin: Erich Schmidt, 1969, pp. 76–86.

Krogmann, Willy. *Der Rattenfänger von Hameln: Eine Untersuchung über das Werden der Sage*. Berlin: Emil Ebering, 1934; rpt. Nendeln, Liechtenstein: Kraus Reprints, 1967.

Krohne, Helmut. "Der Rattenfänger von Hameln." *Magazin für Abenteuer-, Reise- und Unterhaltungsliteratur*, no. 26 (1980), 34–40.

Kunzle, David. "World Upside Down: The Iconography of a European Broadsheet Type." In *The Reversible World: Symbolic Inversion in Art and Society*, ed. by Barbara A. Babcock. Ithaca, New York: Cornell University Press, 1978, pp. 39–94.

Kuusi, Matti. *Parömiologische Betrachtungen*. Helsinki: Suomalainen Tiedeakatemia, 1957.

Kuusi, Matti. *Regen bei Sonnenschein: Zur Weltgeschichte einer Redensart*. Helsinki: Suomalainen Tiedeakatemia, 1957.

Laiblin, Wilhelm (ed.). *Märchenforschung und Tiefenpsychologie*. Darmstadt: Wissenschaftliche Buchgesellschaft, 1969.

Langemeyer, Gerhard, Gerd Unverfehrt, Herwig Guratzsch, and Christoph Stölzl. *Bild als Waffe: Mittel und Motive der Karikatur in fünf Jahrhunderten*. München: Prestel, 1984.

Lauffer, Otto. "Altertumskundliche Beiträge zur Erklärung der Sage von den Hämelschen Kindern." In *Vom Geist der Dichtung: Gedächtnisschrift für Robert Petsch*, ed. by Fritz Martini. Hamburg: Hoffmann und Campe, 1949, pp. 306–315.

Lavalleye, Jacques. *Pieter Bruegel the Elder and Lucas van Leyden: The Complete Engravings, Etchings, and Woodcuts*. New York: Harry N. Abrams, 1967.

Lean, Vincent Stuckey. *Lean's Collectanea: Proverbs (English & Foreign), Folk Lore, and Superstitions, Also Compilations towards Dictionaries of Proverbial Phrases and Words, Old and Disused*, ed. by T. W. Williams. 4 vols. Bristol: J. W. Arrowsmith, 1902–1904; rpt. Detroit: Gale Research Co., 1969.

Lebeer, Louis. "De blauwe huyck." *Gentsche Bijdragen tot de Kunstgeschiedenes*, 6 (1939/1940), 161–229.

Lessmann, Heinrich. *Der deutsche Volksmund im Lichte der Sage*. Berlin: Herbert Stubenrauch, 1937.

Levitine, George. "The Elephant of Goya." *Art Journal*, 20 (1961), 145–147.

Liebrecht, Felix. "Ein Volksvers [He loves me, he loves me not]." *Germania*, 33 (1888), 179–180.

Linfert, Carl. *Hieronymus Bosch*. New York: Harry N. Abrams, 1971.

Lurie, Charles N. *Everyday Sayings: Their Meanings Explained, Their Origins Given*. New York: G. P. Putnam's Sons, 1928; rpt. Detroit: Gale Research Co., 1968.

Lüthi, Max. *Das europäische Volksmärchen: Form und Wesen*. Bern: Francke, 1947; 3d ed. 1968. Translated by John D. Niles with the title *The European Folktale: Form and Nature*. Philadelphia: Institute for the Study of Human Issues, 1982.

Lüthi, Max. *Märchen*. Stuttgart: Metzler, 1962; 7th ed. 1969.

Lüthi, Max. *Das Volksmärchen als Dichtung: Ästhetik und Anthropologie*. Köln: Diederichs, 1975.

McCulloch, Florence. *Medieval Latin and French Bestiaries*. Chapel Hill, North Carolina: University of North Carolina Press, 1960.

Maeterlinck, Louis. *Le Genre satirique dans la sculpture flamande et wallone*. Paris: Jean Schemit, 1910.

Marinese, Lorenzo and Alberto Manfredi (eds.). *Proverbi Figurati di Giuseppe Maria Mitelli*. Milano: Casa Editrice Cerastico, 1963.

Marzell, Heinrich. "Chrysanthemum Leucanthemum L.—Wucherblume." In H. Marzell, *Wörterbuch der deutschen Pflanzennamen*. Leipzig: S. Hirzel, 1943, vol. 1, cols. 956–972.

Marzell, Heinrich. "'Maßliebchen.'" In *Handwörterbuch des deutschen Aberglaubens*, ed. by Eduard Hoffman-Krayer and Hanns Bächtold-Stäubli. Berlin: Walter de Gruyter, 1932–1933, vol. 5, cols. 1861–1863.

Marzell, Heinrich. "Wie heißt die Marguerite im Volksmund?" In *Volkskundliche Gaben: John Meier zum siebzigsten Geburtstag dargebracht*, ed. by Harry Schewe. Berlin: Walter de Gruyter, 1934, pp. 130–137.

Marzell, Heinrich. "Wucherblume." In *Handwörterbuch des deutschen Aberglaubens*, ed. by Eduard Hoffmann-Krayer and Hanns Bächtold-Stäubli. Berlin: Walter de Gruyter, 1938–1941, vol. 9, cols. 817–820.

Mason, Julian. "Some Uses of Folklore in Advertising." *Tennessee Folklore Society Bulletin*, 20, no. 3 (1954), 58–61.

Meißel, Friedrich. *Die Sage vom Rattenfänger von Hameln*. Hameln: L. Warneson, 4th ed. 1924.

Mencken, H. L. *A New Dictionary of Quotations on Historical Principles from Ancient and Modern Sources*. New York: Alfred A. Knopf, 1942; 2d ed. 1960.

Metzger, Michael M., and Katharina Mommsen (eds.). *Fairy Tales as Ways of Knowing: Essays on Märchen in Psychology, Society and Literature*. Bern: Peter Lang, 1984.

Meyer, Herman. "Tradition und Ursprünglichkeit in Sprache und Literatur." In *Tradition und Ursprünglichkeit: Akten des III. Internationalen Germanistenkongresses 1965 in Amsterdam*, ed. by Werner Kohlschmidt and H. Meyer. Bern: Francke, 1966, pp. 18–25.

Meyer, Maurits de. "'De Blauwe Huyck' van Jan van Doetinchem, 1577." *Volkskunde*, 71 (1970), 334–343. A French translation of this essay was published as "'De Blauwe Huyck', La Cape Bleue de Jean van Doetinchem, datée 1577." *Proverbium*, 16 (1971), 564–575.

Meyer, Maurits de. *De volks- en kinderprent in de Nederlanden van de 15e tot de 20e eeuw*. Antwerpen: Standaard Boekhandel, 1962.

Mieder, Barbara and Wolfgang. "Tradition and Innovation: Proverbs in Advertising." *Journal of Popular Culture*, 11 (1977), 308–319.

Mieder, Wolfgang. *Antisprichwörter*. 2 vols. Wiesbaden: Verlag für deutsche Sprache, 1982 and 1985.

Mieder, Wolfgang. "'Der Apfel fällt weit von Deutschland': Zur amerikanischen Entlehnung eines deutschen Sprichwortes." *Der Sprachdienst*, 25 (1981), 89–93.

Mieder, Wolfgang. "Bibliographischer Abriß zur bildlichen Darstellung von Sprichwörtern und Redensarten." In *Forschungen und Berichte zur Volkskunde in Baden-Württemberg 1974–1977*, ed. by Irmgard Hampp and Peter Assion. Stuttgart: Müller & Gräff, 1977, vol. 3, pp. 229–239.

Mieder, Wolfgang. *Deutsche Sprichwörter in Literatur, Politik, Presse und Werbung*. Hamburg: Helmut Buske, 1983.

Mieder, Wolfgang (ed.). *Deutsche Sprichwörter und Redensarten*. Stuttgart: Reclam, 1979.

Mieder, Wolfgang (ed.). *Disenchantments: An Anthology of Modern Fairy Tale Poetry*. Hanover, New Hampshire: University Press of New England, 1985.

Mieder, Wolfgang. "Die drei weisen Affen und das Sprichwort 'Nichts sehen, nichts hören, nichts sagen.'" *Muttersprache*, 90 (1980), 167–178.

Mieder, Wolfgang (ed.). *Ergebnisse der Sprichwörterforschung*. Bern: Peter Lang, 1978.

Mieder, Wolfgang (ed.). *Grimms Märchen—modern: Prosa, Gedichte, Karikaturen*. Stuttgart: Reclam, 1979.

Mieder, Wolfgang. *International Proverb Scholarship: An Annotated Bibliography*. New York: Garland Publishing, 1982.

Mieder, Wolfgang. "International Proverb Scholarship: An Updated Bibliography through 1981." *Proverbium: Yearbook of International Proverb Scholarship*, 1 (1984), 273–309.

Mieder, Wolfgang (ed.). *Mädchen, pfeif auf den Prinzen! Märchengedichte von Günter Grass bis Sarah Kirsch*. Köln: Eugen Diederichs, 1983.

Mieder, Wolfgang. "Modern Anglo-American Variants of 'The Frog Prince' (AT 440)." *New York Folklore*, 6 (1980, published 1982), 111–135.

Mieder, Wolfgang. "Moderne deutsche Sprichwortgedichte." *Fabula*, 21 (1980), 247–260.

Mieder, Wolfgang. "Moderne Varianten des Blumenorakels: 'Er (sie) liebt mich, er (sie) liebt mich nicht.'" In *Festschrift für Lutz Röhrich zum 60. Geburtstag*, ed. by Rolf Wilhelm Brednich and Jürgen Dittmar. Berlin: Erich Schmidt, 1982, pp. 335–345. (*Jahrbuch für Volksliedforschung*, 27/28 [1982/1983], 335–345).

Mieder, Wolfgang. *The Prentice-Hall Encyclopedia of World Proverbs*. Englewood Cliffs, New Jersey: Prentice-Hall, 1986.

Mieder, Wolfgang. "Proverbs in Carl Sandburg's Poem, 'The People, Yes.'" *Southern Folklore Quarterly*, 37 (1973), 15–36.

Mieder, Wolfgang. *Proverbs in Literature: An International Bibliography*. Bern: Peter Lang, 1978.

Mieder, Wolfgang. "Recent International Proverb Scholarship: An Annotated Bibliography for 1982 and 1983." *Proverbium: Yearbook of International Proverb Scholarship*, 1 (1984), 311–350.

Mieder, Wolfgang. "A Sampler of Anglo-American Proverb Poetry." *Folklore Forum*, 13 (1980), 39–53.

Mieder, Wolfgang (ed.). *Selected Writings on Proverbs by Archer Taylor*. Helsinki: Suomalainen Tiedeakatemia, 1975.

Mieder, Wolfgang. "Sexual Content of German Wellerisms." *Maledicta*, 6 (1982), 215–223.

Mieder, Wolfgang. *Das Sprichwort in unserer Zeit*. Frauenfeld: Huber, 1975.

Mieder, Wolfgang. *Spricnwort, Redensart, Zitat: Tradierte Formelsprache in der Moderne*. Bern: Peter Lang, 1985.

Mieder, Wolfgang. "Survival Forms of 'Little Red Riding Hood' in Modern Society." *International Folklore Review*, 2 (1982), 23–40.

Mieder, Wolfgang. "Traditional and Innovative Proverb Use in Lyric Poetry." *Proverbium Paratum*, 1 (1980), 16–27.

Mieder, Wolfgang. "'Wer nicht liebt Wein, Weib und Gesang, der bleibt ein Narr sein Leben lang': Zur Herkunft, Überlieferung und Verwendung eines angeblichen Luther-Spruches." *Muttersprache*, 94 (special issue, 1983–1984), 68–103.

Mieder, Wolfgang. "'Wine, Women and Song': From Martin Luther to American T-Shirts." *Kentucky Folklore Record*, 29 (1983), 89–101.

Mieder, Wolfgang. "'Wine, Women and Song': Zur anglo-amerikanischen Überlieferung eines angeblichen Lutherspruches." *Germanisch-Romanische Monatsschrift*, 65, new series 34 (1984), 385–403.

Mieder, Wolfgang, and Alan Dundes (eds.). *The Wisdom of Many: Essays on the Proverb*. New York: Garland Publishing, 1981.

Moll, Otto. *Sprichwörterbibliographie*. Frankfurt: Vittorio Klostermann, 1958.

Monteiro, George. "'Good Fences Make Good Neighbors': A Proverb and a Poem." *Revista de Etnografia*, 16, no. 31 (1972), 83–88.

Morrison, Lillian. *Touch Blue: Signs and Spells—Love Charms and Chants—Auguries and Old Beliefs—in Rhyme*. New York: Thomas Y. Crowell, 1958.

Moser, Hans. "Gedanken zur heutigen Volkskunde: Ihre Situation, ihre Problematik, ihre Aufgaben." *Bayerisches Jahrbuch für Volkskunde*, no volume (1954), 208–234.

Moser, Hans. "Vom Folklorismus in unserer Zeit." *Zeitschrift für Volkskunde*, 58 (1962), 177–209.

Mounsey, A. C. "England Must Pay the Piper." *Notes and Queries*, 6th series, 9 (29 March 1884), 248–249.

Newell, William Wells. *Games and Songs of American Children*. New York: Harper, 1883; rpt. New York: Dover, 1963.

Nierenberg, Jess. "Proverbs in Graffiti: Taunting Traditional Wisdom." *Maledicta*, 7 (1983), 41–58.

Northall, G. F. *English Folk-Rhymes: A Collection of Traditional Verses Relating to Places and Persons, Customs, Superstitions, etc.* London: Kegan Paul, Trench, Trübner and Co., 1892; rpt. Detroit: Singing Tree Press, 1968.

O'Donnell, James. "Der Rattenfänger von Hameln." *Der Monat: Eine internationale Zeitschrift*, no. 93 (1956), 54–61.

O'Donnell, James. "What Happened to These Children?" *The Saturday Evening Post* (24 December 1955), pp. 26–27 and 54–55.

Opie, Iona and Peter. *The Lore and Language of Schoolchildren*. Oxford: Clarendon Press, 1959.

Opie, Iona and Peter. *The Oxford Dictionary of Nursery Rhymes*. Oxford: Clarendon Press, 1951.

Otto, August. *Die Sprichwörter und sprichwörtlichen Redensarten der Römer*. Leipzig: Teubner, 1890; rpt. Hildesheim: Georg Olms, 1971.

Parsons, Wilfrid. "Lest Men, Like Fishes . . . " *Traditio*, 3 (1945), 380–388.

Petersham, Maud and Miska. *The Rooster Crows. A Book of American Rhymes and Jingles*. New York: McMillan, 15th ed. 1966.

Petzoldt, Leander. *Deutsche Volkssagen*. München: C. H. Beck, 1978.

Petzoldt, Leander. *Historische Sagen*. 2 vols. München: C. H. Beck, 1977.

Piltz, Georg. *Geschichte der europäischen Karikatur*. Berlin: VEB Deutscher Verlag der Wissenschaften, 1980.

Psaar, Werner, and Manfred Klein. *Wer hat Angst vor der bösen Geiß? Zur Märchendidaktik und Märchenrezeption*. Braunschweig: Georg Westermann, 1976; 2d ed. 1980.

Propp, Vladimir. *Morphology of the Folktale*, ed. by Louis Wagner and Alan Dundes. Austin, Texas: University of Texas Press, 2d ed. 1968.

Queenan, Bernard. "The Evolution of the Pied Piper." *Children's Literature*, 7 (1978), 104–114.

Quitard, Pierre-Marie. *Dictionnaire étymologique, historique et anecdotique des proverbes et des locutions proverbiales de la langue française*. Paris: P. Bertrand, 1842; rpt. Genève: Slatkine Reprints, 1968.

Randolph, Mary Claire. "Rat Satires and the Pied Piper of Hamelin Legend." *Southern Folklore Quarterly*, 5 (1941), 81–100.

Ranke, Kurt. "Volkskunde und Kulturgeschichte." *Zeitschrift für deutsche Philologie*, 74 (1955), 337–353.

Remnant, G. L. *A Catalogue of Misericords in Great Britain*. Oxford: Clarendon Press, 1969.

Rendall, Vernon. *Wild Flowers in Literature*. London: The Scholartis Press, 1934.

Ritz, Hans (pseud. Ulrich Erckenbrecht). *Die Geschichte vom Rotkäppchen: Ursprünge, Analysen, Parodien eines Märchens*. Göttingen: Muriverlag, 1981; 3d edition 1983.

Röbbelen, Ingrid. " 'Fast jeder weiß, was in Hameln geschah / vor tausend und einem Jahr . . . ' Hannes Wader: 'Der Rattenfänger.' " *Praxis Deutsch*, no. 35 (May 1979), 51–54.

Rochholz, Ernst Ludwig. *Alemannisches Kinderlied und Kinderspiel aus der Schweiz*. Leipzig: J. J. Weber, 1857.

Roh, Franz. *Pieter Bruegel d. Ä. Die niederländischen Sprichwörter*. Stuttgart: Reclam, 1960; 2d ed. 1967.

Röhrich, Lutz. "Die Bildwelt von Sprichwort und Redensart in der Sprache der politischen Karikatur." In *Kontake und Grenzen: Probleme der Volks-, Kultur- und Sozialforschung: Festschrift für Gerhard Heilfurth*, ed. by Hans Friedrich Foltin. Göttingen: Otto Schwarz, 1969, pp. 175–207.

Röhrich, Lutz. "Folklore and Advertising." In *Folklore Studies in the Twentieth Century*, ed. by Venetia Newall. Woodbridge, United Kingdom: D. S.

Brewer, 1978; Totowa, New Jersey: Rowman and Littlefield, 1980, pp. 114–115.

Röhrich, Lutz. "Der Froschkönig und seine Wandlungen." *Fabula*, 20 (1979), 170–192.

Röhrich, Lutz. *Gebärde-Metapher-Parodie: Studien zur Sprache und Volksdichtung.* Düsseldorf: Pädagogischer Verlag Schwann, 1967.

Röhrich, Lutz. "Das Kontinuitätsproblem bei der Erforschung der Volksprosa." In *Kontinuität? Geschichtlichkeit und Dauer als volkskundliches Problem,* ed. by Herman Bausinger and Wolfgang Brückner. Berlin: Erich Schmidt, 1969, pp. 117–133.

Röhrich, Lutz. *Lexikon der sprichwörtlichen Redensarten.* 2 vols. Freiburg: Herder, 1973.

Röhrich, Lutz. *Märchen und Wirklichkeit.* Wiesbaden: Franz Steiner, 1956; 3d ed. 1974.

Röhrich, Lutz. *Sage und Märchen: Erzählforschung heute.* Freiburg: Herder, 1976.

Röhrich, Lutz. *Der Witz: Figuren, Formen, Funktionen.* Stuttgart: Metzler, 1977.

Röhrich, Lutz, and Wolfgang Mieder. *Sprichwort.* Stuttgart: Metzler, 1977.

Rolland, Eugène. *Flore populaire ou histoire naturelle des plants dans leurs rapports avec la linguistique et le folklore.* Paris: Jean Maisonneuve, 1908 (esp. vol. 7).

Rölleke, Heinz (ed.). *Brüder Grimm: Kinder- und Hausmärchen.* 3 vols. Stuttgart: Reclam, 1980.

Rölleke, Heinz. *"Wo das Wünschen noch geholfen hat": Gesammelte Aufsätze zu den "Kinder- und Hausmärchen" der Brüder Grimm.* Bonn: Bouvier, 1985.

Rooth, Anna Birgitta. *The Cinderella Cycle.* Lund: C. W. K. Gleerup, 1951.

Ruhm, Walter. *Der Rattenfänger von Hameln nach dem Gedicht von Robert Browning.* Hameln: C. W. Niemeyer, 1967.

Rumpf, Marianne. *Rotkäppchen: Eine vergleichende Untersuchung.* Diss. Göttingen, 1951.

Ruskin, John. *Proserpina: Studies of Wayside Flowers.* New York: John W. Lovell, 1885 (esp. vol. 1).

Rysan, Joseph. "Folklore and Mass-Lore." *South Atlantic Bulletin,* 36 (1971), 3–9.

Salamone, Frank A. "The Arrow and the Bird: Proverbs in the Solution of Hausa Conjugal-Conflicts." *Journal of Anthropological Research,* 32 (1976), 358–371.

Sarkar, Benoy Kumar. "The Hindu Theory of State." *Political Science Quarterly,* 36 (1921), 79–90.

Saunders, E. Dale. "Koshin: An Example of Taoist Ideas in Japan." In *Religion in the Japanese Experience,* ed. by H. Byron Earhart. Encino, California: Dickenson, 1974, pp. 76–80.

Savage, Frederick G. *The Flora and Folk Lore of Shakespeare.* Cheltenham: J. Burrow, 1923.

Schenda, Rudolf. "Fisch, Fischen, Fischer." In *Enzyklopädie des Märchens,* ed. by Kurt Ranke et al. Berlin: Walter de Gruyter, 1984, vol. 4, cols. 1196–1211.

Schenda, Rudolf. "Walfisch-Lore und Walfisch-Literatur." *Laographia,* 22 (1965), 431–448.

Scherf, Walter. *Lexikon der Zaubermärchen.* Stuttgart: Alfred Kröner, 1982.

Schilling, Michael. "Die literarischen Vorbilder der Ludwigsburger und Gaarzer Embleme." In *Außerliterarische Wirkungen barocker Emblembücher: Emblematik in Ludwigsburg, Gaarz und Rommersfelden,* ed. by Wolfgang Harms and Hartmut Freytag. München: Wilhelm Fink, 1975, pp. 41–71.

Segalen, Martine. "Le mariage, l'amour et les femmes dans les proverbes populaires français." *Ethnologie française*, 5 (1975), 119–160; and 6 (1976), 33–88.

Seiler, Friedrich. *Deutsche Sprichwörterkunde*. München: C. H. Beck, 1922; rpt. 1967.

Senaltan, Semahat. *Studien zur sprachlichen Gestalt der deutschen und türkischen Sprichwörter*. Diss. Marburg, 1968; Marburg: Erich Mauersberger, 1968.

Simpson, John A. *The Concise Dictionary of Proverbs*. Oxford: Oxford University Press, 1982.

Smith, Arthur H. *Proverbs and Common Sayings from the Chinese*. Shanghai: American Presbyterian Mission Press, 1914; rpt. New York: Paragon and Dover, 1965.

Smith, Grace Partridge. "The Plight of the Folktale in the Comics." *Southern Folklore Quarterly*, 16 (1952), 124–127.

Spanuth, Heinrich. *Baudenkmäler und historische Stätten in Hameln. Ein Führer durch die Rattenfängerstadt*. Hameln: C. W. Niemeyer, 1950; 5th ed. 1976.

Spanuth, Heinrich. *Der Rattenfänger von Hameln*. Diss. Göttingen, 1951.

Spanuth, Heinrich. *Der Rattenfänger von Hameln: Vom Werden und Sinn einer alten Sage*. Hameln: C. W. Niemeyer, 1951; 2d ed. 1969.

Staiger, Emil. "Dialektik der Begriffe Nachahmung und Originalität." In *Tradition und Ursprünglichkeit: Akten des III. Internationalen Germanistenkongresses 1965 in Amsterdam*, ed. by Werner Kohlschmidt and Herman Meyer. Bern: Francke, 1966, pp. 29–38.

Stevenson, Burton. *The Macmillan Book of Proverbs, Maxims, and Famous Phrases*. New York: The Macmillan Company, 1948; 7th ed. 1968.

Stone, Kay F. "Fairy Tales for Adults: Walt Disney's Americanization of the 'Märchen.'" In *Folklore on Two Continents: Essays in Honor of Linda Dégh*, ed. by Nikolai Burlakoff and Carl Lindahl. Bloomington, Indiana: Trickster Press, 1980, pp. 40–48.

Suard, François, and Claude Buridant (eds.). *Richesse du proverbe*. 2 vols. Lille: Université de Lille III, 1984.

Taylor, Archer. "'Audi, vide, tace,' and the Three Monkeys." *Fabula*, 1 (1957), 26–31.

Taylor, Archer. *The Proverb*. Cambridge, Massachusetts: Harvard University Press, 1931; rpt. Hatboro, Pennsylvania: Folklore Associates, 1962; rpt. with an introduction and bibliography by Wolfgang Mieder, Bern: Peter Lang, 1985.

Taylor, Archer. "Sunt tria damna domus." *Hessische Blätter für Volkskunde*, 24 (1926), 130–146.

Taylor, Archer. "'Tom, Dick, and Harry,'" *Names*, 6 (1958), 51–54.

Taylor, Archer, and Bartlett Jere Whiting. *A Dictionary of American Proverbs and Proverbial Phrases, 1820–1880*. Cambridge, Massachusetts: Harvard University Press, 1958.

Thiele, Ernst. *Luthers Sprichwörtersammlung: Nach seiner Handschrift herausgegeben und mit Anmerkungen versehen*. Weimar: Hermann Böhlau, 1900.

Thiselton-Dyer, T. F. *The Folk-Lore of Plants*. New York: D. Appleton, 1889.

Tilley, Morris Palmer. *A Dictionary of the Proverbs in England in the Sixteenth and Seventeenth Centuries*. Ann Arbor, Michigan: University of Michigan Press, 1950.

Tilley, Morris Palmer. *Elizabethan Proverb Lore in Lyly's "Euphues" and in Pettie's "Petite Pallace" with Parallels from Shakespeare*. New York: Macmillan, 1926.

Tolnay, Charles de. *The Drawings of Pieter Bruegel the Elder: With a Critical Catalogue*. New York: The Twin Editions, 1953.

Tylor, Edward B. *Primitive Culture*. 2 vols. New York: H. Holt, 1874.

Unverfehrt, Gerd. "Christliches Exempel und profane Allegorie: Zum Verhältnis von Wort und Bild in der Graphik der Boschnachfolge." In *Wort und Bild in der niederländischen Kunst und Literatur des 16. und 17. Jahrhunderts*, ed. by Herman Vekeman and Justus Müller Hofstede. Erfstadt: Lukassen, 1984, pp. 221–241.

Unverfehrt, Gerd. "'Große Fische fressen kleine': Zu Entstehung und Gebrauch eines satirischen Motivs." In *Bild als Waffe: Mittel und Motive der Karikatur in fünf Jahrhunderten*, ed. by Gerhard Langemeyer, G. Unverfehrt, Herwig Guratzsch and Christoph Stölzl. München: Prestel, 1984, pp. 402–414.

Urdang, Laurence, and Nancy LaRoche. *Picturesque Expressions: A Thematic Dictionary*. Detroit: Gale Research Co., 1980; 2d ed. 1985.

Utley, Alison. *Country Things*. London: Faber and Faber, 1946.

Voigt, Vilmos. "Folklore and 'Folklorism' Today." In *Folklore Studies in the Twentieth Century*, ed. by Venetia Newall. Woodbridge, United Kingdom: D. S. Brewer, 1978; Totowa, New Jersey; Rowman and Littlefield, 1980, pp. 419–424.

Wackernagel, Wilhelm. "Die Farben- und Blumensprache des Mittelalters." In W. Wackernagel, *Kleinere Schriften: Abhandlungen zur deutschen Alterthumskunde und Kunstgeschichte*. Leipzig: S. Hirzel, 1872, vol. 1, pp. 143–240.

Waehler, Martin. "Denkmale als Ausgangspunkt für Sagen: Zur Entstehung der Rattenfänger-Sage." *Volkswerk, Jahrbuch des Staatlichen Museums für deutsche Volkskunde*, 8 (1943), 99–114.

Walther, Hans. *Proverbia Sententiaeque Latinitatis Medii Aevi: Lateinische Sprichwörter und Sentenzen des Mittelalters*. 6 vols. Göttingen: Vandenhoek & Ruprecht, 1963–1969.

Wander, Karl Friedrich Wilhelm. *Deutsches Sprichwörter-Lexikon*. Leipzig: F. A. Brockhaus, 1867–1880; rpt. Darmstadt: Wissenschaftliche Buchgesellschaft, 1964.

Wander, Karl Friedrich Wilhelm (pseud. N. R. Dove). *Politisches Sprichwörterbrevier: Tagebuch eines Patrioten der fünfziger Jahre, zur Charakteristik jener Zeit*. Leipzig: Otto Wigand, 1872.

Wann, Wolfgang. *Die Lösung der Hamelner Rattenfängersage: Ein Symbol des Abendlandes*. Diss. Würzburg, 1949.

Ward, Donald. *The German Legends of the Brothers Grimm*. 2 vols. Philadelphia: Institute for the Study of Human Issues, 1981.

Weber-Kellermann, Ingeborg. *Deutsche Volkskunde zwischen Germanistik und Sozialwissenschaften*. Stuttgart: Metzler, 1969.

Wedemeyer, André. "Das japanische Drei-Affen-Symbol und der Koshin-Tag." *Jahrbuch des Museums für Völkerkunde zu Leipzig*, 16 (1957, published 1959), 28–56.

Weinerth, Lotte. *Was hat die Rattenfängersage von Hameln mit Olmütz zu tun?* Steinheim, Main: Diwisch, 1971.

Whiting, Bartlett Jere. *Early American Proverbs and Proverbial Phrases*. Cambridge, Massachusetts: Harvard University Press, 1977.

Whiting, Bartlett Jere. *Proverbs in the Earlier English Drama*. Cambridge, Massachusetts: Harvard University Press, 1938; rpt. New York: Octagon Books, 1969.

Whiting, Bartlett Jere. *Proverbs, Sentences, and Proverbial Phrases from English Writings Mainly Before 1500*. Cambridge, Massachusetts: Harvard University Press, 1968.

Whitting, C. F. J. *Hausa and Fulani Proverbs*. Lagos: Government Printer, 1940.

Wiegelmann, Günter, Matthias Zender and Gerhard Heilfurth. *Volkskunde: Eine Einführung*. Berlin: Erich Schmidt, 1977.

Wilson, F. P. *The Oxford Dictionary of Proverbs*. Oxford: Clarendon Press, 3d ed. 1970.

Winter, J. L. "Browning's Piper." *Notes and Queries*, 212, new series 14 (October 1967), 373.

Withers, Carl. *A Rocket in My Pocket: The Rhymes and Chants of Young Americans*. New York: Holt, Rinehart and Winston, 1948.

Woeller, Waltraud. *Der soziale Gehalt und die soziale Funktion der deutschen Volksmärchen*. Berlin: Akademie Verlag, 1955.

Woeller, Waltraud. "Zur Entstehung und Entwicklung der Sage vom Rattenfänger von Hameln." *Zeitschrift für deutsche Philologie*, 80 (1961), 180–206.

Woeller, Waltraud. "Zur Sage vom Rattenfänger von Hameln." *Wissenschaftliche Zeitschrift der Humboldt-Universität zu Berlin, gesellschafts- und sprachwissenschaftliche Reihe*, 6 (1956), 135–146.

Wolfers, D. "A Plaguey Piper." *The Lancet*, (3 April 1965), 756–757.

Woodruff, Helen. "The Physiologus of Bern. A Survival of Alexandrian Style in a Ninth Century Manuscript." *The Art Bulletin*, 12 (1930), 226–253.

Wytrzens, Günther. *Eine russische dichterische Gestaltung der Sage vom Hamelner Rattenfänger*. Wien: Verlag der Österreichischen Akademie der Wissenschaften, 1981.

Zingerle, Iganz. *Das deutsche Kinderspiel im Mittelalter*. Innsbruck: Wagner, 1873.

Zipes, Jack. *Breaking the Magic Spell: Radical Theories of Folk & Fairy Tales*. Austin, Texas: University of Texas Press, 1979.

Zipes, Jack. *Fairy Tales and the Art of Subversion: The Classical Genre for Children and the Process of Civilization*. New York: Wildman Press, 1983.

Zipes, Jack. *The Trials and Tribulations of Little Red Riding Hood: Versions of the Tale in Socio-Cultural Context*. London: Heinermann, 1982; published in German translation as *Rotkäppchens Lust und Leid: Biographie eines europäischen Märchens*. Köln: Diederichs, 1982.

# Index

# Text Permissions, continued

John Robert Colombo, "Proverbial Ruth," from *Translations from the English* (Toronto: Peter Martin, 1974). Copyright © 1964 by the author. Reproduced by permission.

David Curry, "Piper," from *Here (Poems, 1965–1969)* (St. Paul, Minn.: New Rivers Press, 1970). Reprinted by permission of David Curry and New Rivers Press.

Florence Boyce Davis, "The Three Wise Monkeys," from *The World's Best Loved Poems*, ed. James Gilchrist Lawson (New York: Harper and Brothers, 1927).

"California Man Goes from Rats to Riches," Associated Press, 1978, reprinted by permission of Associated Press.

"The Children of Hameln" from *The German Legends of the Brothers Grimm*, trans. and ed. by Donald Ward. Copyright © 1981 by the Institute for the Study of Human Issues, Inc. (ISHI). Reprinted with the permission of ISHI, Phila., Penn.

"A Game with Death: Actress Mary Tyler Moore Loses Her Son," from *Time*, Oct. 27, 1980, copyright 1980 Time Inc. All rights reserved. Reprinted by permission from *Time*.

Robert Gillespie, "Snow White," from *Wisconsin Review*, Vol. 6, No. 2 (1971), reprinted by permission of *Wisconsin Review*.

Louise Glück, "Gretel in Darkness," copyright © 1975 by Louise Glück. From *The House of Marshland* by Louise Glück, published by the Ecco Press in 1975. Reprinted by permission.

Arthur Guiterman, "A Proverbial Tragedy," from *The Laughing Muse* (New York: Harper and Brothers, 1915).

Mac Hammond, "The Pied Piper," from *The Horse Opera and Other Poems* (Columbus: The Ohio State University Press, 1950). Reprinted by permission of the publisher.

Sara Henderson Hay, "Juvenile Court," is reprinted from *Story Hours*, copyright © 1982 by Sara Henderson Hay, by permission of the University of Arkansas Press.

A. P. Herbert, "The Problem," from *Tinker, Tailor: A Child's Guide to the Professions*, 1923, reprinted by permission of A. P. Watt Ltd., on behalf of Lady Herbert.

Hyacinth Hill, "Rebels from Fairy Tales," from *The Writing on the Wall*, edited by Walter Lowenfels (New York: Doubleday, 1969). Permission granted by Manna Lowenfels, Literary Executrix for the estate of Walter Lowenfels.

Galway Kinnell, "Kissing the Toad," from *Mortal Acts, Mortal Words*, copyright © 1980 by Galway Kinnell. Reprinted by permission of Houghton Mifflin Company.

Ronald Koertge, "The Pied Piper," from *The Kansas Quarterly*, Vol. 4, No. 1 (1971–72) reprinted by permission of *Kansas Quarterly*.

Gwendolyn MacEwen, "The Pied Piper," from *Magic Animals: Selected Poetry of Gwendolyn MacEwen*. Reprinted by permission of the author and Stoddard Publishing Co., Limited, Toronto, Canada.

A. A. Milne, "Cherry Stones," from *Now We Are Six*. Copyright 1927 by E. P. Dutton, renewed 1955 by A. A. Milne. Reprinted by permission of the publisher, E. P. Dutton, a division of New American Library, and Methuen Children's Books.

Susan Mitchell, "From the Journals of the Frog Prince," copyright © 1978 by Susan Mitchell. Reprinted from *The Water Inside the Water* (Middletown Conn.: Wesleyan University Press, 1983) by permission of Wesleyan University Press. Originally published in *The New Yorker*.

Lisel Mueller, "Reading the Brothers Grimm to Jenny," from *The Private Life* (Baton Rouge, La.: Louisiana State University Press, 1976), first published in *The New Yorker*. Copyright © 1967 Lisel Mueller. Reprinted by permission of the publisher.

John Ower, "The Gingerbread House," from *Kansas Quarterly*, Vol. 11, Nos. 1–2 (1979). Reprinted by permission of the author and *Kansas Quarterly*.

Dorothy Lee Richardson, "Modern Grimm," from *Poetry* Vol. 73, No. 5 (1949). Coyright © 1949 by the Modern Poetry Association, reprinted by permission of *Poetry* and Dorothy Lee Richardson.

Anne Sexton, "Snow White and the Seven Dwarfs," and "The Frog Prince," from *Transformations*. Copyright © 1971. Reprinted by permission of Houghton Mifflin Company and The Sterling Lord Agency, Inc.

"Snow White and the Sincere Mirror," from *Punch*, December 29, 1965, p. 959. © 1965 Punch/Rothco. All rights reserved. Reprinted by permission.

Edward Thomas, "I Built Myself a House of Glass," from *Twentieth Century Poetry*, Harold Monro, ed. (London: Chatto, 1950). Reprinted by permission of Gerald Duckworth and Co. Ltd.

Phyllis Thompson, "A Fairy Tale," from *Artichoke and Other Poems*. Copyright © 1969 by University of Hawaii Press. Reprinted by permission of the publisher.

Peter Udell, "Big Fish, Little Fish," reprinted by permission of Flora Roberts, Inc.

John Stevens Wade, "Daisies," from *Well Water and Daisies* (La Crosse, Wisc.: Juniper Press, 1974), reprinted by permission of Juniper Press.

"Wishing on a Daisy," reprinted by permission of Hallmark Cards, Inc.

## Illustration Permissions

"Assertiveness Training," reproduced from *Saturday Review*, November 1980, p. 77.

Drawing by Auth © 1979, Washington Post Writers Group, reprinted with permission.

Drawing by Randy Glasbergen originally published in *Good Housekeeping* February 1979, reprinted by permission of Randy Glasbergen.

Drawing by Samuel H. Gross originally published in *Good Housekeeping* July 1981, © 1981 by the Hearst Corporation, reprinted by permission of Samuel H. Gross.

Drawing by Mike Peters reprinted by permission of United Features Syndicate, Inc.

Drawing by Jules Stauber from the Swiss satirical weekly *Nebelspalter*. Reproduced by permission.

Cartoon from *The Man in the Cannibal Pot* by Gahan Wilson. Copyright © 1967 by Gahan Wilson. Reprinted by permission of Doubleday & Company, Inc.